LOOKING FOR GOD

LOOKING FOR GOD

A Seeker's Guide to
Religious and Spiritual
Groups of the World

STEVEN SADLEIR

Previously published as
The Spiritual Seeker's Guide

A PERIGEE BOOK

The Twelve Steps and the Twelve Traditions are reprinted with permission of Alcoholics Anonymous World Services, Inc. Permission to reprint the Twelve Steps and Twelve Traditions does not mean that AA has reviewed or approved the contents of this publication, nor that AA agrees with the views herein. AA is a program of recovery from alcoholism. Use of this material in connection with programs and activities that are patterned after AA, but which address other problems, does not imply otherwise.

This book was previously published as The Spiritual Seeker's Guide.

A Perigee Book
Published by The Berkley Publishing Group
A division of Penguin Putnam Inc.
375 Hudson Street
New York, New York 10014

Copyright © 2000 by Steven Sadleir
Cover design by Phaedra Mastrocola

Allwon Publishing Co. edition: 1992
First Perigee edition: October 2000

Published simultaneously in Canada.

The Penguin Putnam Inc. World Wide Web site address is
http://www.penguinputnam.com

Library of Congress Catologing-in-Publication Data
Sadleir, Steven, 1958–
    Looking for God : a seeker's guide to religious and spiritual groups of the world /
Steven Sadleir.
        p.   cm.
    Includes bibliographical references and index.
    ISBN 0-399-52643-9
    1. Religions—Handbooks, manuals, etc. I. Sadleir, Steven, 1958– Spiritual seeker's
guide. II. Title.

BL82 .S33 2000
291—dc21   00-039972

Printed in the United States of America

10 9 8 7 6 5 4 3 2 1

*This book
is dedicated
to those
who seek God*

CONTENTS

ACKNOWLEDGMENTS

This book was made possible through the constructive efforts of every group and person mentioned in it. Each owns a piece of it, and to each I am grateful. I thank Rudy Shur, Fred Keating, and Perigee Books, a division of Penguin Putnam Inc., for all their work to make this a better book. I particularly appreciate the support of my family, friends, and students, and from the depths of my soul, I thank God for making it all possible.

PREFACE

Why are you reading this? What prompted you to pick up this book and start reading these words? Examine your motivation. Observe your choice to examine this text. Could it be that your spirit is guiding you—through your feelings—to be curious about this text?

Within all human beings there is an innate guiding influence causing us to seek God, find our Self, and fulfill our life purpose. You can ignore it for a while, you can distract yourself with other activities, but the desire to find the Truth, to find your Self, and to find God will draw you into people, places, and situations that will persuade you to keep looking, as you are doing now. You are being called to discover who you are and why you were born. It is no coincidence that you are reading these words now.

You are ready to discover something new about yourself, about your life, and about the purpose of your existence, and, remarkably, at just this conjunction of time and opportunity, you find in your hands an overview of the world's great religious and spiritual traditions. The moment for self-discovery is at hand, for each page has something to offer you. This very act of looking develops your soul's ability to see through your eyes and guide you in your search.

Looking for God is my attempt to provide you with the resource I wish that I had had during my years of searching. As a child, I was raised in the religion of my family, but since then, I have explored widely. What I have discovered and what I have experienced have found their way into this book. I am not trying to judge any of these groups or convince you to accept one over another. It is my view that each one has something valuable to offer, and that you will be drawn to the path that you need when you are ready to follow it. Regardless of what we choose to believe or what religions, groups, or teachers we decide to follow, we all have our own unique, individual relationship with life and with our Creator. So, rather than trying to persuade others to think as we do, I feel we should all work to improve ourselves and let others be inspired by our example.

This book reflects my own search for God and inner peace. As a child, I spent most of my free time alone in contemplation and meditation. My paternal grandparents introduced me to Jesus early in my childhood. I was a naturally curious child and had many questions about Jesus, faith, miracles, and more. I used to trek alone from one church to another in my neighborhood trying to find the answers to my questions. In elementary school, I started practicing yoga, rather than participating in the sports that most of the kids played. Later, when I was old enough to drive, I would go out into the wilderness of the Sierra Nevada mountains in California to be alone with my Creator.

It was during a backpacking trip in the Palisades Glacier area of the John Muir wilderness of Inyo National Forest that I got the inspiration to write this book. Sitting on the top of a mountain peak, meditating and praying for guidance, I received the call to study virtually every major spiritual path and tradition in existence. For the next twenty years, this book consumed me, and my search for God was the complete focus of my life. Although I studied a variety of subjects in high school, chose a major in college, and followed a professional career, my real ambition was to realize the Truth and complete this mission in life. In the process, I've read the books I recommend to you, attended the services and rituals I describe to you, participated in the organizations I discuss with you, and personally met most of the teachers referred to you, to provide you an accurate depiction of what these spiritual groups are about. Each group also critiqued what I have written about them to insure that what I have said is fair and accurate.

Over the course of this quest, I have traveled around the world several times. My journeys have taken me from the jungles of Borneo to the icy reaches of the Himalayas, from shamanic initiations in the Mojave Desert to revelations in Gothic cathedrals of Europe, from Wiccan sabats to Holy Eucharists. Everywhere I went, I was guided. Spiritual masters would come to greet me, call for me, or show up unexpectedly without prior notice.

The synchronicity of incidents bringing together the events that shaped this book seems miraculous. In one instance, I had lost contact with a group that had moved away; I wanted to reach them so they could critique what I had written about them. That same afternoon, while shopping at a health food store, I happened to meet the secretary of that very organization, a woman whom I had never met or known before. She just happened to be in town on a short visit, and our paths intersected. To some, that meeting might be considered just a coincidence, but I think it was something more.

To fully experience each path, I participated in the rites and rituals of these groups, took dozens of initiations, and completed several apprenticeships in spiritual disciplines so that I might more completely convey to you the true nature of these organizations, disciplines, and teachers. Moreover, this book has been blessed by almost every preacher, teacher, shaman, spiritual master, saint, guru, or representative mentioned here. All of these group members, leaders, and teachers went out of their way in order to help *you*.

In 1990, the culmination of these years of study took the form of my first book, *The Spiritual Seeker's Guide*. This new revised edition published by Perigee Books is expanded, updated, and more comprehensive. I have divided the text into five large sections, each exploring different major religions, thinkers, or movements. The first delves into the mysteries of the East—Hinduism, Buddhism, Shintoism, Taoism, and more. The second explains the basic teachings of the West and Middle East—Judaism, Catholicism, Protestantism, and Islam, for example. The third investigates the spiritual paths trod by such great spiritual thinkers as Augustine, Francis of Assisi, Teresa of Avila, and dozens of others less well known. The fourth explores a variety of metaphysical teachings, including Theosophy, Scientology, Baha'i, Edgar Cayce, Nostradamus, and Eckankar, among others. The final section looks at other major thinkers and their movements—Maharishi Mahesh Yogi, Mother Meera, Hare Krishna, Ram Dass, and the Sufi Order, for instance. In this way, I have provided you with an unbiased synopsis of most of the world's great spiritual teachings. They are all here, waiting for you to follow *your* path, explore *your* heart, discover *your* truth. Also included are the addresses and telephone numbers of more than 150 groups summarized in this book, as well as selected books and periodicals to help direct you to the best information on these subjects.

Use this book to initiate or to continue your search. Keep an open mind, and you will get a lot more out of your reading. Let your curiosity be your companion, and your spirit will reveal the invisible hand of God guiding you.

Take that hand and walk in peace.

HISTORICAL RELIGIOUS PERSPECTIVE

2000	1500	1250	1000	750	500	250 B.C.	0 A.D.	250

← -4000 B.C.
Adam & Eve
1st Man & Woman
(Traditional Genealogy)

• 400 B.C
Torah or Pentateuch
(in its present form)
accepted as God's
word by Ezra

• 100 A.D.
First fragments
of New Testament

• 2000 B.C.
Abraham goes
to promised land

• 1325 B.C.
Moses leads
Israelites in
Exodus from
Egypt

• 1000 B.C.
King David

• 622 B.C.
King Josiah
recognizes
Deuteronomy as
words of
Moses

• 250 B.C.
Greek translation
of Old Testament
(Septugant)

• 975 B.C
Temple of Solomon
constructed

Prehistoric
Druid/Celtic
culture in
Europe

• 1850 B.C.
Stonehenge III

• 150 B.C.
Essenes Dead
Sea scrolls

• 2nd century
Desert Fathers

• Hittite civilization
at its peak

• 8–4 B.C.
Jeshua Ben Joseph
"Jesus Christ"

Shamans in
North America
& Siberia

• Mycenaean period

• 1st century
Gnostics

• 1700 B.C.
Zoroaster
(traditional date)

• 550 B.C.
Under Cyrus the great
Zoroastrianism flourishes
in Persia

← 2,6000 B.C.
Egyptian Old Kingdom
great pyramids built

• Egyptian Empire
at its peak

• 1200 B.C.
Trojan War

• 750 B.C.
Homer (Greek)

• 400 B.C.
Socrates (Greek)

• 50 B.C.
Caesar
(Roman)

EASTERN

• 1500 B.C.
1st Aryan Invasion

← 8,000 B.C.
Dravidian culture
in India worships
"An" or "Shiva" (Hindu)

• 1300 B.C.
Aryans migrate to
Ganges River basin

500 B.C.   200 A.D.

← 3,200 B.C
Lord Krishna
(Traditional Genealogy)

Upanisads, Sutras & Sastras compiled

• 1400 B.C
Rig Veda in writen form
(Oldest Spiritual Text)

• 1000 B.C
Brahmanas written
(Explanation of Brahman)

• Before 200 B.C.
Mahabharata written
"Bhagavad Gita"

• 500 B.C.
Siddhartha Gautama
"The Buddha"

← Rishis (Great Seers)
expound wisdom of
Sanatana Dharma
"Eternal Truths"

Tantric Yoga practiced in India

• 598 B.C.
Mahavira
"Janism"

• 200 B.C.
Patanjali the
Granmarian

• 203 A.D.
Babaji

• 1 A.D.
Mahayana Buddhist
split from Therada Sect

• 269 B.C.
King Asoka
becomes a Buddhist
Bhakti (Devotional)
worship evolves in India

• 1800 B.C.
Harappan culture (India)
builds sophisticated cities

• 6th century
Lao Tsu writes
Tao Te Ching

• 1st century
present form
of I Ching
evolved

• 551 B.C.
Confucius

Prehistoric Shamans
in China & Tibet

700 B.C   100 B.C

Taoism evolves in China   • Great Wall of China

Shinto in Japan

← Hsia Culture (China)   Shang Period   Chou Period   Chin   Han Period

APPROXIMATE DATES ROUNDED

250	500	750	1000	1250	1500	1750	2000

WESTERN

- 400 A.D. Latin Volgate Bible by Jerome
- 1260 A.D. Meister Eckhart
- 1054 A.D. Eastern & Western churches split
- 1515 A.D. St. Teresa of Avilia
- 1870 A.D. Vatican Council I

- 313 A.D. Emperor Constantine converts to Christianity
- 1274 A.D. Thomas Aquinas
- 1542 A.D. St. Jones of the Cross
- 1964 A.D Vatican Councl II

- 325 A.D. council in Nicaea
- 800 A.D. Emperor Charlemagne
- 1182 A.D. St. Francis of Assisi
- 1350 A.D. Black Plague
- 1575 A.D. Jakob Boehme
- 1915 A.D. Thomas Merton

- 354 A.D Aurelius Augustine
- 1688 A.D. Swedenborg

- 700 A.D. Muslims Invade Iberia/Spain
- 1200 A.D. 1st Inquisition
- 1611 A.D. King James Holy Bible
- 1831 A.D. Helena P. Blavatsky "Theosophy"

- 570 A.D. Prophet Muhammad religion of Islam
- 1100 A.D. First Crusade
- 1351 A.D. Hesychasm
- 1844 A.D. Baha'u'llah "Baha'i Faith"

- 1500 A.D. Europe explores New World

- 675 A.D. Jerusalem captured by Arabs (Islam)
- 1207 A.D. Jalal Ad-Din Runi
- 1517 A.D. Martin Luther Protestant Movement
- 1887 A.D. Earnest Holmes "Religious Science"

| Dark Ages | | Holy Roman Empire | | | Renaissance | Baroque | |

EASTERN

- 1818 A.D. Shiv Daval

- 788 A.D. Adi Shankara

- 1828 A.D. Lahiri Mahasaya

- 1834 A.D. Sri Ramakrishna

800 A.D.   *12th century*   *16th century*

- 1872 A.D. Sri Aurobindo

Vedanta evolves   Vaishnavism flourishes (Devotion to Yishna & Krishna)

- 900 A.D. Shiva Sutras

- 300 A.D. Patanjali of Yoga Sutras
- Taj Mahal built
- 1877 A.D. Sivananda

- 650 A.D. Buddhism introduced in Tibet "Vajrayana"
- 1215 A.D. Zen flourishes in Japan
- 1407 A.D. Kabir
- 1877 A.D. Gurdjieff

- 552 A.D. Ch'an or Zen introduced in Japan
- 1469 A.D. Guru Nanak "Sikhism"
- 1879 A.D. Ramana Maharshi

- 950 A.D. Mongols invade China
- 1882 A.D. Hazrat Inayai Khan

- 500 A.D. Shinto evolves as structured religion in Japan
- 1225 A.D. Genghis Khan
- 1895 A.D. Krishnamurti

960 A.D.   *1279 A.D.*

Tai Chi C'uan Classic

- 1896 A.D. Swami Prabhupada (ISKCON)

1375

| Age of Division | | Tang Period | | Sung Period | Mongol | Ming | Manchu | Republic |

LOOKING FOR GOD

INTRODUCTION

Throughout recorded history, human beings have sought to know God, to know themselves, and to understand the relationship between the two. There are signs that all cultures throughout history have understood there to be some greater being, or force, that set forth into motion this divine drama we know as our existence. Yet so few have been able to discover and convey to us who our Creator is, or what our purpose is in creation. Developing a relationship with the Divine is a central theme in the creation and development of all societies, and discovering purpose to this life experience is at the core of our very existence. Man's eternal quest is to discover meaning in this reality, to seek out the Truth of who we essentially are, and who, or what, "God" is.

BELIEF SYSTEMS

Man's perspectives and opinions of the Divine are as varied as the multitude of cultures and peoples that have inhabited the planet. In ancient societies where man lived closest to nature, he saw God expressed through nature; we have called this belief animism. As societies began to see the divergent character of natural laws, they attributed what they experienced to Divine intervention and gave each expression a name to identify and explain it; we understand this belief as polytheism. Historically, great thinkers came to realize that there was one underlying and unifying force in the Universe, and that force was characterized as having attributes with which man could identify; we call this belief monotheism. And there are those few throughout history who so devoted themselves to the attainment of the Divine that they came to know God through their own personal experience; we understand this to be realization. All are perceiving the Divine through their own perspectives and validate their Truth given the perspective from which they choose to see it. Whoever or whatever God is, he just "is," immutable and unchanging. It is only our perspective of what God is that ever changes.

Most people belong to one of the world's great religions, and accept its belief, or concept of God, on faith. Of the 5.5 billion people of this world, the vast majority are Christian, Islamic, Buddhist, or Hindu. Christianity is the largest religion in the world with approximately 1.5 billion members, 1 billion of whom are Catholic or Orthodox, and the remaining .5 billion of whom are Protestant. There are also around 1 billion members of the Islamic faith, making it the world's second largest religion. They, incidentally, believe in the same God as the Jews and Christians, but refer to God as "Allah." Buddhism comprises the world's third largest religion, and if the Chinese government hadn't banned the practice of religion in China, Buddhism may well have become the world's largest religion. There are some 1 billion Chinese who are now culturally communist—the Chinese government officially does not recognize any religion—but who traditionally align with Buddhist, Taoist, and Confucian teachings. Hinduism, the world's next largest religion, is actually a number of religious systems originating in India. Buddhist teachings are akin to Hindu theology, and together, practicing Buddhists and Hindus make up about 1 billion of the world's population. The remaining 1 billion people of the world's population belong to numerous other smaller religions, spiritual paths, and teachings, or are atheists or agnostics.

Interestingly, all the world's great teachings tend to have very similar messages and counsel: that God is the unifying force in the Universe, and that we should love "him" and obey "his" laws. The differences are primarily cultural and depend upon man's interpretation of the laws handed down by God. Of course, every religion maintains that its interpretation is the correct one, but many interpretations of God's laws have changed over time as human societies have evolved. All religions have adapted their theologies to accommodate changes in society and science. Ultimately, each individual has a unique understanding of, and relationship with, the Divine, and each follows his or her own path.

ADAPTATIONS

Recent history has documented radical changes in the spiritual development of mankind. Churches, temples, and mosques are having to adapt to the new free-thinking ways of a more educated population. In the past, religious leaders proclaimed dictates for their constituents to live by, and those mandates were rarely challenged. Now, the role of the governing religious bodies is to provide guidelines for living, based on their interpretation of the laws of their faith. These days more and more people are taking it upon themselves to live by their own interpretation or understanding of God's law, and they are basing their convictions on their own experiences, rather than purely on faith. For example, we now have more "progressive" Christians who choose the teachings they like and reject the ones they dislike; we have Muslim women who no longer wear the veil to hide their faces; we have Jews who do not "keep a Kosher home." It seems that the more educated a society becomes, the more individuals question, and the better basis they have to evaluate the Truth for themselves.

In the Western civilization, the trend has been to strike out for independent investigation of the Truth. A "New Age" movement was forming at the end of the nineteenth century, with independent thinkers like Emerson, Whitman, and Thoreau developing a "transcendentalist" movement. This philosophy now appears to be in full swing, with a plethora of new spiritual groups espousing transcendental doctrines. Indeed, meditation has come out of the occult closet and is starting to become not only a household word, but a spreading practice. Meditation, introspective studies, and rituals are reentering many religious practices in an effort to add sustenance to ailing dogmas. In our society's drive to know the Truth, many people have delved into ancient esoteric teachings and traditional paths in an effort to uncover the secrets that would animate their spirituality. Still others have looked to the East to gain an understanding from a preserved history, or are consulting with the Masters who have come to realize the Truth for themselves. The one common denominator is that, more than ever, people are looking for God.

OUR SEARCH

In our search for God, we will walk many paths. Because the world's oldest religions originated in the East, we will begin our quest there, examining the great religions of the Eastern tradition: Hinduism, Sikhism, Jainism, Buddhism, Taoism, Confucianism, and Shintoism. Next will come the great religions of the Western and Middle Eastern traditions: Judaism, Christianity, Protestantism, and Islam. In the subsequent section, we will discuss the teachings of the earlier spiritual thinkers, a broad category that includes the indigenous spiritual beliefs of a variety of cultures. Next, we will explore metaphysics—the study of the fundamental nature of existence, knowledge, and truth—and the teachings associated with it. Finally, we will delve into the remaining major spiritual masters and the movements associated with them.

The purpose of this book is to assist *you* in your search for God. By becoming familiar with what others have believed and espoused, you will evolve and develop your own understanding and then use that wisdom to discover the Truth for yourself. No matter what path you follow—whether you even follow a path or not—your relationship with God is personal, and your awareness of who you are is experientially based. The spiritual paths described in this book provide a forum for you to develop an awareness of Truth for yourself.

That which we come to know is expressed through our thoughts, feelings, and actions, and it is conveyed, often quite inadequately, through our very limited form of expression, as words. As you read these humble words, realize that they are being used only to provoke a response that will help awaken in you something that you already knew, deep inside, was true. Allow your personal, direct experience to be your guide.

This book is designed so you can either read it through from cover to cover for a complete overview of the world's spiritual teachings, or flip through it in a leisurely manner to gain insight into areas that you are curious about. Each section is condensed into the essentials in an effort to make the book more readable, and is only intended to provide a brief overview. After you get the gist of the teachings, it is my hope that you will be inspired to investigate one or more of these teachings independently. I could not possibly do justice to any of these spiritual paths in such short space. Please determine the qualities of these spiritual groups through your own research and reflection. After all, in the final analysis, the responsibility for really understanding the messages of these teachings rests with you.

The search for Truth is an adventure, an exploration into the very meaning and purpose of your life. Look around you and notice that so many people don't really *live*, but merely *exist*. Notice that those who make the effort to discover their own spiritual identity begin to wake up to a new and exciting life. They add joy, serenity, and sustenance to their lives.

Imagine living a life with an understanding of who you really are, and what your purpose is in life. Imagine a life with real meaning. I believe there is a purpose and meaning to your existence, and if you don't know it, then you haven't searched deeply enough. When you begin to feel invigorated with life, when you are just naturally happy for no apparent reason, when you understand why certain events in your life are occurring, and when you can cope with life's tests and trials, then you have begun to awaken your inner spiritual nature. Why settle for anything less?

Ask for direction and guidance, and they will be given. Seek out the Truth for yourself, and you will find it. There is no reason that you cannot know the Truth for yourself, but it takes a sustained effort to discover it.

Don't believe anyone, including me. Find out for yourself. Read, explore, understand.

It starts by turning the page.

PART ONE

EASTERN RELIGIONS

Be leery of writers—including me—who make broad generalizations about Eastern thought or religion. Those teachings originating in the East are quite divergent and sometimes contradictory. Moreover, trying to understand Eastern philosophies from a Western perspective is in itself distorting. The broad, holistic, Eastern perspective of the Divine just doesn't fit into the narrow analytical approaches of Western thought. The religions of the Western tradition—Judaism, Christianity, and Islam—evolved from one source, the patriarch Abraham, whereas, in the East, "universal Truths" were revealed to various enlightened individuals at different times and places in history. Western religions stem from the common beliefs that there is only one God and that "He" has set laws that you must obey, but in the East, no one particular philosophy or belief was adopted by the peoples of Asia. In the West, you tend to make judgments about which philosophies and beliefs are "right" or "wrong," whereas in the East, there is generally more freedom to evaluate the Truth for yourself, and you can come to a different conclusion within the multifaceted expression of the Divine.

Eastern religions draw upon the insights of various learned seers and saints. The predominant strains of Eastern thought evolved on the Indian subcontinent, first from the Vedic wisdom of the rishis, or seers, dating back several thousand years, later from the Buddha, who lived approximately 2,500 years ago, and finally from many other enlightened beings since then. The Chinese religions of Taoism and Confucianism have exercised a strong influence on Eastern philosophy, and shamanistic elements have also contributed to those teachings, particularly in Tibetan Buddhism and Japanese Shintoism. Thus, we can view Eastern religion as a vast body of philosophy that provides for flexibility in spiritual thought and practice.

This section begins with Hinduism, which has a number of individual components within it, such as the Vedic religion (scriptural), the Brahmanic religion (societal), and the Bhakti religion (devotional), as well as offshoots to each, such as Vaishnavism and Shivaism. The summary of Hinduism is followed by those spiritual practices that evolved within the Hindu culture, such as Yoga, Tantrism, Sikhism, Jainism, and Buddhism. This section closes with an explanation of the Chinese contributions to Eastern religion, including Taoism and Confucianism, and the Japanese religion of Shinto.

The context for Eastern religions extends from India to Japan. However, I have placed those religions that originated in the Middle East with Western religions, because they have had their greatest influence in the West. Also, I have discussed Zoroastrianism and Sufism in the section called "Early Spiritual Paths," while smaller spiritual orders and spiritual masters from the East are discussed in the section "Eastern Masters and Movements."

HINDUISM

Hinduism is not a religion per se, but rather a variety of religious beliefs and practices making up the major spiritual traditions of the Indian subcontinent. *Hindu* is a Persian word that refers to the people and culture of the Indus River region of northwest India, hence the synonym *Indian*. The word *Indus*, pronounced by Persians, sounds like *Hindus*, and that is why Westerners started calling the people from India *Hindus*.

HISTORY

Unlike other world religions, Hinduism was not founded by any particular person, and it is not based on any one set of beliefs, or dogma. Hinduism is based on the *Sanatana Dharma*, the Eternal Truths, or Laws, that have been realized and expounded by the rishis, or great seers, dating back over ten thousand years ago. Thus, Hinduism is the world's oldest living religion.

The ancient Dravidian culture of India, which dates back several thousand years B.C., worshipped the ancient god An, who is believed to be an early form of Lord Shiva. These early Hindu people appeared to practice various tantric elements (see "Tantrism" on page 22), such as meditation and yoga, and drank a sacred substance called soma, a milky, fermented liquor produced from the soma plant, that brought about intense spiritual experiences and devotional love.

During the second millennium B.C., nomadic Aryan tribes invaded the northern part of India, bringing a culture and theology that became integrated into the beliefs of the various indigenous agrarian communities that existed throughout India at that time. The Aryans brought with them the caste system and laid the foundation for a priesthood and an organization of religious thought. For the most part, the ancient teachings were passed on orally, but eventually many of the ancient hymns, aphorisms, stories, and anecdotes were compiled into the world's oldest collection of spiritual texts, known as the *Vedas*. These texts were written down over a period of thousands of years, and developed into a variety of theologies over time. The *Vedas* consist of over 1,000 hymns describing humanity's relationship with God. No one theology is adopted in the *Vedas*, but rather a cosmology and philosophy that developed out of animistic, polytheistic, and pantheistic mythologies. These, in turn, evolved into a monotheistic relationship.

The oldest Vedic text is the *Rig Veda*, which, in its written form, dates back to 1400 B.C. This Vedic theology further evolved through a collection of philosophical writings called the *Upanishads*, which were compiled between 500 B.C. and A.D. 200. This body of Vedic literature concludes with the Vedantic writings, also known as *Vedanta*, or *End of the Vedas*, which were written between A.D. 200 and A.D. 800. The Vedantic writings developed a clear religious philosophy to explain the purpose of existence, as well as the nature of God and of the Self.

Another important set of spiritual texts that influenced the Hindu culture are the sutras and the sastras, collections of aphorisms or proverbs written from 500 B.C. to 200 B.C. The sutras consist of various instructions for the Brahman priests as to how to conduct various religious acts and ceremonies, and they also serve as a guide for human conduct. The sastras are primarily concerned with matters of personal conduct and a code of ethics.

With the advent of the teachings of Buddha around the year 500 B.C. (see "Buddhism" on page 32), a trend developed in India. Rather than relying on a Brahman priest or rigorous austerities to relate to or commune with the divine, individuals were inspired to develop a personal relationship with God. This popular Hindu tradition began to spread throughout India, evolving into the devotional, or "Bhakti," form of worship that is most prevalent in India today. These devotional practices are outlined in a collection of writings known as the *Puranas*, as well as in the great Hindu epics, the *Mahabharata* and the *Ramayana*.

BELIEF SYSTEM

As the ancient wisdom was revealed and evolved through the different cultures that existed in different parts of India, various forms were adopted to depict the nature of God, and humanity's relationship with God. There are literally thousands of gods and goddesses revered in the Hindu traditions; all are generally accepted as personal forms of the divine. Hindus don't typically argue about which god is "the" god, but rather accept that God can be represented through any and all forms, or through no form at all.

However, there is a general underlying basic belief in a universal principal, or power, known as Brahma, which is omnipotent, omniscient, and beyond all the confines of time, space, and causation. This universal power is typically represented through three major principles: creation, preservation, and destruction. These three attributes are represented by the principal gods in the Hindu pantheon: Brahma, the creative aspect, who is revered but not really worshipped much today in India; Vishnu, the preserver or sustainer of the universe; and Shiva (or Siva), the destroyer (of the illusion of our being separate from God).

It is also generally believed that God dreamed the Universe and all the beings created in it. Each being is asleep and will eventually awaken itself to realize God dwelling within.

Thus, God awakens within us the ability to realize our own true divine nature. In this system, our physical birth is an illusion created in our own mind. We humans have always been, are, and will always be nothing but Brahma. We dream our physical material existence and through this dream, maya, we evolve our conscious awareness through our life experiences until we are ready to fully awaken. The path to awakening consciousness varies between sects, but can generally be divided into four distinct groups, or paths:

1. Raja, the path of yoga and meditation;

2. Bhakti, the path of devotion to God;

3. Jnana, the path of wisdom or self-knowledge;

4. Karma, the path of right action, or selfless service.

To varying degrees, most religious groups incorporate all of these disciplines into their practice. The underlying purpose is to realize God and to help others to realize God.

Through one of the four aforementioned spiritual paths of Raja, Bhakti, Jnana, or Karma yoga, you would awaken to the realization that you yourself are the God that you are seeking, that the notion of individual self is illusionary, and that "beingness-consciousness-bliss" is your true reality. Of course, this self-realization and God-Consciousness are transcendental and, therefore, beyond the abilities of your mind to conceive at this point in time, but they are the ultimate goal and divine purpose of your existence.

Until your soul attains this liberated awareness, your mind will continue to project the illusion of being separate from God, and will appear to reincarnate into various forms and births. These interpretations will vary according to teacher and sect, as well as the level of awareness you have to hear it. Accordingly, other existences may not be in a human form, or even of the physical world. Various spiritual worlds may be projected by your mind, and your perception of reality will vary according to the evolution of your individual consciousness. You will note, for example, that one teacher, or guru, may teach that a soul may take another birth in human form to learn the lessons that it needs to learn; another may teach that the soul will reach another, higher plane of existence, such as a heavenly world; and yet a third will impart that it is all false, that only consciousness exists, that worlds and forms are only a dream, albeit a vivid one, from which you are about to awaken. *Each statement is true* depending on your level of spiritual consciousness.

The most popular of the Hindu gods is Vishnu. His consort, or feminine aspect, is Lakshmi, the goddess of wealth and prosperity. It is through a dream of Vishnu that Brahma creates the universe. In times of great turmoil, Vishnu incarnates into human form to save the world. Vishnu's most important incarnations include Rama and Krishna. Krishna has developed a theology of his own. He is today the most revered god in India, followed in popularity by Rama.

The oldest and most complex of the Hindu gods is Lord Shiva. The Indian archaeological ruins of Mohenjo-Daro and Harappa in western Punjab indicate that an advanced Dravidian culture existed in this area around 2000 B.C. These people worshipped a god identified as Lord Shiva. In these ancient ruins, a pendant was found that showed Lord An, or Shiva, seated in a yogic posture and wearing a trident, a symbol of Shiva. This makes Shivaism the oldest living faith in the world.

Shiva's present personality is partly based on the attributes of three gods: Rudra, the wild god of the *Vedas*; Agni, the god of fire and the first god mentioned in the *Vedas*; and Indra, giver of life. The *Puranas* depict Shiva as the arch-yogi who can deliver the aspirant to the realization of God through his powers of tapasya—the intense fire of inward-turned consciousness. Shiva resides on the earth for mankind, and is often represented by the lingam—a symbolic rounded phallic column—that represents his powers of transcendence. Shiva is often represented in the form of Nataraja, performing the Cosmic Dance inside a mandala of fire, controlling the interplay of creation and destruction.

Shiva's consort, or feminine representation, is called Uma, or Parvati, who signifies the Divine Wisdom and Universal Energy (shakti). This great mother goddess is known under many names and worshipped under many forms. The most prominent aspect depicts her wrathful and terrifying countenance as Kali, or Durga, whose powers destroy man's ego. Shiva's feminine forms represent the destruction of the illusion of physical existence, and the awakening of consciousness. The divine couple has two sons: Ganesha, the elephant-headed deity who provides access to the great gods, and Karikeya, the war god, who rides upon a peacock.

RITUALS AND HOLY DAYS

Hindu religious rites are numerous and varied. Most Hindus have altars in their homes for worship and prayer. Attendance at temples for communal worship, chanting, or individual prayer, as well as pilgrimages to holy sites also play a big part of religious observance. Many holy people, or sadhus, wander from town to town, and it is common for families to feed and sometimes board these wandering sages or go out to visit them and listen to their discourses. Religious festivals are numerous and typically involve the worship of a chosen or family deity, or they commemorate a significant historical religious event.

One of the most popular religious festivals is the Shiva-ratri, or "night of Shiva," which celebrates the birthday of Lord Shiva. It is held on the first new-moon night in January or February. On the day preceding Shiva-ratri, sadhus, or holy men, and devotees fast all day and then stay up all night to perform puja (worship), meditate, pray, and bathe.

Rama-nomi, which celebrates Lord Rama's birthday, is held on the ninth day after the first new moon in March or April. During Rama-nomi devotees recite the Ramayana, which recounts the epic adventures of Lord Rama and Sita, his wife, and enact plays based on the story. They also chant, sing devotional songs, and perform dances.

Janmastami is Lord Krishna's birthday, held in August or September. Devotees of Krishna go into ecstatic dancing while chanting the name of the Lord. This dancing and chanting can continue for days.

The most significant festival in Hinduism, and the single largest spiritual event in the world, is the Kumbha Mela. In 1989, for instance, over thirty million people attended this celebration, which makes it the largest gathering of any type in modern history. The festival is based on the ancient texts. *Kumbha* is Sanskrit for *pitcher* and *mela* means *festival*. Thus, the name refers to the immortalizing pot of nectar—described in the ancient scriptures—that liberates the soul.

The legend claims that in ancient times, Vishnu incarnated into the form of Vamanadevi, a dwarf beggar, in order to oust a king named Bali Maharaja, who had tried to conquer the Universe. After reclaiming the universe by tricking Bali Maharaja, Vamanadevi kicked a hole in the universal shell causing a few drops of water to flow into our mortal world.

This holy water became known as the Ganges River. Originally, the Ganges only flowed among the heavenly planets. Then the great king Bhagiratha desired to purify the earth and prayed for the Ganges to descend to earth. The personified Ganges, mother Goddess Gangadevi, agreed to fulfill his desire; however, since the force of the Ganges was so great, it first had to flow off the head of Lord Shiva. Ever since, Shiva has sustained the Ganges, and pilgrims have been able to purify themselves in her divine waters.

To celebrate this history, every twelve years, when the astrological conditions are right, literally millions of sadhus, or holy people, and pilgrims enter one of four cities—they rotate every dozen years—along the Ganges River. There, they experience a ritual purifying bath, and they pray. The bathing begins with the Nagas, naked holy men with matted hair who have renounced all worldly possessions; they are celibate and perform extreme austerities to purify themselves. After all the holy men and women have sanctified the river, the other millions of pilgrims are allowed to bathe. An informal tent city goes up along the banks of the Ganges, and priests from all sects avail themselves for spiritual rites and services for the pilgrims. Literally thousands of groups are represented, each with its own form of observance. The festival lasts for about a month. Smaller Kumbha Melas are also performed every four years.

Typically, these celebrations are followed by mass feedings. With thousands of Gods to worship in India, there are also thousands of festivals and religious events.

FOR ADDITIONAL INFORMATION

Hindu temples and centers can be found in many major Western cities. A listing of Hindu temples and information on visiting Hindu teachers or priests can be found in the magazine *Hinduism Today*, and I have included a few below. You can also check metaphysical bookstores and health food stores for information on visiting Eastern spiritual masters. (See the other Eastern religions, and "Eastern Masters and Movements" on page 305.) Yoga centers or Indian restaurants may also be places where you could inquire about Hindu places of worship. In larger metropolitan centers, Hindu temples may be listed under "churches" in the telephone book.

Recommended Contacts

There are now many Hindu temples and centers in most states and many countries. For a complete listing, consult the Internet sites on page 16, but here is a sampling from around the country:

Bharatiya Temple
6850 Adams Road
Troy, MI 48098

Hindu Temple of Greater Chicago
c/o Ramalayam Hindu Temple
Box 99
Lemont, IL 60439

Hindu Temple Society of North
    America
45-57 Bowne Street
Flushing, NY 11355

Hindu Temple Society of
    Southern California
1600 Las Vergenes Canyon Road
Calabasas, CA 91302

Vedanta Society
34 W. 71st Street
New York, NY 10023

The Vedanta Society of Southern
    California
1946 Vedanta Place
Hollywood, CA 90068

Vedantic Center
3528 N. Triunfo Canyon Road
Agoura, CA 91301

Recommended Readings

The Classics

Goldman, Robert P., trans. *The Ramayama of Valmiki: An Epic of Ancient India*. Vol. I. Princeton, NJ: Princeton University Press, 1990.

Nikhilananda, Swami, trans. *The Upanishads*. New York: The Ramakrishna-Vivekananda Center, 1977.

Praghupada, Swami, trans. *The Bhagavad-Gita*. New York: The Bhaktibedanta Book Trust, 1972.

Prasada, Rama, trans. *Patanjali's Yoga Sutras*. New Delhi, India: Oriental Books, 1982.

Singh, Jaideva, trans. *The Siva Sutras: The Yoga of Supreme Identity*. New Delhi, India: Motical Banarsidass Publishers, 1988.

Other Readings

Hartsuiker, Dolf. *Sadhus: India's Mystic Holy Men*. Rochester, NY: Inner Traditions International, 1993.

Hebner, Jack, and David Osborn. *Kumbha Mela: The World's Largest Act of Faith*. San Francisco, CA: Mandala Publishing Group, 1991.

Jack, Homer A., ed. *The Gandhi Reader*. Twin Lakes, WI: Lotus Light Publications, 1984.

Maharaj, Sri Nisargadatta. *I Am That*. Durham, NC: The Acorn Press, 1997.

The Vedanta Society

The Vedanta Society keeps a very good catalog of subjects related to Hinduism; for information contact:

Vedanta Catalog
Vedanta Society of Southern California
1946 Vedanta Place
Hollywood, CA 90068–3996
Phone: (213) 856–0322

Recommended Periodicals

Clarion Call
815 Arnold Drive #124
Martinez, CA 94553–9849
Phone: (415) 372–6002

Meditation Magazine
17510 Sherman Way #212
Van Nuys, CA 91406
Phone: (818) 343–4998

EastWest Magazine
P.O. Box 57320
Boulder, CO 80322–7320
Phone: (617) 232–1000

Yoga Journal
P.O. Box 3755
Escondido, CA 92033
Phone: (800) 334–8152

Hinduism Today
Concord, CA 94519
Phone: (808) 822–7032

Recommended Websites

www.asiatica.org

www.hindunet.org

www.mandirnet.org/temple_list.html

www.webhead.com/wwwvl/india

YOGA

Yoga is the science of self-awareness, and the path to God Realization. The word *yoga* is Sanskrit and means *discipline*, or literally *to yoke* or *to harness*, a reference to establishing a union with Divine Consciousness.

HISTORY

The precise origin of yoga has not been determined. As I mentioned in the last section, a pendant found in the ruins of Mohenjo-Daro depicts An (Shiva), the creator of the universe, sitting in a classical yoga posture. This artifact and other objects with similar depictions date back to around 2000 B.C. The *Rig Veda* describes a spiritual ascetic (muni) with abilities attributed to yogis, and the *Atharva Veda* describes a group of ascetics who practice various postures and breathing exercises associated with yoga. Thus the principles of yoga date back at least to the second millennium B.C. The term yoga was first recorded in the *Katha, Shue-tashuatara,* and *Maitri Upanishads,* which were written sometime around 500 B.C.

BELIEF SYSTEM

There may be numerous lineages of yoga practiced around the world today, but all involve some discipline for awakening consciousness. The classical system is called Raja Yoga, "The King of Yoga," which was explained by the arch-yogi Patanjali, sometime around A.D. 300. In Patanjali's *Yoga Sutras,* the methods of attaining enlightenment are established through eight limbs, or levels, known as Ashtanga Yoga, or the "eight-limbed path." Through this yoga practice, the aspirant evolves from "ordinary awareness" (citta) to becoming totally conscious (purusha); from being aware "of" things (subject-object relationship) to becoming one with all that is (The Divine or Supreme Consciousness). This transformation is achieved through various meditation techniques that quiet the mind and senses, allowing clear consciousness to develop naturally. By transcending the mind, the yogi is no longer limited by the constraints of maya (the illusion of separateness from the divine), and becomes liberated (moksha).

Generally, the philosophy of yoga is that you only think you are separate from the Divine. Your ego perpetuates the illusion of being separate from God and everything else that exists (or does not exist). This separation from your God Consciousness creates suffering in your mind, and thus, to transcend that suffering, you must come to a realization of your true nature.

Liberation is achieved through a variety of means, depending on the practices of the school of yoga that is followed. There are perhaps hundreds of schools of yoga, many of which have no clearly defined identity. However, there are four general kinds of yoga practiced, and most schools draw from each of these, to one degree or another. These schools are: Raja Yoga, the path of meditation, Jnana Yoga, the path of wisdom or introspection, Bhakti Yoga, the path of devotion, and Karma Yoga, the path of selfless service to God.

Ashtanga Yoga involves developing eight levels or areas of practice, which include the following:

1. Yama, the restraint of mind and actions;

2. Niyama, developing mental and moral purity;

3. Asana, developing physical purity through yoga postures and exercises;

4. Pranayama, controlling the breath;

5. Pratyahara, detachment of the physical senses;

6. Dharana, the ability to focus the attention on the object of meditation or concentration;

7. Dhyana, meditation;

8. Samadhi, total consciousness: the attainment of a state in meditation in which the difference between "subject" and "object" disappears.

The last one, samadhi, means "to hold together completely," and refers to the state of overcoming the mind and senses, and merging the individual consciousness in total or Divine consciousness. This enlightenment of the consciousness is realization of the Self, of God, and of Existence.

Jnana Yoga involves putting your attention on the nature of the self. Through introspection, self-inquiry, or the grace of a guru—one who is already realized or enlightened—your own nature becomes clear. The nature of the Self becomes self-apparent when sufficiently reflected upon. Jnana yoga involves becoming aware of your own awareness, conscious of your own consciousness.

Bhakti Yoga, on the other hand, involves developing devotion to God. It typically involves chanting and singing devotional songs, as well as performing tasks that show heartfelt love rather than intellectual understanding.

Karma Yoga involves dedicating your actions to serving God. All your actions are performed in the name of God, selflessly and without recognition or expectation of reward.

Some specialized forms of yoga have become popular in the West. For example, Hatha Yoga, the discipline of exertion, is a practice that involves purifying the body and mind through various physical postures (asana), breathing exercises (pranayama), and some form of meditation. Typically, the devotee also adopts a strict diet, usually vegetarian. These controlled exercises develop the practitioner's subtle energies (or spirit)—called shakti—and open the psychic centers within the body—called chakras—where this energy directs the physical energy in the body. Hatha Yoga provides a means of balancing the energies of the body, mind, and spirit, to attain greater insight, clarity, and peace.

In Kundalini Yoga, the yogi learns to draw the life force energy—or Kundalini Shakti—up the spine and into the area of the brain that is dormant in most people. As the kundalini enters the top of the head, it awakens the latent consciousness and with it, the realization of the practitioner's true nature. The purpose is to awaken the latent faculties of higher awareness. This end is achieved through either physical exercises or contemplative techniques, depending on which school the yogi has adopted.

Kriya Yoga involves merging the breath with the mind so that the subtle energies expressed in the individual consciousness merge with the subtle energy expressed within the Divine consciousness (Existence itself), thus liberating the individual consciousness.

Other yogas are even more specialized and may refer either to a specific technique, such as Mantra Yoga, in which the yogi practices chanting mantra, or to the state attained during practice, such as Sahaj Yoga, in which the natural blissful state of Divine union is attained. Still other yogas refer to a lineage's specific teachings, such as Kripalu Yoga, a technique developed by Amrit Desai (see page 318), or Siddha Yoga, associated with the SYDA Foundation and Gurumayi Chidvilasananda (see page 361).

FOR ADDITIONAL INFORMATION

Yoga is traditionally learned from a recognized yogi in an established lineage of instruction. (See "Eastern Masters and Movements" on page 305.) *Yoga Journal* publishes a "Yoga Teacher's Directory" for the entire world in each July/August issue (back issues may be ordered). Hatha yoga classes are often held in neighborhood centers, schools or colleges, and city recreation departments all over the country and in many countries around the world.

Recommended Contacts

The fifth section of this book is called "Eastern Masters and Movements," and much of the material below might have been included there, except that they primarily espouse a physical yoga orientation. Still, they are well-established national yoga training centers and resources, and well worth your investigation:

Ashtanga Yoga
Phone:
New York (212) 982–0753
Encinitas, CA (760) 632–7093
Santa Monica, CA
 (310) 393–5150

Bikram's Yoga College of India
8800 Wilshire Boulevard,
 2nd Floor
Beverly Hills, CA 90211
Phone: (310) 854–5800

Viniyoga
Heart of Yoga Association
971 Manzanita Place
Los Angeles, CA 90029
Phone: (213) 661–1500

White Lotus Foundation
2500 San Marcos Pass
Santa Barbara, CA 93105
Phone: (805) 964–1944

Recommended Readings

Choudhury, Bikram. *Bikram's Beginning Yoga Class*. New York: G. P. Putnam, 1978.

Desikachar, T. K. V. *The Heart of Yoga*. Rochester, NY: Inner Traditions International, 1995.

Feuerstein, Georg. *The Yoga Tradition*. Prescott, AZ: Hohm Press, 1998.

Jois, Sri K. Pattabhi. *Yoga Mala*. India: Hart Productions. 1989.

Lidell, Ludy. *The Sivananda Companion to Yoga*. New York: Simon and Schuster, 1983.

Prasada, Rama, trans. *Patanjali's Yoga Sutras*. New Delhi, India: Oriental Books, 1982.

Venkatesananda, Swami. *The Concise Yoga Vasistha*. Albany, NY: State University of New York Press, 1984.

White, Ganga. *Double Yoga*. Santa Barbara, CA: White Lotus Foundation, 1981.

Recommended Websites

www.alife.com.uk/links/yoga

www.ashtanga.com

www.Bikramyoga.com

www.heartofyoga.org

www.india-web.com/yogaf.htm

www.mandala.co.uk/links/ yoga.htm

www.tigahiyrbak.com

www.whitelotus.org

www.yogafinder.com

TANTRISM

Tantra is the esoteric spiritual discipline that utilizes shakti, the creative power of the absolute, to attain self-realization. It embraces the union of opposites to realize the whole.

HISTORY

There is some evidence that proto-tantric elements existed as far back as 1000 B.C., when phallic lore was well established in India. Tantric elements appear in Hindu—particularly in its yogic disciplines—in Buddhism, and in Taoism. The first tantric written works appear around A.D. 300, through the Buddhist "radical institutions of Manjusri" and the "tantra of secret association" (Guhysamajatantra). The first authentic Hindu text was compiled in the eleventh century and was called *The Tantra of Great Liberation,* or *Mahanirvanatantra.*

Tantrism peaked in India between the ninth and fourteenth centuries, but then as devotional (Bhakti) Hinduism began promoting its puritanical ideology, Tantrism was shunned. Today, it remains a relatively obscure practice. Most tantric practices have never been written down and are only passed on orally from guru to student when the latter proves that he or she is ready. It is considered to be "left handed," or unorthodox and radical, but an accelerated path to God Realization.

BELIEF SYSTEM

Tantrism comes from a Sanskrit word meaning *that which extends, spreads.* It distinctly differs from traditional Hinduism in that it does not adhere to the caste system and is overtly anti-Brahmanical, allowing women and members of lower castes to practice its rites. Tantrists place their emphasis on esoteric yoga practices and meditation. Reliance is placed on a guru (spiritual teacher) rather than on written texts. Hindu tantric scriptures deal with the relationship between God (Shiva) and his Power (Shakti), with the aim of transcending the apparent duality of the spiritual (God) and the material (man) through realization of the union between Shiva and Shakti. Shiva represents the underlying consciousness and latent potentiality, whereas Shakti represents the manifest expression that is Life itself.

Tantra takes what most people would consider obstacles and utilizes them as methods of self-realization. Tantra is considered an accelerated, but sometimes more dangerous, discipline for realization. Ironically, tantric practices are becoming increasingly popular in the West, primarily due to the apparent erotic nature of some of its practices. Most tantric disciplines have nothing to do with actual sexual intercourse, but it would seem that it is the obscure sexual practices of the discipline that have got the attention of the West at the expense of the true esoteric principles.

RITUALS AND HOLY DAYS

The purpose of the tantric ritual practice is to achieve a rapid moksha, or release of the human self (atman) from the cycle of birth and death (samsara). The Tantrist achieves this liberation of the soul through kundalini (life force energy) awakening, and through the union of male and female principles, where the male is characterized as Shiva (consciousness), and the female as Shakti (energy). The achievement of Brahman, or God realization, arises through the union of Shiva and Shakti, where the kundalini rises to the highest centers of awareness at the top of the head. Through the tantric techniques, the dualistic illusion (maya) of this world is dissolved, and the impersonal Absolute is realized.

In tantric practices, the aspirant typically must master a certain degree of control of the body, the mind, and the senses. Buddhist tantric practices tend to be more ritualistic, involving elaborate chanting, visualizations, and meditations, while Hindu and Taoist tantric practices tend to be more yogic, involving meditation, movement, and breath control. In these practices the student learns to raise the "dormant power," or kundalini, from within. In some cases, after the student attains a prescribed degree of mastery in controlling the kundalini, male participants (Shivas) and female participants (Shaktis) work together to raise each other's kundalini shakti.

Tantric practices usually involve some form of meditation. Sometimes various mantras are recited first, and certain pujas, or rituals of worship, are observed. In some tantric practices in India, the participants imbibe generous quantities of vijaya, a drink made with sweetened milk and marijuana, or other substances considered sacred. Once a higher or altered state of consciousness is achieved, the Shivas initiate copulation with the Shaktis. The key in this technique is to keep the consciousness on the divine aspects of the male and female principles, and to refrain from ejaculating throughout the intercourse. The energy generated through the meditation and/or intercourse is raised to the centers of higher consciousness. The achievement of simultaneous control of mind, breath, and semen is believed to be a shortcut to moksha, or spiritual liberation. Some tantric practices can be dangerous if improperly performed, particularly the retaining of semen during intercourse, and proper instruction from a tantric master is advised. Many of the spiritual lovemaking techniques utilized during tantric intercourse were introduced in the Indian classic, *The Kama Sutra*, written sometime between A.D. 100 and A.D. 400.

There is also a rare and clandestine kind of tantric practice called Aghora, in which, in order to overcome attachments to sense perception, the Aghori purposefully engages in activities that would otherwise repulse him due to his sociological and psychological conditioning. These practices can include practicing meditation on top of corpses, eating human flesh, or smearing feces over the practitioner's body. Most Aghoris live in cremation grounds, wear no clothes, and act like lunatics. They often use intoxicants. Frequently, they are said to be assisted by spirits and other disembodied entities.

Tantrists in general, and Aghoris in particular, tend toward the worship of the female aspect of the deity, such as Ma Kali or Durga. I am not familiar with any Aghora practice outside isolated parts of India. Aghoris typically shun Westerners and make themselves unavailable to them.

FOR ADDITIONAL INFORMATION

For more information about Tantrism, see "Eastern Masters and Movements" on page 305, "Tibetan Buddhism" on page 43, and "Taoism" on page 49. Some of the better known tantric teachers are Osho Rajneesh, Mantak Chia, Vethathiri Maharishi, and Yogi Bhajan. Most teachers, particularly the Tibetans, are very discreet about the more radical tantric practices and may not volunteer to share them with a new aspirant.

Recommended Readings

Chia, Mantak, and Michael Winn. *Taoist Secrets of Love*. Santa Fe, NM: Aurora Press, 1984.

Hooper, Anne, ed. *Kama Sutra*. London: DK Publishing, 1994.

Pa, Tsong-Ka. *Deity Yoga: In Action and Performance Tantra*. Ithaca, NY: Snow Lion Publishing, 1987.

Rajneesh, Bhagawan Shree. *The Book of the Secrets*. New York: St. Martin's Press, 1998.

Singh, Jaideva. *The Doctrine of Recognition*. Albany, NY: State University of New York Press, 1990.

Svoboda, Robert E. *Aghora at the Left Hand of God*. Albuquerque, NM: Brotherhood of Life, Inc., 1986.

Recommended Websites

earth.path.net/osho

www.abhidyan.org

www.healingtao.org

www.scand-yoga.org

www.tantra.com

www.yogibhajan.com

SIKHISM

Sikhism is an eclectic faith that includes elements of both Bhakti (devotional) Hinduism and the Sufi Muslims, and is based on the teachings of its founder, Guru Nanak, as well as the nine succeeding Gurus.

HISTORY

The Sikh faith and line of Gurus started in northern India with the birth of Guru Nanak in A.D. 1469. It is believed by the Sikhs that Nanak, at the age of thirty, had gone to bathe in a nearby stream, disappeared in the water, and apparently drowned. During this incident, God spoke to him and gave him a mission to preach. He then miraculously recovered from his "drowning" and returned from the stream. This event is described in detail in his *Janam Sakhis*, or *Birth Stories*.

During Nanak's life, Hinduism and Islam, the dominant religions in northern India, influenced the Sikh philosophy. Sikhism includes elements of both Bhakti (devotional) Hinduism and the Sufi religion. (See "Sufism" on page 221.) Most of Nanak's followers had been either Hindus or Muslims, and now described themselves as "Nanakprasthas" (followers of Nanak's path), or as his disciples—Sikhs. The word *sikh* means *learner* in Sanskrit.

After Nanak came a succession of Sikh Gurus that has continued in an unbroken line to the present day. Before Nanak's death, he appointed a disciple, Angad, to carry on his mission. Angad was succeeded by his disciple, Amar Das, who then nominated his son-in-law, Ram Das Sodhi. From this point on, the role of Guru remained in the Sodhi family. Ram Das nominated his son, Arjun, who compiled the sacred scripture of the Sikhs, the *Granth Sahib*, or *Adi Granth*, which consists of hymns of the first four Gurus, his own compositions, and writings of various Hindu and Muslim saints from northern India.

Arjun then nominated his son, Guru Hargobind, who was succeeded by his grandson, Har Rai. Next came his son, Hari Krishen, who died as a child, so Hargobind's surviving son, Tegh Bahadur, was acclaimed by the Sikhs as their ninth Guru. Tegh Bahadur was at odds with the invading Moguls, and they had him beheaded. Then his only son, Gobind Rai, succeeded him as the tenth Sikh Guru.

On the Punjabi New Year's Day in A.D. 1699, Gobind Rai baptized the Khalsa, or Brotherhood of the Pure Ones, and gave them, as well as himself, the new family name of Singh, which means *lion*. Sikh men keep the name Singh, whereas women use the name Kaur, which means *princess*. In addition to keeping a spiritual name, Sikhs wear their hair unshorn, usually under a turban, grow beards, wear a comb, put on a steel wrist band, and often carry a saber, or kirpan.

Before his death, Gobind Singh proclaimed that the line of Gurus was at an end, and thereafter the *Adi Granth* would be regarded as the living Guru, and be known as Sri Guru Granth Sahib.

According to a 1971 Indian census, there are approximately 10 million Sikhs in the country (slightly less than two percent of the population). Sikhism has also been accepted by many Westerners, and has spread around the world.

BELIEF SYSTEM

Guru Nanak taught that God cannot be perceived in human or any other form, but can be known only through the divine name (Nam). Nanak thought that the aim of life was union with God, and that union could be achieved by blending your light with the eternal light. Meditation or the chanting of various names of God would bring about the inner light and sound, or word of God, that would then free you from the illusion (maya) of the physical world, whereupon you could then come to know God. In order to obtain true knowledge of God, you have to become detached from worldly things and "overcome the base desires and battle with the mind." Nanak thought that realization of Truth comes from within your heart through the light and sound of God.

The Sikh Guru is the mediator of divine grace and closest embodiment of divinity that can be known. Through the direction of the Guru, you can become aware of the "unstruck sound" (anahad shabd) that lies at the heart of creation and thus purify yourself and achieve a higher state of consciousness. The Sikhs believe that you are born in ignorance of God's grace, become awakened to the Truth through the grace of the Guru, and awaken to realize God. It is the bliss of this realization that allows you to approach God.

RITUALS AND HOLY DAYS

Sikhs are expected to rise before dawn, bathe, and then recite the Jap-ji, the sacred prayer, or mantra, of Nanak. Sikhs also recite four other prayers during the day. The Sikh baptism (pahul) is performed in the presence of the *Adi Granth*, which is considered the embodiment of the Guru. Sikhs celebrate the birthdays of their Gurus, the martyrdoms of Guru Arjun and Tegh Bahadur, the anniversary of the Khalsa, as well as the many Hindu festivals of their culture.

On special occasions, the whole of the *Adi Granth* is read out loud. This unbroken reading, or Akhand Path, takes two days and nights to complete. The *Adi Granth*, an object of worship, is placed in the temples at a place of honor on a raised platform, where it is garlanded, fanned, and reverently covered with cloth at night. Devotees bring offerings of specially prepared food, such as a solid porridge made of honey and wheat, or a puffed rice candy. Services typically include the musical reading of the *Adi Granth* from a granthi, or cantor. Sikhs also take pilgrimages to holy places, such as the Golden Temple in Amritsar and Guru Gobind Singh's residence, Anandpur Sahib, in the Himalayan foothills.

FOR ADDITIONAL INFORMATION

Recommended Contacts

Sikh Council of North America   Sikh Dharma
95-30 118th Street   Box 35330
Richmond Hill, NY 11419   Los Angeles, CA 90035

Recommended Readings

McLeod, W. H. *The Sikhs: History, Religion and Society*. New York: Columbia University Press, 1989.

Nanak, Guru. *The Jap-ji*, trans. P. Lal. London: Periplus Line, 1973.

Theosophical Publishing House, trans. *The Gospel of the Guru-Granth Sahib*. Madras, India: Theosophical Publishing House, 1975.

Recommended Websites

www.dancris.com/sikh   www.sikhs.org
www.sikhmuseum.org

JAINISM

The term *Jainism* comes from the Sanskrit word *Jaina*, which means *follower of a Jina*. The latter is a Sanskrit word meaning *conqueror*, or *victor*. Thus, a Jina is one who conquers his inner enemies to bring out his highest qualities. Jainism is a system of asceticism and meditation that teaches Jiva (the soul of each person) how to conquer material existence and achieve liberation from it.

HISTORY

In Jain philosophy, there was a series of twenty-four great teachers known as tirthankaras, or "crossing-makers," who have shown mankind the vehicle to freedom from the bondage of the material world. The founder of Jainism, the first tirthankara, was A-dina-than, or Rsabha. However, modern Jainism is based on the teachings of the twenty-fourth and last tirthankara, known as Mahavira, "the Great Hero," who was born in 598 B.C., near the city of Patna in northeastern India.

Mahavira was born into a warrior (Kshatriya) clan, but abandoned his home at age thirty to become an ascetic. For twelve years, he wandered the countryside, begging and meditating. When, at age forty-two, Mahavira attained complete knowledge (kaiualya), he began teaching, and a following quickly grew up around him. In 527 B.C., Mahavira died and the leadership passed on to the Ganadharas, or "leaders of the assembly." The movement continued to grow throughout India, but not too much outside of India since many Jains refuse to take any form of public transportation, preferring to travel only on foot. Today, there are about 4 million Jains, the vast majority residing within India.

There are two Jain sects: the Digambaras and the Shvetambaras. The former completely renounce most worldly things, including the wearing of clothes, while the latter propagate literature and wear only white monastic robes.

BELIEF SYSTEM

Jainism is based on four main principles:

1. Ahimsa, nonviolence in its broadest sense, including nonviolence in action, speech, and thought;

2. Anekantwad, the belief that there is no "one Truth," but many truths, each represented by a different point of view;

3. Aparigraha, nonattachment to people, ideas, feelings, and material things; and

4. Karma, taking responsibility for your actions, words, and thoughts, which shape our futures. Karma is also involved with the concept of reincarnation—repeated births on the earth in order to learn from our actions, so we can be reborn, or reincarnated, into a new life in the next existence.

The philosophy of Jainism revolves around the concept of soul, Jiva, which is believed to be bound up in your material existence. This bondage is created by karma—your physical actions and inner agitation—which creates material consequences. Your outer actions create an inner turmoil that estranges you from your soul, or Jiva, and this, in turn, causes your suffering in this world.

The goal of the Jain is to free your Jiva from that bondage. The only way to do so is to reduce the inner and outer activity to a bare minimum and finally stop it altogether. Inactivity will impede further accumulation of karma and cleanse the soul. Once freed, the Jiva ascends and abides in its innate perfection. This inner quiet is obtained through meditation.

RITUALS AND HOLY DAYS

Jainism centers around monastic life supported by laypersons. Monks (and in some sects, nuns) take vows to abstain from violence, deceit, theft, sex, and attachment to material things. The thrust of Jainism lies in its meditation techniques. Emphasis is placed on the enhancement of inner experiences and the development of the soul's consciousness.

Emptying the thoughts and energies of the mind and focusing the attention on the knower, or agent of perception, are the key factors in Jain meditation. Developing the inner awareness liberates the soul from the bondage of suffering. Generally, monks adopt the way of life of a wandering beggar, relying on alms from the populace for their survival, retiring to monastic houses or temples only during the rainy season to avoid hurting small animals that swarm in mud. Jains go out of their way to avoid killing any animals, including insects, which they consider sacred.

Laypersons accept a similar but less austere form of life, modified from the five monastic vows, adding almsgiving. Householders practice meditation, fast twice a lunar month, and publicly confess their faults to purify themselves.

Temple rituals include veneration of the Tirthankaras, the early Gurus, by offering flowers and fruits, singing devotional songs, chanting, praying, and meditating before them. Jains are also very much a part of Hindu culture and generally observe the holidays and festivals of those traditions in the regions where they happen to live.

FOR ADDITIONAL INFORMATION

Recommended Contacts

The following is a sample of some of the sites available. For a more complete listing, consult the Internet sites recommended below.

International Nahavir Jain
Mission
722 Tomkins Avenue
Staten Island, NY 10305

Jain Center for Northern
California
2983 Mitton Drive
San Jose, CA 95148
Phone: (408) 274–7864

Jain Center of Southern
California
8072 Commonwealth Avenue
Buena Park, CA 90621
Phone: (714) 994–2266

Jain Meditation Center
176 Ansonia Station
New York, NY 10023
Phone: (212) 362–6483

Jain Society of Southern Florida
8010 South Lake Drive
West Palm Beach, FL 33406
Phone: (305) 595–3833

Recommended Readings

Chitrabhanu, Gurudev Shree. *Realize What You Are: The Dynamics of Jain Meditation*. New York: Dodd, Mead and Co., 1978.

Rampuria, S. *Facets of Jain Philosophy, Religion and Culture*.Columbia, MO: South Asia Books, 1996.

Recommended Websites

www.cs.colostate.edu   www.jainworld.com

BUDDHISM

Buddhism is based on the teachings of its founder, who was known as the Buddha. The term *buddha* is a participle of the Sanskrit verbal root *Budh*, meaning *to awaken*, and is employed as the title, "the Awakened One," or "Enlightened One."

HISTORY

The Buddha, whose given name was Siddhartha Gautama, was born in Kapilavastu in Nepal near the Indian border, and is generally believed to have lived from 560 to 480 B.C. He was born a prince in the kingdom of the Sakyas, and lived in a palace with many luxuries. He is reported to have married a young princess named Yasodhara at the age of sixteen, and to have fathered a son, Rahula. Siddhartha lived a sheltered life as a prince, and was shielded from the suffering that took place in the world. During a rare trip outside of his palace, he was exposed to four sights that deeply moved him: a sick person, an old person, a corpse, and an ascetic. This last man was attempting to escape the problems of suffering and death by renouncing the responsibilities and pleasures of ordinary existence. Gautama reflected upon what he had seen, and made a decision that changed history.

At the age of twenty-nine, Siddhartha left his family and kingdom, renounced his fortune, and became an ascetic. He spent the next six years wandering about the valley of the Ganges, and meeting famous yogis and sadhus, such as Arada Kalama of Vaisali and Udraka Ramaputra of Magadha. Learning from these spiritual masters, he acquired the practice of meditation and yoga. He began the strict practice of austerities, and this gained him a favorable reputation and respect among his peers.

After undergoing many years of strict asceticism without discovering the answers to liberation, Siddhartha abandoned his attachment to the religious systems he had been following. Instead, he adopted a balanced form of discipline—called the Middle Path—in which he avoided the extremes of both self-denial and self-indulgence.

How did he discover this Middle Path? While seated under a banyan tree (the Bodhi Tree, or "Tree of Awakening"), he resolved to sit in meditation and not leave until attaining enlightenment. After a series of temptations and an ordeal of meditation, he awakened from the sleep of ignorance that binds living beings to suffering and attained nirvana (enlightenment). This momentous event occurred along the bank of the river Neranjara at Bodh Gaya, near Gaya in modern Bihar, India. At the time, Gautama had attained the age of thirty-five.

As a result of this "enlightenment," the Buddha began teaching his Middle Way to all who would listen, regardless of caste, race, or sex—a practice that was unusual in the Hindu caste society of India at the time. His first sermon was to a group of five ascetics; these men were his old colleagues from Deer Park at Isipatana, now Saranath, near Benares, India. Naturally, the Buddhists consider this site sacred and hold it as a major holy place.

For the next forty-five years, he and his disciples wandered throughout the larger Ganges River basin, proclaiming his teachings. Buddhism rapidly spread, as many were in search of truth and found this new teaching sensible and appealing. Since then, over hundreds of years, Buddhism has spread to Tibet, China, Japan, and beyond. Today, Buddhism is practiced around the world, with some 500 million adherents, concentrated primarily in the Asian countries.

BELIEF SYSTEM

Buddhist teachings center on the theme of liberation from suffering and repeated incarnations into a perfectly peaceful and enlightened state of transformed consciousness referred to as nirvana. The key to achieving this liberation, or moksha, lies in the cessation of selfish desires and attachments. Inherent in these beliefs are the twin Hindu principles of karma—the actions you take in your life—and dharma—righteousness. The latter, which the Buddha referred to as "the lovely" (kalyana), denotes serene peace, in which the twin fires of self-centered desire and attachment are extinguished. Buddha's teachings focus on dharma as the primary means of acquiring liberation.

The Buddhist believes that you are born into suffering, but through righteous actions, you are able to evolve yourself to attain enlightenment. Faithfully following the Buddhist teachings will bring you to nirvana, or enlightenment. At the core of the Buddha's teachings are the Four Noble Truths. These truths consist of:

1. Duhkha, the universal fact of suffering;

2. Samudaya, the cause of suffering;

3. Nirodha, the defeat of suffering; and

4. Magga, the way of overcoming suffering.

The way of overcoming suffering is through "The Noble Eightfold Path," another concept central to Buddhist teaching. This Noble Eightfold Path consists of practicing: (1) right understanding, (2) right thought, (3) right speech, (4) right action, (5) right livelihood, (6) right effort, (7) right mindfulness, and (8) right concentration (meditation). Practice of this spiritual path is considered the method of acquiring dharma and achieving nirvana during one's lifetime.

Within Buddhism, there lie two main schools of thought and practice: Theravada-Hinayana, or "small vehicle," also known as "The School of Elders" (Theras), which was the original line of teachings; and the Mahayana, or "Great Vehicle," which is the larger group. The Theravada is generally considered more orthodox Buddhism, and is primarily practiced in Ceylon, Bangladesh, and Southeast Asia. Mahayana is more of a reform teaching that developed later, and is followed principally in China, Tibet, and Japan. The Mahayana group includes several large sects, such as Madhyamika, Vijnanavada, T'ien-t'ai, Hua-Yen, and Ch'an, or Zen.

RITUALS AND HOLY DAYS

Religious festivals within Buddhism fall into three categories: those that celebrate the person of the Buddha; those that celebrate his teachings (dharma); and those that celebrate the founding of monastic orders (Sangha). As festivals within the Theravada and Mahayana schools vary considerably, they will be described separately in the following pages.

FOR ADDITIONAL INFORMATION

I highly recommend the book *Buddhist America*, edited by Don Morreale, for it describes the various Buddhist sects and provides the addresses of various centers and retreat facilities throughout the Americas. There are also numerous Buddhist temples and centers throughout North America, usually in Asian communities. Look up "Buddhism" in your telephone directory, or consult your metaphysical bookshop or health food store for more information. You could also peruse the periodicals suggested on page 35.

Recommended Contacts

American Buddhist Congress
4267 W. Third Street
Los Angeles, CA 90020

Buddhist Sangha Council of
Southern California
928 S. New Hampshire Ave.
Los Angeles, CA 90006

Recommended Readings

Each Buddhist sect has its own preferred scriptures. Thus, see also "Theravada" on page 37, "Mahayana" on page 40, "Tibetan" on page 43, and "Zen Buddhism" on page 46. Although there is no one source of Buddhist doctrine used by all believers, the following should prove useful:

Kaviratna, Harischandra, trans. *The Dhammapada, Wisdom of the Buddha*. Pasadena, CA: Theosophical University Press, 1980.

Morreale, Don, ed. *Buddhist America*. Boston, MA: Shambhala Publications, 1998.

Rahula, Walpola. *What the Buddha Taught*. New York: Grove Press, 1959.

Watson, Burton, trans. *The Lotus Sutra*. New York: Columbia University Press, 1994.

Woodward, F. L. *The Minor Anthologies of the Pali Canon*. Somerville, MA: Wisdom Publications, 1935.

Recommended Periodicals

Shambhala Sun
1585 Burrington Street,
   Suite 300
Halifax, Nova Scotia
Canada B3J128
Phone: (877) 786–1950
Website: www.shambhalasun.com

Turning Wheel
BPF National Office
P.O. Box 4650
Berkeley, CA 94704
Phone: (510) 655–6169
Website: www.bpf.org/tw.html

Tricycle: The Buddhist Review
92 Vandam Street
New York, NY 10013
Phone: (212) 645–1143
Website: www.tricycle.com

Recommended Websites

www.buddhanet.com

www.buddhism.org

www.ciolek.com/wwwvl.Buddhism.
  html

www.llamalinks.com/buddhism.
  html

THERAVADA BUDDHISM

Within Buddhism, there are two major schools, Theravada Buddhism, discussed in this section, and Mahayana Buddhism, discussed in the next. The former comes from the Sanskrit *theravada*, which means *elders*, referring to those who were present at the inception of the sect.

HISTORY

After the Buddha's Parinibbana, or final liberation from the cycle of birth and death, some five hundred living disciples convened at what is known as the First Great Council of the Theras, or "elders." All of the disciples were Arahants (fully enlightened beings) who met in an effort to preserve the entire body of Buddha's teachings for mankind. The body of knowledge preserved by the First Great Council of the Theras, plus its later commentary, comprises over 20,000 pages. It is known as the *Pali Canon*, and has served as foundation and guide for the Theravadans ever since the First Great Council.

BELIEF SYSTEM

The core of Buddhist discipline lies in the eradication of cravings, and ideally, this is achieved through the practice of the Noble Eightfold Path. This path can be divided into three categories: (1) moral conduct, which includes right speech, right action, right livelihood; (2) mental discipline, which includes right effort, right mindfulness, right concentration; and (3) intuitive wisdom, which includes right views and right intentions. Essentially, you must not commit any harmful or negative action, deed, or thought; you should discipline the mind and gain control over it; and you should develop your inner awareness through contemplation and introspection.

The Theravadans also believe that there is no permanent self or soul, only that you are a combination of what they call the five aggregates (skandhas): matter, sensation, perception, predisposition, and consciousness. Moreover, they believe that as you realize that your self is only a fluctuating state of physical and psychical phenomena, you can eliminate your egotistical tendencies and attachments to worldly desires. It is only through this eradication of ignorance, lustful cravings, and selfish thoughts that you can eliminate karma and repeated rebirths, and achieve the state of bliss called nirvana.

RITUALS AND HOLY DAYS

Theravada Buddhism is a discipline in which an individual is engaged in ascetic practices in order to achieve salvation or liberation (moksha) for himself by himself. Buddha's teachings of Theravada are meant for both the monastic and the layperson, each living in harmony with and mutual support of one another. In this manner, the monastics insure the continuity of the Vinaya—Buddha's teachings for the uprooting of all greed, aversion, and delusion—and provide spiritual services to the community. By supporting the renunciates and the monastic way of life, householders provide themselves with dharma and meditation teachers.

The holiest festival for the Theravadans is Buddha's Day or Visakha Puja, which is celebrated on full-moon day of the lunar month of Visakha (April-May). This day commemorates the birth, enlightenment, and death of the Buddha, which is believed to have happened miraculously on the same day of the week. On this day, devotees flock to monasteries to listen to a traditional sermon on the life of the Buddha, solemnly walk in procession about the reliquary, water the sacred Bodhi Tree, lustrate their sacred Buddha images, and renew their dedication to the Five Precepts: not to kill, steal, lie, abuse sex, or take intoxicants. The Buddha's First Discourse, *Dhammacakkappavattana Sutra*, or *Setting the Wheel of the Law in Motion*, is also honored on the full moon of Asalha, in the eighth lunar month. This is a time of reflection on the Buddha's teaching. This is a time of resolution to stay on the path.

Other religious holidays center around different cultural events and the founding of religious orders; these vary with each country and sect. Buddha rituals are also a part of harvest festivals, new year ceremonies, and celebrations at the end of the monsoon season; these also vary with each geographic region and sect.

FOR ADDITIONAL INFORMATION

Recommended Contact

DharmaNet International
3115 San Ramon Rd.
Concord, CA 94519-2226
Website: www.dharmanet.org

Recommended Readings

Bhikku, Thanissaro. *The Wings to Awaken: An Anthology from the Pali Canon*. Barre, MA: Dhammadana Publishers, 1996.

Thera, Ven. Nyanaponika. *The Heart of Buddhist Meditation*. York Beach, ME: Samuel Weiser, 1976.

Recommended Websites

www.dhamma.com

www.dharmanet.org

www.std.com

www.zip.com/au

MAHAYANA BUDDHISM

As I mentioned at the beginning of the last section, there are two schools of Buddhism, the Theravada and the Mahayana. In this section, I will discuss the Mahayana, which comes from the Sanskrit word *Mahayanam*, which means *great vehicle*.

HISTORY

Elements of the Mahayana tradition began developing one hundred years after Buddha's physical incarnation, as arguments occurred within the Sangha relevant to the interpretation and implementation of Buddha's words. The first group to split from the Theras were the Mahasanghikas, who were the forerunners of the Mahayana school. Five hundred years after Buddha's time, around the year A.D. 1, several major points of dissension had developed as the laity began to reject the "orthodox" and monastic forms of practice in favor of taking a more active and personal role in the worship and exercise of their religion. Mahayanan adherents claimed that they were only revealing doctrines that had previously been considered too sacred to be shared with the laity.

In Tibet, Mahayana first completely replaced the Theravada tradition, and then merged with the indigenous religion of Bon to become the esoteric branch of Buddhism called the Vajrayana, which will be dealt with separately. (See "Tibetan Buddhism" on page 43.)

BELIEF SYSTEM

There are several striking differences between Theravada and Mahayana schools of Buddhism. Unlike the Theravadan, for example, the Mahayana tradition is likened to a broad river that accommodates all manner of craft, and the religion has spread far and wide, due to its willingness to assimilate cultural elements that were new and foreign to it. Also, unlike the Theravadan tradition, in Mahayana Buddhism there is the concept of the bodhisattva; rather than attaining individual enlightenment, the bodhisattva takes a vow to forgo the joy of nirvana until all beings have become enlightened. And, unlike the Theravadans, the

Mahayana Buddhists believe that everyone possesses the Buddha nature and is capable of becoming a Buddha, or enlightened one.

In that tradition, the concept of Buddha developed into the idea that there is an eternal Buddha who embodies the absolute Truth. Reality is held to be knowledge experienced before the perception of duality, a predifferentiated state of sunyata, or "emptiness," which underlies the fundamental nature of all reality. Achieving this awareness of nonduality is "enlightenment," and you do have the capacity to realize this true nature within yourself. Thus, you do have the Buddha nature within, and your goal is to reawaken this Buddhahood for the benefit of all mankind.

As I mentioned in the previous section on Buddhism, there are several schools within the Mahayana tradition, each emphasizing a different aspect of that tradition. For instance, the Madhyamika school, founded by Nagarjuna in the second century A.D., contends that what is produced by causes does not, in and of itself, exist. Moreover, their belief holds a number of paradoxes: that nothing comes into being, and nothing disappears; that nothing is eternal and nothing has an end; and that nothing is identical or differentiated. It is believed that, with these precepts, no attachment to thoughts can be created, and the inner awareness is thus freed.

Another, the Vijnanavada (Yoga Cara) school, founded by Asanga and Vasubandhu around the fourth century A.D., contends that individuals have no direct perception of the external world; therefore, the whole world is only a mental representation or "ideation." Then there is the T'ien-t'ai school, which posits that the Absolute is one and undifferentiated, but is, nevertheless, diverse and particular in its function; therefore, your work as a layman is one with that of the Buddha, and strides should be made to realize that single beingness. Similarly, the Hua-Yen ("Kegon" in Japan) school states that you are all sons of the Buddha and possess the Buddha-nature within you. Finally, the Ch'an (or Zen) school emphasizes a simple and direct method of meditation in order to realize your Buddha nature within. Regarding the latter: Because of its familiarity and popularity in the West, Zen Buddhism will be discussed at greater length as a separate religion later in the text.

RITUALS AND HOLY DAYS

In Mahayana Buddhist traditions, devotees typically celebrate the birth of the Buddha, the Enlightenment of the Buddha, and the death or ascension of the Buddha. Depending on the culture and sect of the teaching, these festivals are held on different days and celebrated in different ways. The procession and bathing of Buddha images is a special characteristic of Buddha's Day celebrations in China, Korea, and Japan. The *Mahasttva Sutra* designates the eighth day of the fourth lunar month as the most propitious time to purify the Buddha images in order to achieve rewards and good luck. Buddha images may be honored as a physical representation of the enlightened one (Tathagata) or of celestial Buddhas, and therefore, it is typical to have individual ceremonies honoring particular Buddha images. It is also common to take a pilgrimage to sacred Buddhist sites, such as Bodh Gaya, where the Buddha attained enlightenment, or Sarnath, where Buddha first taught the Four Nobel Truths and The Eightfold Path; or to visit a site that houses a relic of the Buddha. For instance, the festival of the tooth relic is held in Kandy (Sri Lanka) each year during the lunar month of Asalha (late July). The *Lotus Sutra*, or *Saddharmapundarika Sutra*, which is the basic text of the T'ient'ai and Nichiren schools, is also the object of worship and annual celebration in China, Korea, and Japan.

FOR ADDITIONAL INFORMATION

Recommended Readings

Chang, Garma C. C. *A Treasury of Mahayana Sutras*. University Park, PA: The Pennsylvania State University Press, 1983.

Thich, Nhat-Hahn. *The Sutra on the Eight Realizations of the Great Beings*. Carole Melkonian, trans. Berkeley, CA: Parallax Press, 1987.

Wong, Mou-Lam, trans. *The Diamond Sutra*. Boston, MA: Shambhala Publications, 1990.

Recommended Websites

buddhanet.net   www.dharmanet.org

buddhism.tqn.com   www.edharma.com

TIBETAN BUDDHISM

Tibetan Buddhism, often referred to as the Vajrayana (or Diamond Vehicle), is a tantric form of Mahayana Buddhism indigenous to Tibet.

HISTORY

Buddhism was introduced to Tibet during the reign of Srong-brtsan-sgam-po, the thirty-second king of Tibet, around A.D. 650. The king had married Chinese and Nepalese princesses, who were both Buddhist. They were able to sway the king away from the prevailing religion, called Bon, and convince him to adopt Buddhist teachings. As a result, King Srong-brtsan-sgam-po built several Buddhist temples, and had many Buddhist books from India translated into Tibetan.

By the seventh century, a form of Indian Tantrism called the Vajrayana, or "Diamond Vehicle," was established; it taught formulas for sudden enlightenment, *The Direct Path*, for example. In A.D. 747, a reform movement was spearheaded by the great teacher from India, Guru Padmasambhava, who reestablished the ethical and intellectual heritage of older Buddhism and initiated the building of the first monastery in Tibet, the Samyas, which was completed in A.D. 787. In the following centuries, a vast number of religious texts, such as the *Kanjur* and *Tanjur*, were compiled, and tension mounted between the ethical-intellectual and magical-ritualistic elements of Buddhism in Tibet.

In the fourteenth and fifteenth centuries, the Dalai Lama, who is believed to be the reincarnation of a bodhisattva (an enlightened being), was established as the spiritual and temporal head of Tibet. With the advent of the Communist insurgency of 1959 in China, the Dalai Lama was forced to flee to India, awaiting a favorable time to return to Tibet and reestablish the Buddhist government. Today, Tibetan Buddhism is gaining interest in the West, with lamas (monks) coming to the United States and Europe to teach the dharma, or spiritual law.

BELIEF SYSTEM

Tibetan Buddhism is founded on the Four Noble Truths established by the Buddha (see "Buddhism" on page 32). The object is to obtain the ultimate release of all sentient beings from the suffering of the endless cycle of reincarnations (samsara). In Tibetan Buddhism, enlightenment, or nirvana, is found through the bodhisattvas, who are liberated themselves, but forgo nirvana in order to bring salvation to others. Tibetan Buddhism centers around a monastic way of living, though some of the teachings are available to the public through books and discourses.

Tibetan dharma is a sophisticated philosophy involving years of study. The meditations are highly intellectual, yet utilize magical formulas and cultic devotions. As a Tantric tradition, Tibetan Buddhism integrates the capacities of the mind with physical and emotional disciplines toward the search for salvation. Tibetan Buddhists not only strive to attain enlightenment, but forgo the bliss of nirvana until all sentient beings achieve enlightenment. Thus, every Buddhist serves to awaken humanity through contemplation, prayer, and good works.

There are four major orders of Tibetan Buddhism. These sects are:

1. The Nyingruapa, or "ancient ones," who trace their lineage back to Padmasambhava;

2. The Kargyupa, an oral tradition founded by Marpa in the eleventh century, is based on the fundamental teachings of Naropa;

3. The Saskyapa, founded in the eleventh century, was the first to establish a priestly monarchy; and

4. The Gelugpa, or "merit system ones," is led by the Dalai Lama, the spiritual leader of the Tibetan people and Buddhist followers.

RITUALS AND HOLY DAYS

In Tibet, the seminal events of the Buddha's life are celebrated independently. Buddha's conception is honored on the fifteenth day of the first lunar month, whereas his enlightenment is celebrated on the eighth day, and his death on the fifteenth day of the fourth month. Elaborate processions and ceremonies mark each of these festivals. In Tibet, each monastery also annually honors the particular tantra, or sacred text, to which the school ascribes special importance, and all schools celebrate the commemoration of the *Kalachakra Tantra*—revealed by Shakyamuni Buddha—on the fifteenth day of the third lunar month. This celebration always includes reading the *Kalachakra* and contemplating its meaning.

FOR ADDITIONAL INFORMATION

Recommended Contact

Tibet House
32 West 15th Street
New York, NY 10011
Phone: (212) 807–0563
Website: www.tibethouse.org

Recommended Readings

Chang, Garma C. C., and Mi-La-Ras-Pa, trans. *The Hundred Thousand Songs of Milarepa*. Boston, MA: Shambhala Publications, Inc., 1999.

Cutler, Howard C., and the Dalai Lama. *The Art of Happiness*. New York: Riverhead Books/Penguin Putnam, 1998.

Fremantle, Frances, and Chogyam Trunpa. *The Tibetan Book of the Dead*. Boston, MA: Shambhala Publications, Inc., 1975.

Gyatsho, Tenzin [The Dalai Lama of Tibet]. *The Opening of the Wisdom-Eye*. Pasadena, CA: Theosophical Publishing House, 1986.

Mullin, Glenn H. *The Practice of Kalachakra*. Ithaca, NY: Snow Lion Publications, Inc., 1991.

Rinpoche, Kalu. *The Gem Ornament of Manifold Oral Instructions*. Ithaca, NY: Snow Lion Publications, Inc., 1976.

Trungpa, Chogyam. *Shambhala: The Sacred Path of the Warrior*. Boston, MA: Shambhala Publications, Inc., 1988.

Recommended Websites

www.dharma-haven.org

www.dharmapress.com

www.fpmt.org

www.kalavinka.org

www.nyingma.org

www.quietmountain.com

www.rokpa.org

www.shambhala.com

www.shambhala.org

www.snowlionpubl.com

www.vajrayana.org

ZEN (CH'AN) BUDDHISM

Zen is the Japanese pronunciation of the Chinese word *ch'an*, which means *meditation*. Zen is a highly refined form of Mahayana Buddhism, which emphasizes the aim of enlightenment.

Zen, or Ch'an, is a Chinese synthesis and adaptation of the two schools of Mahayana Buddhism that had their origins in India: The Madhyamika school, which emphasizes that all forms and thought are essentially empty in nature, and utilizes the way of negation and intuitive thought; and the Yoga Cara school, which emphasizes that consciousness alone is real, and utilizes meditation as the principal discipline.

HISTORY

As early as the fifth century A.D., the Indian teacher Kumarajiva and the meditation master Buddhabhadra were preparing the way for Zen. In fact, one of Kumarajiva's disciples, Tao-sheng, is credited by some as the actual founder of Zen. By tradition, Zen has its origin in the esoteric teachings of the Buddha, when the Buddha stood on Vulture Peak, holding a lotus, and remained silent before his disciples. Through the silence, the disciple Mahakasyapa achieved nirvana, or enlightenment, and from him the "lamp of enlightenment" was passed on to the twenty-eighth patriarch, Bodhidharma, who carried the "lamp" to China and founded the Ch'an (Zen) tradition.

Little is known about the patriarchs and about the evolution of Zen from Bodhidharma until the Fang dynasty (A.D. 618–906). During the T'ang dynasty, a revolutionary form of Ch'an was developing that rejected sutra study, ritual, and the veneration of images, and instead preached the methods of "sudden enlightenment."

Ch'an forms of Buddhism were introduced to Japan from Korea in A.D. 552, and flourished under the patronage of Prince Shotoku (d. 621). It was during the Kamakura period (1185–1333) that Zen was established in Japan, primarily through the efforts of two Japanese monks, Eisai and Dogen. Eisai, who died in 1215, traveled to China and trained with Lin-Chi, or Rinzai meditation masters, and brought the sect to Japan in 1191. Ch'an was readily accepted by the Shoguns and Samurai of Japan, and it flourished as Rinzai Zen. Dogen, who died in 1253, is credited with the founding of the Soto sect in Japan, and with establishing the first Zen temple in 1236.

Zen has also impacted the West. With Zen Master Soyen Shaku's appearance at the World Parliament of Religions at the Chicago World's Fair of 1893, and decades of work by Dr. D. T. Suzuki, who died in 1970, Zen practice has steadily grown, particularly in California and Hawaii.

BELIEF SYSTEM

Zen is fundamentally a school of Mahayana Buddhism, and shares traditions, sutras, rules, and rituals with other Mahayanists. However, the Zen tradition has veered away from scholasticism and emphasizes the direct personal experience of enlightenment, or Satori. Fostering, deepening, and expressing the experience of the Buddha-mind are the primary focal points of Zen Buddhism. The aim of enlightenment is the unfolding of the inner mind experience through meditation. Zen is characterized by the doctrines of sunyata (emptiness) and bodhi (enlightenment). The direct experience of enlightenment, the Buddha-mind, is believed to express itself in every detail of nature and in every activity.

RITUALS AND PRACTICES

At the heart of Zen practice is monasticism. Monastic life combines simplicity and discipline, and involves the practices of seated meditation (za-zen) in a zendo (meditation hall), with instruction from a roshi, or Zen master. In Rinzai sects, emphasis is placed on seated meditation in which the concentration is intensified through the use of an "encouragement stick," which is applied to your back in order to rouse and deepen your concentration during meditation. Another tool used in Rinzai is the koan exercise. An abstract thought, or riddle, is given to the student to contemplate, such as, "What is the sound of one hand clapping?" In Soto sects, emphasis is placed on identifying za-zen itself with enlightenment, and being fully present, or mindful, within each moment. In both disciplines meditation is the key to the practice, and understanding comes from a direct personal experience with Truth rather than from an intellectual understanding.

FOR ADDITIONAL INFORMATION
Recommended Readings

Cleary, Thomas. *Zen Essence*. Boston, MA: Shambhala Publishing, 1995.

Hahn, Thich Nhat. *Being Peace*. Berkeley, CA: Parallax Press, 1996.

Kapleau, Roshi. *The Three Pillars of Zen*. New York: Anchor, 1989.

Suzuki, Daisetz Teitaro. *The Awakening of Zen*. Boston, MA: Shambhala Publishing, 1987.

Suzuki, Shunryu. *Zen Mind, Beginner's Mind*. Trumbull, CT: Weather Hill, 1972.

Watts, Allen. *The Spirit of Zen*. Rowesville, SC: Grove Press, 1969.

Recommended Websites

www.angelnet.com   www.kwanumzen.com

www.buddhanet.net   www.mbzc.org

www.dharmanet.org   www.sfzc.com

www.emptygatezen.com   www.zendo.com

www.izs.org

TAOISM

Tao is the ancient Chinese word for *way* or *the way*. Taoism is both a Chinese philosophical system and a religious teaching.

HISTORY

The origin of Taoism is obscure, but it is generally believed to have evolved around 700 to 100 B.C. The earliest Taoist classic, the *Tao Te Ching*, was composed by Lao-tzu around the sixth century B.C. Lao-tzu, who lived in the province of Honan, China, was an older contemporary of Confucius. Both Confucianism and Taoism have played an integral part in forming Chinese and other Eastern thought and cultures. But whereas Confucianism (see page 58) is more concerned with day-to-day rules of conduct and ethics, Taoism is more concerned with the spiritual aspect of being. Taoism has evolved considerably since its inception, and will be explained herein in both its philosophical and religious contexts.

BELIEF SYSTEM

The Tao is "the way," the source and essence of existence. Tao is the creator (Tsao-Wu Chu), impersonal and inseparable from creation. The Tao is viewed as both the source of creation, or "nonbeing" (wu, or "nothing"), and as creation itself manifested physically or mentally, or "being" (yu, or "to exist"). In this manner, human beings and the rest of existence are inseparable. All aspects or manifestations of existence are part of the one, the Tao. The first sentence of the *Tao Te Ching* states: "The Tao that can be told is not the eternal Tao." By being aware of what is, you transcend the understanding of it. Thus Taoist philosophy leads one beyond the very mind that strives to understand it. The Tao just IS.

In Taoism, the life-giving or sustaining energy is manifested as the chi (literally, "breath," "vapor," or "air"). This force moves in cycles throughout nature, from a positive pole to a negative pole and back. This movement is known as "reversal" (fan), and is characterized as the cycles of night and day, life and death, fortune and misfortune. It is perceived as responsible for the perceived chaos of existence. Later, this belief evolved into the concept of Yin and Yang, with Yin representing the "nonbeing" and Yang representing the "being" aspects of creation. Lao-tzu taught that one could not transcend the cycle of creation, but by learning to flow with the tides of change, one could find inner peace and tranquillity. The Tao is nonpurposeful, nondeliberate, and continually changing. This is believed to be the way for human beings to live at peace with themselves and with the world around them.

The Taoist philosophy states that when you are not at one with the Tao (the way things are), you experience suffering. In order to attain serenity, you need to find peace within yourself. To find that inner peace, you should stop wanting, stop trying, stop thinking, stop desiring things to be different from what they are. Rather, you should allow nature to provide everything by being at peace with it and without requiring payment from it. Thus, you should work with and learn from nature. You should be conscious of it and how it works. Moreover, the Truth comes naturally to a clear and open mind, and you gain all by giving up all. In other words, you should simply "be." Peace will come to a mind serene. This is the highest aspiration of man.

Tao-Chiao, "the teaching of the way," is a series of religious movements that worship the Tao (the way). These religious movements characteristically involve observing various ritual, alchemical, and meditative practices aiming at immortality. Taoist movements have involved frequent revelations based on direct communication with divine powers, and are often messianic, with visions of the ending of an old order and the coming of a new age.

The precepts of Taoism involve moral self-restraint, humility, and unselfishness. As Taoists perceive spirit and matter as being a part of the whole (nonbeing and being), the goal is not to obtain liberation of the soul (spirit) from matter (as is characteristic in many other religions), but rather to conserve, harmonize, and transform the chi (body/mind energy). By nourishing the chi, the cycle of progression from life to death, Yang to Yin, can be reversed, and move back from death to life, Yin to Yang, in order to reach an eternal state of transcendent being called the Chen Jen (true human). Thus the soul, not the physical body, achieves immortality, the goal in the Taoist religion.

RITUALS AND HOLY DAYS

Various rituals and techniques are used in the different Taoist movements to achieve immortality. For example, control of the chi (vital energy) through various deep and controlled breathing exercises is a common practice among Taoists, as are various meditative techniques usually done in conjunction with breath control. Another means is to eat foods and herbs that contain energies for the various life-sustaining bodily organs. Hygiene and exercise are also regarded as part of the required discipline. Practices of sexual restraint, both mental and physical, are also often used by the Taoist. This discipline might include either celibacy or the retention of seminal fluids normally ejaculated; or it might involve the suppression of orgasms during sexual intercourse in order to conserve the vital energies used to achieve spiritual immortality. Control over the worldly passions is seen as conserving vitality and is practiced in order to restore personal harmony with the Tao.

Taoism does not contain religious festivals per se. Within the Chinese culture, which integrates Taoist, Confucian, and Buddhist traditions, religious ceremonies, practices, and holidays have evolved, but they vary considerably within each province. Typically, a time is selected to honor a patriarch of an order, commemorate the new year, worship the ancestors, and mark seasonal changes relating to agriculture, such as planting and harvesting periods.

FOR ADDITIONAL INFORMATION

Facts can be best obtained through Chinese medical practitioners, healing centers (acupuncturists or herbalists, for example), and schools that practice the martial arts, such as Ta'i Chi and Kung Fu. In addition, you might consult Asian cultural centers, or search the Internet.

Recommended Contacts

Abode of the Eternal Tao
1991 Garfield Street
Eugene, OR 97405
Phone: (800) 574–5118

College of Tao
1314 Second Street
Santa Monica, CA 90401
Phone: (310) 917–2202
Website: www.yosan.edu

Dhan Tao Center
3053 West Olympic Boulevard
Los Angeles, CA 90006-2558
Phone: (213) 381–3893

Taoist Esoteric Yoga Center
   and Foundation
P.O. Box 1194
Huntington, NY 11743
Phone: (800) 497–1017

Taoist Sanctuary of San Diego
4229 Park Boulevard
San Diego, CA 92116
Phone: (619) 692-1155
Website: www.taoistsanctuary.org

Recommended Readings

Chan, Wing Tsit. *A Source Book in Chinese Philosophy*. Princeton, NJ: Princeton University Press, 1963.

Chia, Mantak, and Michael Winn. *Secrets of Love*. Santa Fe, NM: Aurora Press, 1984.

Hua-Ching, Ni. *Tao: The Universal Subtle Law*. Los Angeles, CA: College of Tao, 1979.

Lao-tzu. *The Tao Te Ching*. Gia-Fu Feng and Jane English, trans. New York: Vintage, 1997.

Lao-tzu. *The Tao Te Ching*. Stephen Mitchell, ed. New York: Harper Perennial Library, 1992.

Ming-Dao, Deng. *Everyday Tao: Living with Balance and Harmony*. San Francisco, CA: Harper, 1996.

Towler, Solala. *Embarking on the Way*. Eugene, OR: Abode of the Eternal Tao, 1998.

Recommended Periodical

The Empty Vessel: A Journal of Contemporary Taoism
The Abode of the Eternal Tao
1991 Garfield Street
Eugene, OR 97405
Phone: (800) 574–5118

Recommended Websites

www.abodetao.com   www.tao.org

www.edepot.com/taoism   www.taoismandpoetry.org

www.healingtao.org   www.taoist.org

TAI CHI CH'UAN

Tai Chi is the Chinese classical martial art of self-defense. *Tai Chi Ch'uan* literally means *supreme ultimate boxing*. Although it was used as a form of self-defense, it is now more popular as a form of active meditation.

HISTORY

The original study of T'ai Chi—with that ancient spelling—dates back to the founder Chang San-Feng, who wrote the *T'ai Chi Ch'uan Classic* during the Sung dynasty (A.D. 960–1279). This art form was further developed during the Ming dynasty (A.D. 1368–1644), by the great master Wang Chung Yueh, who wrote both the *Treatise on T'ai Chi Ch'uan* and *Mental Elucidation of the Thirteen Postures*. Within these three classics are the principles from which the techniques were derived. Tai Chi was very popular up until the Cultural Revolution in China, when the government suppressed the practice of ancient Chinese traditions, but it is reclaiming its popularity once again. Moreover, Tai Chi has become quite popular in many Western cultures, and is practiced by thousands throughout North America and Europe. Some forms serve as a martial art for self-defense, and others as a practice for health, longevity, and higher awareness. Tai Chi is taught in thousands of cities throughout the world, in martial arts studios, community recreation departments, and Taoist centers. Qigong and Kung Fu martial arts also typically utilize Tai Chi Ch'uan principles.

BELIEF SYSTEM

The classics from which Tai Chi Ch'uan was founded were based upon the philosophy of Taoism and the principles of the *I Ching*. The underlying principle of Tai Chi is becoming aware of, and cultivating, "chi," which is described as, "The one through which the Tao manifests itself and then differentiates into two forces (Yin and Yang) that interact to produce the world phenomena." The belief is that this life force energy, chi, can be generated in the area approximately two inches below your navel, known as the "Tan T'ien" or "Field of Cinnabar," and that this chi will then circulate throughout your body, providing increased vitality and intrinsic strength. The techniques of Tai Chi cultivate this chi in the Tan T'ien, and the practice of the moving postures develops the ability to direct and utilize your chi energy. This intensified energy can be used to neutralize your aggressive actions, increase your body's vitality and stamina, and heighten your faculties of awareness.

The practice originally involved thirteen postures: Ward Off, Roll Back, Press, Push, Pull, Split, Elbow-Stroke, Shoulder-Stroke, Advance, Retreat, Gaze to Left, Look to Right, and Central Equilibrium. Now the complete "long style" sequence includes up to 150 postures (depending on how you count them), which are performed in slow, circular movements. The mind directs the chi, and the chi directs the muscles and bones; and through your practice of Tai Chi, you learn to control the mind and body.

Tai Chi consists of a system of rounded, fluid, balanced movements that you should perform under the guidance of a qualified Tai Chi master. As you complete the postures, you become increasingly aware of the movement of chi within you, and learn how to integrate the energies within yourself—and between yourself and another, perhaps, even an opponent.

FOR ADDITIONAL INFORMATION
Recommended Contacts

Consult the telephone directory for the nearest martial arts studio or supply store, and ask where classes are scheduled. Many city recreation departments, YMCAs, and youth groups also offer classes in Tai Chi; most are oriented toward the personal growth aspects of the art. Also look into Taoist centers, martial arts centers—qigong or kung fu—and the periodicals on Tai Chi for other classes.

Boston Kung Fu Tai Chi Institute
361 Newbury Street
Boston, MA 02115
Phone: (617) 262–0600
Website: www.taichi.com

The School of Tai Chi Chuan
5 East 17th Street, 5th floor
New York, NY 10003
Phone: (888) 882–4424
Website: www.taichichuan.org

Tai Chi Chuan Center
125 West 43rd Street
New York, NY 10036
Phone: (212) 221–6110
Website: www.chutaichi.com

Taoist Tai Chi Society of the
USA
1310 North Monroe Street
Tallahassee, FL 32303
Phone: (904) 224–5438
E-mail: usa@taoist.org

United States Martial Arts
Association
8011 Mariposa Avenue
Citrus Heights, CA 95610
Phone: (619) 727–1486
Website: www.mararts.org

The World Martial Arts
Information Center
P.O. Box 10911
Canoga Park, CA 91309
Phone: (818) 704–5638
Website: martialinfo.com

Recommended Readings

Dang, Tri Thong. *Beginning Tai Chi*. Boston: Charles Tuttle, 1994.

Kauz, Herman. *Tai Chi Handbook*. New York: Doubleday, 1974.

Liang, T. T. *T'ai Chi Chuan, for Health and Self-Defense*. New York: Random House, 1977.

McFarlane, Stewart, and New Hong Tan. *Complete Book of Tai Chi*. New York: DK Publishing, 1997.

Recommended Periodicals

T'ai Chi and Alternative Health
Maybank Road, South
Woodford, London E18 1ET
United Kingdom
Phone: 0184–502–9307

T'ai Chi Magazine
Wayfarer Publications
P.O. Box 26156
Los Angeles, CA 90026
Phone: (213) 665–7773

Recommended Websites

www.wustyle.com

www. xiongjing.com

QIGONG

Another form of mental discipline is Qigong, the Chinese science of cultivating the body's internal energy, which is called Qi (or Chi).

HISTORY

Qigong has its roots dating back to sometime before 1122 B.C., and became increasingly more popular during the Han dynasty (206 B.C.) when Buddhism and its meditation methods came to China from India. During the Liang dynasty (A.D. 502–557), Qigong developed into a martial art form and, over hundreds of years, maintained a strong following. With the conversion of China to communism after World War II, however, many of the Chinese Qigong masters fled China for Hong Kong, Taiwan, and the United States. Since that time, Qigong has grown to even greater popularity.

BELIEF SYSTEM

As the natural force that fills the universe, Qi is found in all living things and forces of nature. By learning to attune and balance the flows of Qi within you and around you, devotees believe you can harmonize these natural forces and use them for many practical benefits. Qi is utilized in the healing arts, including acupuncture, herbal treatments, massage, and acupressure. Qi is also used in the various martial arts—in Iron Shirt, Iron Sand Palm, and Cavity Press, as well as Kung Fu—and it is often used to enhance spiritual development, or enlightenment.

RITUALS AND EXERCISES

Qigong exercises are practiced in order to develop more Qi and learn to direct or channel the Qi to the points where it is needed. Through controlled movements, breathing, and concentration, the practitioner moves the Qi in, up, out, down, or around, and develops polar (bio-magnetic) fields of strength throughout the body.

The effect and purpose of the Qigong ritual is to awaken, develop, and express the highest potential of the body-mind-spirit of the individual. A Qigong Master instructs the student in the Qigong exercises, and the student practices regularly to develop proficiency.

FOR ADDITIONAL INFORMATION

Recommended Contacts

I would recommend you contact Taoist centers, martial arts studios that utilize Chinese martial arts forms, alternative healing centers (such as acupuncture), or review the periodicals on the subject. See also "Taoism" on page 49 and "Tai Chi Ch'uan" on page 53.

Qigong Association of America
2021 NW Grant Avenue
Corvallis, OR 97330
Phone: (541) 752–6599
Website: www.qi.org

The World Martial Arts
 Information Center
P.O. Box 10911
Canoga Park, CA 91309
Phone: (818) 704–5638
Website: www.martialinfo.com

United States Martial Arts
 Association
8011 Mariposa Avenue
Citrus Heights, CA 95610
Phone: (619) 727–1486
Website: www.mararts.org

Recommended Reading

Yang, Jwing-Ming. *The Root of Chinese Qigong.* Roslindale, MA: YMAA Publication Center, Inc., 1997.

Recommended Periodical

Qi Magazine
Box 18476
Anaheim Hills, CA 92817
Phone: (714) 779–1796
 or (800) 787–2600
Website: qijournal.com

CONFUCIANISM

Confucianism is a system of thought based on the teachings of Confucius and his successors. *Confucius* is the Latinized form of the Chinese name *Kung Fu-tzu*, which means *Great Master Kung*.

HISTORY

Confucius was born around 551 B.C. in the small feudal state of Lu, located in present-day Shantang, China. He came from a *shih* family, members of a lesser nobility, and when his father passed away prematurely, the family suffered many hardships. As a young man, Confucius held various minor posts in government—overseer of granaries and minister of state—married, and had a son and daughter. He later held higher posts in government and was recognized for his provocative ideas.

At around the age of fifty, Confucius left his native state of Lu and began wandering from state to state in an attempt to initiate political and social reforms. During this time, he developed a considerable following. After thirteen years of teaching, Confucius returned to his native state, where he was reported to have edited the Confucian classics:

- *The Book of Poetry*, or *Shih Ching*, 305 poems of the early Chou dynasty;

- *The Book of Rites*, or *Li Ching*, philosophical discussions of ritual;

- *The Book of History*, or *Shu Ching*, a documentary of Chinese history from the time of Emperor Yao, in the third millennium B.C., to the early Chou dynasty (1122–249 B.C.), which included discussions of leaders who served as paragons of his political ideologies;

- *The Spring and Autumn Annals*, or *Ch'un Ch'iu*, a history and comment on events that occurred during Confucius' time in his state of Lu; and

- *The Book of Changes*, or *I Ching*, which is based on the ancient practices of divination, and used as a practical guide for taking the wisest course of action.

BELIEF SYSTEM

The teachings of Confucius emphasize moral and ethical standards within social, political, and religious thought. He did not preach a religious belief per se, but rather incorporated high spiritual values into a way of living. These concepts include humaneness (Jen), where in order to achieve peace in this world, you must practice benevolence toward others. Moreover, you should do good without expectation of recognition of that good. He believed heaven could best be understood through the study of history and of how the influences of heaven affected the world throughout its history. He taught that rites and music should fully express their potential to encourage virtuous behavior.

Confucius believed that you should act according to your position, that is, you should know your place in the world and do your duty accordingly. Thus, the human ideal is outlined in the doctrine of rectification of names (Cheng-Ming), wherein a king acts within the ideals established for him as a king, a father acts as an ideal father, and so forth, down to the lowest clerk. The bulk of Confucius' teachings center around the concept of "The Gentleman" (Chun-tzu); you should never lose sight of the virtuous or higher nature of your humanity, and always take responsibility for your actions. These teachings have been a cornerstone of Chinese philosophy and culture for hundreds of years.

Another principal tenet of Confucianism holds that your human nature is initially good, not evil, not neutral. It is through your recognition of this higher inner nature and seeing your relation to heaven that you can realize your full human potential for goodness. Your purpose is, then, to realize your own higher nature and live up to your own intrinsic higher ideal.

Confucianism is primarily philosophical. It is based on the writing of the classic texts that delineate its principle tenets. In addition to the ones mentioned on page 58, these include: *Meng-tyu (Menicus), Shu-ching (Book of History), Chung Yung (Doctrine of the Mean)*, and *Ta-hsueh (Great Learning)*. However, the most informative source on the life and teachings of Confucius is *The Analects (Lun-Yu*, or *Discourses)*. Compiled over a century after his death, *The Analects* contains the reputed sayings and conversations of Confucius and summarize his teachings. Additional insights will be found in the *Book of Rites (Li Chi)*, which stresses personal moral cultivation as the means for achieving inner, personal, and world peace.

RITUALS AND HOLY DAYS

During the Han Dynasty (206 B.C.–A.D. 220), Confucianism was established as the state of orthodoxy, and other canons developed. Temples began to be erected, the concepts of Yin and Yang were introduced (see "Taoism" on page 49), and various cults formed. Over the years, Confucianism has continued to evolve, and now only two major schools exist: the School of Principle (Li-Hsueh) and the School of Mind (Hsin-Hsueh). Both are considered neo-Confucian, and emphasize more of an internal search for principle rather than the external intellectual investigation that was traditional in Confucianism. The School of Mind focuses on the internal experience of the self, and often utilizes meditation techniques. Religious rites are still performed for the layman; however, the influence of Confucianism has greatly diminished with the advent of the Communist government, which has subdued Confucianism's role in Chinese culture. Confucianism does not advocate any particular religious observances or holidays per se; however, Chinese custom and tradition are rich with colorful rites and services that incorporate Confucian, Taoist, and Buddhist traditions.

FOR ADDITIONAL INFORMATION

Recommended Contacts

I am not familiar with any Confucian teachers or groups in North America. This wisdom is typically integrated into general Chinese philosophy, particularly Taoism. The best sources of information will be found in the classic Confucian texts. See also "I Ching" on page 61.

Recommended Readings

Legge, James, ed. *Confucius: Confucian Analects, The Great Learning, and the Doctrine of the Mean.* New York: Dover, 1971.

Meng-tzu. *The Mencius.* D. C. Lau, trans. New York: Viking Press, 1970.

Waley, Arthur, trans. *The Analects of Confucius.* Vancouver, WA: Vintage Books, 1989.

Recommended Websites

chineseculture.miningco.com   www.confucius.com

www.chinapage.com   www.confucius.org

I CHING

Of the Confucian classics, the *Book of Changes (I Ching)* is the most well-known and popular in the West. It is the foundation of much of Chinese philosophy. It originated in the Mandarin *yi*, meaning *divination*, and *jing*, meaning *classic book*.

HISTORY

The *I Ching*—pronounced *ee-jing*—represents one of the first efforts of the human mind to place itself within the context of the universe. It dates back to Chinese antiquity and has influenced both Chinese culture and literature for three thousand years. It was first established as a book of oracles, and used as a predictive instrument—a way of divining the future. It evolved over time into a book of wisdom, providing ethical and spiritual guidance. It has had a significant impact on both Confucian and Taoist philosophies.

According to tradition, the present system, described below, was originally represented by yarrow sticks. During the reign of King Wen (1150–249 B.C.), progenitor of the Chou dynasty, these sticks were combined to form the symbols used in interpreting the future.

Confucius is said to have made many commentaries concerning the *I Ching*, and brought it into common usage in China. Today, it is one of the most established cultural, philosophical, and religious resources in the world, and consulted by millions around the globe.

BELIEF SYSTEM

The philosophy espoused in this text views changes in terms of cycles that move in opposites (e.g., expansion and contraction, rise and fall), and incorporates the concept of Yin and Yang. The latter refers to your active, male, hard, or expansive pole, and the former to your passive, female, soft, or contracting pole. Thus, changes occur in cycles. When one pole is reached (Yin or Yang), your movement invariably is directed to the opposite pole. Therefore, as changes occur in you, in your nature, and in your society, your attitude should be to accept the cosmic order and to flow with it.

The *I Ching* is mainly used for the ancient practice of divination. You would consult the *I Ching* to determine which course of action to take in various instances. The book deals with eight "trigrams," which use broken lines to represent Yin, the female principal; and solid lines to represent Yang, the male principal. These are connected to sixty-four "hexagrams," each composed of two trigrams, in a variety of possible combinations. To each hexagram is ascribed a particular action or judgment (t'uan) and archetype or image (Hsiang). When you manipulate the stalks of the yarrow plant (typically), lines that represent the various hexagrams are formed in a variety of patterns. When you have identified the hexagrammatic pattern, its corresponding judgment and image would indicate the appropriate course of action to take in a particular situation. In this manner, the *I Ching* would be a guide to right action in problematic times.

FOR ADDITIONAL INFORMATION

Recommended Contacts

I suggest you contact Chinese healers, perhaps in herbal medicine stores, acupuncture or acupressure centers, or Taoist centers for T'ai Chi or Qigong. See also periodicals for Taoism, Qigong and Tai Chi. See also "Taoism" on page 49, and "Confucianism" on page 58.

Recommended Reading

Naturally, you could also consult the *I Ching* itself. I recommend this edition:

Wilhelm, Richard, and Cary F. Bayness, trans. *The I-Ching: Book of Changes*. Princeton, NJ: Princeton University Press, 1997.

Recommended Websites

www.iching.com   www.iching.org

FENG-SHUI

The Chinese characters for Feng-Shui literally mean *wind/water*, referring to the balance of the elements. Feng-Shui is a practice of acknowledging the natural order of the universe and living in harmony with it. It particularly refers to working with the elements of nature and hidden forces that direct and shape the course of life itself.

HISTORY

Along with the general Taoist and Confucian philosophical works, the fundamental elements of Feng-Shui date back well over three thousand years. The origins of the practice are clouded in mystery, but two written works from the fourth and fifth centuries A.D. have greatly influenced the Feng-Shui masters. These are *The Burial Classic* and *The Yellow Emperor's Dwelling Classic*. Based somewhat on the teachings of Confucius, modern Feng-Shui moves from an intellectual or philosophical view of the world to a more practical arrangement of the elements of creation, always seeking harmony and serenity between the practitioner and the environment.

Respected and practiced for thousands of years throughout the Far East, Feng-Shui is now growing in practical use in many Western countries.

BELIEF SYSTEM

In the eleventh century A.D., Confucian philosopher Chou Tun-yi wrote: "The Great Ultimate, through movement, generates yang. When its activity reaches its limit, it becomes tranquil. Through tranquility, the Great Ultimate generates the yin. When tranquility reaches its limit, activity begins again. Thus, movement and tranquility alternate and become the root of each other, giving rise to the distinctions of yin and yang, and these two modes are thus established. By the transformation of yang and its union with yin, the five agents of water, fire, wood, metal, and earth arise. When these five material forces (chi) are distributed in harmonious order, the four seasons run their course."

The practice of Feng-Shui serves to create the harmonious flow of chi within the environment you create, such as a temple, a grave, or your home. The Feng-Shui Master knows the nature in which chi flows, and helps to orient building foundations, walls, windows, furniture, plants, and objects to optimize the natural order of things within your environment. The Feng-Shui Master may also utilize a special Pa Tzu compass to help direct the lucky or unlucky directions within the environment in question. The master may make suggestions to improve the chi flows, such as moving objects in a room, placing a plant, mirror, or water fountain in a certain location, or on the other hand, removing something that is blocking the movement of chi in the room or building. By optimizing the circulation of chi, or natural life-force energy, in your home or office, you can improve your health, create greater prosperity, and achieve greater happiness and peace in your life.

FOR ADDITIONAL INFORMATION
Recommended Contacts

For more information on Feng-Shui, consult your local metaphysical bookstore or visit a Taoist center in your area.

The Feng Shui Directory of
   Consultants
P.O. Box 6701
Charlottesville, VA 22906
Phone: (804) 974–1726
Website: www.fsdirectory.com

Feng Shui Works
P.O. Box 5293
Somerset, NJ 08875
Phone: (732) 828–6559

Recommended Readings

There are books and kits that can teach you the basics to practice on your own:

Kwok, Man-Ho, and Joanne O'Brien. *The Feng-Shui Kit*. Boston, MA: Charles E. Tuttle Company, 1995.

Spear, William. *Feng Shui Made Easy*. San Francisco, CA: Harper, 1995.

Too, Lillian. *The Complete Illustrated Guide to Feng-Shui*. Rockport, MA: Element Books, 1996.

Recommended Websites

www.fengshui.com   www.fsdirectory.com
www.fengshui.org

SHINTOISM

Shinto is the indigenous religion of Japan. The word *shinto* means *way of the kami*, or gods. It is as old as the Japanese nation itself, evolving out of prehistoric religious practices as primarily a nature religion with tribal characteristics.

HISTORY

As Japan evolved from a hunting-gathering culture into an agrarian culture, fertility rites were practiced and festivals commemorating the seasons and the harvest were integrated into the culture. By A.D. 500, Chinese culture and the organized religion of Buddhism began to influence the Japanese culture and Shinto practices. Shinto took on more structure as a religion and developed more theology regarding the veneration of ancestors and kami, or spirits. During the Meiji period (1867–1912), Shinto developed into a form of national patriotism and ideology that is now referred to as "State Shinto," which was more naturalistic than religious. However, after 1945, with the defeat of the Japanese in World War II and the occupation of Japan by American forces, State Shinto was disestablished, although smaller sects of "Shrine Shinto" remain active to this day. Shinto is practiced primarily in Japan, and almost exclusively by people of Japanese descent.

BELIEF SYSTEM

To the ancient Japanese, each aspect of creation was a living being: The sun and moon, the rivers and ocean, the mountains, trees and herbs all had consciousness. Even the "Great-Eight-Island-Country" (Japan), was a supernatural being. The divine kami Izanagi (male) and Izanami (female) were responsible for creating the sun goddess Amaterasu Omikami, the great ancestor of the emperor. In Shinto, ancestors are venerated, and the head (male) of each family clan is the priest. The emperor, or head of the imperial family, is the highest priest and was considered a kami incarnate. In Shinto, the "gods are immortal men, and men are mortal gods." When a person dies, the soul leaves the body; nevertheless, dead people are believed to have consciousness. Moreover, in death, a soul may either descend below the earth to the land of darkness, "Yomi-no-Kuni," or ascend to the High Plain of Heaven, "Takama-ga-Hara," the abode of the heavenly gods.

Shinto has developed into more of an ethnic intellectual religion that emphasizes your sincerity, truthfulness, uprightness, patriotism, and loyalty to the emperor. It is your life goal to live up to these values to the best of your ability.

RITUALS AND HOLY DAYS

Shinto festivals are held to ensure the continued material success (particularly good harvests), physical well-being (safety from pestilence and natural disaster), and spiritual well-being within the community. This is achieved through a matsuri, where gods (kamis) and souls (tamas) are entertained and attended to. A typical matsuri begins with purification rites (monoimi) that are intended to cleanse the participants of polluting forces. Offerings of rice cakes (mochi), rice wine (sake), and ritual prayers (norito) serve to please the spirits, who then offer their assistance. A communion meal (naorai) is often shared by both the humans and gods. Ceremonies also often include a lively procession of the kami in a portable shrine (mikoshi), ceremonial dancing (kagura), and special events such as tug-of-war games, and horse and boat racing.

The most important festivals are held during the spring and autumn in conjunction with agricultural cycles. During the spring planting days, Shinto festivals invoke the blessings of the kami who have descended from the mountains to the fields. During the autumn harvest, festivals of thanksgiving for a bountiful crop are performed for the deities who then return to the mountains. Summer and winter festivals are held to avert natural disasters. Although there are over 80,000 shinto shrines throughout Japan for worship, prayer, and contemplation, veneration of the kami is primarily the duty of the Shinto priest.

FOR ADDITIONAL INFORMATION

I suggest that you visit cultural centers in your closest Japanese community. Some larger cities with a high percentage of people of Japanese descent have Shinto shrines, and universities that offer courses in Asian studies may offer helpful information.

Recommended Contacts

Church of World Messianity
960 S. Kenmore Avenue
Los Angeles, CA 90006

Taishakyo Shinto
215 N. Kukui Street
Honolulu, HI 96817

Honkyoku Shinto
61 Puiwa Road
Honolulu, HI 96817

Tenrikyo Mission Headquarters
  in America
2727 E. First Street
Los Angeles, CA 90033
Phone: (323) 261–3379

International Shinto Foundation
777 United Nations Plaza
Suite WCRP-9A
New York, NY 10017
Phone: (212) 661–9117
Website: www.shinto.org

Recommended Readings

Kato, Genchi. *A Study of Shinto.* London: Curzon Press, 1971.

Lowell, Percival. *Occult Japan: Shinto, Shamanism and the Way of the Gods.* Rochester, NY: Inner Traditions International, 1990.

Sokyo, Ono. *Shinto: The Kami Way.* Boston, MA: Charles E. Tuttle Co., 1994.

Recommended Websites

www.japan/guide.com

www.jinja.or.jp

www.shinto.org

www.webaissance.com/shinto-templesandshrines.htm

Reiki

In Japanese, *reiki* means *universal life energy*, and refers to the method of restoring and balancing your own vital energy for greater health and well being.

HISTORY

The ability to tap into and channel your life-force energy was rediscovered by Dr. Mikao Usui in the mid-nineteenth century, while reading a 2,500-year-old Sanskrit sutra. Dr. Usui taught several others this technique, and they carried on the tradition of the Reiki masters.

In the mid-1930s, Hawayo Takata, an American-born Hawaiian woman of Japanese descent, traveled to her parents' home in Japan, because of a severely debilitating illness. While in Japan, she discovered a Reiki clinic and began several months' treatment that completely restored her health. Intrigued, she stayed on to receive further training in Reiki. Later, she returned to the United States where she instructed others in the science before she died.

Reiki continued to gain in acceptance and is now a very popular form of both holistic healing and spiritual discipline designed to raise consciousness and attain spiritual awakening.

BELIEF SYSTEM

The actual techniques are only to be transferred from a recognized master to student through formal initiation, and there are several degrees of mastery. The techniques generally involve learning how to tune into the natural life-force energy that flows around you and through you. Affirmations, visualizations, and focused concentration are used to develop and channel this life-force energy. Esoteric symbols, breathing, and sound may also be used to help develop and focus this energy.

FOR ADDITIONAL INFORMATION

Recommended Contacts

I recommend that you consult with metaphysical bookstores and centers, holistic healing centers, and health food stores in your area. You may also consult:

The International Center for Reiki Training
21421 Hilltop, #28
Southfield, MI 48034
Phone: (800) 332–8112
    or (248) 948–8112
Website: www.reiki.org

Recommended Readings

Baninski, Bodo, and Shalila Sharamon. *Reiki, Universal Life Energy.* Mendocino, CA: Liferhythm, 1988.

Honervogt, Tanmaya. *The Power of Reiki: An Ancient Hands-On Healing Technique.* New York: Henry Holt & Company, 1998.

Rand, William L. *Reiki, the Healing Touch: First and Second Degree Manual.* Southfield, MI: Vision Publications, 1998.

Recommended Websites

www.awarinst.com   www.reiki.com

www.eastwest.com

PART TWO

WESTERN AND MIDDLE EASTERN RELIGIONS

Western and Middle Eastern religions generally refer to the Judeo-Christian-Islamic heritages. The religions of Judaism, Christianity, and Islam all share common origins and hold some similar beliefs, although their spiritual practices, philosophical perspectives, and other beliefs differ greatly. One commonality is the concept of monotheism, or the belief in one almighty God. From the Western and Middle Eastern perspectives, God is both omnipresent and omnipotent, and yet very personal, with apparent feelings and emotions, such as love and compassion, jealousy and anger. Although this God is called by different names—Yahweh or Elohim by the Jews, Jehovah or God by the Christians, and Allah by the Muslims—this same God is considered to be the one and only God.

Another common belief held by all three religions is that, after creating the universe, God created man "in his own image" out of the dust from the ground (thus humans did not evolve from other, lower life forms). Then God breathed into man's nostrils the breath of life, and man became a living soul. Woman was later created out of the rib of man, and these first two humans are called Adam and Eve. Man and woman were created in the Garden of Eden, believed to have been Mesopotamia (modern Iraq). Since then, their descendants have populated the entire earth.

The story of the creation of mankind is told in the book of Genesis, which is the first book in the Torah (Jewish scripture) and in the Holy Bible (Christian scripture), and the second sura of the Koran, or Qur'an (Islamic scripture). In this account, God expressly tells Adam that he can eat of all fruits in the Garden of Eden except for one—the fruit of the "tree of knowledge of good and evil"—which is forbidden. A serpent in the Garden of Eden tempts Eve into trying this forbidden fruit, and she in turn convinces Adam to taste it as well. This serpent represents the forces of evil—Satan, or the Devil—a "fallen angel" whose influence ever since has tested and tainted mankind. Thus, man's disobedience of God's laws has created a "sin." It has estranged man from God, and created a necessity for man to be forgiven by God.

In Western and Middle Eastern religions, emphasis is placed on living in accordance with God's laws, as recounted by the prophets, whom God has sent to guide us. Thus all of mankind needs redemption in order to live in God's grace, and live in eternal peace. This belief in redemption means that if you are forgiven by God, after the death of the physical body, you will live with God eternally in Heaven, enjoying unimaginable pleasures. However, if you are not forgiven, then you are destined for an eternal existence in Hell, suffering unimaginable torture and pain.

But how is it decided whether you merit heaven or hell? The principal differences among these three religions is in how they believe redemption will be obtained. Jewish prophecy holds that a Messiah (deliverer) will be sent by God to establish a Holy Kingdom upon the earth and to rule over the Jewish people and over the entire earth. Jews maintain that the Messiah has yet to come, and do not accept the belief that Jesus Christ was the Messiah, or that Mohammed is the prophet of God, because neither one has yet fulfilled the Jewish prophecy.

Christians, however, believe that Jesus of Nazareth did fulfill the prophecy, that he demonstrated he was the Messiah, or Christ, by the miracles he performed, the love and compassion he exemplified, and his triumph over death. Christians believe that Christ will come again to rule on Earth, and that you can be saved by accepting Jesus Christ as your personal Savior and following his teachings.

Muslims believe that Jesus was a prophet of God (Allah), but as the people were still not obeying God's laws, God sent another prophet, Mohammed, to teach mankind. Muslims believe that Mohammed is

God's last prophet, and that the Qur'an is a revision of God's law as directed through his prophet.

All three religions base their beliefs on faith, and maintain their convictions based on the scriptures that they accept to be the word of God.

I begin this section with an examination of the most ancient of these religions, Judaism, and then move on to Christianity, dealing especially with the Eastern Orthodox and the Roman Catholic faiths. Historically, the next great movement was the "protest" against the strict orthodoxy of the pope in Rome and the dawn of the Protestant Reformation, with its reliance on a more personal interpretation of Scripture. In this context, I will examine a number of Protestant sects, such as Lutheran, Anglican, Baptist, and more. I will also delve into modern Christian movements like the Salvation Army, Mormons, Unitarians, and Jehovah's Witnesses, among others. Finally, I will take up an examination of Islam, or Mohammadism. My hope is that your exploration of these different faiths will open doors to you and present opportunities for you in your search for God.

Interpretations and beliefs about God and his laws vary considerably among and within each of the great Western and Middle Eastern religions. Even fundamental generalizations about each of these religions can be challenged by sects within each one, so keep in mind that every tenet interpreted here only represents the majority opinion. Within that faith, other opinions may be equally valid. The following serves as a brief overview of those religions that have had the most influence on Western and Middle Eastern civilizations.

JUDAISM

Judaism is the religion of the Jewish people. They believe its origins began with the creation of mankind, and its foundation as a religion began with the covenant between the patriarch Abraham and God, or Yahweh.

HISTORY

Abraham lived in the city of Ur in Mesopotamia, between the Tigris and Euphrates rivers, around 2000 B.C. Following God's call, Abraham left his home and migrated with his family and flocks to the "Promised Land," called Canaan, where he settled in Shechem. Soon, however, he was driven out when a severe drought devastated the land. After traveling through Egypt during this difficult time, he returned to Canaan where, after proving his faith in Yahweh, he was given a son, Isaac. To further test Abraham's faith, God asked him to sacrifice Isaac, his only son. Abraham was ready to do the will of God, but he was spared from the ordeal only at the last moment. After Abraham had thus once again proven his loyalty, God assured him that he would be the father of a great people in the land of Canaan, also known as Palestine, now Israel. In addition to his son, Isaac, he had another son, Ishmael, the ancestor of the twelve tribes of Israel; he was the grandfather of Jacob, whose name means "Israel." Traditionally, then, Abraham is regarded as the father not only of Judaism, but also of Christianity and Islam.

The people of the land of Canaan and of Abraham's religion are collectively known as the Hebrews. After Abraham's death at the age of 175, famine forced the Hebrews to flee from the Holy Land into Egypt, where they were known as Israelites. They stayed in Egypt for several centuries under oppressive rule, as slaves.

Around the year 1300 B.C., the Israelites were delivered from their oppression in Egypt by the noble leader and prophet Moses. In this exodus from Egypt, Moses led the Israelites southeast through the wilderness of what is now called the Sinai Peninsula. Suffering many hardships, the Israelites began to lose faith in their deliverance, whereupon Moses climbed up Mount Sinai and communed personally with God. It was during this trying time that the Lord gave Moses the famous Ten Commandments to guide his people:

1. Do not worship any other Gods but me.

2. Do not make any images or idols of God to worship.

3. Do not use the Lord's name in vain (dishonor God).

4. Keep the Sabbath day holy, and do not work on this day.

5. Honor your mother and your father.

6. Do not kill.

7. Do not commit adultery.

8. Do not steal.

9. Do not bear false witness against your neighbor.

10. Do not covet your neighbor's wife or property.

The Israelites spent some forty years in the desert before entering again into the Promised Land of Canaan. After their successful fight to wrest control of the Holy Land, they cultivated the earth and prospered as a people. However, the history of the Israelites, or Jews, is fraught with acts of war and persecution, even to the present day. For thousands of years, the Jews were an exiled people. The struggle to keep the Promised Land has persisted for over 3,000 years. Today, a portion of the Holy Land has been reclaimed by the Jewish people as the state of Israel, and although the Jewish people are now spread throughout the world, they maintain a cohesive unity in faith and cultural heritage. Many believe that this reemergence of a Jewish homeland in Israel is evidence of the fulfillment of the ancient prophesy of a promised land, and the harbinger of an era of happiness and peace. There are currently about 13 to 14 million Jews in the world, the vast majority living in either Israel or the United States.

BELIEF SYSTEM

Judaism was instrumental in the Western acceptance of monotheism, the belief in one God. The sacred name for God was represented by the tetragrammaton (spelled in Hebrew without vowels) YHWH, generally believed to be pronounced "Yahweh," which means "I am that I am." This name of God is so revered that it is generally not uttered by the devout Jew. This patriarchal God is both loved and feared: Absolute obedience to God's laws and conformity to his divine will is rewarded both spiritually and physically, but disobedience brings the threat of spiritual and physical exile.

Central to the Jewish faith are the covenants that the Jewish patriarchs made with God, such as the sacred act of circumcision (cutting off the male foreskin at birth), to remind God of his promise of genealogical continuity. Another central Judaic belief is the messianic ideal of a universal reintegration of mankind; this will be accomplished with a spiritual monarchy headed by the Jews as "God's chosen people," followed by an era of peace and well-being on earth.

In Judaism, there is a strong emphasis placed on adherence to God's laws, and in observances of moral and ethical conduct. God is conceived as exclusively one and indivisible; he is omnipresent and omniscient. Humans are seen as conscious beings comprised of both spirit and matter, body and soul, with the inherent capacity and potential for ethical conduct, and with both the duty and destiny to actualize this higher potential.

Your relationship with God is mainly one of ethical consideration. As a human being, you are given the destiny to elevate yourself to the Divine. Through faith, prayer, good works, and obedience to God's laws, you are brought closer to God.

The primary source of God's revelation is the Torah, which comprises the books of Genesis, Exodus, Leviticus, Numbers, and Deuteronomy in both the Hebrew and Christian versions of the Bible. Also esteemed were the books of the Prophets and the Writings, which are also recounted in the Bible. Knowledge of God's will is further pursued in the study of Judaic texts like the *Midrash*, the *Mishnah*, and the *Talmud*—which comment on and interpret the books of the Bible—or the *Aggadah*, which emphasizes study of God's love. The study of the mystical or esoteric aspects of Judaism is developed through disciplined contemplation of the *Kabbalah* (see "Kabbalism" on page 175) and through the *Zohar*, or *Book of Splendor*, a more mystical text. Jewish religious study encourages philosophical debate, which is believed to foster a greater understanding of God and his laws. Community prayers are emphasized in community synagogues and temples. Children are encouraged to study God's laws in Hebrew, and at the age of thirteen a boy's spiritual maturity is celebrated in what is called a Bar Mitzvah, and girls of the same age are given a Bat Mitzvah. The Sabbath is observed for twenty-four hours beginning on

Fridays at sundown; for that period, religious study is encouraged and work is forbidden.

There are three major Jewish sects: Orthodox, Reform, and Conservative. *Orthodox* schools are the strictest in adhering to Mosaic laws, including dietary and Sabbath observances. In *Reform* synagogues, Mosaic laws have been modified to conform to circumstances in modern life; for instance, men and women are seated together, rather than being seated apart, as they are in the Orthodox synagogues. *Conservative* Judaism is the centrist movement within contemporary Judaism, and is the largest of the sects in America.

There are also different movements within Judaism. A major one is called Hasidism, which developed from two socio-religious movements in medieval and modern Jewish history, in Germany and Eastern Europe. This movement is more mystical, with a focus on the notion of "devekut," or communion with God's presence in all things, trying to sanctify the everyday.

There is also an international reconstructionist movement gaining ground in recent years, in which adherents attempt to adapt and evolve Judaism within a changing society. Finally, there is Messianic Judaism, which accepts Jesus Christ as the Messiah but honors Jewish customs and culture.

In traditional Judaism, death is not an end of human existence. However, since Judaism is primarily focused on how you live your life in the present, very little dogma is given to afterlife. For this reason, there is much room for personal opinion.

The place for spiritual reward for the righteous dead in Judaism is not "heaven" but Olam Ha-Ba (the World to Come) or Gan Eden (the Garden of Eden). Nevertheless, it is possible for an Orthodox Jew to believe that the souls of the righteous dead go to a place similar to the Christian heaven, that they reincarnate through many lifetimes, or that they simply wait for the coming of the messiah, at which time they will be resurrected. An Orthodox Jew may also believe that the souls of the evildoers may be tormented by demons of their own creation, that they simply cease to exist, or that they are destroyed at death.

RITUALS AND HOLY DAYS

The most holy day for many Jewish people is the Sabbath. Other primary religious observances include the high holy days of Rosh Hashanah and Yom Kippur, as well as the popular holidays of Hanukkah, Purim, and

Passover. Rosh Hashanah celebrates the beginning of the Jewish new year, beginning in late September or October. This two-day solemn occasion is the beginning of a ten-day period of introspection and penance. During lengthy synagogue services, the ram's horn is traditionally blown as a wordless form of prayer.

This rite of purification is concluded on the tenth day celebrated as Yom Kippur, or Day of Atonement. During Yom Kippur, virtually the entire day is spent in the synagogue petitioning God to pardon sins and bestow blessings for the coming year. On this day, it is forbidden to eat, drink, wear leather, or have sexual relations, as an act of purification.

Celebrated in December, Hanukkah—which means *dedication*—commemorates the ancient Jewish revolt, led by Judas Maccabee in 168 B.C., against the Hellenists. For each of the eight days, single candles are lit at nightfall in an eight-branch candelabra, known as a menorah, until all eight have been lit. During these days of Hanukkah, families exchange gifts, sing songs, eat special foods, and play games with a dreidel (spinning top). In terms of religion, Hanukkah is of little significance, but in modern times, it takes on a secular importance because of its Christian counterpart in December (Christmas).

Purim, observed in February or March, commemorates the deliverance of the Jewish community from Persia, as recorded in the Book of Esther in the Bible. Observances include reading from the Book of Esther in the synagogue, parading in costume, exchanging delicacies, and giving to the poor.

Passover, celebrated in March or April, expresses gratitude to the Angel of Death in "passing over" the Israelite boys during the Jewish bondage in Egypt. As the last and most terrible of the plagues visited upon the Egyptians by God, it had been decreed that all first-born Egyptian males would be slain. The Jews were delivered from this fate, however. They slaughtered and ate the sacrificial lamb, and smeared its blood on their entrance door; in this way, the Angel of Death would "pass over" the Jewish homes. To commemorate this deliverance, the celebration begins with a special dinner called a Seder, and the story of the Exodus is recounted. It is in Exodus that the story is told of how Moses led the Jewish people, how they stood up to the Pharaoh, how God sent the plagues, and finally, how Moses led his people out of slavery to become a free people in the promised land of Canaan.

FOR ADDITIONAL INFORMATION

I would suggest that you look under "synagogues" or "temples" in the telephone book, or sometimes also under "churches." You could also consult your local Chamber of Commerce. Jewish colleges and universities also provide religious and theological instruction. For mystical teachings, see "Kabbalism" on page 175.

Recommended Contacts

Orthodox

Orthodox Union
11 Broadway
New York, NY 10004
Phone: (212) 613-8233
Website: www.ou.org

Rabbinical Council of America
305 7th Avenue
New York, NY 10001–6008
Phone: (212) 807–7888
Website: www.rabbis.org

Conservative

Jewish Theological Seminary
3080 Broadway
New York, NY 10027
Phone: (212) 678–8000
Website: www.jtsa.edu

The United Synagogues of
   Conservative Judaism
Rapport House
155 Fifth Avenue
New York, NY 10010-6802
Phone: (212) 533–7800
Website: www.uscj.org

Reform

Central Conference of American
   Rabbis
355 Lexington Avenue
New York, NY 10017
Websites: www.rj.org
   also: www.shammash.org

Hebrew Union College-Jewish
   Institute of Religion
In California:
3077 University Avenue
Los Angeles, CA 90007
Phone: (213) 749–3424
Website: www.huc.edu

In New York:
1 West 4th Street
New York, NY 10012
Phone: (212) 674–5300
Website: www.huc.edu

In Ohio:
3101 Clifton Avenue
Cincinnati, OH 45220
Phone: (513) 221–1875
Websites: www.huc.edu
   also: www.rj.org

The Union of American Hebrew Congregations
633 Third Avenue
New York, NY 10017-6778
Phone: (212) 650–4227
Websites: www.rj.org   also: www.shammash.org

Hasidism, or Chassidism

Chabad-Lubavitch in Cyberspace
770 Eastern Parkway
Brooklyn, NY 11213
Phone: (718) 953–2444
Websites: www.chabad.org   also: www.nishmas.org

Reconstructionist

Shir Hadash Reconstructionist Synagogue
P.O. Box 632
Northbrook, IL 60065
Phone: (847) 498–8218
Websites: www.shir-hadash.org   also: www.ariga.org

Messianic, or Jews for Jesus

Jews for Jesus
60 Haight Street
San Francisco, CA 94102
Phone: (415) 864–2600
Website: www.jewsforjesus.org

Menorah Ministries
P.O. Box 460024
Glendale, CO 80246-0024
Phone: (303) 355–2009
Website: www.menorah.org

Other Recommended Jewish Contacts

Conversion to Judaism Resource
   Center
74 Hauppauge Road, Room 53
Commack, NY 11725
Phone: (516) 462–5826
Website: www.convert.org

University of Judaism
15600 Mulholland Drive
Bel Air, CA 90077
Phone: (310) 476–9777
Website: www.uj.edu

Project Genesis, Inc.
17 Warren Road #2B
Baltimore, MD 21208
Phone: (410) 602–1350
Website: www.torah.org

Recommended Readings

Donin, Hayim Halevy. *To Be a Jew*. Boulder, CO: Basic Books, 1991.

Dosick, Wayne D. *Living Judaism: The Complete Guide to Jewish Belief, Tradition and Practice*. San Francisco: Harper, 1998.

Frank, Anne. *Anne Frank: The Diary of a Young Girl*. Otto H. Frank and Mirjam Pressler, eds. New York: Bantam Books, 1997.

Kolatch, Alfred J. *The Jewish Book of Why*. Middle Village, NY: Jonathan David Publishers, 1983.

Neusuer, Jacob, trans. *The Mishnah*. Harrisburg, PA: Trinity Press International-Morehouse, 1992.

The Torah, The First American Edition. New York: Henry Holt and Company, 1996.

Whiston, William, trans. *The Complete Works of Josephus*. Grand Rapids, MI: Kregal Publications, 1981.

Recommended Periodical

Jewish Affairs
235 W 23 Street
New York, NY 10011
Phone: (212) 989–4994

Recommended Websites

www.jewfaq.org

www.jewsforjewdaism.org

www.jewishstore.com

www.judaica.com

www.jews.com

www.utj.org

www.jews.org

CHRISTIANITY

Christianity is a religion based on the belief of the fulfillment of the ancient Jewish prophecy foretelling the coming of the Messiah—the expected deliverer and ruler of the Jewish people. Nearly two thousand years ago a special being was born in a manger outside the city of Bethlehem, and recognized by many to be the Messiah, or the Christ. *Christ* is Greek for *anointed one*.

This Messiah was named Yeshua ben Joseph, but he is more commonly known by the Greek name of Jesus. Christians believe that Jesus Christ has fulfilled the prophecy of the Messiah for four basic reasons. First, events that had been prophesied centuries before were fulfilled in his lifetime. Second, he demonstrated selfless humility, wisdom, and love during his ministry. Third, he performed numerous miracles during that period. Finally, by his resurrection, he triumphed over death. Those who believe in and follow the teachings of Jesus Christ are called Christians, and the source of his teachings is the Holy Bible, believed to be the word of God.

HISTORY

Jesus was born a Jew sometime around 8 to 4 B.C., and died around A.D. 27 to 30—the curious dates being the result of different calendar revisions. He preached the word of God from his enlightened understanding of it, and exemplified it through selfless acts and unconditional love. Christianity developed when a small group of Jews gathered around the rabbi (teacher) Jesus, and began to follow his teachings. The central theme of his teachings was to turn to God in preparation for the coming "Kingdom of God." He preached repentance in order to prepare for the impending judgment, which was a motif in apocalyptic Judaism at that time. Jesus is thought of as both a reformer and a humanitarian. By representing himself as the Messiah and by calling for changes in the dogmas and commercialized practices in the synagogues (such as money changing), he challenged the Jewish people and caused them to question many established beliefs and practices. This eventually led to his conviction and crucifixion. By healing the sick, exorcising demons, and raising the dead, Jesus gained a reputation as the messenger of God, and the deliverer of not just the Jewish people, but of all people who believe in him and accept him into their hearts and lives.

Jesus' ministry lasted only about three years. As his teachings and his influence on the Jewish people were perceived as threatening by the Jewish priests of the time, they pressured the Romans, who occupied the region, to condemn Jesus to death. The Roman procurator, Pontius Pilate, acceded to the pressure and gave the order to crucify Jesus. His soldiers nailed Christ to a wooden cross to die at Calvary.

Three days after Christ's physical death on the cross, he was resurrected—restored to life—and appeared to the apostles and several disciples, such as Mary Magdalene and the pilgrims at Emmaus. After a final meeting with his apostles, he ascended to Heaven where he awaits those who follow him.

Christ's martyrdom compelled the disciples, and particularly Jesus' twelve Apostles, to preach the gospel throughout the world. Most of the disciples traveled into the lands of the Gentiles—non-Jews—who were more receptive to the Christian theology than were the Jews. Most influential of the early Christian missionaries were the apostles: Paul (Saul), Peter, Barnabas, Philip, and Mark. They traveled north of the Holy Land into the areas now known as Syria, Turkey, Greece, Cyprus, and Italy. The writings of the evangelists Matthew, Mark, Luke, and John have also been tremendously influential in the development and acceptance of Christian theology and faith.

By the end of the first century, Christianity was represented throughout southern Europe, North Africa, and the Middle East. By the third century, Christianity had spread and become the predominant religion throughout the Mediterranean. Of enormous importance was the fact that Charlemagne, King of the Franks, declared, on Christmas Day, A.D. 800, that his entire Holy Roman Empire would henceforth be Christian.

Through the strong missionary efforts of the Christian churches, Christianity has now spread to every corner of the globe and is currently the largest religion in the world, with over 1.5 billion believers. Christianity remains a strong evangelical movement to this day.

BELIEF SYSTEM

According to the disciple Paul, you are assured that, through the sacrifice on the cross of God's only begotten son, Jesus, you are given the opportunity to be forgiven for your sins in this life. By believing in Jesus Christ as your lord and savior, you are offered redemption and assured a place in

Heaven, beside Jesus and God, in the next life. Christians also believe that if you do not accept Jesus Christ as your personal Lord and Savior, and do not follow his precepts, you will suffer in Hell for all eternity. You were born in sin, but have been given a chance for redemption, an opportunity to live in peace with God in Heaven by accepting Jesus Christ as your Lord and Savior.

Christian theology is based on Christ's teachings as recorded in the Holy Bible, particularly in the New Testament, which is an account of Christ's life, the acts of the Apostles, and the conduct of the early Church.

Interpretations of scripture and perspectives of Christ and his teachings vary among churches. There are three principal branches of Christianity: Eastern Orthodox, Roman Catholic, and Protestant churches. However, generally Christians share a common belief that Jesus Christ is the only Son of God, and that he is the Word of God made flesh. Moreover, as Lord, Christ preached the gospel of God, and the Bible is believed to be a pure representation of God's word. Central to Christ's teachings was the command to love God and to live by his laws, and to love your fellow man. Christians maintain the faith that Jesus Christ will come again at the end of the world, at the famous battle of Armageddon, in which the forces of God and Satan come to a final confrontation. During this purging of sin, God will pass judgment over humanity, destroying evil, while the faithful will be saved by Christ and live in eternal peace with God and Christ in a Holy Kingdom on earth.

Christianity is practiced through adherence to God's word as preached in the Holy Bible. Christians are encouraged to study the Holy Scripture, either through sermons from the clergy or by personal readings and reflection. Fundamental to Christianity is the personal relationship with Jesus Christ and God by way of prayer and contemplation.

RITUALS AND HOLY DAYS

Central to Christian practice is attendance at and participation in church services, which typically include sacred rituals, sermons, singing of hymns, blessings, and prayers. The Christian Sabbath is typically observed on Sunday, which is reserved for church attendance, rest, and contemplation of God's word.

A primary observance in Christianity is the Holy Eucharist, or the sacrament of Holy Communion, in which bread and wine are consecrated and consumed in recognition of Christ's sacrifice on Calvary. The Eucharist represents Christ's flesh and blood, or in the case of the Roman

Catholic Church, is believed to *be* the body and blood of Christ under the *appearance* of bread and wine.

A common sacrament, or sacred rite, in many churches is baptism, where the spirit of God cleanses the soul through the symbolic immersion in or sprinkling of water. In another rite, confirmation, those who are of an age to personally accept Jesus into their lives ratify the vows taken in baptism. There are also other sacraments: marriage, in which two people pledge their life-long fidelity to each other and beg God's blessing on their union; holy orders, in which a priest consecrates his life to God; extreme unction, in which the priest administers the "last rites" to the dying; and reconciliation, in which the penitent confesses his or her sins to God.

One of the most important holidays in Christianity is Easter, which usually occurs in March or April. *Easter* comes from *Eostre*, the Anglo-Saxon Goddess of Spring. Thus, what had been a pagan feast now celebrates Christ's resurrection from the tomb on the third day after his crucifixion. Easter is observed through special services or mass by the church. In the Roman Catholic, Orthodox, Anglican, and some Protestant churches, Easter services are preceded by forty days of penance and fasting called Lent, which culminates in Holy Thursday, recalling the institution of the Eucharist, and Good Friday, commemorating the crucifixion and death of Christ. The modern customs of Easter eggs, rabbits, new clothes, and flowers reflect the lingering pre-Christian customs celebrating the coming of spring.

The most popular Christian holiday is Christmas, celebrated in the West on December 25, and in the Eastern Orthodox Church, on January 6. Christmas honors the birth of Jesus Christ and is celebrated by special services, songs, food, plays, and traditions recounting the story of his nativity. This celebration dates back to the middle of the fourth century in Rome and the celebration of Sol Invictus—in Latin, *Unconquered Sun*—the pagan feast of the winter solstice. This pagan feast was appropriated by the early Church for its own religious purposes. The current traditions of Santa Claus (Saint Nicholas), Father Christmas, Christmas trees, and the exchange of gifts are all modern European adaptations. As with other rites, holidays and customs differ among the different churches; they will be discussed in the separate sections that follow.

FOR ADDITIONAL INFORMATION

Look up "churches" in your telephone directory or contact your local Chamber of Commerce. It may also be helpful to look under the specific denomination that you are looking for in this book. See also Christian bookstores in your area.

Recommended Readings

Each denomination will generally have its own reading material. Books by the denomination's founder are generally mentioned in the description of the organization. Other books, magazines, and other media can be recommended by members of the congregation or by the ministers. The following suggested reading material is popular among a broad-based group of Christians.

The Holy Bible

Perhaps, the best place to start is with *The Holy Bible*. There are several translations that are used today, but I have found the following to be the most popular and accepted:

The Holy Bible: The New International Version. Grand Rapids, MI: Zondervan Publishing House, 1998.

The Holy Bible: New Revised Standard Version. Fort Collins, CO: Ignatius Press, 1994.

The Holy Bible: New American Bible. Walton-on-Thames, UK: Thomas Nelson, 1988.

The Holy Bible: King James Version. Grand Rapids, MI: Zondervan Publishing House, 1985.

The Living Bible. Chicago, IL: Tyndale House Publishing, 1977.

Recommended Readings Related to The Holy Bible

Bowker, John Westerdale. *The Complete Bible Handbook*. New York: DK Publishing, 1998.

Calvocoressi, Peter. *Who's Who in the Bible*. New York: Penguin USA, 1989.

Mead, Frank S. *Handbook of Denominations*. Samuel S. Hill, ed. Nashville, TN: Abingdon Press, 1999.

Strong, James, ed. *The New Strong's Exhaustive Concordance of the Bible*. Walton-on-Thames, UK: Thomas Nelson, 1997.

Other Recommended Readings

Bonhoeffer, Dietrich. *The Cost of Discipleship*. New York: Simon & Schuster, 1989.

Bunyan, John. *Pilgrim's Progress*. Chicago, IL: Moody Press, 1985.

Fosdick, Harry Emerson. *The Meaning of Prayer*. Nashville, TN: Abingdon Press, 1980.

Fox, Emmet. *The Sermon on the Mount*. San Francisco: Harper Books, 1989.

Graham, Billy. *How to Be Born Again*. Chicago: World Books, 1989.

King, Jr., Martin Luther. *Strength to Love*. New York: Fortress Press, 1986.

Lewis, C. S. *A Case for Christianity*. New York: Touchstone Books, 1952.

Lucado, Max. *No Wonder We Call Him the Savior*. New York: Multnomah Publications, 1993.

Peale, Norman Vincent. *The Power of Positive Thinking*. New York: Ballantine Books, 1996.

Schuller, Robert H. *Life Is Not Fair But God Is Good*. Walton-on-Thames, UK: Thomas Nelson, 1991.

Recommended Periodicals

Bible Review
41st Street, NW
Washington, D.C. 20016
Phone: (202) 364–3300
   or (800) 687–4444

Christianity Today
P.O. Box 11618
Des Moines, Iowa 50340
Phone: (800) 999–1704
Website: www.christianity.org

Christian History
465 Gundersen Drive
Carole Stream, IL 60188
Phone: (800) 873–6986

Discipleship Journal
P.O. Box 54479
Boulder, CO 80322
Phone: (800) 877–1811

Christian Research Journal
P.O. Box 7000
Rancho Santa Margarita, CA
   92688-7000
Phone: (888) 700–0CRI

Moody
Moody Bible Institute
820 N. La Salle Blvd.
Chicago, IL 60610
Phone: (800) 284–9551

Recommended Websites

Bible Studies Foundation
www.bible.org

Christian Answers.Net
www.christiananswers.net

Christian Research Institute
www.equip.org

Crosswalk.com, Inc
www.crosswalk.com

Internet Christian Library
www.iclnet.org

EASTERN ORTHODOX CHURCHES

The word *orthodox* in Greek means *straight opinion* or *right belief*. It was in the eastern part of the Roman Empire, with its capital at Byzantium—later, Constantinople, or now Istanbul—that Christian doctrine, liturgy, and spirituality were shaped.

HISTORY

The early fourth century marks the end of the persecutions of the Christians, the formation of the Christian church, and the dawn of the medieval period. It was the Emperor Constantine (A.D. 288–337) who converted to Christianity and ended the persecution of the pagans. In A.D. 324, he decreed that Christianity would be the state religion, giving the Christian Church a foothold as a world religion. In A.D. 330, after Constantine had become sole emperor, he moved the capital of the Roman Empire east to the old Greek city of Byzantium, later renamed Constantinople in his honor.

During these formative years, the Church held a series of seven ecumenical councils that formed the basis of modern Christian theology and development. In A.D. 325, during the first ecumenical council in Nicaea, now Iznik, Turkey, the Church fathers proclaimed what is known as the Nicene Creed. This doctrine affirmed the full deity of Jesus Christ as being "of the same substance" as God the Father. (See "Christian Mysticism" on page 186.) Other councils further established the creeds of the Trinity, the person of Christ, and the incarnation.

During the third century, a decentralized system had developed whereby churches were grouped in provinces, and were generally self-governing. Nevertheless, the greater honor was given to the "metropolitan," or the bishop, of the capital city (metropolis) of each province. During the ecumenical council of A.D. 325, the dioceses of Rome, Alexandria, and Antioch were recognized, and in the council of A.D. 381, Constantinople, as the "New Rome," was given a second place to old Rome. This legislation received further confirmation at the fourth council of Chalcedon in A.D. 421, which, in effect, laid the foundation for a split between the power bases of the Eastern (Constantinople) and Western (Roman) churches. To this day, both remain autonomous, but the Eastern Church has never recognized any papal authority over them.

Eastern churches were established in Constantinople, Alexandria, Antioch, Jerusalem, Russia, Romania, Bulgaria, Serbia, Georgia, Greece, Cypress, Poland, Czechoslovakia, and Finland. In recent years, as much of the East has either converted to Islam or become Communist, the Eastern Orthodox Church has diminished in size. However, it is still well represented in the United States, Australia, and Europe, and is gaining in popularity again in the newly freed Baltic countries.

BELIEF SYSTEM

The tradition of the Eastern Church is transmitted through the Bible, in the creeds and canons established in the ecumenical councils, and in local customs and attitudes.

In the Eastern Church, the purpose of worship and ritual is to achieve a mystical union with God. The aim of Christian life is to acquire the Holy Spirit, and to attune the individual human will with the divine will. God became man so that man might become divine. This unity is realized in the holy sacrament of the Eucharist.

RITUALS AND HOLY DAYS

Like the Roman Catholic Church, the Orthodox Church observes the seven sacraments: baptism, confirmation, holy orders, penance, the Eucharist, matrimony, and extreme unction. Baptism is administered by a triple immersion in sanctified water, followed by a rite of confirmation called "Holy Chrismation," whereupon you confirm your faith in Christ. Holy orders are monastic vows through which ordained men and women devote their lives to Christ and perform good works for the Church. Penance is the practice of acknowledging sin before God, requesting forgiveness from God, and practicing an austerity as an act of redemption to God. The Eucharist is the affirmation of Christ within yourself through consumption of sanctified bread and wine, which holds the body of Christ's spirit. Matrimony is the union of man and woman as husband and wife before God and the Church. Finally, "the last rites," or extreme unction, are performed in preparation for death in this world and the reunion of the soul with God and Christ in the next world.

The Orthodox Church observes substantially the same holy days as the Catholic Church, but these are calculated in a different manner, so they are observed on different days. There is also the widespread use in churches and homes of sacred images of Christ and the saints in such forms as paintings, mosaics, or other icons. The faithful do not actually worship the icons themselves, but venerate them as examples of the Holy Spirit within man.

FOR ADDITIONAL INFORMATION

Recommended Contacts

Look in your phone directory or Chamber of Commerce directory of churches under "Orthodox," or variation thereof, such as Greek Orthodox or Russian Orthodox. For a more complete source of Orthodox Churches and centers contact the following sources:

The Orthodox Ministry
8-10 E. 79th Street
New York, NY 10021
Phone: (212) 570–3500
Website: www.goarch.org

Spirit Works Ministries
P.O. Box 325
Lexington Avenue Station
New York, NY 10028
Phone: (887) 774–0217
Website: www.spiritworks.com

Recommended Readings

Constantelos, Demetrios J. *Understanding the Greek Orthodox Church.* New York: Hellenic College Press, 1988.

Eusebius of Caesarea. *The History of the Church.* G. A. Williamson, trans. New York: Penguin, 1990.

Konstantopoulos, Elaine. *Meditations on the Lord's Prayer.* New York: Cappadocia Press, 1999.

Timiadis, Emilianos. *Towards Authentic Christian Spirituality.* Markos Nickolas, ed. Boston: Holy Cross Orthodox Press, 1998.

ROMAN CATHOLICISM

Catholic means *universal,* and *Roman Catholic* refers to the Latin Western church founded by Jesus Christ and headed since that time by a continuous succession of popes.

HISTORY

After the ascension of Christ into heaven, his apostles became missionary zealots, especially Paul and Peter. They traveled from the Holy Land into southern Europe and Asia. The writings of the evangelists Matthew, Mark, Luke, and John were influential in the acceptance of Christian theology. By the end of the first century, Christianity was represented throughout southern Europe, North Africa, and the Middle East. By the third century, Christianity had become the predominant religion throughout the Mediterranean.

After the emperor Constantine granted freedom of religion to Christians with the Edict of Milan in A.D. 313, the entire Roman Empire was converted to Christianity. Thus, most of the Mediterranean and much of Europe became Christianized. From the fourth century on, the Church was identified with the Roman Empire. But as the fortunes of Rome declined, the power of the empire shifted eastward to Constantinople, which resulted in a split between the Eastern and Western churches in A.D. 1054. (See "Eastern Orthodox Churches" on page 89.)

The Middle Ages represented the classic period for Roman Catholicism. Numerous majestic cathedrals were constructed throughout Europe to glorify God; religious orders such as the Franciscans and Dominicans were formed; and the Church flourished and spread in every direction.

In the eleventh century, a philosophical system known as "scholasticism" was introduced into the Church. Scholastics attempted to synthesize traditional faith and values with the logic and reason of the Greek philosopher Aristotle. The theologian Thomas Aquinas (A.D. 1225–1274) was particularly influential in reconciling faith and reason, and his ideas dominated Catholic thought for seven centuries.

Since the sixteenth century, "Roman Catholic" has meant the Christian religious body that acknowledges the pope as head of the universal

Church and the center of ecclesiastical unity. Papal authority is based on the doctrine of apostolic succession, which holds that the authority of the Church was given to the apostle Peter, the first Bishop of Rome, by Jesus Christ himself. This authority has been passed down through successive bishops of Rome to the current pope. The first Vatican Council, held in 1870, declared that the pope has primacy of jurisdiction over the whole Church and that, under specific conditions, he is infallible—that is, he cannot make an error—in proclaiming doctrines of faith and morals. In 1964, Vatican Council II further explained infallibility and set it in the context of the Church and the college of bishops.

Today, Christianity is the largest religion in the world, and the Roman Catholic church is the largest branch of Christianity, with over a billion adherents. The religion is represented around the world, particularly in Southern Europe, Ireland, Latin America, and South America.

BELIEF SYSTEM

The Roman Catholic church believes in the traditional Christian creeds and the Trinity of God as:

1. God, the Father, All-Governing;

2. Jesus Christ, the Son of God, who was begotten by the Holy Spirit from the Virgin Mary and was crucified by Pontius Pilate, died, rose from the dead on the third day, ascended into Heaven, and sits at the right hand of the Father. At the end of the world, Christ will come again to judge the living and the dead.

3. The Holy Spirit, who, through God's grace, awakens faith in you as it has in the Holy Church itself.

Catholics also believe in the concept of "original sin," which states that mankind is inherently sinful due to the disobedient acts of Adam and Eve, the first man and woman, and thus needs to be saved. Although confession, repentance, and absolution are means of rectifying your individual sins, salvation is achieved only through God's grace. Catholics believe that God so loved you that he allowed his only son, Jesus Christ, to suffer and die on the cross in atonement for your sins. In turn, it is your acceptance of Christ as Lord that redeems you and assures your eternal life with God and Jesus in Heaven.

RITUALS AND HOLY DAYS

Roman Catholics observe the seven sacraments, venerate saints, particularly the Virgin Mary (Christ's mother), and acknowledge the presence of the Holy Spirit. The Eucharist, or Mass, is the center of church life, in which bread and wine are transformed into the body and blood of Christ—a phenomenon known as transubstantiation. The physical ingestion of the body and blood of Christ in Holy Communion confers grace upon the believers. Catholic beliefs and doctrines are interpreted by the pope, who is regarded as infallible, under certain conditions, in matters of faith and morals, and by the clergy, who are deemed properly prepared to interpret the word of God for the believers. (See "Christianity" on page 82, and "Eastern Orthodox Churches" on page 89.)

FOR ADDITIONAL INFORMATION

Recommended Contacts

Look in your phone directory or Chamber of Commerce list of churches, or consult the resources listed below. (See also "Christian Mysticism" on page 186.)

Catholic Online
1701 Westwind Drive, Suite 219
Bakersfield, CA 93301
Phone: (805) 869–1000
Website: www.catholic.org

Catholic Press Association
3555 Veteran's Memorial
  Highway, Unit O
Ronkonkoma, NY 11779
Phone: (516) 471–4730
Website: www.catholicpress.org

Catholic Television Network
1531 West 9th Street
Los Angeles, CA 90015
Phone: (213) 251–3308
E-mail address: ctn@supal

The Catholic Information Center
150 Werimus Lane
Hillsdale, NJ 07642-1223
Phone: No listing
Website: www.catholic.net

Eternal World Network
5817 Old Leeds Road
Irondale, AL 35210
Phone: (205) 271–2900
Website: www.ewtn.com

National Association of Religious
  Broadcasters
7839 Ashton Avenue
Manassas, VA 22110
Phone: (703) 330–7000
Website: www.nrb.com

The National Conference of
Catholic Bishops
3211 4th Street, N.E.
Washington, D.C. 20017-1194
Phone: (202) 541–3000
Website: www.nccbuscc.org

WEWN World Wide Catholic
Radio
1500 High Road
Vandiver, AL 35176
Phone: (800) 585–9396

Recommended Periodicals

Catholic Digest
P.O. Box 64090
St. Paul, MN 55164
Phone: (612) 962–6749

Our Sunday Visitor
200 Noll Plaza
Huntington, IN 46750
Phone: (219) 356–8400

National Catholic Register
33 Rossotto Drive
Hamden, CT 06514
Phone: (800) 421–3230

US Catholic
205 West Monroe Street
Chicago, IL 60606
Phone: (312) 236–7782

National Catholic Reporter
P.O. Box 419281
Kansas City, MO 64141
Phone: (816) 531–0538

Recommended Readings

Bokenkotter, Thomas S. *Concise History of the Catholic Church*. New York: Image Books, 1990.

Chaliha, Joya, and Edward LeJoly, eds. *Mother Teresa: A Complete Authorized Biography*. San Francisco, CA: Harper, 1998.

Davies, Brian. *The Thought of Thomas Aquinas*. New York: Clarendon Press. 1993.

The Holy Bible: New Revised Standard Version. Fort Collins, CO: Ignatius Press, 1994.

John Paul II. *Prayers and Devotions: 365 Daily Meditations*. New York: Penguin USA, 1998.

John Paul II. *Crossing the Threshold of Hope*. New York: Random House, 1995.

John Paul II. *Catechism of the Catholic Church*. Vatican City: Urbi et Orbi Communications, 1994.

Szulc, Tad. *Pope John Paul II: The Biography*. New York: Pocket Books, 1996.

Recommended Websites

www.cathcom.net

www.catholicgoldmine.com

www.catholicsonline.com

www.christusrex.org

www.community.catholic.org

www.cwnews.com

www.diocesenet.com

www.Roman-Catholic.org

www.vatican.va

PROTESTANTISM

Protestantism embraces those churches that place a great emphasis on a personal interpretation of the Holy Bible. All Protestant churches have their origin in the Reformation begun by Martin Luther, who like other reformers, protested against the power of the pope and the Roman Catholic Church. In this section, we will delve into the history of Protestantism, beginning in the fourteenth century, then explore those beliefs that most Protestants hold in common, and finally, examine the major Protestant sects that grew out of the Reformation.

HISTORY

The English reformer John Wycliffe (1329–1384) protested against the power of the pope, and argued that believers are directly responsible to God. He placed his emphasis on the Bible itself as the source of God's word, rather than on the authority of the pope and the Catholic Church. Later, the teacher and priest John Huss (1369–1415), inspired by Wycliffe, led a reform party in Bohemia that based its theology on Biblical interpretation, and called for church reforms. Huss was later burned as a heretic, but this only served as a catalyst for further rebellion against the Church of Rome.

The permanent Protestant reform began shortly after the invention of the printing press because the public at large had greater access to the Holy Bible. During a two-decade period, Martin Luther (1483–1546) in Germany, John Calvin (1509–1564) in France, and Huldreich Zwingli (1484–1531) in Switzerland—and numerous reformers in the Netherlands, Scotland, and England—broke away from Roman Catholicism. The Protestant Reformation had begun.

BELIEF SYSTEM

As we said previously, Protestantism embraces those churches where the emphasis is placed on a personal interpretation of the Holy Bible. These churches grew out of the Reformation, in which various individuals protested against the strict interpretations of Rome, preferring their own interpretation of the scriptures. Others called attention to abuses like the selling of indulgences, or adopted different philosophical positions on the religious issues of the day, problems like papal infallibility, infant salvation, and predestination.

Interpretation of the scripture may vary, but reliance on the written word of the Bible itself, rather than on papal dictates or religious doctrine is what separates Protestant churches from Catholic or Orthodox churches.

Protestants generally recognize two of the seven sacraments that the Orthodox and Catholic churches recognize. They believe in baptism, through which a human spirit is cleansed of "original sin" and endowed with a new kind of life with Jesus Christ, and Holy Communion—the Lord's Supper or the Eucharist—a representation of Christ's sacrifice on Calvary.

Protestantism is divided into three main groups, although there are many other secular and nondenominational churches. These three main branches are Lutherans, Presbyterians, and Anglicans—or Episcopalians, as they are known in America. Because the various churches share so much in common, I will emphasize those areas in which they differ significantly from their brethren.

FOR ADDITIONAL INFORMATION

Protestantism is a broad-based term applied to those churches that broke off from the Roman Catholic Church, were never a part of the Orthodox Church, or are modern movements that base their teachings on the Bible. Most Protestant churches are listed under other, more specific sect names, such as Lutheran or Presbyterian, as in the sections that follow. The resources listed below provide general information on Protestantism, in general.

Recommended Contact

Reformed Churches of America
475 Riverside Drive, 18th Floor
New York, NY 10115
Phone: (800) 722–9977
Website: www.rca.org

Recommended Readings

Bainton, Roland Herbert. *The Reformation of the Sixteenth Century*. New York: Beacon Press, 1985.

Miller, Donald E. *Reinventing American Protestantism*. Berkeley, CA: University of California Press, 1997.

Recommended Websites

Christian World
www.christianworld.com

The Interactive Bible
www.bible.com

Protestant Reformed Churches
in America
www.prca.org

Protestant Reformed Network
www.reformednet.org

Reformed Churches' Network
www.reformed.net

Lutheran Church

Martin Luther, a German friar, is credited with starting the Reformation after nailing his ninety-five theses—protests against the Catholic Church—on the door of a church at Wittenberg, Germany, in 1517.

HISTORY

Lutheran was a derisive nickname given to the followers of Martin Luther and other reformists by their enemies in the early days of the Protestant Reformation. Lutheranism now stands for the movement that denies the divine authority of the pope, emphasizes Holy Scripture as the basis of faith, and Jesus Christ as the authoritative source of the Word of God.

Martin Luther was a German friar who helped initiate the reformation of Christianity and the Protestant movement by "protesting" against the actions of the Catholic Church, such as offering redemption through financial contributions to the Church. He had no wish to begin a new religion; rather, he hoped to "reform" the Catholic Church from within through vigorous protest. Thus, in 1517, Luther nailed his theses of ninety-five protests to the door of the Church in Wittenberg, Germany. This action ignited a flame in Germany that spread across a Europe that was already a theological tinderbox ready to explode.

In 1529, Luther wrote his longer and shorter catechisms. A year later, Philip Melanchthon (1497–1560), a scholarly associate of Luther's, published a statement of faith known as the Augsburg Confession. These documents were among the articles that served to form the basis of Luther's theology and inspired other reformers of his day to think in new ways and "protest," as well. The Reformation had begun. At first, Lutheranism spread primarily into northern and eastern Europe. The new religion found its way to the United States mainly through the influence of immigrants from Germany and Scandinavia. The first service in North America was in 1619 in Hudson's Bay in Canada, and in 1623, another was held on Manhattan Island by Dutch immigrants. Lutheranism is today the oldest and largest Protestant denomination worldwide.

BELIEF SYSTEM

Lutheranism separated itself from the Catholic Church that had dominated European religious theology, and served as the cornerstone of the Protestant movement by declaring that the Roman Catholic Church and the papacy had no divine right to things spiritual; that the pope was not infallible; that the scripture, not a priest or the church, had final authority over conscience.

Luther believed that you are forgiven and absolved of your sins, not by the performance of good works or the imposition of church rite, but by the grace of the Holy Spirit, which is empowered to turn you from sin to God. This ideology set the standard for the Reformation.

Lutherans believe that in Holy Communion, Christ is "really present" in the bread and wine in a mystical and miraculous way, although not in the literal sense of the Catholic doctrine of transubstantiation. With many other Christians, they also believe in baptism, confirmation, marriage, and ordination of priests. Sunday services consist of prayer, meditation, homily, and readings from scripture.

FOR ADDITIONAL INFORMATION

Recommended Contacts

Look in your neighborhood telephone directory or Chamber of Commerce directory under "churches," or consult any of the following resources:

Evangelical Lutheran Churches
  in America
8765 W. Higgins Road
Chicago, IL 60631
Phone: (800) 638–3522
Website: www.elca.org

Lutheran World Federation
150 Route de Ferney CH-1211
Geneva 2, Switzerland
Phone: 41–22 791–61–11
Website: www.lutheranworld.org

Recommended Readings

Braaten, Carl E. *Principles of Lutheran Theology*. Minneapolis, MN: Fortress Press, 1983.

Luther, Martin. *Luther's Prayers*. Herbert F. Brokering, ed. Minneapolis, MN: Fortress Press, 1994.

Marius, Richard. *Martin Luther: The Christian Between God and Death*. Chicago, IL: Belknap Press, 1999.

Recommended Websites

Churchonline.com
www.churchonline.com

Indiana Lutherans
www.in.lcms.org

*The Lutheran Magazine and
Web Guide*
www.thelutheran.org

Presbyterian Church

Presbyterians are also known as Calvinists. The word *presbyterian* comes from the Greek word *presbuteros*, meaning *elder*, a reference to those who direct the operations of the church.

HISTORY

Presbyterians—and members of reformed churches—are Protestants who trace their denomination to a reformer from France, John Calvin. In his *The Institutes of the Christian Religion*, Calvin outlined a comprehensive system of Protestant doctrine. He moved to Geneva, Switzerland, where he preached his beliefs, which spread rapidly through Europe. One of his disciples, the Scottish reformer John Knox, brought Calvin's ideas to the British Isles. Presbyterianism then spread to America and the rest of the world. The Presbyterian and reform churches comprise the second largest and second oldest Protestant churches.

BELIEF SYSTEM

Calvin's theology emphasized God's sovereignty over us all, where humans are completely dominated by and dependent upon God, and our lives are unconditionally predestined. Calvinists, and later, Presbyterians, lived rather austere lives, and sought to reform Christianity by living morally clean and wholesome lives. Calvin's reforms include education, liberation of the oppressed, and the establishment of democratic forms of government both in church and state.

RITUALS AND HOLY DAYS

The Presbyterian rituals and holy days would be comparable to those of other Protestants. However, Presbyterians also believe that in Holy Communion the consecrated bread and wine must be regarded as symbols, or "representations," of the Lord's body and blood.

FOR ADDITIONAL INFORMATION

Recommended Contacts

Look in your neighborhood phone directory or Chamber of Commerce directory, or contact any of the following:

The Associated Reformed
  Presbyterian Church
1 Cleveland Street, Suite 110
Greenville, SC 29601-3696
Phone: (864) 232–8297
Website: www.arpsynod.org

The Orthodox Presbyterian
  Church
Box P
Willow Grove, PA 19090
Phone: (215) 830–0900
Website: www.opc.org

The Presbyterian Church
100 Witherspoon Street
Louisville, KY 40202
Phone: (502) 569–5000
Website: www.pcusa.org

Presbyterian Church in America
Website: www.pcanet.cjb.net

The Reformed Presbyterian
  Church
26550 Evergreen Road
Southfield, MI 48076
Phone: (248) 356–3932
Website: www.reformed.com

Recommended Readings

Calvin, John. *The Institutes of the Christian Religion*. Henry Beveridge, trans. Louisville, KY: William B. Eerdmas Publishing Co., 1995.

Knox, John. *Humanity and Divinity of Christ*. Cambridge, UK: Cambridge University Press, 1967.

Lingle, Walter Lee, and John W. Kuykendall. *Presbyterians, Their History and Beliefs*. Louisville, KY: John Knox Press, 1983.

Weeks, Louis B. *To Be a Presbyterian*. Louisville, KY: John Knox Press, 1983.

Episcopal Church

Episcopalians are the American Anglicans. The name *Episcopal* comes from the Greek word *episkopos*, which means *bishop*.

HISTORY

Founded by King Henry VIII of England (1491–1547), the Anglican Church is composed of the Church of England and seventeen other autonomous national churches, including the Protestant Episcopal Church. Pope Clement VII refused to grant King Henry an annulment of his marriage to Catherine, daughter of the King of Spain—a close ally of Rome. Henry then repudiated the papal authority, and proclaimed himself head of the Church of England. This was the beginning of the Anglican Church, and eventually opened the door to the reform movement in all the British Isles.

The Anglican communion is a worldwide fellowship, and is the third oldest and third largest family of Protestant churches.

BELIEF SYSTEM

Anglicans retain Catholic tradition while accepting the basic insights of the Protestant reform. The church is essentially loyal to the "doctrine, discipline and worship of the one, holy, catholic, and Apostolic Church" in all its essentials, but permits great liberty in "nonessentials," a term that is interpreted differently in various sects. The church allows for variation, individuality, independent thinking, and religious liberty. Furthermore, it places emphasis on the Holy Scriptures of the Old and New Testaments to be the Word of God and source for all that is necessary for salvation.

FOR ADDITIONAL INFORMATION
Recommended Contacts

Check your neighborhood telephone directory, the Chamber of Commerce directory, or the following sources:

The Anglican Catholic Church
1607 Dewitt Avenue
Alexandria, VA 22301
Phone: (703) 683–3343
Website:
   www.anglicancatholic.org

The Anglican Church in America
4807 Aspen Drive
West Des Moines, IA 50265
Website: www.acahome.org

The Anglican Communion
   Secretariat
157 Waterloo Road
London, SE1 8UT, England
Website:
   www.anglicancommunion.org

The Episcopal Church
815 Second Avenue
New York, NY 10017
Phone: (212) 867–8400
Website: www.ecusa.org

The Episcopalian Organization
P.O. Box 399
Amberidge, PA 15003
Phone: (724) 266–0669
Website: www.episcopalian.org

Recommended Readings

Griffiss, James E. *The Anglican Vision*. Boston: Cowley Publications, 1997.

Holmes, David L. *A Brief History of the Episcopal Church*. Cambridge, UK: Trinity Press International, 1993.

Webber, Christopher L. *A User's Guide to the Book of Common Prayer*. Atlanta, GA: Morehouse Publishing Co., 1997.

Recommended Websites

The Anglican Domain
www.anglican.org

The Society of Archbishop Justus
Justus.anglican.org

Congregational Church

The Congregational Church, also known as the Puritans or as the United Church of Christ, also had its origins in the Protestant Reformation. People of the United States generally associate these believers with the traditional feast of Thanksgiving.

HISTORY

Congregationalism has its roots in the Reformation. Groups of dissenting church members in England sought a better way than the one they had experienced in their established church—the Church of England. As the Reformation developed, the dissenters formed a Puritan movement, with the Congregationalists becoming the most extreme wing. It was said that their mission was to "reform the Reformation." They were among the most fundamental in their biblical studies and the most austere in their lifestyle.

For example, they would permit no consumption of alcohol, no work on Sunday, and no dancing. You had to read the Bible and devote your entire existence to the glory of God.

The Puritans were instrumental in laying their ideological foundation in the New World, and were among the first to colonize there. It was a Puritan group that set off from England in the *Mayflower* to start a new life and church in New England.

In America they became known as the Pilgrims and established colonies throughout New England. Our celebration of Thanksgiving was first celebrated by the Puritans by expressing gratitude to God for deliverance from harm and for a bountiful harvest. In 1957, the Congregational Church merged with the Evangelical and Reform Church, a Calvinist body, to form the United Church of Christ.

BELIEF SYSTEM

The Congregationalists and Puritans were staunchly independent, and adhered strictly to literal biblical interpretation. The United Church of Christ has placed its emphasis on faith: "We believe in God the Father, infinite in wisdom, goodness, and love; and in Jesus Christ, His Son, our

Lord and Savior, who for us and our salvation, lived and died and rose again and liveth evermore; and in the Holy Spirit, who taketh of the things of Christ and revealeth them to us, renewing, comforting, and inspiring the souls of men."

FOR ADDITIONAL INFORMATION

Recommended Contacts

Look in your neighborhood telephone directory, check with the Chamber of Commerce, or contact the following:

Conservative Congregational
   Christian Conference
7582 Currell Boulevard, #108
St. Paul, MN 55125
Phone: (612) 737–1474
Website: www.ccccusa.org

The Hall of Church History
P.O. Box 4000
Panorama City, CA 91412
Phone: (805) 295–5777
Website: www.gty.org

National Association of
   Congregational Christian
   Churches
8473 South Howell Avenue
P.O. Box 1620
Oak Creek, WI 53154-0620
Phone: (414) 764–1620
Website: www.congregational.org

United Church of Christ
700 Prospect Avenue
Cleveland, OH 44115
Phone: (216) 736–2222
Website: www.gmcc.org

Recommended Readings

Di Gangi, Mariano, ed. *A Golden Treasury of Puritan Devotion*. Laurinburg, NC: Presbyterian and Reform Publications, 1999.

Miller, Perry. *The American Puritans*. New York: Columbia University Press, 1982.

Ovid. *Metamorphoses*. Mary Annes, trans. New York: Viking Press, 1987.

Youngs, William J. *The Congregationalists*. Westport, CT: Praeger Publications, 1998.

Zikmund, Barbara Brown, and John B. Payne, eds. *The Living Theologica Heritage of the United Church of Christ*. Elkton, MD: Pilgrim Press, 1997.

Recommended Websites

Fire and Ice
www.puritansermons.com

Soli Deo Gloria Ministries
www.sdgbooks.com

Baptist Church

This group of Protestants was influenced by the doctrine of another reform church called the Anabaptists, whose members did not believe in infant baptism. Today, the Baptists comprise the largest Protestant family of churches in America.

HISTORY

The Baptists have their origins as a church in England and Holland during the sixteenth century. Scattered groups began a quiet reform, based on the conviction of faith: They wished to rebaptize adults who had once been christened as children. The principle was taken directly from an incident in the Bible in which Jesus himself was blessed and immersed in the Jordan River by John the Baptist, not because he needed to be "saved," but so as to bear witness to his faith in God. Similar movements also began to arise in Germany and Switzerland.

In Holland a group of Mennonites (see "Mennonite Church" on page 117) met with a group of British Separatists who were taking refuge in Amsterdam from the persecution of King James I. The Separatist leader, John Smyth, became inspired by the Mennonite argument for individual confirmation of faith in Jesus Christ through holy baptism. In 1909, John Smyth founded the first English Baptist Church, and over the years, members of his congregation began moving back into England. Later, Calvinist theology (see "Presbyterian Church" on page 103) influenced the formation of more Baptist churches in Europe. They adopted the practice of holy baptism for the adult, because the initial baptism had been received as an infant, a baby too immature to really make a lifelong commitment to God and his church.

The Anabaptists were considered "the left wing" of the Reformation. In dogmatic matters, they believed in a literal application of the word of God. In community matters, they refused to pay taxes or interest, would not run for public office, declined to give an oath in court, and opposed capital punishment.

Baptists began coming over early during the colonization of America, and then became one of the most represented denominations in North America with a strong evangelical emphasis. Baptist congregations have now covered the globe. They have traditionally been very independent of each other, and individual churches have moved away from associations with other churches, although at other times, they have come together to form associations and conventions with them.

BELIEF SYSTEM

Baptists place emphasis on the salvation of souls through the evangelical practice of witnessing the gospel of Jesus Christ. They are generally fundamentalists, receiving God's word directly from the Holy Bible—as opposed to church doctrine or individual creed—and take the Word of God in the Bible very literally, where other denominations might view passages more metaphorically. For instance, Baptists would believe the literal Biblical interpretation of creation, rather than accept the scientific belief in evolution. Baptists place emphasis on adult confirmation of their faith in God by a baptism, a total immersion of the body in water, thereby witnessing the gospel of Jesus Christ. Members emphasize the reading of Scripture and regular observance of the Lord's Supper.

FOR ADDITIONAL INFORMATION

Recommended Contacts

Look in your neighborhood telephone directory, check with your local Chamber of Commerce, or consult the following:

The Alliance of Baptists
1328 16th Street, NW
Washington, D.C., 20036
Phone: (202) 745–7609
Website: www.bonitara.com

American Baptist Association
4605 State Line Avenue
Texarkana, TX 75503
Website: www.abaptist.org

American Baptist Evangelicals
P.O. Box 128
Librany, PA 15129
Phone: (412) 851–1060
Website: www.abonline.org

American Baptist Churches USA
P.O. Box 851
Valley Forge, PA 19482-0851
Phone: (610) 768–2000
Website: www.abc-usa.org

Baptist.Org
P.O. Box 23428
Nashville, TN 23438
Phone: (615) 414–0142
Website: www.baptist.org

Conservative Baptist Association
    of America
P.O. Box 66
Wheaton, IL 60189-0066
Phone: (630) 260-3800
Website: www.cbamerica.org

General Association of Regular
    Baptist Churches
1300 N. Meacham Road
Schaumburg, IL 60173-4806
Phone: (888) 588-1600
Website: www.garbc.org

Cooperative Baptist Fellowship
P.O. Box 450329
Atlanta, GA 31145-0329
Phone: (770) 220-1600
Website: www.cbonline.org

National Association of Free Will
    Baptists
5233 Mt. View Road
Antioch, TN 37013
Phone: (615) 731-6812
Website: www.nafwb.org

Recommended Readings

Bradus, John A. *Baptist Confessions, Covenants and Catechisms*. Timothy George, ed. Spokane, WA: Broadman & Holman Publishers, 1996.

Brom, J. Newton. *The Baptist Church Manual*. Los Angeles, CA: Judson Press, 1982.

Bush, L. Russ, and Tom J. Nettles. *Baptists and the Bible*. Spokane, WA: Broadman & Holman Publishers, 1999.

Leonard, Bill J., ed. *The Dictionary of Baptists in America*. Macon, GA: Smyth & Helwys Publishers, 1999.

Recommended Websites

Baptist Bible Fellowship
International
www.bbfi.org

Baptist Bookstore
www.baptistbookstore.com

Baptist Standard
www.baptiststandard.com

Baptist Today
www.baptisttoday.org

Fundamentalist Baptist Fellowship
www.f-B-F.org

National Baptist Convention
www.nbcusa

Primitive Baptists' Web Station
www.pb.org

Southern Baptist Convention
www.sbc.net

Methodist Church

Also known as the Wesleyan Church, after its founder, the Methodist Church dates back to the eighteenth century. The term *methodist* refers to one who methodically searches the Bible as a source of divine wisdom and guidance.

HISTORY

The Methodist Church was founded in England, about 1735, by John Wesley, a student at Oxford University who was preparing for the Anglican ministry. At Oxford, Wesley became a leader of a group of students who sought spiritual renewal through methodical diligence in study and worship. The term "Methodists" was originally a nickname given to this study group. Later, as an Anglican priest, Wesley traveled across England encouraging a revival of the Church of England. John and his brother Charles preached among the poor and desperate commoners and inspired a grass roots movement among the populace. Soon, he formed his own church, which spread rapidly throughout the country.

The movement may have flourished, but when the Church of England would not ordain Wesley's priests, he left for America, arriving in Georgia in 1736. His ministry of two years was initially unsuccessful, but when he returned to England, conditions improved, his reputation grew, and converts flocked to the church.

Later, his ordained clergy established a mission in America. In 1769, they built their first chapel in New York and the church flourished. Methodists now constitute the second largest Protestant denomination in the United States.

BELIEF SYSTEM

The Methodist Church teaches the doctrine of the Trinity, the natural sinfulness of humankind, the fall of Adam and Eve—who represent all humanity—and the need for conversion and repentance. It also teaches the doctrine of free will, the need for salvation through God's grace, and the necessity to strive for perfection. Emphasis is placed on living right, and accepting Jesus Christ into your heart.

FOR ADDITIONAL INFORMATION

Recommended Contacts

Look in your neighborhood telephone directory, talk to the local Chamber of Commerce, work through their central offices that list affiliate churches, or consult the following resources:

The General Board of Church
and Society
100 Maryland Avenue, NE
Washington, D.C. 20002
Phone: (202) 488–5625
Website: www.umc_gbcs.org

The General Board of Global
Ministries
475 Riverside Drive, #1439
New York, NY 10015
Phone: (212) 870–3637
Website: www.gbgm-umc.org

The Official United Methodists
Church Homepage
Phone: (800) 251–8140
Website: www.umc.org

United Methodist Publishing
House
Phone: (800) 672–1789
Website: www.umph.org

Recommended Readings

Heitzenrater, Richard P. *Wesley and the People Called Methodists*. Nashville, TN: Abingdon Press, 1994.

Kempis, Thomas A. *The Imitation of Christ*. Nashville, TN: Image Books, 1955.

Law, William. *A Serious Call to a Devout and Holy Life*. John Meister, ed. Louisville, KY: Westminister John Knox Press, 1968.

Witherington, Ben. *How United Methodists Study Scripture*. Nashville: TN: Abingdon Press, 1994.

Quakers

The Quakers represent a relatively small church also known as the Society of Friends.

HISTORY

The Society of Friends is a puritanical group that is descended from the Church of England. In the seventeenth century, its founder, George Fox, was considered a rebel because he did not believe in showing reverence to anyone but God. He even refused to doff his hat to his earthly monarch, the king, and urged his followers to do the same. For maintaining such beliefs and attitudes, he and his Quaker followers were persecuted.

Seeking religious freedom, Fox and his adherents sailed to America in 1671, and started settlements in Maryland, Rhode Island, and Pennsylvania. This church remains relatively small and concentrated in the eastern United States.

BELIEF SYSTEM

George Fox, who founded the Society of Friends, or Quakers, developed the doctrine of the "Inner Light," which holds that God is ever present within every human being, and that he can be approached and experienced directly by anyone who sincerely seeks him. The emphasis is therefore placed on personal experience with God, and less on theories and practices. Quakers generally value simple, ascetic lives and are extreme pacifists. According to their creed, no true Quaker gambles, plays the stock market, wagers on or owns race horses, drinks alcoholic beverages, uses narcotics, or takes up arms against a fellow human being.

FOR ADDITIONAL INFORMATION
Recommended Contacts

Friends General Conference
1216 Arch Street, #2B
Philadelphia, PA 19107
Phone: (215) 561–1700
Website: www.quaker.org

Friends United Meeting
101 Quaker Hill Drive
Richmond, IN 47374
Phone: (765) 962–7573
Website: QuakerLife@xc.org

Recommended Readings

Ingle, H. Larry. *First Among Friends: George Fox and the Creation of Quakerism*. New York: Oxford University Press, 1966.

Smith, Robert Lawrence. *A Quaker Book of Wisdom*. New York: William Morrow & Co., 1998.

West, Jassamyn, ed. *The Quaker Reader*. Wallingsford, PA: Pendle Hill Publications, 1992.

Recommended Websites

Evangelical Friends International
www.evangelical_friends.org

George Fox Website
www.georgefox.edu

Mennonite Church

Mennonites got their name from a former Roman Catholic priest named Menno Simons (1492–1559). For theological reasons, he had left the Catholic Church and joined the Anabaptists. However, so great was his charismatic leadership that the movement adopted his name, and its adherents were subsequently called Mennonites.

HISTORY

Mennonites are direct spiritual descendants of the Anabaptist movement, which was founded in Zurich, Switzerland, in 1535. These people were considered the left wing of the Reformation, and were persecuted by Catholics, Lutherans, and Calvinists for their extreme beliefs, especially their contention that only adult believers could be baptized. About 1683, many of these persecuted Protestants fled to America and settled in the area around Germantown, Pennsylvania. Later, other Mennonite settlers came to America, but these people have tended to keep to themselves. Members of the Mennonites include the Amish, the Hutterian Brethren, and some smaller denominations.

BELIEF SYSTEM

The Mennonite belief is based on a "confession of faith" signed in Holland in 1632, with very traditional beliefs in faith in God as creator and Christ as the son of God. Moreover, the creed asserts the belief in our fall from grace, in our restoration at the coming of Christ, in our redemption through his death on the cross, and in obedience to his law in the gospel. Mennonites see the necessity for repentance of sin, for conversion to the will of God, for salvation through the cross, and for the use of baptism as a public testimony of faith. They tend to interpret every word of the Bible literally. They live very austere lives, are complete pacifists, and dress simply.

RITUALS AND HOLY DAYS

Mennonites would follow roughly the same rituals and holy days as any other Protestant sect. However, there are some differences. These include the serving of the Lord's Supper twice each year; baptism by the pouring of water, rather than immersion; and the ritual washing of the feet, especially in connection with the Lord's Supper during Holy Week.

FOR ADDITIONAL INFORMATION

Recommended Contact

Mennonite orders are not common, unless you happen to live in Pennsylvania. For additional information contact the following source:

MennoLink
3720 10th Avenue, South
Minneapolis, MN 55407
Phone: (612) 823–5779
Website: www.mennolink.org

Recommended Reading

Denlinger, Martha. *Real People: Amish and Mennonites in Lancaster County, Pennsylvania.* Scottdale, PA: Herald Press, 1993.

Evangelical Church

HISTORY

Evangelical Churches comprise many different sects with different origins and methods of practice, including the Evangelical Christian Churches, which started with the Arminian preacher Horace Bushnell (1802–1876). He was a follower of the teachings of Jacobus Arminius (1560–1609), who preached that God bestows forgiveness and salvation on all men who believe in Jesus Christ, not just the elect. Arminius was controversial at the time, because his teachings opposed those of the Calvinists, who believed in predestination. (See "Presbyterian Church" on page 103.)

In 1894, the Evangelical Congregational Church broke off from Bushnell's Evangelical Church to form its own group. Another sect, the Evangelical Covenant Church of America, goes back to the Protestant Reformation in Sweden. Still another, the Evangelical Free Church of America, is the result of a union between the Swedish Evangelical Free Church and the Evangelical Free Church in 1950.

Today, an "evangelical" church could be used in association with any number of Protestant sects or even with independent churches.

BELIEF SYSTEM

Evangelical churches tend to be fairly "mainstream fundamental" believers, that is, they follow biblical scripture literally and emphasize the need for salvation. In their teachings, they generally follow Arminius (1560–1609), the Dutch theologian, in holding that God saves all who repent of their sins and who sincerely believe in Jesus Christ. Only because he knows all things from all eternity has God foreseen the belief or unbelief of all individuals, and has, therefore, determined the fate of each.

FOR ADDITIONAL INFORMATION
Recommended Contacts

I suggest you look in your neighborhood telephone directory, check with the local Chamber of Commerce, or consult the sources listed below. Note that the term "evangelical" may appear in the names of many churches that have no formal relation to the Evangelical Church described above. You might also see "Evangelists" on page 140.

Evangelical Christian Publishers'
   Association
1969 East Broadway, Suite Two
Tempe, AZ 85282
Phone: (480) 966–3998
Website: www.ecpa.org

Evangelical Covenant Church
5101 North Francisco Avenue
Chicago, IL 60625
Website: www.covchurch.org

Evangelical Free Church of
   America
901 East 78th Street
Minneapolis, MN 55420
Website: www.efca.org

Recommended Readings

Hale, Frederich. *Trans-Atlantic Conservative Protestantism in the Evangelical Free and Mission Convenant Traditions*. North Stratford, NH: Ayer Company Publishers, 1979.

Hanson, Calvin B. *The Trinity Story*. Berkeley, CA: Next Step Resources, 1983.

Swindoll, Charles R. *Living on the Ragged Edge*. Chicago: World Books, 1990.

Recommended Websites

Evangelical Anabaptist Fellowship
www.eaf.org

Evangelical Outreach
www.internetsermons.com

World Evangelical Fellowship
www.worldevangelical.org

MODERN CHRISTIAN MOVEMENTS

Not all Christian churches grew out of the reaction, or reformation, against Roman Catholicism or Eastern Orthodox. Others grew out of a personal vision of someone seeking God. Yet, they too speak to their followers in very powerful ways. In the pages that follow, we will examine fourteen different denominations.

Salvation Army

HISTORY

A Methodist minister, William Booth, left the pulpit in 1861 to become a freelance evangelistic preacher. This work led him to the slums of London, where he dedicated his life to the poverty-stricken unchurched masses in that area. In 1878, he founded the Salvation Army to build an army of crusaders to save the souls of people in need. The movement has grown rapidly and spread around the world, along with many community services and outreach programs.

BELIEF SYSTEM

Booth believed service to the Lord was not merely worship, but involved cutting the chains of injustice, freeing the oppressed, sharing food with the hungry, housing the homeless, clothing the naked, and tending to family duties. He and his "army" fought sweatshops and child prostitution in their "war" against social and economic injustice; their crusade continues to this day.

RITUALS AND HOLY DAYS

Members of the Salvation Army would follow roughly the same rituals and holy days as any Protestant sect. They are particularly zealous at Christmas, manning charity stands as "sidewalk Santas."

FOR ADDITIONAL INFORMATION

Recommended Contact

Look in your local telephone directory, check with the Chamber of Commerce, or consult the following resource:

The Salvation Army
P.O. Box 269
Alexandria, VA 22312
Phone: (703) 684–5500
Website: www.salvationarmy.org

Recommended Readings

Brooks, Stephen. *God's Army: The Story of the Salvation Army.* London, UK: MacMillan, 1999.

Winston, Diane H. *Red Hot and Righteous: The Urban Religion of the Salvation Army.* Cambridge, MA: Harvard University Press, 1999.

Recommended Website

The Red Shield
www.redshield.org

Foursquare Gospel

The Foursquare Gospel began under the evangelistic work of Aimee Semple McPherson.

HISTORY

Around 1890, Aimee Semple McPherson was born in Canada into a Salvation Army family. She married a Pentecostal missionary named Robert Semple, but was soon widowed when he died in China in 1910. She returned to North America with her daughter and decided to carry on his evangelistic work. An inspired American speaker and faith healer, she settled in Los Angeles and built the famous Angelus Temple, which opened in 1923. She had her own radio station, Bible school, magazine, and social service network.

BELIEF SYSTEM

This group is strongly "fundamentalist" in its teachings. It has an active missionary program and broadcasts from several radio stations around the country.

FOR ADDITIONAL INFORMATION

Recommended Contact

You might consult your local telephone directory, Chamber of Commerce, or the following:

The Foursquare Gospel
1910 West Sunset Boulevard
P.O. Box 26902
Los Angeles, CA 90026
Phone: (213) 989–4234
Website: www.foursquare.org

Recommended Readings

Cleave, Nathanial Van. *The Vine and the Branches*. Los Angeles: ICFG Publishing, 1999.

Cox, Raymond. *The Foursquare Gospel*. Los Angeles: ICFG Publishing, 1999.

Unitarian Universalist Church

The Unitarian view was expounded as early as the fourth century A.D. by Arius of Alexandria, who taught that Jesus was sent from God, but was not actually God incarnate. Similar views continued to be manifested over the centuries by English and European intellectuals.

HISTORY

The first Universalist congregation was established by a former Wesleyan minister named John Murray. He left England in 1770 to emigrate to the United States, where he preached the doctrine of universal salvation. He became known as the "Father of American Universalism."

The Unitarian movement first emerged as an organized denomination in 1819, under the leadership of William Ellery Channing, an American clergyman from New England, who had a well-deserved reputation as a powerful preacher. Later in the nineteenth century, Unitarian ideas were expressed by Ralph Waldo Emerson and Theodore Parker, who helped to foster an independent and free-thinking approach to Christian theology.

In 1961, the Universalists merged with the Unitarians to form the Unitarian Universalist Association, which remains a relatively small group of churches today.

BELIEF SYSTEM

The Unitarian Universalist Association's stated purpose is, "To cherish and spread the universal truths taught by the great prophets and teachers of humanity in every age and tradition, immemorially summarized in the Judaeo-Christian heritage as love to God and love to man." They consider Jesus Christ to be one sent by God to lead men into the way, the truth, and the life, but do not regard him as divine. Rather, they place great emphasis on individual freedom of belief, and leave each member to "seek the truth for himself."

FOR ADDITIONAL INFORMATION

Recommended Contact

You might consult your local telephone directory, Chamber of Commerce, or the following:

Unitarian Universalist Association
25 Beacon Street
Boston, MA 02108
Phone: (617) 742–2100
Website: www.uua.org

Recommended Readings

Lach, William, ed. *The Green Sound: Nature Writings from the Living Tradition of Unitarian Universalism*. Boston: Skinner House of Books, 1992.

Owen, Tom. *The Gospel of Universalism: Hope, Courage, and the Love of God*. Boston: Skinner House of Books, 1993.

The Church of Jesus Christ of Latter-Day Saints

The Church of Jesus Christ of Latter-Day Saints is erroneously referred to as "The Mormon Church." Adherents believe their mission is to correct the errors of other churches and restore the true teachings of Jesus Christ.

HISTORY

The Church of Jesus Christ of Latter-Day Saints was started by a man named Joseph Smith, Jr., who was born in Sharon, Vermont, in 1805. At the age of fourteen, Smith had a series of visions and was visited by an angel named Moroni. The angel began to prepare him to reform the Christian church in preparation for the second coming of Jesus Christ. During a vision, Moroni directed Smith to a box of golden plates inscribed with hieroglyphics. The angel also provided a pair of instruments—called Urim and Thummim—which enabled Smith to read the tablets and dictate an English translation. The result was the *Book of Mormon*, said to be written by a prophet named Mormon. Published in 1829, this other testament of the Bible tells of Christ visiting a lost tribe of Israelites who migrated to America in 600 B.C., and ends with a prophecy that the Church of Christ would be restored in America by a group of "Latter-Day Saints." Their mission would be to correct the errors of other churches and restore the communal life of the New Testament Christians.

The first Church of Jesus Christ of Latter-Day Saints was first organized on April 6, 1830, in Fayette, New York. Shortly thereafter, due to religious persecution, the Latter-Day Saints were forced to move en masse from the Finger Lakes region of western New York to Kirtland, Ohio, then to Jackson County, Missouri, and then to Commerce, Illinois, where they started the community of Nanvoo. Their influence started spreading, and within three years, they had over 20,000 members. The Mormons were persecuted for their "unorthodox" Christian views and practices. Smith, for example, practiced polygamy and took several "spiritual wives." When he and his brother were arrested in 1844, an angry mob of more than one hundred men broke into the Carthage jail and murdered them.

Later, Brigham Young, Smith's successor, led a group of Mormon settlers to the valley of the Great Salt Lake in Utah, and started a Latter-Day Saints congregation. As others came and settled in the area, this settlement flourished. Today, the Church of Latter-Day Saints has millions of members all over the world, with one of the strongest missionary efforts in Christianity.

BELIEF SYSTEM

In addition to the Holy Bible, Mormons regard the *Book of Mormon* as Holy Scripture, and believe that Joseph Smith was a prophet of God. One distinguishing difference from traditional Protestant doctrine is that Latter-Day Saints believe that God is a flesh-and-bones person who became supreme by mastering universal knowledge, and that all human beings have an unremembered preexistence in the spirit world. Mormons also observe strict rules of personal morality, scrupulously avoiding alcohol, tobacco, and gambling.

RITUALS AND HOLY DAYS

Latter-Day Saints follow the same religious holidays as Protestants. Young men, however, are expected to commit to a two-year missionary program, and all members are expected to tithe 10 percent of their income to the church. They also have an internationally recognized geneological center in Salt Lake City that is available to the public.

FOR ADDITIONAL INFORMATION

Recommended Contact

You might consult your local telephone directory, Chamber of Commerce, or the following:

The Church of Jesus Christ of Latter-Day Saints
50 East Street, North Temple Road
Salt Lake City, UT 84150
Phone: (888) 537–7111
Website: www.lds.org

Recommended Readings

Smith, Joseph, trans. *The Book of Mormon*. Salt Lake City, UT: Signature Books, 1999.

Smith, Joseph, and Scott H. Fairbring, eds. *An American Prophet's Record: The Diaries and Journals of Joseph Smith*. Salt Lake City, UT: Signature Books, 1999.

Recommended Website

Morman Website [Unofficial]
www.morganut.com

Seventh-Day Adventist Church

Early in the nineteenth century, in America and in Europe, a movement developed around the belief that the second coming of Christ was at hand.

HISTORY

The church was formally organized in 1863, in Michigan, by Mrs. Ellen White (1827–1915). She was said to have experienced during her lifetime some two thousand visions and prophetic dreams. She was an advocate of good health, and emphasized the preparation of church members, and the world, for the second coming of Christ. This church is now represented around the world, part of an international revivalist movement.

BELIEF SYSTEM

Adventists are fundamentalists who emphasize the Biblical prophecies found in the apocalyptic books of Daniel and Revelation. The Adventists are convinced that the promised "Second Advent" of Christ is near, but do not state or proffer to know exactly when. This church has a strong missionary program and maintains many medical facilities. Most Adventists are vegetarians, and the church promotes an austere and conservative lifestyle.

RITUALS AND HOLY DAYS

Adventists would follow roughly the same rituals and holy days as most Protestant sects.

FOR ADDITIONAL INFORMATION

Recommended Contacts

Look in your neighborhood telephone directory, check with the Chamber of Commerce, or consult the following resources:

Seventh-Day Adventist Church
12501 Old Columbia Pike
Silver Spring, MD 20904-6600
Phone: (301) 680–6000
Website: www.adventist.org

Seventh-Day Adventist Reform
  Movement
P.O. Box 7240
Roanoke, VA 24019-0240
Phone: (540) 362–1800
Website: www.sdarm.org

Recommended Readings

Moore, Marvin. *Conquering the Dragon Within*. Nampa, ID: Pacific Press Publishing, 1996.

Mosley, Stephen R. *Deepen My Heart*. Hagarstown, MD: Review and Herald Publishing, 1998.

Church of Christ, Scientist

Founded in the latter part of the nineteenth century by Mary Baker Eddy, the church emphasizes spiritual, not medical, healing.

HISTORY

The Christian Science Church was formally established in 1879 by Mrs. Mary Baker Eddy. Raised as a Congregationalist, she had been frequently ill as a young woman. In the 1860s, she had tried every kind of medication without much success. Then, in 1862, she suffered a serious fall, and she remained in critical condition for several days. Nevertheless, after reading Biblical accounts of Christ's healing a man bedridden with palsy, Mrs. Eddy said a prayer, arose from her bed, dressed herself, and walked out of the hospital on her own. From this event grew one of America's major religious denominations, one which is now represented around the world.

BELIEF SYSTEM

Christian Scientists believe that God is "infinite good," and that all "reality" in the universe is necessarily good because God created it.

The evil, sickness, and death that men think they see in the world could not have come from God; therefore, these things are essentially unreal. This church emphasizes spiritual healing, and adherents will refuse blood transfusions and other medical interventions inconsistent with their faith.

Mrs. Eddy's book *Science and Health with Key to the Scriptures*, published in 1875, is typically read in addition to the Bible at Sunday services. The church also sponsors reading rooms containing Christian Science literature in most major cities.

RITUALS AND HOLY DAYS

Christian Scientists observe the same religious holidays as other Protestant denominations, and their services are similar. However, they do not have ministers. *The Holy Bible* and *Science and Health* serve as pastor; they are read with the spirit of Christ attending through the readers and the congregation. Healing prayers are also emphasized.

FOR ADDITIONAL INFORMATION

Recommended Contact

I suggest you look in your local telephone directory, check with the Chamber of Commerce, locate a Christian Science Reading Room, or consult the following resource:

The Church of Christ, Scientist
175 Huntington Avenue
Boston, MA 02115
Phone: (617) 450–2000
Website: www.tfccs.com

Recommended Readings

Eddy, Mary Baker. *Science and Health with Keys to the Scriptures*. Claremont, CA: Aequus Institute, 1997.

Grekel, Doris. *The Founding of Christian Scientist*. Boston: Healing Unlimited, 1999.

Wright, Helen M., *God's Great Scientist, Book I*. Boston: H. M. Wright Publishers, 1998.

Recommended Websites

Healing Unlimited
www.christianscience.org

Christian Science Monitor
www.csmonitor.com

Pentecostal Church

The Pentecostal Church is also known as the Church of God or the Assemblies of God. They share an emotional approach to spirituality.

HISTORY

The Pentecostal movement was an outgrowth of the popular religious revivals that swept the world during the latter part of the nineteenth century. This movement comprises over twenty organized denominations, plus thousands of independent local churches, predominantly within the United States.

BELIEF SYSTEM

Pentecostals are Protestant fundamentalists who believe that authentic religious conversion is an ecstatic experience that should be accompanied by all the "signs" that attend the outpouring of God's Holy Spirit, as it did with the first Christian apostles. This experience may include "the gift of tongues," meaning that while filled with the Spirit, believers may be able to speak and understand many strange languages that they never learned. The common bond between various Pentecostal churches is their intensely emotional approach to religion.

RITUALS AND HOLY DAYS

Pentecostals observe the same religious holidays as other Protestant denominations, and their services are similar, as well.

FOR ADDITIONAL INFORMATION
Recommended Contacts

I suggest you look in your neighborhood telephone directory, check with your local Chamber of Commerce, or consult one of the following resources:

Assemblies of God
12445 Boonville Avenue
Springfield, MO 65802
Phone: (417) 862–2781
Website: www.ag.org

International Pentecostal
  Holiness Church
P.O. Box 12609
Oklahoma City, OK 73157
Phone: (405) 787–7110
Website: www.iphc.org

Pentecostal World Conference
P.O. Box 4815
Cleveland, TN 37320-4815
Phone: (423) 478–7260
Website:
    www.Pentecostalworldconf.org

Worldwide Church of God
P.O. Box 92463
Pasadena, CA 91109-2463
Phone: (800) 309–4466
Website: www.wcg.org

Recommended Readings

Blumhofer, Edith L. *The Assemblies of God: A Chapter in the Story of American Pentecostalism*. Oklahoma City, OK: Gospel Publishing House,1989.

Duewel, Wesley L. *Ablaze for God*. Nashville, TN: Wesley Heritage Press, 1989.

Mansfield, Patti Gallagher. *As by a New Pentecost: The Dramatic Beginning of the Catholic Charismatic Renewal*. Steubenville, OH: Franciscan University Press, 1998.

Tyson, James L. *Early Pentecostal Revival*. Hazelwood, MO: Pentecostal Publishing, 1992.

Recommended Websites

Assemblies Links
www.assemblies.org

Church of God International
www.chofgod.org

Pentecostal Evangelical Magazine
www.berean.edu

Pentecostal Links
www.pentecostal-issues.org

Pentecostal Research Centers
www.pctii.org

Jehovah's Witnesses

The Watchtower Bible and Tract Society, better known as Jehovah's Witnesses, was founded in Allegheny, Pennsylvania, in 1872, by Charles Taze Russell.

HISTORY

The Jehovah's Witnesses, formally incorporated as The Watchtower Bible and Tract Society, was organized by Pastor Charles Taze Russell (1852–1916). The first group that Russell organized was formed in Pittsburgh in 1872. Known earlier as Millennial Dawnists, and International Bible Students, they first incorporated in 1884. In 1909, they moved to New York, and in 1956, changed their name to the Watchtower Bible and Tract Society. Russell attracted large crowds with pronouncements of Christ's impending Second Coming.

Today, this church is one of the fastest growing religious bodies in the United States. However, with the Watchtower's strong missionary efforts, they have also built their church internationally, spreading throughout Europe, Latin America, and Africa.

BELIEF SYSTEM

Witnesses meet in Kingdom Halls, not churches, and do not believe in separation into clergy or laity. They give time generously to proclaiming their faith and "witnessing" the bible in their communities.

Their theology emphasizes the imminent battle of Armageddon, where Christ will lead an army of the righteous composed of the "host of heaven, the holy angels," and will completely annihilate the army of Satan. The righteous of the Earth will watch the battle but not participate in it. Those who are true believers in God will be saved and be his servants here in this world. Henceforth, those saved will repopulate the earth, live freely in peace, and be governed under Christ as King.

RITUALS AND HOLY DAYS

Witnesses do not celebrate Christmas, Easter, or birthdays, as these are considered pagan holidays.

They also refuse to salute the flag, bear arms, or participate in the affairs of government. They hold that the Bible is the sole source of laws that should govern men.

FOR ADDITIONAL INFORMATION

Recommended Contact

Look in your neighborhood telephone directory, check with the local Chamber of Commerce, or contact the following:

The Watchtower Bible and Tract Society
25 Columbia Heights
Brooklyn, NY 11201-2483
Phone: (718) 625–3600
Website: www.watchtower.org

Recommended Readings

Many books about Jehovah's Witnesses are written by *other* Christian groups who do not believe in the Witnesses' theology and so condemn them. I suggest you contact the headquarters in Brooklyn, or get in touch with a Kingdom Hall to receive reliable information published by their own organization. There are, however, two principal texts that I can recommend:

Mankind's Search for God. Brooklyn, NY: Watchtower Bible and Tract Society of New York, 1990.

Revelation—Its Grand Climax at Hand. Brooklyn, NY: Watchtower Bible and Tract Society of New York, 1988.

Unification Church

The official name of this church is The Holy Spirit Association for the Unification of World Christianity. People outside the church often refer to its members as "Moonies," but this term is incorrect and is considered derogatory.

HISTORY

The church was founded in Korea in 1954 by Reverend Sun Myung Moon. According to the Unification Church tradition, Jesus Christ appeared to Reverend Moon on Easter morning in 1936, and asked him to take responsibility for establishing the Kingdom of God on earth. Rev. Moon also communicates with Moses and Buddha, among other spiritual masters, as he "travels in the spirit world." From Korea, the church has spread to over 120 countries, including Japan, Western Europe, and the United States.

BELIEF SYSTEM

Moon's lectures about the revelations that he has received are in his text, *Won-li Kang Mon*, or *Lectures of Principle*. The basic belief is that humanity is to be restored to its original perfect state by a "principle of indemnity," by which all sin and wrong in the world must be put right at the proper time. Adam and Eve are considered the first parents, and because they sinned, a second set of parents came to "indemnify" the fall of mankind and reestablish the true family ideal.

According to Rev. Moon, Jesus came as the second Adam. He was not God himself, but he was related to God "as the body is related to the mind," Moon says in his *Divine Principle*. Because Jesus' contemporaries did not support him, and therefore he did not marry, he could only complete a spiritual restoration through the Holy Spirit, who played the role of Eve. The material world has remained under the power of Satan to the present day, but he will soon be vanquished by the new Messiah.

Reverend Moon teaches that the coming of a new Messiah is near and will occur in Korea. This second coming will complete the restoration. This Messiah will marry a new Eve, found a sinless humanity, and establish God's kingdom on earth. Members of this church are directed to follow puritanical sexual mores, since the misuse of love is believed to have been the original sin of not only Adam and Eve, but of the archangels, as well.

Reverend Moon takes responsibility for arranging marriages between members of the church and may unite hundreds of couples in matrimony in mass ceremonies in order to help create harmony among different nationalities, races, and religions of the world.

RITUALS AND HOLY DAYS

Members of the Unification Church honor the same holidays as Protestant Christians, but marriages are arranged by Reverend Moon himself. In this capacity, he may bring thousands of couples together—some of whom have never met previously—and marry them in a mass ceremony.

FOR ADDITIONAL INFORMATION

Recommended Contact

I suggest you contact the International Headquarters for the closest church in your area:

Unification Church
HAS-UWA
4 West 43rd Street
New York, NY 10036
Phone: (212) 997–0050
Website: www.unification.org

Recommended Readings

Moon, Sun Myung. *Blessing and the Ideal Family.* New York: HSA Publications, 1998.

Moon, Sun Myung. *The Tribal Messiah.* New York: HSA Publications, 1998.

OTHER CHRISTIAN CHURCHES

In this final section, we will take a brief look at other Christian churches, like the Church of Jesus Christ, Church of Christ, Church of the Nazarene, Church of God, and more.

HISTORY

There are literally thousands of independent Christian churches, and they may or may not be affiliated with other churches or organizations. There are at least twenty religious bodies in the United States alone that bear the name "Church of Jesus Christ." The largest of these is headquartered in Cleveland, Tennessee, and was chartered by Bishop M. K. Lawson in 1927; it has since both grown and splintered into several other groups with the same or similar names. For example, there is the Church of our Lord Jesus Christ of the Apostolic Faith that was organized by an R. C. Lawson in Columbus, Ohio, in 1919 and is now represented in thirty-two states and many countries around the world.

The Church of the Nazarene is an amalgamation of several church entities, including the Association of Pentecostal Churches in New England and the Church of the Nazarene in California, which joined in 1907; they later merged with the Holiness Church of Christ in the South in 1908. These Nazarenes are generally considered Methodists, but they emphasize "sanctification" of the soul through living a holy life and cleansing the heart of original sin.

The Church of Christ encompasses numerous independent churches, each with its own history. Nevertheless, they are related to each other in the fact that they are a part of the restoration movement that attempts to "restore" faith in the hearts of the people and bring them back to God. The movement would also include the work of James O'Kelly in Virginia, Abner Jones and Elias Smith in New England, Barton Stone in Kentucky, and Thomas and Alexander Campbell in West Virginia.

Other smaller movements include: Churches of God General Conference started by John Winebrenner (1797–1860) in Maryland; Churches of God, Holiness, founded by K. H. Burruss in Atlanta in 1914;

The Churches of the Living God formed by William Christian in Arkansas in 1889, and The National Council of Community Churches, which formed in the mid-1800s. Many of these groups have since joined others or splintered off on their own.

BELIEF SYSTEM

The commonality to these independent churches is in the emphasis on reading the Holy Bible and personally accepting Jesus Christ as your Lord and Savior. There is a saying among many independent churches that they have "no creed but Christ." Even among church organizations, the teachings can vary among the individual churches and their ministers. Typically, individuals are encouraged to find a personal relationship with Jesus through their reading of the Bible and through prayer, and find fellowship and support through their congregations.

RITUALS AND HOLY DAYS

Most independent Christian churches follow the same rituals and holy days as other Protestant denominations. However, there are some that do not adopt the celebration of Christmas or Easter because of their roots in pre-Christian culture.

FOR ADDITIONAL INFORMATION
Recommended Contacts

Look in your neighborhood telephone directory, consult your local Chamber of Commerce, or contact any of these sites:

The Church of God
P.O. Box 450
Charleston, TN 37310
Phone: (423) 559–1916
Website:
    www.thechurchofgod.org

The Church of God, Inc.
P.O. Box 406
Temperance, MI 48182
Phone: (888) 470–6222
Website:
    www.the-church-of-god.org

Church of God, International
P.O. Box 2525
Tyler, TX 75710
Phone: (909) 825–2525
Website: www.cgi.org

Church of the Nazarene
6401 The Paseo
Kansas City, MO 64131-1213
Phone: (816) 333–7000
Website: www.nazarene.org

The Global Church of God
P.O. Box 501111
San Diego, CA 92150-1111
Phone: (619) 675–2222
Website: www.gcg.org

National Council of the
Churches of Christ in the
USA
475 Riverside Drive, #850
New York, NY 10115
Phone: (212) 870–2227
Website: www.ncccusa.org

National Directory for the
Churches of Christ
903 South Main Street
Searcy, AR 72143-7314
Phone: (501) 268–9886
Website: www.outbound.org

The United Church of Christ
700 Prospect Avenue
Cleveland, OH 44115
Phone: (216) 736–2222
Website: www.ucc.org

Recommended Readings

Brown, Barbara, and John B. Payne, eds. *The Living Theological Heritage of the United Church of Christ*. New York: Pilgrim Press, 1997.

Church of God. Charlottesville, VA: Evangelical Press, 1994.

Lockhart, Douglas. *The Dark Side of God: A Quest for the Lost Heart of Christianity*. Rockport, MA: Element Books, 1999.

Mead, Frank S. *Handbook of Denominations*. Samuel S. Hill, ed. Nashville, TN: Abingdon Press, 1987.

Middendorf, Jesse C., ed. *The Church Rituals Handbook*. New York: Beacon Hill Press, 1997.

Needham, Nicholas R. *2000 Years of Christ Power*. Charlottesville, VA: Evangelical Press, 1998.

Norris, Kathleen. *Amazing Grace: A Vocabulary of Faith*. New York: Riverhead Books, 1999.

Strobel, Lee. *The Case for Christ*. South Barrington, IL: Zondervan Publishing, 1988.

Tracy, Wesley. *What Is a Nazarene? Understanding Our Place in the Religious Community*. Boston: Beacon Hill Press, 1998.

Evangelists

An evangelist is one who proclaims the gospel of the Holy Bible. Evangelists date back to the time of Jesus Christ, approximately two thousand years ago, particularly with the gospel writings of Matthew, Mark, Luke, and John. In the early Catholic Church, the evangelists were those who first brought the gospel to a city or a region. Later, they were itinerant preachers, usually powerful and charismatic speakers. The term later broadened to mean any person marked by evangelical enthusiasm for a cause—a crusader, for example. In this context, we apply the term to charismatic ministers who typically preach in revivals and special crusades, but especially with the advent of television and the Internet, those who have reached millions and developed their own followings.

FOR ADDITIONAL INFORMATION

Today, there are numerous Christian television and radio networks, and dozens of interactive websites transmitting the Word of God. To obtain a comprehensive listing of all the programming available to you, check your local television guide for Christian television programs, and your local newspaper for Christian radio programs. You might also consult any of the resources listed below, including the more popular evangelical organizations and television or radio evangelists that follow. You might also consult the "Crusades" inset that begins on page 142 for information on the three major crusades: the Campus Crusades for Christ, Promise Keepers, and the Harvest Crusade.

Recommended Contacts

Evangelical Christian Publishers
    Association
1969 East Broadway, Suite Two
Tempe, AZ 85282
Phone: (480) 966–3998
Website: www.ecpa.org

Foundation for Evangelism
551 Lakeshore Drive
P.O. Box 985
Lake Junaluska, NC 28745
Phone: (828) 456–4312
Website: www.evangelize.org

Global Online Service Helping
Evangelize Nations
c/o Media Management
P.O. Box 21433
Roanoke, VA 24018
Phone: (540) 989–1330
Website:
www.mediamanagement.net

The Institute of Evangelism
500 East College Avenue
Wheaton, IL 60187
Phone: (630) 752–5904
Website: www.wheaton.edu

Recommended Websites

ChristiaNet
www.christianet.com

EvangeLists
www.evangelists.org

Web Evangelism
www.webevangelism.org

Billy Graham

The Reverend Billy Graham was born in 1918 in North Carolina. Inspired at an early age to preach the gospel, he was ordained in 1939 as a minister of the Southern Baptist Convention. In 1943, after graduating from Wheaton College in Illinois, he married Ruth Bell. After building a reputation as a charismatic preacher, Graham launched his 1949 crusade in Los Angeles that vaulted him to national prominence. Since then, he has preached on every continent—to over 200 million people in 185 countries and territories—and converted millions to Christianity. Graham has become a friend and counselor to many public figures, including nine presidents. He is a modern evangelist, using television, the media, and the Internet to advantage. His son, Franklin Graham, has gained wide respect in his own right as a nationally recognized evangelist.

FOR ADDITIONAL INFORMATION

Recommended Contact

Billy Graham Evangelistic Association
P.O Box 779
Minneapolis, MN 55440
Phone: (877) 247–2426
Website: www.billygraham.org

Recommended Readings

Graham, Billy. *Angels*. Chicago: World Books, 1996.

Graham, Billy. *Death and the Life After*. Chicago: World Books, 1995.

Crusades

Part of the evangelist phenomenon is the crusade, a large-scale movement often involving thousands of people coming together to listen to the word of God, accept Christ into their hearts, and develop a sense of community and mutual support. We will look at three of the most successful crusades, the Campus Crusades for Christ, Promise Keepers, and the Harvest Crusade.

The Campus Crusades for Christ has a staff of millions of Christians—whom they have trained—who have taken the gospel to more than one billion people during the past forty years, tens of millions of whom have indicated their desire to receive and follow Christ. Bill Bright is the founder and President, Dr. Billy Graham is Chairman, and Dr. Ted Engstrom is President Emeritus of their World Vision program. For information:

> Campus Crusades for Christ International
> 100 Lake Hart Drive
> Orlando, FL 32832
> Phone: (407) 826–2000
> Website: www.ccci.org

Promise Keepers is a Christ-centered ministry dedicated to uniting men, through vital relationships, to become godly influences in their world. In 1990, Bill McCartney and Dave Wardell were

Pat Robertson

Marion Gordon "Pat" Robertson was born in 1930 in Lexington, Virginia. He graduated with a juris doctor degree from Yale University Law School in 1955, and received a Master's degree from New York Theological Seminary in 1959. The following year, Robertson raised the funds to purchase a radio station, and in 1961, the Christian Broadcasting Network went on the air for the first time. Today, CBN is one of the world's largest television ministries with programs aired in ninety countries around the globe. His flagship program, *The 700 Club*, is one of the longest-running religious television shows. It reaches an average of 1.5 million viewers daily. He also produces and distributes family entertain-

inspired to bring thousands of men together for Christian discipleship, then, in 1991, a group of over 4,000 men gathered at the University of Colorado as the first Promise Keepers. Since then, over two million men have attended their convocations. For information:

Promise Keepers
P.O. Box 103001
Denver, CO 80250-3001
Phone: (888) 888-7595
Website: www.promisekeepers.org

The Harvest Crusade Fellowship grew out of a bible study group of thirty people led by Greg Laurie, a nineteen-year-old from Riverside, California. Laurie had studied under Calvary Chapel minister Chuck Smith (see "Chuck Smith" on page 148), and then started the Harvest Christian Fellowship in 1982. Since then, a new movement has begun, with Harvest Crusades filling up sports stadiums and thousands accepting Christ into their lives. To date, over two million have heard Greg Laurie preach. For information:

Harvest Crusade
6115 Arlington Avenue
Riverside, CA 92504
Phone: (909) 687-6902
Website: www.harvest.org

ment programming, operates a university in Virginia Beach, Virginia, and has been a candidate for president, representing the "religious right" in America.

FOR ADDITIONAL INFORMATION

Recommended Contact

Christian Broadcasting Network
Centerville Turnpike
Virginia Beach, VA 23463
Phone: (757) 226–7000
Website: www.the700club.org

Recommended Readings

Robertson, Pat. *The End of the Age*. Chicago: World Books, 1998.

Robertson, Pat. *The New World Order*. Chicago: World Books, 1992.

Robert Schuller

Robert Schuller fulfilled his life's dream of becoming a minister in 1950. After receiving his Bachelor's degree from Hope College, and a Master's of Divinity degree from Western Theological Seminary, he was ordained by the Reform Church. He preached for five years as a minister at Ivanhoe Reformed Church in Chicago, then moved with his family to Garden Grove, California. There, he began preaching in a drive-in theater, where he would exhort the congregation from atop the snack bar. Nevertheless, because of his sincerity and charisma, his ministry flourished. Today, he is one of the most popular television evangelists in the world. His "Hour of Power" has been on the air for over thirty years, and is now the most widely viewed religious program in America. His Crystal Cathedral is a landmark in Southern California, and several of his books are bestsellers.

FOR ADDITIONAL INFORMATION
Recommended Contact

The Crystal Cathedral
13280 Chapman Avenue
Garden Grove, CA 92840
Phone: (714) 971–4000
Website: www.crystalcathedral.org

Recommended Readings

Schuller, Robert. *Be Happy Attitudes*. Chicago: World Books, 1997.

Schuller, Robert. *Turning Hurts Into Halos and Scars Into Stars*. Nashville, TN: Thomas Nelson Publishers, 1999.

Oral Roberts

Oral Roberts was born in 1918 in Pontotoc County, Oklahoma. He received his formal education at Oklahoma Baptist and Phillips Universities, but resigned his pastorate in 1947 to enter an evangelistic ministry. Since then, he has conducted over three hundred evangelistic and healing crusades on six continents. In 1963, Roberts chartered the university that bears his name. Later, he received an honorary doctor of divinity degree from the International Church of the Foursquare Gospel in 1988. He has written over 120 books, and is currently building up his Golden Eagle Broadcasting, a Christian television network that features Christian family programming, including his *Miracles Now* weekly show.

FOR ADDITIONAL INFORMATION
Recommended Contact

Oral Roberts University
7777 South Lewis Avenue
Tulsa, OK 74171
Phone: (800) 678–8876
   or (918) 495–6566
Website: www.oru.edu

Recommended Readings

Roberts, Oral. *Expect a Miracle: My Life and Ministry.* Nashville, TN: Thomas Nelson, 1998.

Roberts, Oral. *Something Good Is Going to Happen to You.* Tulsa, OK: Albury Publishing, 1996.

Jerry Falwell

Jerry Falwell was born in Lynchburg, Virginia, in 1933. At first, he studied engineering, but after a religious epiphany, attended the Baptist Bible College in Missouri, where he was ordained in 1956. He later founded the Thomas Road Baptist Church and began the radio and television broadcasts of *The Old-Time Gospel Hour.* In 1971, Falwell founded the Lynchburg Baptist College, and in 1979, he established the secular conservative political organization known as "The Moral Majority." Today, Falwell is known as one of America's most popular evangelists, and spokesperson for a large sector of American Christian conservatives.

FOR ADDITIONAL INFORMATION

Recommended Contact

Jerry Falwell
c/o Postmaster
Lynchburg, VA 24514
Phone: (804) 237-0770
Website: www.falwell.com

Recommended Reading

Falwell, Jerry. *Wisdom for Living.* Lynchburg, VA: Scripture Press, 1984.

Chuck Swindoll

Charles R. Swindoll was born in El Campo, Texas, in 1934. He initially served several pastorates in Texas, Massachusetts, and California, before being ordained into the gospel ministry in 1963. He received an honorary Doctor of Divinity degree from Talbot School of Theology in 1977, and has received several such degrees since then. In 1979, his radio ministry, "Insight for Living," was born, and now airs worldwide over 1,400 times daily.

FOR ADDITIONAL INFORMATION

Recommended Contact

Insight for Living
P.O. Box 69000
Anaheim, CA 92817-8888
Website: www.kcbi.org

Recommended Readings

Swindoll, Chuck. *Stress Fractures*. Weston, ON (Canada): David C. Cook Publishing, 1992.

Swindoll, Chuck. *Living Above the Level of Mediocrity*. Chicago: World Books, 1990.

James Dobson

James Dobson holds a Ph.D. in child development from the University of Southern California. He served fourteen years as associate clinical professor of pediatrics at the USC School of Medicine, and concurrently, seventeen years on the staff of the Los Angeles Children's Hospital. His Christian-based radio program, "Focus on the Family," began in 1977 in a two-room suite in Arcadia, California, and has since grown into an international organization with the broadcasts heard over 4,000 facilities worldwide. Ten magazines published by his organization are sent to more than 2.3 million people each month, and he has written numerous award-winning books dealing with family issues, and produced numerous videos on the same topic.

FOR ADDITIONAL INFORMATION

Recommended Contact

Focus on the Family
Colorado Springs, CO 80995
Phone: (719) 531–3328
Website: www.family.com

Recommended Readings

Dobson, James. *Love for a Lifetime*. Sisters, OR: Multnomah Publishers, 1998.

Dobson, James. *The New Dare to Discipline*. Wheaton, IL: Tyndale House Publishers, 1996.

Chuck Smith

In 1965, Chuck Smith left the pulpit of a small church in Corona, California, to become the pastor at Calvary Chapel in Costa Mesa, California. Since then, he has seen Calvary grow from a tiny congregation of only twenty-five on his first Sunday morning, to a nationwide movement of millions today. In fact, he is credited with fostering the "Jesus Movement" of the '60s and '70s. In 1993, Smith founded the Calvary Satellite Network, which currently broadcasts to over 160 stations around the world. Today, Pastor Smith's radio and television programs, including his *The Word for Today*, can be heard in any time zone on Earth.

FOR ADDITIONAL INFORMATION

Recommended Contact

The Word for Today
P.O. Box 8000
Costa Mesa, CA 92628
Phone: (800) 272–WORD
Website: www.thewordfortoday.org

Recommended Readings

Smith, Chuck. *Harvest*. Costa Mesa, CA: Word for Today Publishers, 1993.

Smith, Chuck. *What Is in the World Coming*. Costa Mesa, CA: Word for Today Publishers, 1993.

Bishop T. D. Jakes

Bishop Thomas T. D. Jakes, Sr., was called to ministry at the age of seventeen and first began preaching part-time while a student at West Virginia State College. In 1979, Pastor Jakes opened the doors of his first church. Located in Montgomery, West Virginia, it began with only ten members and was called the Temple of Faith. Bishop Jakes founded the T. D. Jakes Ministries in 1994, and began airing his popular television program, *The Potter's House*, which now broadcasts internationally to millions.

FOR ADDITIONAL INFORMATION
Recommended Contact

T. D. Jakes Ministries
P.O. Box 5390
6777 West Kiest Boulevard
Dallas, TX 75236
Phone: (800) BISHOP-2
Website: www.tdjakes.net

Recommended Readings

Jakes, T. D. *The Lady, Her Lover, and Her Lord*. New York: Putnam Publishers, 1998.

Jakes, T. D. *Water in the Wilderness*. Pneuma Life Publications, 1996.

J. Vernon McGee

John Vernon McGee was born in Hillsboro, Texas, in 1904. After completing his Th.D. at the Dallas Theological Seminary in Texas, he pastored churches in Georgia, Tennessee, and Texas. At this point, he and his wife moved west, settling in Pasadena, California, at a Presbyterian church. Dr. McGee began teaching his famous "Thru the Bible" series in

1967, and set up radio headquarters in Pasadena. Today, the program airs on over four hundred stations and is heard in more than fifty languages around the world. Dr. McGee died in 1988, but his radio ministry is still heard around the world through the technology of taped messages.

FOR ADDITIONAL INFORMATION

Recommended Contact

Thru the Bible Radio
P.O. Box 7100
Pasadena, CA 91109
Phone: (626) 795–4145
Website: www.ttb.org

Recommended Readings

McGee, J. Vernon. *Proverbs*. Nashville, TN: Thomas Nelson, 1997.

McGee. J. Vernon. *Thru the Bible*. Volumes 1–5. Nashville, TN: Thomas Nelson, 1997.

ISLAM

In Arabic, *Islam* means *purity, by submission to Allah's will,* and *obedience to Allah's laws*. Allah is the one God of infinite perfection and beauty. Islam is a religion based on the revelations and teachings of Allah to his prophet Muhammad (Mohammed).

HISTORY

Muhammad was born in the city of Mecca in Arabia, in the year A.D. 570. He was orphaned as a child, and was raised in abject poverty by his uncle. He later married a widow and had three daughters. During this period, Mecca was a city where pagans made pilgrimages to worship idols at various shrines. After retreating to a cave near Mecca to pray and contemplate, Muhammad was visited by the angel Gabriel. It was Gabriel who presented the message of Islam: Confirm what the previous prophets of Judaism and Christianity had taught, and correct adulterations that had perverted those teachings. Gabriel told Muhammad that he had been chosen to correct these errors, and to complete the divine revelation that had begun with the older faiths of Judaism and Christianity.

Having received these revelations, Muhammad went to the people of Mecca to proclaim the absolute unity of Allah, denounce idolatry, and urge the rich to give to the poor.

At first, his message was not well received, but he did make some converts at Yathrib, an agricultural community to the north. These people invited him to come there and mediate some local disputes, so he migrated north with some of his followers. This migration is called the Hegira, and it marks the beginning of the Muslim era.

Because of Muhammad's good works in Yathrib, the name of the town was changed to Medina, or "the city of the prophet." Muhammad gradually gained a large following, and by A.D. 630, he was able to return to Mecca as a victorious leader of this new movement. Muhammad's words spread quickly throughout the Arab world. Within ten years, the whole of the Arabian Peninsula was converted to Islam. Within one generation, an area almost the size of the continental United States was converted, and within a century, Islam had spread as far as Spain and Morocco in the west and India and Thailand in the east. Today, Islam is one of the world's largest religions (there are over a billion Muslims), and is represented around the world, with the largest followings in East Asia and the Middle East.

BELIEF SYSTEM

Islam is predicated upon the Six Articles of Belief, which are as follows: (1) Allah (God) is one; (2) The Qur'an (Koran) is Allah's truly revealed book; (3) God's angels are heavenly beings created to serve God, and they are opposed to evil; (4) God sends his prophets to earth at stated times for stated purposes. The last of these prophets was Muhammad, and Allah makes no distinction among messengers; (5) The Day of Judgment will find good and evil weighed in the balance; (6) The lives and acts of people are foreordained by the all-knowing Allah.

Human beings are considered the builders of their own destiny and are free to make or mar their future. Central to Islamic faith is submission to Allah's law and will, and a Muslim (Moslem) is one who adheres to the religion of Islam, or is "one who submits to Allah." Thus, we are born with the ability and express purpose to live under the law of Allah, and will find peace and eternal pleasure in so doing. The deeds of a lifetime are weighted in the balance, and their preponderance of good or of evil determines an eternity of bliss or tribulation. The Qur'an—or Koran—is the guide for man to follow to find enduring happiness and peace.

The revelations of the Qur'an focus on the gifts or rewards that Allah will bestow upon the faithful in the hereafter and the severe punishments that will go to those who were unfaithful and disobedient. Muslims believe in the Law of Moses, the Psalms of David, and the Gospel of Jesus Christ (who is thought of as one of Allah's prophets), but believe that those Scriptures are superseded by the revelations given to Muhammad.

A second major scriptural source, under the Qur'an, is the Sunna of the Prophet Muhammad, which recounts what Muhammad said and did when asked religious questions while in Medina. The verbal traditions about the Prophet's Sunna are known as the Hadith, which help lay the foundations for Islamic social behavior and ritual performance.

There are two primary sects of Muslims: Sunnites and Shi'ites. Over 90 percent of the world's Muslims are Sunnites. Sunnite Muslims accept four caliphs, or spiritual leaders, in direct succession from Muhammad—and no others. They practice a moderate form of Islamic interpretation. Shi'ite Muslims are much more literal in their interpretation and application of the Qur'an, and they tend to be more militant. The highest concentration of Shi'ite Muslims is in Iran, where their spiritual leader is referred to as the Ayatollah. There is also a mystical sect called Tasawof, or Sufism, which is discussed in the section "Spiritual Paths." (See "Sufism" on page 221.)

RITUALS AND HOLY DAYS

Central to the practice of this faith is the fulfillment of the "Five Pillars of Islam," namely:

1. Recitation of the Shahadah, or "confession," which states: "There is no God but Allah, and Muhammad is the prophet of Allah";

2. Five daily prayers (Salat or Namaz) in Arabic, including genuflection and prostration in the direction of the holy city of Mecca;

3. Almsgiving (Zakat), and regular charitable contributions;

4. Fasting (Saum or Ruzeh) during the entire month of Ramadan, where no food or drink is taken from sunrise to sunset for self-discipline and the atonement of sins;

5. A pilgrimage (Hajj) to Mecca, the holy city in Saudi Arabia, at least once in one's lifetime.

Reading the Qur'an is also an important part of Islamic practice, as well as study of the *Hadith*, which is a collection of sayings and reported actions of Muhammad; it provides guidance for the political and social structure of Islam. Muslims practice congregational prayers several times a day in mosques, which are found throughout the Islamic world. Muslims also follow a strict moral and ethical code.

A major religious observance and holiday within Islam is Ramadan, which takes place during the entire ninth month of the Islamic (lunar) calendar. The period is traditionally believed to be the month in which the first revelation of the Qur'an was given. Ramadan is a time of personal and communal abstention and religious discipline. It gives the Muslim a period of self-examination and repentance. During the entire month of Ramadan, a Muslim fasts from dawn until dusk; this trial is believed to cleanse the believer's heart, particularly when done in conjunction with increased religious devotions, such as reading the Qur'an and praying. Ramadan ends with the Little Festival, *id al-saghir,* or Festival of Breaking Fast, *id al-fitr,* which is marked by feasting and exchanging gifts.

The other great spiritual occasion is the Hajj, which every Muslim is asked to undertake at least once in a lifetime. The Hajj is a pilgrimage to the holy city of Mecca during the twelfth (lunar) month. It begins with the settling of your affairs prior to leaving, and praying for God's protection on the journey. Before entering the sacred territory which surrounds Mecca, you perform a rite of sacralization (ihram), which includes the donning of a simple white garment worn by all pilgrims, regardless of status. At this point, you become subject to certain prohibitions, including that against sexual relations. After arriving in Mecca, you go to the Kaaba—built by Abraham at Allah's command—the central shrine of Islam within the Mosque of Mecca. Here, you touch, or kiss, the southeastern corner of the shrine. This is said to contain the sacred black stone believed to be the "cornerstone" or "foundation" of the house, and "navel of the earth." It is also believed to lie directly under the seven heavens and the throne of Allah. You then proceed to perform several passages around the Kaaba while reciting prescribed prayers.

After making seven circuits around the Kaaba, you go to the nearby maqam Ibrahim ("station of Abraham"), where you pray before (but not to) the sacred stone, which, it is said, miraculously retains the footprint of Abraham. You follow this by going to the well of Zamzam and drinking from it before leaving the mosque.

Much of the Hajj is spent reenacting key biblical events. For example, you might call for aid from God, as Hagar did, after she and her son Ishmael had been abandoned by Abraham; or you might gather pebbles to throw at the Devil, as Abraham had done.

At the end of the Hajj, you would sacrifice an animal. If you were a man, you would then shave your head, or if a woman, cut a lock of hair. This is followed by three days of feasting and celebration called the Great Festival, *al-id al-kabir*. In some sects of Islam, Muslims do celebrate the prophet Muhammad's birthday, whereas it is forbidden in other sects.

FOR ADDITIONAL INFORMATION

Recommended Contacts

Islamic Centers can be found in most metropolitan areas; mosques are located in most major cities around the world today. You can also check with your Chamber of Commerce, consult telephone directory assistance under "Islamic Centers" or "Mosques," or contact the following resources:

American Muslim Council
1212 New York Avenue, NW
Washington, DC 20005
Phone: (202) 789–2262
Website: www.amermuslim.org

Islamic Circle of North America
166-26, 89th Avenue
Jamaica, NY 11432
Phone: (718) 658–1199
Website: www.icna.com

Human Assistance &
    Development International
P.O. Box 4598
Culver City, CA 90231-4598
Phone: (310) 397–8899

The Islamic Shura Council of
    Southern California
10573 West Pico Boulevard, #35
Los Angeles, CA 90064
Phone: (500) 446–9704
E-mail: www.iscsc@islam.org

The Institute of Islamic
    Information & Education
P.O. Box 41129
Chicago, IL 60641-0129
Phone: (773) 777–7443
Website: www.dar-es-salaam.com

Islamic Society of North America
P.O. Box 38
Plainfield, IN 46168
Phone: (317) 839–8157
Website: www.isna.net

Recommended Readings

Ahmad, Kassim. *Hadith*. Boca Raton, FL: Universal Unity, 1997.

Ali, A. Yusuf, trans. *The Holy Qur'an*. Brentwood, MD: Amana Corporation Publishers, 1983.

Bakhtiar, Laleh. *Mohammed's Companions: Essays on Those Who Bore Witness*. Chicago: Kazi Publications, 1993.

Dunn, Ross E. *The Adventures of Ibn Battuta: A Muslim Traveler of the 14th Century*. Berkeley, CA: University of California Press, 1990.

Esposito, John L. *Islam, The Straight Path*. London, UK: Oxford University Press, 1998.

al-Haddad, Imam, and Abdullah, and Ibn Alawi. *The Lives of Man*. Mustofa al-Badawi, trans. Fons Vitae, 1998.

Haykal, Muhammad Husayn. *The Life of Muhammad*. Plainfield, IN: Islamic Book Service, 1995.

Maalouf, Amin, and Jon Rothschild, trans. *The Crusades Through Arab Eyes*. New York: Schochen Books, 1989.

Pinault, David. *The Shi'ites: Ritual and Popular Piety in a Muslim Community*. New York: St. Martin's Press, 1993.

Recommended Websites

Fiqh Council of North America
www.moonsights.com

Global Islamic Movement
www.ummah.org.uk

Islamic Education Institute
www.mpac.com

Islamic City
www.islam.org

Library of Islamic Information
www.islaminfo.net

Moslem Organizations' Directory
www.moslem.org

Musalman Directory
www.musalman.com

Muslim Links
www.muslimlinks.com

NATION OF ISLAM

HISTORY

The Nation of Islam has its origins in the arrival of Master Fard Muhammad from Mecca, Saudi Arabia, to the United States in 1930. It was Master Fard who brought the message of Islam to all people, but especially to the black people. He is considered a prophet, or "Mahdi," and known as the founder of the Black Muslim movement in the United States. According to Master Fard, he came in search of the Lost and Found members of the Tribe of Shabazz, the black people's race, to establish the Truth, and to uplift the race from the servitude of white supremacy. It was he who chose the Honorable Elijah Muhammad (formerly Elijah Poole) as his first minister, and later entrusted him to teach and fulfill the prophecy. Under Islam, it is believed that the black race will attain freedom from white bondage and take their place as the leaders of the world thus creating a world community that may live together in peace. It was with this objective in mind that the Nation of Islam began.

Today, Abdul Haleem Farrakhan, or Louis Farrakhan, is the leader of the Nation of Islam, and prophet of their religion. He was born Louis Eugene Wolcott in the Bronx, New York. Farrakhan had been a nightclub singer who joined the Nation of Islam in the late 1950s, and served briefly under its famous leader, Malcolm X. With his musical talent, oratorical skills, and absolute dedication to Elijah Muhammad, Farrakhan quickly moved up the ranks and achieved a leading position in the Boston Mosque. He later dropped his last name—which he considered to be a scar of slavery—and became known as Minister Louis X. After the defection and death of Malcolm X, Farrakhan was designated the leader of the Harlem mosque in New York City.

Upon Elijah Mohammed's death in 1975, Elijah's son Wallace became the official leader. Under his leadership, the Nation of Islam distanced itself from what were considered radical racial policies, and began admitting white people and other races into its membership. Farrakhan then led a "purist" movement within the Black Muslim body, instituted a new Nation of Islam in 1978, and became their leader.

Farrakhan enforces a strict dress code, supports community advancement of his people, and promotes individual dignity. In 1995, Farrakhan organized the Million Man March in Washington, D.C., a peaceful daylong demonstration by African-American males from across the nation. The demonstrators pledged greater fidelity to their families, greater pride in themselves, and greater acceptance of responsibility for their actions. Farrakhan is now heard weekly on radio and television stations nationally, and has membership reported in the tens of thousands.

BELIEF SYSTEM

The Nation of Islam is fundamentally Islamic, with an emphasis on promoting cultural independence from the white community, encouraging economic self-sufficiency, and developing high moral virtue through the teachings of Islam. They have faith in the one God whose proper name is Allah. They profess belief in the Holy Qur'an, in the truth of the Bible, and in the Scriptures of all the prophets of God. They also believe that the Bible has been "tampered with" and must be "reinterpreted" so that mankind will not be snared by the falsehoods that have been added to it. They also hold that the black race in America has a right to its own territory and sovereignty, free from the subjugation of the white race. The purpose of the Nation of Islam adherent is to become a good Muslim by serving Allah.

RITUALS AND HOLY DAYS

Islamic holidays, such as Ramadan, are celebrated. Reading the Qur'an is also an important part of Islamic practice, as well as study of the *Hadith*, the collection of sayings and actions reputed to Muhammad. Nation of Islam adherents practice congregational prayers several times a day in area mosques. They also follow a strict moral and ethical code, and service work in the community is extensive.

FOR ADDITIONAL INFORMATION

Recommended Contact

For information on the Nation of Islam, consult your telephone book, check with the Chamber of Commerce, or contact the following resource:

Nation of Islam
4855 South Woodlawn Avenue
Chicago, IL 60615
Phone: (773) 602–1230
Website: www.noi.org

Recommended Readings

Farrakhan, Louis. *Torchlight for America*. Chicago, IL: FCN Publications, 1993.

Haley, Alex, forward. *Autobiography of Malcolm X*. New York: Ballantine Books, 1992.

Muhammad, Elijah. *History of the Nation of Islam*. Chicago, IL: Secretarius Publications, 1996.

PART THREE

EARLY
SPIRITUAL
PATHS

"Spiritual Paths" is a broad category that generally refers to the spiritual teachings of various cultures, and the secret teachings evolving from within established religions. These spiritual teachings either existed before the advent of one of the major Western religions, or developed within the established religious institutions as a subculture or movement. Because many of these teachings were practiced privately to avoid persecution by the predominant religious institutions in their society, they are sometimes considered "occult" or "esoteric," meaning that the teachings contain a secret or hidden knowledge intended for or understood by only a select few.

In this section, we will discuss a number of these varied groups and individuals, especially the ones that influenced the thinking of others. We will begin with Druidism, the spiritual practice of the people of Western Europe before the influx of, first, the Roman culture, and, later, the Christian missionaries. Because of the repression of Druidic culture by outside influences, their teachings went underground and have stayed there to the present day. Yet Druidic teachings appear to have heavily influenced the Wiccan teachings and the practice of witchcraft in Europe and abroad. Because the widespread acceptance of Christianity in the Western world led to the persecution of indigenous religions, the practice of Wicca and witchcraft had remained underground until the 1990s.

Another influential path we will explore is Zoroastrianism. This was the principal religion of Persia before the conversion to Islam. Although Zoroastrian theology appears to have influenced the monotheistic theology of the Western religions, it was considered a pagan religion, and was therefore shunned by the newly evangelized cultures. Most Zoroastrians migrated to other cultures that were more tolerant, with the heaviest concentration being in India, where they are known as Parsis. Also within the Islamic culture, a group of mystics known as Sufis have maintained a tradition of knowing God through personal experience (gnosis), and have influenced both Western and Eastern theology and spiritual practice. Thus, within Jewish, Christian, and Islamic cultures, a mystical element has been preserved for those who are inclined to know God through personal experience.

We will look into Kabbalism, the esoteric spiritual teachings of the Jews. While these teachings are recognized within Judaism as a legitimate and authoritative science, they have never been taught to the masses and have only recently been made available to the public. Nevertheless, the Kabbalah has influenced such spiritual studies and beliefs as astrology, numerology, and tarot. Also, the Freemasons, the Builders of the Adytum, and many secret societies, Wiccan groups, and new age teachings have also borrowed heavily from Kabbalah. These teachings appear to have influenced the Essenes, Gnosticism, and Christian Mysticism, as well.

In this section, we will also examine the early Christian mystics, who were known as Gnostics (knowers of Truth). They were eventually eradicated by the institutional Christian churches; nevertheless, the elements of mysticism gained a foothold within the churches through individuals who, often at great risk to themselves, shared their inner mystical experiences with their spiritual brothers and sisters. Saint Augustine of Hippo, The Desert Fathers, Saint Francis of Assisi, Meister Eckhart, Saint John of the Cross, Saint Teresa of Avila, Jakob Boehme, Emanuel Swedenborg, and Thomas Merton, among others, played an important role in preserving the aspect of mysticism and personal gnosis (knowledge) within the context of Christian theology.

We will also explore other, smaller groups that have been able to preserve some of their own culture and spiritual practices in other parts of the world. Although most have been heavily influenced by the world's major religions, they have adapted to the cultural infusion and strengthened their beliefs. For example, shamanistic practices are now common throughout Siberia and North America. Indigenous tribal groups, such as the Native Americans, have been able to preserve their rites and maintain their communion with the Earth Mother, despite strong resistance from orthodox "new" religions. In Hawaii, a group of Shamanistic teachings known as Huna has reemerged within public view to preserve the cultural and spiritual heritage of the Hawaiian Islands. In Africa, the Caribbean, and parts of South America, native peoples have developed a spiritual practice that combines the essence of their original African spiritualism with the archetypes of Catholicism. This blended religion is generally referred to as voodoo, santeria, or macoumba. In Jamaica, the native people have developed and adapted their spirituality to new circumstances and created a new religion known as Rastafarianism. Thus, these cultures appear to have been able to preserve some of their cultural heritage, yet still maintain a personal relationship with their creator through mystical experiences.

It is human nature to be skeptical of anything that is new or not understood. People who have been brought up in structured theological belief systems often find mystical experiences strange or frightening, and consider those things that they don't understand to be evil. However, once the symbol systems have been interpreted and the experiences explained, mystical traditions become easier to understand and accept. Individuals ultimately discover the truth through their own independent investigation.

The traditional spiritual paths discussed in this section serve as alternatives to the generally accepted modes of understanding God, and provide a means of preserving cultural inheritances.

FOR ADDITIONAL INFORMATION
Recommended Periodicals

Circle Network News
P.O. Box 219
Mt. Horeb, WI 53572
Phone: (608) 924–2216

Connections: The Journal of
Community, Philosophy
and Magik
1705 14th Street, #181
Boulder, CO 80302
Phone: (303) 650–9285

Gnosis, A Journal of the Western
  Inner Traditions
P.O. Box 14217
San Francisco, CA 94114-0217
Phone: (714) 821–7566

Kindred Spirit: The Guide to
  Personal and Planetary Healing
Foxhole, Dartington
Totnes, Devon
TQ9 6EB England
Phone: (01803) 866686

Magical Blend
P.O. Box 421130
San Francisco, CA 94142
Phone: (415) 673–1001

New Worlds of Mind and Spirit
P.O. Box 64383, Dept. 976
Saint Paul, MN 55164-0383
Phone: (800) The Moon

The Quest, A Quarterly Journal of
  Philosophy, Science, Religion &
  Arts
P.O. Box 270
Wheaton, IL 60189–0270
Phone: (415) 548–1680

Shaman's Drum, A Journal of
  Experimental Shamanism
P.O. Box 430
Phone: (707) 459–0486

Wildfire Shamanistic Naturalist
P.O. Box 9167
Spokane, WA 99209
Phone: (509) 326–6561

DRUIDS

The Druids were the Magi, or philosopher-magicians, of the early Celtic civilization in northeastern Europe. Several meanings are offered for the word *druid*, including: *a servant of truth, all knowing, wise man, an oak*, and *equal in honor*. Generally, a Druid is considered one with gnosis, or spiritual awareness. Many Druids consider themselves to be "pagans," a much broader term.

HISTORY

The history of the Druids dates back to the migration of the Indo-European-speaking people in the second millennium B.C., about 4,000 years ago. Nomadic tribes who occupied the area around the Caspian Sea in southern Russia began to migrate toward the southeast into the Indus Valley, and toward the west into Asia Minor, the Balkans, and the fertile plains of Europe. Around the tenth century B.C., a people recognizably Celtic began to emerge from Bohemia, in western Czechoslovakia. In the eighth to the sixth centuries B.C., they began to migrate south into Italy and Spain, as well as farther west into France and Belgium.

Eventually, these Celtic groups found their way into the British Isles, where they became known as the Celts. These people were generally tall in stature and industrious by nature. They gained a justified reputation for being skilled horsemen, metalworkers, and warriors. Subsequently, according to *The Welsh Triads* or *Traditional Chronicles*, one Hu Gadarn, or "Hu the Mighty," a descendant of the patriarch Abraham, led a party of settlers from Asia Minor to the British Isles. There, he established a religious practice among the Celts that we now refer to as Druidism. Thus, within the Celtic culture there existed a brotherhood, or perhaps a class of priests, known as the Druids, who served as the spiritual leaders and wise men of their day. Because the Druids did not keep a written record of their spiritual practices or culture, most of what is known about them comes from the records of their conquerors and the myths and legends of the bards of the period.

The Romans considered the Druids to have been an established institution by the fourth century B.C. The Roman philosopher-historian Posidonius (c.135–c.51 B.C.) had traveled throughout Gaul during the time of the Druids, and had written about them in his *Histories*. Unfortunately, these writings were lost, but portions were later referred to by the historian Strabo (63 B.C.–A.D. 21). The best records by people who lived during the time of the Druids are *Caesar's Conquest of Gaul* and *Natural History*, both authored by Pliny the Elder (A.D. 23–79). By A.D. 37, Gaul and much of Britain were under Roman control, and Rome prohibited Druidic practices altogether. Nevertheless, such beliefs and practices were passed on through oral traditions within secret circles throughout Europe.

In the latter part of the eighteenth century, Druidic cults and societies appeared all over western Europe. One of the first was the Ancient Order of Druids, founded by an Englishman, Henry Hurle. Later, the Ancient Order of Druids became more of a benefit society, and some of the members, who were more interested in the esoteric side of Druidism, formed other orders. These include the British Circle of the Universal Bond; the Order of Bards, Ovates and Druids; and the Order of the Golden Dawn.

Today, there are numerous orders throughout Western societies; however, most of the older traditional ones do not solicit or even admit members unfamiliar to them. Consequently, it is difficult to estimate their numbers.

BELIEF SYSTEM

Druids believe in the eternal nature of the Soul, and see a living spirit in all forms of creation. There is an ancient saying attributed to the Druids: "Spirit sleeps in the mineral, breathes in the vegetable, dreams in the animal, and wakes in man." Druids hold that souls can be contacted after death, and that souls reincarnate (are reborn). The universe is the Druid's living bible, written directly by the hand of God. Moreover, mankind is seen as evolving and unfolding in its awareness of itself.

Within the spiritual makeup of creation is a group of gods and goddesses, each representing some attribute of nature. Some of the most recognized are:

• Taranis, the father of the gods, associated with the oak tree;

• Belenos, the god of the Sun, celebrated on Beltane, or May Day;

• Cernunnos, the horned god of the hunt, who rules the dark side of the year (winter);

• Lugh, the many-skilled;

- Esus, the pastoral god and magician;

- Teutatis, the warrior god and ruler of the people;

- Epona, the horse goddess, associated with fertility;

- Morrigan, the goddess of war;

- Caridwen, the mother goddess and triple goddess of fire, water, and air;

- Rhea, the mistress of life and sovereign of time; and

- Diana, the huntress and goddess of the moon.

There were also many other gods and goddesses known by many names, depending on the region and period of time.

Druids are, typically, homeopathic healers and astrologers. However, Druids are principally the teachers of Truth. They assist their followers in seeing the divine spirit within themselves, and indeed, within all things. Druids use natural science and experience to verify truths. For them, spiritual development is an interactive process, not a faith.

Druids see humans as one of God's marvelous creations. They believe you are intended to live in accordance with God's laws in order to bring about harmony and peace within yourself and in the Universe. A major Druidic symbol is the triad with the three fundamental principles of wisdom:

1. Obedience to the Laws of God;

2. Effort for the welfare of mankind; and

3. Heroically enduring the unavoidable ills of life.

Like the ancient Greeks, Druids believe that tragedy in your life is inevitable. What matters is how you learn from your grief, how you seek to help others in similar circumstances, and how you obey the laws of the creator.

RITUALS AND HOLY DAYS

The influence of the Druids on the Celtic culture, and on Western civilization, has endured for thousands of years. Seasonal celebrations and festivals have been adopted by and adapted to the new Christianized cultures of Europe. Examples would be the observance of Christmas at the winter solstice and the celebration of the Druid festival of Samhain, or All Hallows Sabbath, which we now call Halloween. Moreover, Druid beliefs and customs, such as kissing under the mistletoe, have also been passed down to the present day.

Wiccan groups appear to be heavily influenced by the Druids. However, because any form of "pagan" worship was repressed in Christian societies, such rituals were practiced very discreetly and little is known or available to the public. Thus, to this day, many Druidic practices are not open to the public.

Druids are the interpreters of the gods. They are considered judges and teachers, astronomers and seers, as well as physicians and healers. Rites and rituals are generally held outdoors, typically in an oak grove or around a stone circle; Stonehenge is a favorite site.

Druids celebrate the four major Sabbaths:

1. Samhain, or All Hallows, or Halloween;

2. Imbolc, or the Feast of Lights, or Candlemas;

3. Beltane, or May Day; and

4. Laghnasadh, or Lammas, the Feast of Bread.

They also celebrate the four lesser Sabbaths related to the changing of seasons, namely, the spring and autumn equinoxes, and the summer and winter solstices. Druidic rites are generally merry occasions, with feasting, dancing, and singing. Warm feelings of love for the gods and goddesses are expressed and an appreciation for nature's abundance is celebrated.

FOR ADDITIONAL INFORMATION

Recommended Contacts

Often metaphysical bookstores will have information available, or refer to the following resources. See also "Wicca and Witchcraft" on page 168.

The British Druid Order
P.O. Box 29
St. Leonard's-on-Sea, East Sussex,
   TN39 7YP, England
Website:
   www.druidorder.demon.co.uk

A Druid Fellowship
P.O. Box 115259
Ann Arbor, MI 48106-5259
Phone: (734) 485-2722
Website: www.adf.org

Henge of Keltria
P.O. Box 17969
Long Beach, CA 90807-7969
Website: www.keltra.org

Order of Bards, Ovates, and Druids
P.O. Box 1333
Lewis, East Sussex, BN7 1DX,
   England
Phone: 011–44–1273–480485
Website: www.druidity.org

The Pagan Federation
BM Box 7097
London, WC1N 3XX, England
Phone: 01928 770909
Website:
   www.paganfed.demon.co.uk

Reform Druids of North America
Phone: (507) 646–4205
Website:
   www.student.carleton.edu/orgs/
   druids

Recommended Readings

Ellis, Peter Berresford. *Dictionary of Celtic Mythology*. New York: Oxford University Press, 1994.

Llywelyn, Morgan. *Druids*. Ivy Books, 1993.

Matthews, Caitlin. *The Encyclopaedia of Celtic Wisdom*. Boston, MA: Element Books, 1996.

Matthews, John, ed. *The Druid Source Book*. New York: Sterling Publishing, 1998.

Nichols, Ross, John Matthews, and Philip Carr-Gomm. *The Book of Druidry: History, Sites and Wisdom*. London, UK: Thorsons Publishing, 1992.

Recommended Websites

www.druid.net
www.monmouth.com
www.neopagan.net

Sacred Sites of Ancient Britain
www.amamchara.com/celtic/photos.htm

WICCA AND WITCHCRAFT

Wicca, or witchcraft, is the old religion of Europe, and apparently evolved from Druidism. Wiccan is generally a term applied to a "wise one" or "magician," and Wicca is the practice of "magic," which is the application and utilization of natural laws.

HISTORY

Wicca is the modern version of the old Druid craft of Europe. (See "Druids" on page 163.) As it competed as a religion with Christianity—the "new" religion—in the Christianized Western world, it came to be considered a form of paganism called "witchcraft." It was therefore repressed as a primitive teaching. Given this evil stigma by the establishment, it was not practiced openly. However, with the repeal of the English Witchcraft Act in 1951, many covens, or congregations, have opened up to the public, and many new groups have formed. There are now dozens of Wiccan organizations in the United States and Europe, with perhaps thousands of active Wiccans and witches.

Most witches practicing the craft publicly are considered to be white witches, that is, they use their knowledge for positive purposes. They practice the Wiccan Creed, "Ye hurt none, do as ye will." On the other hand, black witches—which have received notoriety out of proportion to their numbers—are generally not visible to the public and use their knowledge for selfish or evil means.

BELIEF SYSTEM

Witchcraft generally involves some form of god or goddess worship, and many forms involve the invocation of spirits and guides as well. Witchcraft is a very individualized religion, and each person chooses his or her own deities to worship. Generally, the supreme being is considered genderless and is comprised of many aspects that may be identified as masculine or feminine in nature, and thus a god or a goddess. Originally, the horned God of hunting—perhaps Cernunnos, although the name varied by region—represented the masculine facet of the deity, whereas the female qualities were represented in the fertility goddess, perhaps Epona, but, again, the names varied from kingdom to kingdom. The gods and goddesses form the personalities of the supreme being, and are a reflection of the attributes that the worshipers seek to emulate. To commune with the particular aspect of the deity with which they identify, Wiccans may draw upon the ancient civilizations of the Druids, Egyptians, Greeks, Romans, or other polytheistic cultures. Some favorite gods include Osiris, Pan, Cernunnos, and Bacchus. Favorite goddesses include Isis, Caridwen, Rhea, Selene, and Diana.

Wiccans see humans as instruments to bring spirit into this world, and live in accordance with Nature. This is achieved by becoming aware of how Nature functions and working cooperatively with it.

RITUALS AND HOLY DAYS

Like the Druids before them, Wiccans generally observe the four greater Sabbaths of Samhain, Imbolc, Beltane, and Laghnasadh; and the lesser Sabbaths—the spring and autumn equinoxes and the summer and winter solstices. These celebrations are typically free-spirited, and are sometimes held "sky clad" (naked) or in various styles of robes. Other rituals include handfasting (marriage), handparting (divorce), and wiccaning (birth rite). Regular meetings called Esbats are also held, at which magic and healing rites are performed. Wiccans meet in a small group (up to twelve) called a coven, which typically joins with other covens to form a "grove."

Rituals are typically held in the open air. They usually consist of forming a circle and erecting the temple (consecrating the circle); invoking; praising; soliciting assistance from gods, goddesses, and elementals; observing the change of seasons and the energies represented by the various seasons; singing; dancing; "cakes and ale" (sharing of bread and wine); and, finally, clearing the temple. Personal practice includes meditation, prayer, divination, and development of personal will and psychic abilities through spells and various forms of healing. Most witches have altars where they burn candles and incense, and practice their ceremonies. To perform their rituals, other tools of the craft are used. These might include a handmade and consecrated knife, a sword, or a wand. Sometimes special jewelry, amulets, or talismans—magically empowered objects—would be used, and sometimes these objects would be inscribed with magical writings.

Joining a coven or grove typically involves an initiation, which is stylized by each individual group, but generally involves the confirmation that the initiate understands principles of Wicca and is willing to take an oath of secrecy.

FOR ADDITIONAL INFORMATION
Recommended Contacts

Check with local metaphysical bookstores or any of the following resources. (See also the preceding section on Druids):

Abaxion Links
236 W. East Avenue, #216
Chico, CA 95926
Phone: (530) 898–0791
Website:
　www.maxinet.com/shadows/
　witchlink.htm

Church and School of Wicca
P.O. Box 297-IN
Hinton, WV 2591-0297
Website: www.wicca.org

The Circle Guide to Pagan
　Groups
P.O. Box 219
Mt. Horeb, WI 53572
Phone: (608) 924–2216
Website: www.circlesanctuary.org

Covenant of the Goddess
P.O. Box 1226
Berkeley, CA 94701
Website: www.cog.org

The Pagan Federation
BM Box 7097
London, WC1N 3XX, England
Website:
　www.paganfed.demon.co.uk

The Witches' League for Public
　Awareness
P.O. Box 8736
Salem, MA 01971
Website: www.celticcrow.com

The Witches' Voice
P.O. Box 4924
Clearwater, FL 33758-4924
Website: www.witchvox.com

Recommended Readings

Adler, Margot. *Drawing Down the Moon*. New York: Penguin USA, 1997.

Chuvin, Pierre. *A Chronicle of the Last Pagans*. B. A. Archer, trans. Cambridge, MA: Harvard University Press, 1990.

Cooper, Phillip. *Basic Magick: A Practical Guide*. York Beach, ME: Samuel Weiser, 1996.

Cunningham, Scott. *Wicca: A Guide for the Solitary Practitioner.* St. Paul, MN: Llewellyn Publishing, 1990.

Dunwich, Gerina. *The Wicca Spellbook.* Secaucus, NJ: Citadel Press, 1994.

Pepper, Elizabeth, ed. *The Witches' Almanac.* Witches' Almanac, Inc., 1999.

Ravenwolf, Silver. *American Folk Magick: Charms, Spells and Herbals.* St. Paul, MN: Llewellyn Publishing, 1998.

Ravenwolf, Silver. *To Ride a Silver Broomstick: New Generation Witchcraft.* St. Paul, MN: Llewellyn Publishing, 1993.

Recommended Websites

Alliance for Magical and Earth Religions
www.monmouth.com

Black Raven
www.black-raven.com

Catala's Wiccan
www.silvermoon.net

The Celtic Connection
www.wicca.com

Fantasy Realms
www.fantasyrealms.simplenet.com

Gaia Web
www.gaia-web.org

Llewellyn
www.llewellyn.com

Magickal Moon
www.magickalmoon.com

New Age Info
www.newageinfo.com

Pagan and Wiccan Networking
www.witchnet.org

Sun Dragon Wiccan
www.wiccan.com

Witches' Web
www.witchesweb.com

ZOROASTRIANISM

The Zoroastrian religion was founded in south-central Asia, in modern Iran, by the prophet Zoroaster, or Zarathustra, after whom it is named.

HISTORY

The Zoroastrian religion has endured through the many conquests of Persia, and has had a profound influence upon the development of monotheistic ideology in world history. Zoroastrianism is the ancient religion of the Indo-European, or Aryan, people. According to legend, the Aryans were a people that originally lived north of modern Siberia, now Russia, and migrated south into Persia, India, and Europe around twenty thousand years ago. Around 8000 B.C., as their people spread out across the land, their God, Ahura Mazda, sent the prophet Zarathustra to Persia, now modern Iran, to revive the faith. Thus by historical account, Zoroastrianism is the oldest living religion in the world.

The religion first started to gain wide acceptance during the Achaemenid (Hakhamanian) Empire under Cyrus the Great (600–529 B.C.), the first emperor of Persia. The religion began to decline during the rule of the Seleucid Empire (330–250 B.C.), after Alexander the Great defeated Darius III and subsequently destroyed the Nasks—the sacred scriptures of the Zoroastrians.

The Zoroastrians gained strength again during the Parthian Dynasty (250–218 B.C.), and reached its height as a state religion during the rule of the Sassanid dynasty (A.D. 226–651). However, in the seventh century, the Arabs conquered Iran and gradually imposed their own religion of Islam. Early in the tenth century, a small group of Zoroastrians seeking freedom of worship left Iran and eventually settled in India, where they are known as Parsis. Due to pressure and coercion from the Islamic government in Iran, many Zoroastrians have converted to the Islamic faith. The Zoroastrian population in Iran is now about 90,000, and some 13,000 now live in North America.

BELIEF SYSTEM

Zoroastrian concepts included the idea of a single god, or monotheism; heaven and hell; god's adversary, called Satan; resurrection and final purification of the world; a virgin birth; and the savior of humanity in preparation for the coming kingdom of heaven on earth for all. These Zoroastrian precepts are believed to have influenced the newer religions of Judaism and Christianity, as Abraham—the patriarch of the Jews— was born in the Persian city of Ur during a period when Zoroastrianism was prevalent in that area. (See "Judaism" on page 74.)

Zoroastrians believe in one God, known in Avestan, the ancient Iranian language, as *Ahura Mazda*. Zarathustra describes him more specifically as, "The one Supreme God . . . who is All Wise, All Good, and Eternal, conceived [as the] ideal creation, in accordance with the principle identified with Asha (the truth)." The Zoroastrian God is a friend to all, not to be feared.

These teachings about Ahura Mazda and the revelations of Zarathustra are expressed in poetic form in the *Gathas*, a collection of sacred hymns. Zarathustra emphasized the virtue of righteousness, and his philosophy involved the practice of good thoughts, good words, and good deeds. The events of this world are seen as a contest between the powers of good and evil. Upon death, the soul is believed to cross the Chinvat Bridge, or "Bridge of the Separator," which widens to permit easy passage to heaven—a place of eternal peace, health, and joy—for the righteous, but shrinks to a knife-edge for the wicked, so that they fall into a life of hell below.

RITUALS AND HOLY DAYS

Zoroastrians worship in what are known as Fire Temples, where a fire always burns as the symbol of divine power, presence, and purity. Fires may also be burned in services in homes of the believers. Prayers are said in Avestan, the ancient language, rather than in modern vernaculars, since the pronunciation of these sounds has a mantra-like or meditative quality to them. Zoroastrians receive a white undershirt, called a *sudreh*, and a hollow woven cord, called a *kusti*, which are to be worn under their clothing the rest of their lives, except while bathing. Several times a day the follower reties the kusti while saying certain fixed prayers. In addition to meditation and prayer, Zarathustra emphatically stated, "Those who served God best were those who rendered active service to God's creations which include fellow human beings." Service to others is therefore an integral part of Zoroastrian practice. Your purpose on earth is to serve both God and fellow human beings.

FOR ADDITIONAL INFORMATION

Recommended Contacts

There are Zoroastrian centers and temples in several major cities around the world, but the following resources would be best to contact:

California Zoroastrian Center
8952 Hazard Avenue
Westminister, CA 92368
Phone: (714) 893–4737
Website: www.czc@iname.com

Global Directory of Zoroastrian
  Fire Temples
Dhunmai Bldg. 667 Lady
  Jehangir Road, Dadar
Mumbai, Maharashtra, 40014, India
E-mail: Giara@bom5.vsnl.net.in

The World Zoroastrian
  Organization
135 Tennison Road

South Norwood, London SE25
  5NF, England
Website: www.w-z-o.org

The Zarathushtrian Assembly
1814 Bayless Street
Anaheim, CA 92802
Phone: (714) 520–9577
Website: www.zoroastrian.org

Zoroastrian Association of
  Chicago
8615 Meadowbrook Drive
Hinsdale, IL 60521
Phone: (630) 789–1983

Recommended Readings

Avesta, Yasna. *Gathas of Zarathustra*. New York: AMS Press, 1947.

Clark, Peter. *Zoroastrianism: An Introduction to Ancient Faith*. Sussex Academic Press, 1999.

Cooper, D. Jason. *Mithras: Mysteries and Initiation Rediscovered*. York Beach, ME: Samuel Weiser, 1996.

Darmesteter, James. *The Zend Avesta of Zarathustra*. Edmonds, WA: Holmes Publishing, 1984.

Nigosian, Solomon A. *The Zoroastrian Faith: Tradition and Modern Research*. McGill Queens University Press, 1993.

Recommended Websites

Avesta Links
www.avesta.org

Federation of Zoroastrian
  Associations of North America
www.fezana.org

Zoroastrianism Business and
  Shopping Links
www.zarathusht.com

Zoroastrianism Links
www.zoroastrianism.com
www.zoroastrianism.org

KABBALISM

Kabbalism is the esoteric doctrine of the Jewish faith. In Hebrew it is called QBLH, *qabalah*, which is derived from the root QBL, *qibel*, which means *to receive*. The Kabbalistic teachings were kept secret, and were only transmitted orally, so the exact date of the origin of the teachings cannot be pinned down.

HISTORY

It is purported by some believers that the Kabbalah was first taught by God himself to a select company of angels, who then imparted the sacred knowledge to Adam. From Adam the teachings were passed down to Noah, and then to Abraham, who emigrated to Egypt, where the Egyptians obtained some knowledge of it. From Egypt, other Eastern teachers introduced it into their philosophical systems.

Moses was said to have been initiated into the sacred Kabbalah and studied it throughout his life; it is even said he had been instructed in it by one of the angels. Moreover, Moses is said to have covertly laid down the principles of this secret doctrine in the first four books of the Torah (Genesis, Exodus, Leviticus, and Numbers), but withheld it from Deuteronomy. These teachings were further transmitted, by an unbroken line of verbal tradition, until the time of the destruction of the second temple in A.D. 68. During this period, Rabbi Simen Ben Jochai's treatises were collated after his death by his son Rabbi Eleazar and his disciples. From these writings was composed the main and most significant written text of the Kabbalah, known as the Zohar, or the Book of Splendor. However, the bulk of the various treatises that comprise the Zohar were written by Moses de Leon, and published in Spain around 1285. The Kabbalah movement appears to have arisen in eleventh-century France and spread from there, notably to Spain.

After the Jews were forcibly expelled from Spain in 1492, the believers apparently changed their emphasis, becoming more messianic, that is, attempting to hasten the arrival of the Messiah through the intense study of the Kabbalah. This form of Kabbalism has many followers. It was also a major influence in the development of the Jewish sect, Hasidism.

BELIEF SYSTEM

The Kabbalah contains the keys that unlock the hidden meaning within the Bible (Torah), which has been withheld from those considered unworthy or unprepared to understand its significance. It is based on the belief that every word, number, letter, and even accent of the Scripture contains mysteries. It places emphasis on symbology and numbers in trying to understand the mysterious teachings in the Bible (Torah).

The Kabbalah discusses such topics as the hierarchy of being, mankind as a microcosm of the spiritual worlds, how moral purity is a precondition to spiritual enlightenment, and how you can purify yourself and return to the Divine One. Kabbalah is the science of cause-and-effect relationships and the practice of developing your awareness to understand, and commune with, the Holy One.

Understanding Kabbalah requires going beyond mental constraints. By using various contemplative and meditative techniques that alter your modes of perception, you can pierce the illusion of your reality and gain insight into, and reach harmony with, the source of all being. Moreover, the Kabbalah teaches that intuitive contact with spirit carries the divine power, or creative energy, and by developing this creative energy, you can sustain a harmonious relationship with God.

The Kabbalah has had influences in other areas besides philosophy and religion. For instance, modern numerology and Western astrology were both developed through Kabbalistic practice, but both were also originally used as a means of understanding the process of evolving the consciousness and liberating the soul. In addition, the Kabbalah has held a strong influence upon other arcane teachings. For example, you will also find the Kabbalah adapted and used by other sects, such as Christian Mysticism, Gnosticism, and Tarot. I will discuss its connections in these sections as I take them up. (See pages 186, 182, and 215.)

Kabbalists believe humans are here on Earth as a naturally evolving process of the Divine order. Your purpose is to learn the lessons you need in order to fulfill your Divine destiny. This evolution is achieved through the study of Kabbalah.

RITUALS AND HOLY DAYS

Kabbalists of the Jewish tradition observe the Sabbath and high holidays of the Jewish religion. In addition to orthodox observances, many Kabbalists might practice various forms of meditation, contemplation, and prayer that are described in the Kabbalist teachings.

FOR ADDITIONAL INFORMATION
Recommended Contacts

I suggest that you contact the following sources:

Bnei Baruch Organization
P.O. Box 584
Bnei Brak, 51104, Israel
Phone: 972–3–619–1301
Website: www.kabbalah-web.org

The Kabbalah Connection
1721 45th Street
Brooklyn, NY 11204
Phone: (718) 854–4139
Website: www.jewishinfo.org

The Kabbalah Center
1062 So. Robertson Boulevard
Los Angeles, CA 90035
Phone: (310) 657–5404
Website: www.kabbalah.com

Kabbalah Society
100 Broadway
P.O. Box 531
Lynbrook, NY 11563
Phone: (516) 887–4957
E-mail: limetree@gn.apc.org

Kabbalah and Chassidut
Gal Einai Institute
P.O. Box 1439
Kiryat Arba, 90100, Israel
USA Phone: (888) 522–6768
Website: www.inner.org

Recommended Readings

Aaron, David. *Endless Light: The Ancient Path of the Kabbalah to Love, Spiritual Growth, and Personal Power.* New York: Berkley Publishing, 1998.

Berg, Philip S., trans. *Parashat Pinchas: The Zohar Series,* vol. 1. Los Angeles: Kabbalah Learning Center, 1986.

Levi, Eliphas. *Book of Spendour.* York Beach, ME: Samuel Weiser, 1973.

Scholem, Gershom. *Kabbalah.* New York: New American Library, 1989.

Scholem, Gershom. *Sabbatai Sevi: The Mystical Messiah.* Princeton, NJ: Princeton University Press, 1973.

ESSENES

The Essenes were a society of ascetic Jews who lived throughout the Holy Land before the time of Christ, but apparently concentrated around the area of the Dead Sea, in the area now in the modern state of Israel.

HISTORY

Although opinions differ as to the origins and history of the Essenes, archaeological excavations at Khirbat Qumran provided documents known as the Dead Sea Scrolls, which support a date around the middle of the second century B.C. It is generally held that the Essene brotherhood evolved in the early part of the second century B.C. This might have occurred as a countermovement to the Hellenization of Judaea, first by the Ptolemys (Greek rulers of Egypt) and the Seleucids (Greek rulers of Syria), and others who officially promoted the Greek ideal throughout Judaea. The decline of their society is believed to have begun after the earthquake in 31 B.C.

The Essenes were the smallest of four sects of Jews, the others being the Pharisees, Sadducees, and Zealots. Most of what is known about the Essenes comes from the commentaries of two Jewish historians, Philo of Alexandria and Flavius Josephus, from the first century A.D. Both historians estimate their numbers to be 4,000 at that time. After the destruction of the temple in Jerusalem by the Romans in A.D. 70, the Essene brotherhood apparently disintegrated.

Unfortunately, the principal source of documentation of the life and practices of the Essenes, the Dead Sea Scrolls from Qumran, have not been made available to the public—except for small sections—by the scholars working on them. So a great deal more about this group is yet to be learned.

BELIEF SYSTEM

The Essenes were first and foremost Jews. They believed in the one almighty God, Yahweh, and followed the laws of God as set forth by the patriarch Moses. (See "Judaism" on page 74.) According to Josephus, the Essenes believed that the body is corruptible at death, but the soul is immortal and will endure forever. They also believed that good (pious) souls would be liberated and rewarded by God, and that bad (ungodly) souls would be doomed to Hades (Hell). Many of the Essenes, but not all, lived in communes, and all of them shared income and property equally among themselves. They had disdain for accumulated material possessions and for lascivious behavior. On the other hand, they had esteem for self-restraint and conquest over passions. They were strong advocates of peace and justice, and did not believe in animal sacrifices at the temples, which was the norm at the time. The most distinctive attributes of the Essenes were their beliefs in the imminent battle between the forces of good and evil, and in the coming of the Messiah to deliver and lead their people.

The Essenes were a select group, accepting members only after testing the candidates over a period of several years. For one year, the candidate would live with them so that his character and temperament could be observed and tested. After that time, if the candidate passed these rigors, he would then participate in a purification by bathing in water. For two more years, the neophyte would be tested before being accepted into the brotherhood. An oath was also required that the brother maintain piety toward God and justice toward men. The initiate must harm no one, maintain fidelity to his fellow man, value honesty, and uphold the secrecy of the Essene doctrines. Those who broke this oath were cast out of the society.

There is evidence that the Essenes may have integrated into the early Christian Church, because of their similarities in apocalyptic faith, the practice of ritual bathing, the initiation rites by immersion in water, and the emphasis on moral purity and nonattachment to material existence.

Essenes saw themselves as serving to help bring forth the Divine plan of establishing a Heavenly Kingdom on Earth. This Kingdom was to be created through those who lived in accordance with God's law and lived righteously.

RITUALS AND HOLY DAYS

The Essenes studied the writings of the ancients, and had knowledge of medicinal roots and stones. They held prayers first thing in the morning and before the afternoon meal, after a ritual bath for purification, as well as before the evening meal. They were strict in observing the Sabbath on the seventh day, and would not even cook food on this day. They were also noted for wearing white robes and observing periods of silence.

FOR ADDITIONAL INFORMATION

Recommended Contacts

I am not familiar with any direct lineage of the Essene brotherhood. However, the International Biogenic Society (see page 270) has founded their organization on the principles of the Essenes, as researched by Edmond Bordeaux Szekely.

Other smaller groups have adopted Essene beliefs, or have "channeled" the teachings. Independent investigation of these groups through metaphysical organizations or the Internet is suggested. You could also contact the following resources:

The Essene Church
E-mail: Essene@mindspring.com

Mount Shasta, CA 96067-2636
Phone: (887) 808–8098
Website: www.awarinst.com

The Essene Church of Christ
45 N. 3rd Street
Creswell, OR 97426
Phone: (541) 895–2190
Website: www.essene.org

International Biogenic Society
P.O. Box 849
Nelson, B.C., V1L 6A4, Canada
E-mail: Awarinst@gate.net

The Essene Network
    International
"Windwood" 22 Avenue Road
Christchurch, Dorset, BH23 2BY,
    England
E-mail: Seth_Haniel@hotmail.com

Quamran, Essene, Dead Sea
    Scrolls Discussion Forum
Website: www.quamran.com

Essene New Life Church
110 Smith Street, Suite A

Recommended Readings

Cannon, Delores. *Jesus and the Essenes*. New York: Macmillan, 1992.

Meurois-Givassdan, Anne. *The Way of the Essenes*. Rochester, VT: Inner Traditions International, 1992.

Pagels, Elaine. *The Gnostic Gospels*. New York: Vintage Books, 1989.

Robinson, James M., ed. *The Nag Hammadi Library in English*. San Francisco: Harper, 1990.

Szekely, Edmond. *The Gospel of the Essenes*. C. W. Daniel Company, 1988.

Vermes, Geza. *The Complete Dead Sea Scrolls in English*. New York: Penguin USA, 1998.

Whiston, William, trans. *Josephus: The Complete Works*. Nashville, TN: Thomas Nelson Publisher, 1998.

GNOSTICISM

The word *gnosticism* comes from the Greek *gnosis* meaning *knowledge*, referring to the inner, hidden knowledge or transcendental understanding of God gained experientially.

HISTORY

Gnosticism is a mixed and diverse body of thought. Although its origins seem to have been in pagan and Jewish (perhaps Kabbalistic) sects before the coming of Jesus Christ, the term Gnostic generally refers to the teachings of those Christians in the first century A.D. who were not members of the orthodox Christian churches. By the second and third centuries, Gnosticism had grown into numerous scattered groups. These generally fell into two main schools, the Basilideans and the Valentinians, both of which were considered heretical by the orthodox Church authorities.

The Basilideans were founded by Basilides of Alexandria, born early in the second century A.D., who claimed to have received his esoteric doctrines from Claucias, an apostle of St. Peter. The Basilidean sect worshiped Abraxas, an ancient Egyptian name for God, as the Supreme Being, and believed that Jesus Christ emanated from Abraxas. As early Christianity spread into Egypt, it adopted the mystical and mythological attributes of the inner experience of God. The mystic word *abracadabra* was derived from his name.

The Valentinians were a sect influenced by the second century Christian mystic Valentinus of Phrebonis, in Egypt, later known as Saint Valentine—after whom the holiday celebrating love was named. Valentinians believed that God is infinite, without beginning or end, encompassing all creation; that God is self-unfolding through the multiplicity of being, while remaining its unity; that God is also androgynous, having both masculine and feminine aspects. You, as an independent being, have an innate longing to know the one undifferentiated wholeness of being that is God. This longing, or *sophia*, brings you back to the Almighty through *gnosis*, or direct knowledge or experience of God.

Until recently, all that was generally known of Gnosticism was recorded by its critics, theologians, and thinkers of the time, men like

Irenaeus, Hippolytus, Tertullian, Origen, and Plotinus. However, in 1945, the "Apocryphal Documents," which are believed to contain the scriptural basis for Gnostic beliefs, were discovered at Nag Hammadi, an architectural dig in Egypt. These Gnostic gospels include The Apocryphon of James; the Gospel of Truth; the Gospel of Thomas (Jesus' brother); the Gospel of Philip; the Exegesis of the Soul; the Origin of the World; the Dialogues of the Savior; the Apocalypse of Paul; the Acts of Peter and the Twelve Apostles; and the Gospel of Mary (Magdalene), as well as many others. These Coptic texts profess and document the teachings of Adam, Jesus Christ, and the disciples, among others. They also help to explain many of the esoteric or "hidden" teachings of Judaism and Christianity.

BELIEF SYSTEM

Gnosticism generally emphasizes one's individual pursuit of spiritual knowledge and personal experience with the Holy Spirit, in preference to the established beliefs, or dogma, of the Church of Rome. Gnostics apparently reject the Church doctrines of blind faith and the belief that accepting Jesus Christ as the Savior is the sole source of salvation. Gnostics appear to perceive Jesus as an enlightened Spiritual Master, or God Man, who shows the way to salvation by providing a means of attaining Gnosis, or experiential knowledge, through his Grace. Mere faith is not sufficient for salvation; you had to come to know God to be saved. Gnostics seek freedom from the illusory material world by means of spiritual insight and development of their inner awareness.

The Nag Hammadi documents present a significantly different interpretation of Christian theology. This accounts for the Gnostics' being so heavily persecuted by the churches and almost all the ancient writings being destroyed. These esoteric documents give new accounts about Adam and Eve's discovery of knowledge in Eden; the inner light of God, which is something actually experienced, not merely a metaphor; meditation techniques; experiences of leaving the physical body, traveling to the heavenly spheres, and returning again; and various other esoteric teachings. It suggests the possibility of attaining a realization of God through techniques that Jesus himself taught—through self-inquiry and personal experience, for example.

Gnostics believe that your purpose is to receive salvation through Christ, and establish God's Kingdom of Heaven here on Earth.

RITUALS AND HOLY DAYS

Modern Gnosticism is practiced either through independent research and contemplation or through traditional services, which are quite similar to the Catholic Mass. Traditional services include the celebration of the Holy Eucharist, but they also include unorthodox services, such as the "Feast of the Holy Mary Magdalene" and various healing services. Gnostic practices place emphasis on individual "gnosis" rather than on faith or on rules to live by. With English translations of most of the Nag Hammadi library only becoming available in the last decade, only a few people have become familiar with their contents. But as more thinkers are questioning traditional dogmas, Gnostic congregations continue to grow.

FOR ADDITIONAL INFORMATION

Recommended Contacts

I suggest that you contact the following resources:

The Christian Coptic Orthodox
   Church of Egypt
4909 Cleland Avenue
Los Angeles, CA 90042
Phone: (323) 254–3333
Website: www.lacopts.org

The Gnostic Center
4885 Melrose Avenue
Los Angeles, CA 90029
Phone: (323) 467–1542
E-mail: Gnosisla@earthlink.net

The Gnostic Society
4516 Hollywood Boulevard
Los Angeles, CA 90029
Phone: (213) 467–2685
Website: www.gnosis.org

Thelesis Camp, OTO
P.O. Box 34872
Philadelphia, PA 19101-4872
Website: www.thud.org

Recommended Readings

Holroyd, Stuart. *Elements of Gnosticism*. Boston, MA: Element Books, 1994.

Pagels, Elaine. *The Gnostic Gospels*. New York: Vintage Books, 1989.

Robinson, James M., ed. *The Nag Hammadi Library in English*. San Francisco: Harper, 1990.

Rudolph, Kurt. *Gnosis. The Nature and History of Gnosticism*. San Francisco: Harper & Row, 1983.

Whiston, William, trans. *Josephus: The Complete Works*. Nashville, TN: Thomas Nelson Publisher, 1998.

Recommended Periodical

Gnosis, A Journal of the Western Inner Traditions
401 Terry A. Francois Boulevard, #110
San Francisco, CA 94107
Phone: (415) 974–0600

Recommended Websites

Academic Information on
  Gnosticism
www.academicinfo.net/
  gnostic.html

Early Church History
www.gtu.edu

First Gnostic Church
www.1gnostic.com

Gnosticism Links
www.thepearl.org

Gnostic Network
www.trufax.org/menu/gnostic.html

Hermetic Links
www.hermetic.com

Living Gnosis
www.living-gnois.org

The Mystica
www.themystica.com

OMCE: Order Militia Crucifera
  Evangelica
www.omcesite.org

Ouroboros: The Gnostic Ring
www.gnostikos.co

CHRISTIAN MYSTICISM

Christian Mysticism is a rather broad category of belief that generally pertains to personal experiences with Jesus, or God. The literature of this field spans about 2,000 years, beginning with the advent of Christ and continuing to evolve even to the present day. The themes generally involve the individual inner experiences of various saints written in the form of guides, poems, and autobiographies. Most of the literature comes from ascetic monks and nuns within the Roman Catholic Church, who describe such things as the necessary discipline of the mind and body to receive mystical experiences, the nature of those experiences, and the effect that these occurrences had on their lives. Another type of mystical experience would involve visits by or visions of angels. (See the Inset on "Angels" on page 187.)

We begin with Saint Augustine, whose *Confessions* catalogs one of the most difficult spiritual battles in religious history. We examine the Desert Fathers, who lived their mysticism daily, and Saint Francis of Assisi, who communed with God himself and was granted the stigmata— the five physical wounds of Christ on the cross of Calvary. We will note the mystical teachings of Meister Eckhart and Hesychasm. We will delve into the mystical visions of John of the Cross, Teresa of Avila, Jakob Boehme, and Thomas Merton. Finally, we will explore the spirit world and Emanuel Swedenborg, the Swedish mystic.

FOR ADDITIONAL INFORMATION
Recommended Contacts

Christian Mysticism is a broad and deep subject which cannot adequately be covered by the scope of this book. Use the following resources to begin your investigation, and then see the few mystics and saints that I have highlighted in the following sections. For additional research you may also want to look into the teaching of both the Orthodox and Catholic Churches, and into their monastic orders.

Angels

Angels are God's celestial beings who serve as intermediaries between the divine and human realms. In the Bible, angels are mentioned frequently either as messengers—like the Angel Gabriel who told Mary she was to be the mother of the Messiah—or as those in heaven that praise God.

In the sixth century, Dionysius the Areopagite, a Greek churchman, categorized angels into a hierarchy of nine orders. Ranging from most important to least, they are seraphim, cherubim, thrones, dominations, virtues, powers, principalities, archangels, and angels. Some Christians also believe that each person has a "guardian angel" that provides individual counsel, grace, and guidance, especially during times of temptation.

Christian theology also sees one fallen angel, Lucifer, as the Lord of the damned who resides in Hell eternally, tempts humanity seductively, and brings to this world ceaselessly the evil that causes our suffering. Lucifer has several names: Satan, Beelzebub (*Ba'alzevuv* in Hebrew), and the Devil. It is God's angels—Michael the Archangel, for example—who serve to help combat the presence of Lucifer's demonic presence, and guide humanity to a righteous path to Heaven through Jesus Christ.

If you would like to know more about angels, you might read a book by James R. Lewis called *Angels A to Z*, published by Visible Press, in 1995, or consult the *Encyclopedia of Angels*, by Rosemary Ellen Guiley. You can also subscribe to a periodical, *Angel Times*, by writing to P.O. Box 1325, Duluth, GA 30096, or calling 800–36ANGEL. On the Internet, there is an excellent site for saints and angels at: www.goarch.org/access/companion

Recommended Readings

Johnston, William, trans. *The Cloud of Unknowing and Book of Privy*. Nashville, TN: Image Books, 1996.

King, Ursula, and Constance Herndon. *Christian Mystics*. New York: Simon and Schuster, 1998.

Mascetti, Manuela Dunn. *Christian Mysticism*. New York: Hyperion, 1998.

Sandoval, Annette. *The Dictionary of Saints: A Concise Guide to Patron Saints*. New York: E. P. Dutton, 1996.

Recommended Websites

Beatification and Canonization
www.knight.org/advent/cathen

Carmelite Literature on the Net
www.ocd.or.at/lit/eng.htm

Christian Classics Ethereal
 Library
www.ccel.org/

Christian Mysticism
www.gigiserve.com/
 mystic/Christian

Inner Explorations
Box 520
Chiloquin, OR 97625
Website:
 www.innerexplorations. com

Medieval Source Book
www.fordham.edu/halsall
New Advent Fathers of the
 Church
www.newadvent.org/fathers

ORB: The On Line Reference
 Book for Medieval Studies
www.Orb.rhodes.edu

Saint Pachomius Library Global
 Index
www.ocf.org/orthodoxpage/reading

Saints & Angels
www.catholic.org/saints/
 index.shtml
Saints of the Orthodox Church
www.goarch.org/access/
 companion

The Website of Unknowing
www.anamchara.com/mystics

Who's Who in the History of
 Mysticism
www.clas.ufl.edu/users

SAINT AUGUSTINE

Aurelius Augustinus (A.D. 354–430), a North African bishop of Hippo Regius in what is now Algeria, is one of the most influential theologians in Christian history.

HISTORY

Born in A.D. 354, Augustine was anything but saintly in his youth, committing sins of the flesh and of the mind. His mother was Monica, also a saint of the Catholic Church. It was upon her death, when he was thirty-two, that he mended his ways and began to seek God in earnest. He wrote his powerful *Confessions*, not to satisfy anyone's curiosity about such a wicked life, but to demonstrate the infinite capacity of God to forgive even the most grievous sins.

As a young man, he went to Carthage to study and was actually first in his class in rhetoric. However, he achieved so much only out of vanity and ambition, he later admitted. Indeed, he went on to what he thought was a successful career in rhetoric and grammar, but still continued his drinking and loose living. Then, at the urging of a visitor from Africa, Pontitian, he read the epistles of Saint Paul. These had such a remarkable effect upon him that he immediately gave up his wicked ways and reformed. Subsequently, he performed difficult austerities, strictly controlled his passions, and opened his heart to the mercy of God. After three years of prayer, fasting, and meditation, he became a priest, and, in A.D. 395, he was consecrated Bishop of Hippo in North Africa. He served in that post for thirty-five years, until his death in A.D. 430.

BELIEF SYSTEM

Augustine conversed freely with nonbelievers, and often invited them to eat with him. On the other hand, he would not eat with Christians whose behavior was publicly scandalous, but rather spoke out against them. He always opposed injustice, no matter who was at fault, and was himself unfailingly courteous, meek, and charitable.

Augustine's writings established a precedent in acknowledging mystical experience as an important aspect of spiritual practice. His writings showed a shift in emphasis from *Faith*—in God's promise to you—to *Will*—God's intentions for you—to perfect *Love*. Thus, when you love God, your own love is reciprocated, and salvation is assured. The emphasis changed from theological to experiential, from faith to conscious awareness of God's presence in your life.

FOR ADDITIONAL INFORMATION

Recommended Reading

Augustinus, Aurelius. *The Confessions of Saint Augustine*. Rex Werner, trans. New York: New American Library, 1978.

THE DESERT FATHERS

If Augustine introduced mysticism to Christianity and gave it credibility, it was the Desert Fathers who put it into practice and promoted it to the masses, largely by example. The Desert Fathers were the early Christian monks, mystics, and hermits who were a major influence from the late second to fourth centuries.

HISTORY

The early Christian monks who came to be known as the Desert Fathers lived in the wilderness, away from worldly life and church authorities. They were rebels, and followed a personal and more independent Christian faith. In Lower Egypt, the hermits tended to live alone, but in Upper Egypt, monks and nuns lived in communities. In Nitria and Scetis some lived solitary lives, others in groups of three or four, often as the disciples of a master. For the most part they were simple peasants from villages by the Nile; few were educated.

The literature produced by these monks is not very sophisticated. As an austerity, most of them kept silent. Their words were sparse and not meant for intellectual examination. Rather, they tended to utter life-affirming words that sustained their faith and resolve. Eventually, a few of the various narratives were written down by disciples. Sometimes, the stories were grouped by the names of the monks who were inspired by them, while others were grouped by category, such as, "solitude and stability," "discipline," or "obedience." As the church grew stronger, these outcasts were eventually either purged as heretics or absorbed into the church as one of the monastic orders.

BELIEF SYSTEM

The theological goal of the Desert Fathers was to find inner spiritual peace in this world and eternal salvation in the next. As Friar Antony said, "For the sake of Greek learning, men go overseas. But the City of God has its foundations in every human habitation. The Kingdom of God is within. The goodness that is in us asks only the human mind."

The Desert Fathers had a reputation for being fiercely independent. They lived ascetic lives, spent time in solitude, and engaged in deep meditation and humble prayer. They tried to follow Jesus' example in all things.

FOR ADDITIONAL INFORMATION

Recommended Readings

Cistercian Studies 59. *The Sayings of the Desert Fathers*. Cistercian Publications, 1987.

Waddell, Helen, trans. *The Desert Fathers: Translations from the Latin*. New York: Vintage Books, 1998.

Recommended Websites

The Orthodox and Catholic Churches and their monastic orders are some of the best sources of information. See also the following resources on the Internet:

The Paradise of the Desert Fathers
www.cin.org/dsrtftit.html

Desert Fathers
www.christdesert.org

SAINT FRANCIS OF ASSISI

Saint Francis (1182–1226) is probably the most popular and best known of the Christian mystics.

HISTORY

Originally Giovanni Bernadone, Francis entered the world as the son of a wealthy merchant of Assisi, Italy. In his youth, he loved music and became familiar with the language of the troubadours, so much so that he acquired the nickname, *Il Francesco*, or "the little Frenchman," hence, Francis. He enjoyed his wealth and all that it could buy. He was not interested in his father's business affairs or in the university and its heavy tomes. Rather, he focused on enjoying himself to the fullest. That changed soon enough.

During a visit to Rome, Francis, as he was now known, had a vision of Christ, who told him to rebuild his Church. Francis took the vision literally and attempted to repair the church buildings, selling all he had, even his own clothes, armor, and horses, and giving the money to the Church fathers. He renounced this worldly life, and devoted his days to working among the poor and the lepers. In the last two years of his life, Francis was given the "gift" of the stigmata, sustaining the five wounds that Christ himself received on the cross of Calvary. Francis was canonized a saint in 1226.

BELIEF SYSTEM

Francis's simplicity, charity, and love of nature have set an example for the Christian brotherhood. Francis is the founder of the Order of the Friars Minor (OFM), or Franciscan Fathers, which has evolved, over time, into liberal, moderate, and conservative wings. He was assisted in his religious works by Clare of Assisi (1194–1253), who, with him, founded an order of nuns, the Poor Clares. These Franciscan orders are founded upon the principles of their founders, mainly humility, charity, and submission to the will of God. Each novice priest or nun takes the vows of poverty, chastity, and obedience, but the Franciscans, like their founders, empha-size the first, denying all ownership of material goods for themselves.

FOR ADDITIONAL INFORMATION

Recommended Readings

Chesterton, G. K. *Saint Francis of Assisi.* Nashville, TN: Image Books, 1987.

Green, Julian. *God's Fool: The Life and Times of St. Francis of Assisi.* San Francisco: Harper, 1987.

Recommended Websites

There are numerous Franciscan monasteries across the nation. Consult your local telephone directory or Chamber of Commerce. You could also contact the following Internet sources:

The Franciscan Web Page
www.listserve.american.edu/catholic/franciscan

Internet Franciscan Fraternity
www.multimania.com/iff

MEISTER ECKHART

Meister Eckhart (1260–1327) was a Dominican friar from Germany. He is one of the best known of the Christian mystics.

HISTORY

Johannes Eckhart, later called Meister Eckhart, was born in Hochheim, near Gotha, Germany, in 1260. After an unremarkable childhood, he entered the Dominican order of the Roman Catholic Church; studied and taught in Paris; acted as prior of Erfurt; and became vicar of his order for Thuringia. He continued to advance in the priesthood, becoming provincial in Saxony and vicar-general in Bohemia. So great was the demand for his lectures, he then became an itinerant preacher in 1312, moving from Strasbourg to Frankfurt to Cologne. Because his teachings regarding mysticism were regarded as blasphemous, he was accused of heresy in 1325 by the bishop of Cologne. Two years after his death in 1327, his writings were condemned by Pope John XXII.

BELIEF SYSTEM

Eckhart's ideas were condemned by the Church. He emphasized that you must strip your mind of all active thoughts and images in order to obtain mystical experiences. Eckhart taught that through such mystical experiences, you would come to know the "Eternal Word of the Soul."

Eckhart was himself prone to mystical experience. He explained the importance of mystical experience in his search to know God, stating: "It is the nature of the Holy Spirit that I should be consumed in him, and transformed wholly into love. Whoever is in love and is wholly love, feels that God loves nobody other than themselves."

FOR ADDITIONAL INFORMATION

Recommended Readings

Backhouse, Halcyon, ed. *Best of Meister Eckhart*. Crossroads Publishing, 1993.

Davis, Oliver, ed. *Meister Eckhart: Selected Writings*. New York: Penguin USA, 1995.

Recommended Websites

I suggest that you consult the following Internet sources:

The Eckhart Society
www.op.org/eckhart

Meister Eckhart Home Page
www.wwisp.com

Mysticism in World Religion
www.digiserve.com/mystic/christian/eckhart

HESYCHASM

The Eastern Orthodox mystical practice of Hesychasm gains its name from the Greek *hesychastes*, meaning *recluse* or *one who is quiet or still*.

HISTORY

The roots of Hesychasm go back to the early church and the Desert Fathers who sought to know God through the mystical experiences found in the solitude of deep contemplation on God. (See "Desert Fathers" on page 190.) The early friar, Clement of Alexandria (150–230) departed from traditional Christianity by esteeming a true gnosis—experiential knowledge of God—above faith or theological understanding. But it was Gregory Palamas (1296–1359), a Byzantine priest from Constantinople, who most notably defended the practice of hesychasm against its opponents. Although excommunicated for his beliefs in 1344, Gregory was later restored to the Church, consecrated Bishop of Thessaloniki, and canonized a saint after his death.

Gregory taught that although God is ultimately unknowable, you can experience his energies through the sacraments and through mystical experiences. Gregory had lived in solitude for almost twenty years on the island of Athos, and in a series of tracts, described his mystical experiences with God. He was an advocate of the Jesus Prayer that, in combination with controlled breathing and spiritual mindfulness, would induce mystical experience and the inner knowledge called *gnosis*.

Largely through the influence of Palamas, hesychasm was given theological justification and received as official doctrine of the Greek Orthodox church in 1351.

BELIEF SYSTEM

Hesychasm is a spiritual discipline that prepares the body and soul for mystical union with God. Through constant contemplation on God and his perfection, the mind and the heart meld into union with him.

In this process, you would control your breathing while praying to unite the body and soul and create one wholeness of being with Christ. The experience of the uncreated light, or inner light, opens your inner vision to see the union with God. Thus, through contemplation, meditation, and prayer, you are able to discover God's presence within you.

FOR ADDITIONAL INFORMATION

Recommended Readings

Lossky, Vladimir. *The Mystical Theology of the Eastern Church.* St. Vladimis Seminary Press, 1977.

Meyendoff, John. *Gregory Palamas.* Mahwah, NJ: Paulist Press, 1988.

Recommended Websites

I would suggest that you contact an Eastern Orthodox church in your area, consult a telephone directory, or connect with one of the following Internet sources:

Anthem-Hesychasm
www.geocities.com/athens/aegean

Orthodox-Christianity
www.suite101.com/welcome.cfm/orthodox-christianity

SAINT JOHN
OF THE CROSS

Saint John (1542–1591) was a mystic and reformer who was a member of the Carmelite order.

HISTORY

John de Yepes was born to a poor family in Fontiveros in Old Castile, Spain, in 1542. At the age of twenty-one, he became a Carmelite friar at Medina, taking the name of John of Saint Matthias. When Saint Teresa of Avila visited Medina to initiate reforms among the Carmelites, she spoke with John. Teresa told him she had experienced a vision in which she had been told he would be an instrument of God. Soon thereafter, the first monastery of ascetic discalced, that is, barefooted, Carmelite friars was formed. They were led by John and two others. In the process, the three renewed their vows, and John now took the name of John of the Cross.

The new name was appropriate, for in his new station, John was subject to all sorts of terrible trials and temptations. These are described in his moving *The Dark Night of the Soul*. Eventually, he was appointed to a convent in Avila, where he was arrested because he refused the secular order of a local official. Imprisoned in Toledo in 1577, he escaped the following year, again assuming a life of poverty and contemplation. He lived in illness in the monastery at Ubeda, where he died in 1591. He was canonized in 1726 and declared a Doctor of the Church in 1926.

BELIEF SYSTEM

The poems of John of the Cross are recognized as among the finest in the Spanish language. Saint John is popularly known for his explorations in *The Dark Night of the Soul*, describing the struggles one must go through in purifying oneself and receiving God's grace. In one section, for example, he details a temptation of the flesh from a seductive woman. John did not throw holy water, wave a cross, or seek to escape; rather, he used gentle words and argument to show her the error of her ways and encourage her to repent. Through such visions did he defeat Lucifer and find serenity in the grace of God.

FOR ADDITIONAL INFORMATION

Recommended Readings

John of the Cross. *The Dark Night of the Soul*. Allison Peters, trans. Nashville, TN: Image Books, 1959.

Krabbenhoft, Kenneth, trans. *The Collected Poems of Saint John of the Cross*. New York: Harcourt Brace, 1999.

TERESA OF AVILA

Saint Teresa (1515–1582) was a mystic and reformer within the Carmelite order. She was a contemporary of Saint John of the Cross.

HISTORY

Teresa was born near Avila in Castile, Spain, in 1515. After an uneventful childhood, she entered the Carmelite convent in 1533. Two years later, her austerities and strong spiritual desires brought her to such a state of asceticism that she experienced ecstasies. Also, God began to visit her with intellectual visions and quiet communications. The fame of her sanctity spread far and wide.

In 1562, she received papal permission to found the Convent of Saint Joseph and to reform the Carmelite order. In her lifetime, over thirty convents or monasteries adopted her reforms. She died in 1582, and was canonized forty years later.

BELIEF SYSTEM

Because of her intense love of God and her strict austerities, Teresa underwent a spiritual transformation and began to have visions and mystical experiences, or raptures. She was favored by the "prayer of quiet," and also by the "prayer of union." These often went on for some time, with a corresponding increase in joy and love. One day, for example, while she was reciting the hymn *Veni Creator Spiritus*, she was seized with a glorious rapture. In this state, she heard a loving voice saying that henceforth, she would speak, not with men, but with angels.

Her journals and other works, especially *The Way of Perfection*, are considered some of the most powerful in Christian mysticism.

FOR ADDITIONAL INFORMATION

Recommended Readings

Cohen, J. M., trans. *The Life of Saint Teresa of Avila by Herself*. New York: Penguin USA, 1988.

Peers, E. Allison, trans. *The Way of Perfection*. Nashville, TN: Image Books, 1991.

Recommended Websites

I recommend that you check with a local Catholic church or consult any of the following Internet sources:

The Carmelites Call
www.Carmelnet.org/chas

Catholic Information Network
www.cin.org/7thmans.html

The Teresian Carmel
www.or.at/eng/teresa.html

JAKOB BOEHME

Jakob Boehme (1575–1624) was a German lay theologian and mystic.

HISTORY

Boehme was born to poor parents in Altseidenberg, Germany. As a lad, he tended cattle and later worked as a shoemaker. However, in 1600, he had a mystical experience and from that point on, devoted his life to meditation on and writing about things divine. His first published work was *Aurora*, which describes his visions. It was condemned by the ecclesiastical authorities of Gorlitz, and he was cruelly tormented by the populace. Nevertheless, he was not deterred and continued to publish. His ideas spread throughout northern Europe, and the great minds of the age argued his propositions. Boehme's writings were influential in the Theosophy Movement started by Helena Petrovna Blavatsky and Henry Alcott in 1875 (see also "Theosophy" on page 255). Thus, although denounced by the Lutheran clergy, he has been an inspiration to many Christians seeking mystical experiences.

BELIEF SYSTEM

Boehme's books, principally *Aurora, The Way of Christ,* and *Mysterium,* discuss his revelations and meditations on Man, Nature, and God. They show a thorough knowledge of the Bible and a familiarity with sorcery and alchemy. His main themes focused on the origins of things, especially how evil came to exist in the world. He conceived of God as the original and entire unity, at once everything and nothing. It is through the "principle of negation" that creation can be explained, including the existence of evil. And it is through the "principle of contradiction" that the great philosophical problems can be explained.

Through his own symbolic language, he describes a step-by-step method of attaining union with Christ. For example, he suggests a system of triads, based on the doctrine of the Trinity, to explain the relationship among Man, Nature, and Divine, and ultimately, to bring the believer closer to God.

FOR ADDITIONAL INFORMATION

Recommended Readings

Boehme, Jacob. *The "Key" of Jacob Boehme*. William Law, trans. Grand Rapids, MI: Phanes Press, 1991.

Weeks, Andrew. *Boehme: An Intellectual Biography of the Seventeenth-Century Philosopher and Mystic*. Albany, NY: State University of New York Press, 1991.

Recommended Websites

Check the following Internet sites:

Jacob Boehme
www.kheper.auz.com/topics/christianmysticism/JacobBoehme.htm

The Ecole Initiative
www.cedar.evansville.edu/ecoleweb

THOMAS MERTON

Thomas Merton (1915–1968) is perhaps the best known of the modern-day mystics and the most influential theologian among monastics in recent history.

HISTORY

Merton was born in Prades, France, in 1915. His parents were of New Zealand and American stock. He studied at Columbia University in New York, taught English there, and also investigated a variety of religions. In 1938, he became a baptized Catholic and in 1941, joined the Trappist order of monks at the Cistercian abbey in Kentucky. Subsequently, he published his most famous work, *The Seven Storey Mountain,* a biography that became a bestseller and inspired many to seek the contemplative life of a monk. He wrote on a broad range of topics, including Eastern spirituality, for the rest of his life. He died in Bangkok, Thailand, while attending a conference.

BELIEF SYSTEM

Merton's work catalogues the intense tensions he experienced between his contemplative needs and his community needs. Nevertheless, his Cistercian superiors respected his views and found ways to allow him to balance his competing obligations. His writings emphasize discipline, meditation, and contemplation, while acknowledging spiritual experiences as a test of spiritual development. His life is proof that self-discipline and struggle against temptation can bring you closer to God.

FOR ADDITIONAL INFORMATION

Recommended Readings

Merton, Thomas. *The Seven Storey Mountain.* New York: Harcourt Brace, 1978.

Merton, Thomas. *New Seeds of Contemplation.* New York: W. W. Norton & Co., 1974.

Recommended Websites

Merton Center at Bellarmine College
www.bellarmine.edu/mertoncenter

Thomas Merton Links
www.ucl.ac.uk

Thomas Merton Resources: Gethsemane
www.monks.org/merton.

Thomas Merton Society
www.ucl.ac.uk/ucylpmp/home.htm

SWEDENBORGIANISM

Swedenborgianism, or the Church of New Jerusalem, is based upon the teachings of Emanuel Swedenborg, a Swedish mystic.

HISTORY

Swedenborg was born in Stockholm, Sweden, in 1688. He was a distinguished scientist in the fields of cosmology, mathematics, geology, and anatomy before turning seriously to theology. Swedenborg was uniquely gifted as a scientist, as he was able to communicate with the "other world." In 1743, he had a religious experience, described in his *Journal of Dreams*, which he interpreted as direct visions of the spiritual world, of heaven and hell. He even had frequent conversations with spirits.

Through these experiences, Swedenborg learned that a new church was to be born, and that his writings were to be part of its teachings. Swedenborg himself never preached or founded a church, but in 1772, his followers formed a group to disseminate his teachings. They considered him to be a divinely inspired seer and messenger. An organized church was established in London in 1789, when a follower named Robert Hindmarsh gathered friends to discuss Swedenborg's teachings.

The first Swedenborgian society in America formed in Baltimore in 1792. The Church of New Jerusalem developed from these societies, and today remains a relatively small congregation of several thousand followers, mostly in northeastern Europe and on the East Coast of the United States.

BELIEF SYSTEM

Swedenborg held that "God is Man," and that the origin of all that is truly human is in one God. Christ, as God incarnate, glorified his humanity, and thereby established a new unity between the spiritual and natural dimensions of reality, a unity in which each person can now participate. Church doctrine includes beliefs that:

- There is One God, in whom there is a Divine Trinity; and that He is the Lord Jesus Christ;

- Your faith will save you if you believe in Him;

- You are born to evils of every kind, but unless through repentance, you remove them in part, you remain in them, and he who remains in them cannot be saved;

- Good actions are to be done, because they are of God and from God;

- These are to be done by you as from yourself; nevertheless, you should believe they are only done by you through and with the help of the Lord.

Swedenborgians accept that Christians receive salvation through Jesus Christ, that they live to establish a life on Earth as God intended, and that they thereby assure eternal life in Heaven with God.

FOR ADDITIONAL INFORMATION

Recommended Contacts

Emanual Swedenborg Association
278-A Meeting Street
Charleston, SC 29401
Website: www.swedenborg.net
  www.swedenborg.net

The Wayfarer's Chapel
5755 Palos Verdes Road South
Rancho Palos Verdes, CA 90274
Phone: (213) 377–1650

The Swedenborgian Church
112 E. 35th Street
New York, NY 10016
Phone: (646) 685–8967

Recommended Readings

Hallengren, Anders, and Inge Jonnon. *Gallery of Mirrors: Reflections of Swedenborgian Thought.* West Chester, PA: Swedenborg Foundation, 1998.

Swedenborg, Emanuel. *Heaven and Hell.* George F. Dole, trans. West Chester, PA: Swedenborg Foundation, 1990.

Recommended Websites

The New Earth Swedenborg
www.netaxas.com/mvd/swedenborg.html

The Swedenborg Homepage
www.ozemail.com.au/sllandec

MYSTICISM

Mysticism is a broad-based term referring to the inquiry into the nature of the unknown, the unseen, or the occult. It is rooted in the notion of *mysteria* found in the mystery religions of the ancient Greek world, dating back several centuries B.C. Nevertheless, as the word applies today, it cuts across cultural and religious boundaries. As a practice, mysticism may involve a scientific understanding of the nature of the universe, an inquiry into a universal order, or any personal experience which may transcend intellectual understanding or sense perception.

Mystical orders appear within virtually all of the world's religions, as the more contemplative or meditative sects sought personal experience with the Divine. Mysticism forms the basis of most native and shamanistic traditions, and it is the underlying focus of the New Age religions and self-improvement movements.

Common to all mystical traditions is the underlying assumption that there is an innate intelligence within the universe, and an orderly and universal way in which this Divine mind is expressed. This universal intelligence appears within the order and movement of celestial bodies, through the universal language of numbers or vibrations, and through universal symbols, colors, and images. Therefore, in this section, a brief overview of the beliefs and practices of astrology and tarot will be discussed.

FOR ADDITIONAL INFORMATION

Information on mysticism and the occult crosses over many boundaries. I have selected independent topics that are sufficiently defined to have their own sections—Christian Mysticism, Kabbalah, Wicca, Astrology, and Tarot, for example—but for those areas that are more general, the following resources may be useful. Moreover, I have omitted sections specifically focused on the dark side of spirituality and Satanism as they, by definition, run counter to searching for God in the classical sense. Those interested in learning more about such topics may find them under these resources as well.

Recommended Readings

Freake, James. *Three Books of Occult Philosophy*. St. Paul, MN: Llewellyn Publishing, 1994.

Hall, Manly P. *The Secret Teachings of All Ages*. Los Angeles: The Philosophical Research Society, 1977.

Robb, Alexander. *Alchemy and Mysticism: Hermetic Museum*. Taschen America, 1997.

Steiner, Rudolph. *Anthroposophy in Everyday Life*. Brian Kelly, trans. Anthroposophic Press, 1995.

Steiner, Rudolph. *Intuitive Thinking As a Spiritual Path: A Philosophy of Freedom*. Michael Lipson, trans. Anthroposophic Press, 1995.

Underhill, Evelyn. *Practical Mysticism*. Alpharetta, GA: Ariel Press, 1988.

Wasserman, James, ed. *Art and Symbols of the Occult: Images of Power and Wisdom*. Rochester, VT: Inner Traditions, 1993.

Recommended Websites

Avatar-Occult Links
www.avatarsearch.com

The Facade
www.facade.com

The Mystica
www.themystica.com

Mystical World Wide Web
www.mystical-www.co.uk

Occult Chat
www.chathouse.com

The Occult
www.occultinfo.cx

The Philosophical Research
  Center
www.prs.org

Rudolf Steiner (Anthroposophy)
www.elib.com/steiner
www.goetheanum.ch

ASTROLOGY

Astrology is a form of divination based on the ancient belief that the movements of the sun, moon, stars, and other celestial bodies influence human affairs and may even determine human events. It is also a tool for providing insights into the evolution of consciousness within individuals and society.

HISTORY

Astrologers have existed since earliest times. Their influence grew out of a need to explain the existence and movements of the moon, sun, stars, and other heavenly bodies. They also made connections between those movements and human affairs. A famous example is that of the Magi in the Bible who followed the Star of David. The Chaldaeans and the Assyrians believed that human events are predetermined by the movements of celestial bodies, and even developed a system of divination from this belief, one that did not depend upon deities but upon the stars and celestial movements.

During the Middle Ages, astrologers held important posts in almost all of the courts of Europe; their major task was to forecast the future, to divine if the stars were favorable to this or that enterprise. Their influence was diminished by the rise of Christianity, with its emphasis on the power and grace of God and the free will of man. During the Renaissance, interest in things astrological became popular once more, due to the heightened interest in science, especially new discoveries in astronomy. Nevertheless, Church authorities waged war against astrology, and Pope Sixtus V condemned the practice in 1585.

Ironically, in their studies to chart the heavens, astrologers did learn much about the motions and positions of celestial bodies, and this gave rise to the science of astronomy. Astrology is still popular, however, as millions of people, from ordinary to presidential, consult their daily horoscopes, have individual readings done, or plan their activities around the movements of the stars.

BELIEF SYSTEM

Most people are familiar with the act of divining the future through horoscopes and learning of their natural disposition through interpretations of sun signs and planetary aspects. However, there is also the relation of karmic imprints that mold our destiny and learning experiences, providing opportunities for us to evolve and grow in consciousness.

The horoscope is a map of the position of the planets in the heavens at the exact time and place of birth. This map represents a circle of 360 degrees, the path which the sun appears to follow through the sky (actually Earth's orbit around the sun), which is called the ecliptic. This path is divided into twelve 30-degree sectors that are represented by constellations in the universe known as the signs of the zodiac, or sun signs. These twelve signs include Aries, the Ram; Taurus, the Bull; Gemini, the Twins; Cancer, the Crab; Leo, the Lion; Virgo, the Virgin; Libra, the Scales; Scorpio, the Scorpion (or Eagle); Sagittarius, the Centaur; Capricorn, the Goat; Aquarius, the Water Bearer; and Pisces, the Fish, two swimming in opposite directions. Each sign is ruled by a different planet, or the moon, and each projects or represents various traits, vibrational characteristics, and attributes. In some manner, they influence everyone born, depending on when and where they were born in relation to the constellation at their time of birth. For example, someone born during a time when the sun was in one particular sign would be "imprinted" with more of the attributes of that sun sign.

In addition to the twelve signs of the zodiac and the effects of the sun, planets, and moon, there are also twelve arcs of time and space that divide the passage of time. Referred to as the "houses" of the birthchart, these twelve configurations of time and space represent the cycles of life and learning experience that all souls progress through periodically in order to learn and grow. Whereas *signs* are subdivisions of the Earth's revolution around the Sun, the *houses* are subdivisions of the Earth's rotation on its axis. At the time of your birth, the constellation that was raising up wherever you happened to be became the first house (time frame), and as the Earth continued to rotate, that passed through all the other constellations in twenty-four-hour cycles.

The sign that was arising at your birth is called the Ascendant, and it represents aspects that are reflected in your outward personality. The opposite point is the Descendant, and the place between them is the Midheaven. The basic purpose of the horoscope is to answer the question "Who am I?" Practitioners believe that universal energies are conducting the forces that set forth into motion all your life's activities and circumstances. *Transits* and *progressions* indicate when certain effects are likely to occur, and the *houses* show us where (in our lives) the action is taking place. The general characteristics of the houses would include the following.

- First house, your body;

- Second house, your possessions, property, resources;

- Third house, your brothers and sisters;

- Fourth house, your environment, the place where you live;

- Fifth house, your soul;

- Sixth house, the comforts of life;

- Seventh house, marriage and partnership;

- Eighth house, influence of others;

- Ninth house, spirit;

- Tenth house, honor, prestige, business;

- Eleventh house, friendships and associations; and

- Twelfth house, service.

So the *planets* represent those energies that are operating in your life. The *signs of the zodiac* represent how the individual uses those energies. The *houses* represent where these energies play out in your life, and what circumstances bring them about. In addition, the angles and degrees between the planets describe how relatively difficult or easy some aspects will be as they relate to each other. Some will complement and offer smooth sailing, and others will oppose and create stress.

Understanding the ways in which all these energies interact is the study of astrology. Obviously, this study can get very complicated; therefore, it is best to consult an astrologer for guidance and direction.

An astrological conception of your purpose on Earth would be for you to live in accordance with the natural laws of the universe, and in so doing, achieve greater balance, understanding, and harmony in your life.

FOR ADDITIONAL INFORMATION

Recommended Contacts

Astrologers can be found in every major city. They are listed in the phone book, and often network through metaphysical bookstores. Because the proficiencies of astrologers vary considerably, you should ask for references. To get accurate and meaningful readings, get a full chart done; just knowing your sun sign or reading a daily horoscope will not tell you much that is unique, or pertinent, about you.

The Association for Astrological
 Networking
8306 Wilshire Boulevard, #537
Beverly Hills, CA 90211
Phone: (800) 578–AFAN
Website: www.afan.org

National Council for Geocosmic
 Research
P.O. Box 38866
Los Angeles, CA 90038
Phone: (818) 761–6433
Website: www.geocosmic.org

International Society for
 Astrological Research (ISAR)
P.O. Box 38613
Los Angeles, CA 90038
Website: www.isarastrology.com

Recommended Readings

Goodman, Linda. *Linda Goodman's Love Signs*. San Francisco: Harper-Collins, 1992.

Hickey, Isabel M. *Astrology: A Cosmic Science*. Waltham, MA: Fellowship House, 1987.

Lau, Theodora. *The Handbook of Chinese Astrology*. San Francisco, CA: HarperCollins, 1995.

Moore, Marcia, and Mark Douglas. *Astrology: The Divine Science*. York Harbor, ME: Arcane Publications, 1977.

Pottenger, Rique. *American Ephemeris 2001-2010*. San Diego, CA: ACS Publications, 1997.

Sakoian, Frances, and Louis S. Acker. *The Astrologer's Handbook*. San Francisco, CA: HarperCollins, 1989.

Spiller, Jan. *Astrology for the Soul*. New York: Bantam Books, 1997.

Spiller, Jan, and Karen McCoy. *Spiritual Astrology.* New York: Fireside, 1988.

Recommended Periodicals

Horoscope
1270 Avenue of the Americas
New York, NY 10020
Phone: (800) 888–6901

The Mountain Astrologer
P.O. Box 970
Cedar Ridge, CA 95924
Phone: (800) 287–4828

Recommended Websites

To look up your sign, obtain charts, horoscopes, and readings, I suggest you contact one or more of the following:

Astrology Net
www.astrology.net

Horoscopes
www.4horoscope.com

Astrology Online: Megasite
www.astrology-online.com

Indian Astrology
www.astrosurfindia.com

Astronet
www.astronet.com

Signs, Houses and Planetary
    Rulers
www.djay.com/astrol/ztable.html

Atlas-Timezone Database
www.astro.ch/atlas

Chinese Astrology
www.found.cs.nyu.edu/
    liaos/horoscope.html

TAROT

The tarot is a series of seventy-eight images, usually in the form of pasteboard cards, that have been used for centuries to reveal the puzzles of the past, the patterns of the present, and the events of the future. In quite a different approach, the tarot has also been used for deeper esoteric and philosophical insights, even being used to impart the teachings and mystical interpretations of the ancient Kabbalah (Jewish Mysticism).

HISTORY

The origins of the tarot cards are obscure. There are three major lines of investigation to account for their introduction: the Egyptian mystery schools, the European gypsies, and the Kabbalah.

The first, popularized by Alliette, a writer who lived during the French Revolution, argued that the tarot originated in the Egyptian mystery schools. He cited archeological evidence claiming the Egyptian Magus used such cards. He said the word *tarot* is derived from the Egyptian words *tar*, meaning *path*, and *rog*, meaning *royal*, and the two together mean *the royal path of life*. This view is supported by Count de Gebelin, another eighteenth-century writer. He claimed that he had found remnants of the ancient Egyptian tarot in the old Italian *tarocchi* cards, that the originals had been distorted, and that their true meanings and knowledge had been lost—except to a select few. He argued that the Egyptians had sailed the Mediterranean, trading with the peoples they found, and spreading their culture—including the tarot.

Another scholar who favors this theory is Samuel Liddell MacGregor Mathers, former head of the Hermetic Order of the Golden Dawn, a secret society that studies alchemy, astrology, numerology—and the tarot. He claims the latter is derived from the Egyptian *taru*, meaning *to require an answer* or *to consult*.

A second theory on the origin of the tarot ascribes it to the European gypsies. One who favors this approach is the nineteenth-century writer De L'Hoste Ranking, who says the word *tarot* is derived from the Hungarian gypsy word *tar*, meaning a pack of cards. This, in turn, originated in the Hindustani *taru*, meaning roughly the same thing. Another writer of the period, Vaillant, who lived with the gypsies for many years, supports this view, as does Papus, a later writer who penned *The Tarot of the Bohemians*, published in 1889.

The third theory on the origin of the tarot is that it is descended from the Hebrew Kabbalah. In this view, tarot was developed as a pictorial form of the secret teachings in order to simplify the material for initiates. The use of these ancient symbols to convey the Kabbalistic teachings probably dates back to the age of Moses, approximately 1300 B.C. The deck is full of Kabbalistic symbols, especially the Wheel of Fortune, with its Hebrew inscriptions, and the Hebrew letters, YHWH, which spell out *Jehova*.

The Kabbalistic traditions were initially handed down orally; then some were carved on rocks and in caves, others on tablets and parchment. With the advent of the printing press in 1440, by Johannes Gutenberg (1400–1468), cards could be mass-produced. Pilgrims, traders, crusaders, and other travelers could have acquired the cards, brought them back to their own country, and changed the symbolism to coincide with their own cultures. In the process, the Kabbalistic meanings have been lost or distorted, except for those who have been instructed in them.

These days, tarot cards are best known for their use in divination, telling fortunes, or predicting the future. However, I believe the primary use of the symbols represented in the tarot deck is as a meditative discipline. Reflecting on the symbols represented on the cards will develop your psychic perceptions, stimulate your inner awareness, and ultimately elevate you to a higher psychic plane.

BELIEF SYSTEM

Each card represents a different aspect of life and contains keys to an innate understanding or intuitive awareness stored within the subconscious. This awareness is evoked when those symbols are contemplated. Each card will have a picture that holds a meaning; numbers, colors, and astrological references may also be used to incite a psychic memory.

In descending order, the tarot cards consist of: The Fool, The Magus, The Priestess, The Empress, The Emperor, The Hierophant, The Lovers, The Chariot, Adjustment, The Hermit, Fortune, Lust, The Hanged Man, Death, Art, The Devil, The Tower, The Star, The Moon, The Sun, The Aeon, and The Universe. There is also a Knight, Queen, Prince, Princess, Ace, and two to ten of Wands, Cups, Swords, and Disks.

Typically, if you are using the card for inner reflection, you will contemplate the area in which you are seeking guidance and direction; you will often use an invocation to acknowledge the inner spirit guiding you. Randomly and intuitively, you would choose the cards from the Tarot deck and lay them out in various configurations, depending on the form or purpose of the reading. When the cards are turned over and the pictures exposed, the reader reflects upon the symbols in the context of the position of the card in the order of cards laid out. Each position represents a different consideration, such as the nature of the problem, the direction to be taken, the decisions to be made, the opportunities and obstacles to be dealt with, the lesson to be learned, and the solutions possible. By reflecting upon these aspects of the problem, you are given spiritual insight and intuitively guided toward making conscious decisions. In this way, you may evolve your consciousness to its highest potential. You will find great fulfillment in reaching your greatest potential and ascending to the highest levels of consciousness.

FOR ADDITIONAL INFORMATION

Recommended Readings

Greer, Mary K. *Tarot for Your Self*. Newcastle Publishing, 1987.

Sharman-Burke, Juliet. *The Complete Book of Tarot*. New York: St. Martin's Press, 1996.

Recommended Websites

Tarot readers and classes are available typically at metaphysical bookstores, Wiccan and pagan groups, fortune telling centers, and through the Builders of the Adytum (see BOTA on page 234).

You should obtain a good set of tarot cards. One that I recommend is *The Original Rider Waite Tarot Pack*, a book and deck set authored by A. E. Waite and published by United States Games Systems, 1993.

The following two Internet sources should also prove useful:

Tarot Resources
www.kenaz.com/resources/tarot.htm

Tarot Weekly
www.tarot.readers.com

SPIRITUALISM

Spiritualists believe that there are two modes to existence, the physical and the spiritual. They place great reliance on communing with "those on the other side," that is, in the spiritual world, in enhancing their lives on this side.

HISTORY

The Spiritualist Movement began in the early 1900s with the popularity of mediums, seances, clairvoyance, Ouija boards, and communicating with spirits, which grew out of a general interest in Christian mysticism and the occult at the time.

Many spiritualist groups meet without benefit of any organized body, but there are several organizations representing this movement. One of the earliest is the National Spiritualist Association of Churches, organized in 1893 in Chicago. In addition to a nationwide church body, it offers a seminary, The Morris Pratt Institute, to train ministers, and it offers national conventions to meet and share ideas. The Progressive Spiritual Church was founded in Chicago in 1907 by G. Cordingley, and now has several dozen churches around the country. The National Spiritual Alliance of the U.S.A. was founded by G. Tabor Thompson in 1913 in Lake Pleasant, Massachusetts, and most of its churches are in Massachusetts and Connecticut. The International General Assembly of Spiritualists was organized in Buffalo, New York, in 1936, and is a cooperative body designed to establish unity within the spiritualist movement with hundreds of churches around the country.

BELIEF SYSTEM

Although many of the beliefs and practices vary among the different spiritualist churches and groups, a central teaching in spiritualism is that "God is Love." Christ is often thought of as a medium and his message as being channeled from the spirit world. The National Spiritual Alliance uses the following Declaration of Principles to explain their religious beliefs:

- We believe in Infinite Intelligence;

- We believe that the phenomena of Nature, both physical and spiritual, are the expression of Infinite Intelligence;

- We affirm that a correct understanding of such expression, and living in accordance therewith, constitutes true religion;

- We affirm that the existence and personal identity of the individual continue after the change called death;

- We affirm that communication with the so-called dead is a fact scientifically proven by the phenomena of Spiritualism;

- We believe that the highest morality is contained in the Golden Rule;

- We affirm the moral responsibility of the individual, and that he makes his own happiness or unhappiness as he obeys or disobeys Nature's physical and spiritual laws;

- We affirm that the doorway to reformation is never closed against any human soul, here or hereafter; and

- We affirm that the practice of Prophecy, as authorized by the Holy Bible, is a divine and God-given gift, reestablished and proven through mediumship by the phenomena of Spiritualism.

In addition to regular services held in a church, which may include a sermon, readings, and singing, spiritualist services may include channeled information from the spirit realm.

Seances, where a medium contacts a departed soul or non-incarnated entity, may take place during church or in the privacy of the follower's home. In some groups, individuals are taught to leave their physical body in their "astral body" or "soul body" to travel in the "astral planes" or "spirit realms" to gain spiritual insights.

Sometimes, spiritualists use the Ouija board as an avenue for spirits to contact practitioners. All participants put their hands on the Ouija board, which has on it letters, numbers, and symbols. The spirit can communicate by tipping the board in the direction that spells out or otherwise points to the answer to be conveyed.

Sometimes, a spirit may use other forms of communication, such as elevating the table being used, or moving another object. Some spirits may materialize in a light body or ethereal form, or communicate by making a sound, such as tapping or speaking through another person—channeling. (See "Channeling" on page 289.) Spirits may also communicate through tarot cards, which depict symbols representing various ideas, feelings, and lessons that are communicated through the tarot card reader. Similar readings can take place through tea leaves, runes (symbols on stones from Nordic traditions), or sticks.

Spiritualists see your purpose in life is to learn and evolve as spirit, to improve the quality of life on the planet, and to bring the wisdom and love of the spiritual world into the physical world. This is achieved by learning what you can of life—and of yourself—and contacting those beings (incarnate or not) on the other side, to gain the information and insights needed. You are here to grow and evolve in consciousness, thus providing even greater happiness and fulfillment in your life.

FOR ADDITIONAL INFORMATION

Recommended Contact

Look up "spiritualist churches" in the telephone directory. You might also inquire at metaphysical bookstores or centers in your area. You may also contact the following group:

General Assembly of Spiritualists
27 Appleton Street
Rochester, NY 14611
Phone: (716) 464–9419
Website: www.hispirit.org.au

Recommended Readings

Houdini, Harry. *Miracle Mongers and Their Methods*. Prometheus Books, 1993.

Lagrand, Louis E. *After Death Communication: Final Farewells*. St. Paul, MN: Llewellyn Publishing.

Lakhani, M. P. *Spiritualism and Mysticism: Experiences of a Disciple*. Stosius Inc., 1985.

Massey, Gerald. *Concerning Spiritualism*. Kessinger Publishing, 1997.

SUFISM

Sufism is the English name given to the religion known as *Tasawof* in Arabic. The term *Sufism* is derived from the word *sufi*, which, in both Arabic and English, refers to one who follows the Tasawof religion. The word *sufi* may be derived from the Arabic word *safa*, meaning *honesty* and *purity*; from the Arabic word *suf*, meaning *wool* (referring to the traditional dress of the Sufi); or from the Arabic word *suffe* meaning *platform*, referring to the platform on which the prophet Mohammed used to worship and instruct. The East Indian followers of this religion are known as dervishes.

HISTORY

Sufism is generally considered to be the mystical teaching of the religion of Islam. The origins of the Sufi movement are obscure. The root of the religion comes from the teachings of the prophet Mohammed, the founder of Islam, who was born in Mecca, Arabia, about A.D. 572. Mohammed taught his disciples the way to true knowledge of Allah (God), and out of these teachings evolved the mystical sect that later became known as Tasawof, or Sufism. As these disciples went off and gathered more disciples, centers of Sufism were formed in different parts of the land, including Baghdad, Khuzistan, Shiraz, Kurdistan, and Karaj. Sufism has spread throughout the Arab world and Persia, and as far as India, Indonesia, West Africa, and quite recently, the United States. Because many great Sufi masters have established their own interpretations of Sufi theory, Sufism, as it has been introduced in the West, has adopted its own style and form. Sufi sects can be found around the world in small numbers, typically inconspicuously, as they have not been readily accepted by Islamic fundamentalists.

BELIEF SYSTEM

The practice of Sufism is explained in the very derivation of the Arabic word for the religion: *Tasawof*. As one of Mohammed's disciples, Imam Ali, explains, the word *Tasawof* is a combination of four words embodying three concepts each. These are as follows:

- *Ta,* to shun everything other than God; *toubeth,* meaning *repentance;* and *tougha,* meaning *purification.*

- *Sa,* signifying *safa,* which means *purity and honesty; sabr,* which means *patience;* and *sedgh,* which means *truthfulness.*

- *Wo,* signifying *wafa,* which means *faith; werd,* which means *remembrance of God;* and *woud,* which means *love.* And

- *Fe,* embodying *faghr,* which means *poverty; fana,* which means *to become one with God;* and *fard,* which means *individuality.*

From all of this, we learn the aim of the Sufi is to renounce all physical desires and attachments; purify the heart so only thoughts of God remain; develop and maintain complete faith and love for God; and finally, give up the self completely to become one with God.

Sufis can be of different sects, such as Sunni or Shi'ite, and maintain different beliefs and practices, depending on the school the Sufi had studied in. Some sects of Sufis believe that you can attain the Kingdom of Heaven on Earth through God Realization. Sufis are Muslims, and as such, believe that you are here to submit to God's will and abide by his laws. In so doing, you live a more righteous life, and are assured a greater life after death, in heaven.

Whatever the sect, all Sufism is based on Islam, and therefore, the primary scriptural source is the Qur'an (or Koran). Other great Sufi works include *Kashf Al Mahjub,* by Ali Hujwiri, perhaps the oldest Persian treatise on Sufism, written sometime late in the tenth century. Another Sufi theologian and poet, Mawlana (Jalal ad-Din arRumi), inspired the Sufi order Tariaa, popularly known as Whirling Dervishes, referring to a spiritual dance that puts the salek—the spiritual seeker—into an ecstatic state. Mawlana also wrote such Sufi collections as *Ma'navi* and *Divan-e Shams-i Tabrizi.* Other great works include *Ghoshairi's Treatise,* by Abol Ghasem Ghoshairi, and *Ihya ulum ad-din,* by Abu Hamid al-Ghazali.

RITUALS AND HOLY DAYS

In Sufism, the aspirant to wisdom, or *salek,* places complete trust in his Sufi Master, a *Murshed* (or *Ghotb, Agha,* or *Pir*). Upon being accepted as a salek, the novice is instructed by the Murshed in the proper use of a spiritual word (similar to a mantra), which is known as a *zekr.* In addition to personal zekrs, there are special ceremonies that take place in the Khanegheh (place of worship) called the "circle of zekr," where worshipers sit in a circle on the floor, with their knees touching, and chant in unison another zekr. These spiritual exercises assist the salek to be purified of all worldly desires, so that he may come to know God.

The aim of the salek is to pass through some forty stages of spiritual development. This process starts with "willingness" and ends with "gnosis," or the achievement of true self-knowledge and knowledge of God.

FOR ADDITIONAL INFORMATION
Recommended Contacts

Bawa Muhaiyaddeen Fellowship
5820 Overbrook Avenue
Philadelphia, PA 19131
Phone: (215) 879–6300
Website: www.bmf.org

Halveti-Jerrahi Mosque of
   Dervishes
864 Chestnut Ridge Road
Chestnut Ridge, NY 10977
Phone: (914) 352–5518
Website: www.jerrahi.org

International Association of
   Sufism
25 Mitchell Boulevard, Suite 2
San Rafael, CA 94903
Phone: (415) 472–6959
Website: www.ias.com

Khaniqahi-Nimatullahi
306 W. 11th Street
New York, NY 10014
Phone: (212) 924–7739
Website: www.nimatullahi.org

The Sufi Order
P.O. Box 30065
Seattle, WA 98103
Phone: (206) 525–6992
Website: www.sufiorder.org

Recommended Readings

Barks, Coleman, trans. *The Essential Rumi*. NJ: Castle Books, 1997.

Haeri, Shaykh Fadhlalla. *The Elements of Sufism*. Element Books, 1997.

Khan, Pir Vilayat Inayat. *The Call of the Dervish*. Santa Fe, NM: Sufi Order Publications, 1981.

Shah, Idries. *The Sufis*. New York: Anchor Books, 1971.

Recommended Periodical

Sufi
306 W. 11th Street
New York, NY 10014
Phone: (212) 924–7739

FREEMASONRY

The Society of Free and Accepted Masons is the oldest worldwide men's fraternal club in existence. The organization meets primarily for social purposes and stresses the importance of civic, patriotic, and charitable activities among its members. However, Masons, as they are commonly called, differ from most fraternal bodies in that a belief in God is a necessary qualification for admission, and great emphasis is placed upon members' maintaining the highest moral standards and constantly endeavoring to improve themselves spiritually. Despite the fact that *individuals* may be of varying religious faiths, the Masons *unite* men in brotherhood and the universalism of one God by means of their charitable and service work in the community.

HISTORY

The Society of Free and Accepted Masons was founded in the seventeenth century in England. The founders were "gentlemen," not laborers such as stone cutters or carvers, as is commonly believed. These men formed clubs called lodges, not only for social purposes, but to discuss and advance their knowledge in the liberal arts and in science, which was in its infancy at that time.

The union of the local lodges was made in 1717, when four London lodges formed the first "Grand Lodge." Grand Lodges were subsequently formed in Scotland and Ireland, and Freemasonry quickly spread from the British Isles throughout the world. Freemasonry is now the largest fraternity in the world, with over 4 million members, 3 million in the United States. The Eastern Star, composed of female relatives of Masons, is the world's largest women's fraternity. Many prominent figures in history were Masons, including George Washington, John Hancock, Benjamin Franklin, John Paul Jones, Charles Lindbergh, Henry Ford, Rudyard Kipling, David Crockett, and Norman Vincent Peale. Many English kings and thirteen U.S. Presidents have been Masons, including, recently, Truman and Ford.

It should be noted that there are numerous texts suggesting an association between Freemasons and the masons who built the cathedrals of Europe, and even the pyramids of Egypt, and implying that the teachings are occult. While ancient masons may have had occult or esoteric knowledge, the organization of Freemasonry is *not* associated with those masons or any such knowledge. Also, the architectural symbols of Masonry, such as the compass and square, are merely used to explain the principles of building a strong moral foundation for the temple for the soul.

Currently, there are about 4 million members in the world, mostly in the United States and other English-speaking countries.

BELIEF SYSTEM

The seventeenth-century founders of Freemasonry, having formed their lodges in imitation of actual operative lodges of masons, decided that they would illustrate the teachings of Freemasonry by the use of the working tools of the operative mason. An example: "The Plumb is an instrument made use of by operative Masons to try perpendicular; the Square, to square their work; and the Level, to provide horizontals; but we, as Free and Accepted Masons, are taught to make use of them for more noble and glorious purposes. The Plumb admonishes us to walk uprightly in our several stations before God and man, squaring our actions by the Square of virtue, and ever remembering that we are traveling upon the Level of time to 'that undiscovered country from whose bourn [kingdom] no traveler returns.'"

Many of the activities conducted by Masons focus on charitable causes, such as support of youth organizations, public schools, and hospitals. Masons emphasize service to the community, and do not as a whole speculate on religious philosophy; rather, they build in flexibility for all members to accept their faith according to their individual consciences.

RITUALS AND HOLY DAYS

Masons advance in what are called "degrees" within the fraternity. In one degree, for example, a candidate learns the first principle tenet of Freemasonry, which is brotherly love. A candidate for membership is asked to memorize the following: "By the exercise of Brotherly Love, we are taught to regard the whole human species as one family, the high and the low, the rich and the poor, who, as created by one Almighty Parent, and inhabitants of the same planet, are to aid, support and protect each other. On this principle Masonry unites men of every country, sect, and opinion; and causes true friendship to exist among those who might otherwise have remained at a perpetual distance."

In the United States, meetings are opened by repeating the Pledge of Allegiance to the Flag, which was written by a Mason, and reciting a nondenominational prayer. The rituals, however, are private, and explanations for the various rites are provided only as the members progress in degrees of understanding and service.

FOR ADDITIONAL INFORMATION
Recommended Contacts

The Grand Lodge of Free and Accepted Masons of Virginia
4115 Nine Mile Road
Richmond, VA 23223-4926
Phone: (804) 222-3110
E-mail: www.glva@web-span.com

The Most Worshipful Grand Lodge of Free and Accepted Masons of California
1111 California Street
San Francisco, CA 94108

Recommended Readings

MacNulty, W. Kirk. *Freemasonry: A Journey Through Ritual and Symbol*. Thames and Hudson, 1991.

Roberts, Allen E. *The Craft and Its Symbols*. MacOy Publishers, 1985.

Robinson, John J. *Born in Blood: The Lost Secrets of Freemasonry*. New York: M. Evans and Company, 1990.

Wilmhurst, W. L. *The Meaning of Masonry*. Bell Publishing Co., 1996.

Recommended Websites

Internet Lodge
www.internetlodge.org.uk

Masonic Services
www.msana.com

THE ANCIENT AND MYSTICAL ORDER ROSAE CRUCIS

The Ancient and Mystical Order Rosae Crucis, or AMORC, is a fraternity of men and women who strive to attain knowledge of the higher truths through the study of preserved ancient teachings.

HISTORY

The AMORC traditionally traces its lineage to the mystery schools of ancient Egypt. These mystery schools are said to have begun as early as 5000 B.C.; however, the first known pharaoh to conduct private classes on the arcane arts and sciences was Ahmose I (1580–1557 B.C.). Thutmose III (1500–1447 B.C.) is credited with the organization of the first secret brotherhood for the preservation and dissemination of these teachings. This brotherhood has come to be called the Illuminati. It was Amenhotep IV, also called Akhnaten (1378–1350 B.C.) who introduced the rose and the cross as the symbols of that brotherhood. Also, it was Akhnaten who is traditionally credited with the construction of a cross-shaped Illuminati temple at the city of al-Amarna in Egypt. During the centuries that followed, this brotherhood—sometimes called the Great White Brotherhood—achieved a reputation as a center of knowledge for arcane teachings of higher truth. Seekers came from throughout the world to become initiates of the brotherhood, study its teachings, and disseminate its wisdom.

Many great teachers are said to have been members of this early Rosicrucian brotherhood: Hermes Trismegistus (1399–1257 B.C.); Solomon, who came to the temple at al-Amarna around 1000 B.C.; Pythagoras, who entered the Illuminati in 529 B.C.; as well as the Greek philosophers Democritus, Socrates, Plato, and Aristotle. The biblical Moses is said to have been a High Priest of this brotherhood. As these Rosicrucian workers carried their knowledge into other lands, they became known as the Essenes in Palestine, and as the Therapeuti in

Greece. It is said that Jesus the Christ was a Master, and that his disciples were high officers of this Great White Brotherhood.

It was during the pre-Christian era that the Rosicrucian Order entered a period of active (visible) and inactive (invisible) cycles of 108 years. Some of the periods of important revival include the reign of Charlemagne, around A.D. 778; early seventeenth-century Germany, where the invention of the printing press rapidly accelerated the dissemination of Rosicrucian teachings; and, most recently, the 1915 establishment of the AMORC in the United States of America by Harvey Spencer Lewis (1883–1939).

Lewis was a writer, artist, and student of the occult who lived in New York City around the turn of the century. He formed the New York Institute for Psychical Research, an interest group for investigation of the occult. A few years later, in 1908, he met Mrs. May Banks-Stacy, a member of the Rosicrucian Order, who introduced him to the organization. The following year, he traveled to Europe, where he was initiated and granted authority to found groups in America. AMORC, founded in 1915, immediately gained a wide circle of adherents. After several moves around the nation, the order settled in San Jose, California. In the 1930s, Lewis developed a headquarters complex that included a university, a planetarium, a research library, and the famous Egyptian Museum. Currently, the Rosicrucian Order is represented by thousands of members throughout the world; it publishes two magazines and numerous texts and monographs for its members.

BELIEF SYSTEM

As the Rosicrucian Order is not a religion, it does not exclude the adherents to any religious belief from its brotherhood. The Order seeks to guide you to a greater understanding of your own being and a recognition of your purpose of earthly existence. Through personal experiences, you learn of the invisible cosmic influences that can be utilized to shape life through the attainment of higher levels of consciousness. The lessons, or monographs, can be received by mail and studied in the privacy of your home. Simple experiments are also provided to allow you to demonstrate the principles studied. The underlying belief is that you have certain lessons to learn here on Earth, and as you do learn those lessons, you evolve yourself to your highest potential, eventually fulfilling your life's purpose.

RITUALS AND HOLY DAYS

It is said that the rituals of the Rosicrucian Order are modeled on those of the ancient Egyptians. Rituals are conducted in private, and devotees are committed to secrecy.

FOR ADDITIONAL INFORMATION

Recommended Contact

The Rosicrucian Order, AMORC
1342 Naglee Avenue
San Jose, CA 95191
Phone: (800) 882–6672
Website: www.rosicrucian.org
www.amorc.org

Recommended Readings

Lewis, H. Spencer. *Rosicrucian Questions and Answers with a Complete History*. San Jose, CA: Supreme Grand Lodge of AMORC, 1969.

Lewis, H. Spencer. *Rosicrucian Manual*. San Jose, CA: Rosicrucian Press, 1938.

ROSICRUCIAN FELLOWSHIP

The Rosicrucian Fellowship is an international association of Christian mystics. Despite the similarity in symbol and name, the Rosicrucian Fellowship should *not* be confused with the Ancient and Mystical Order Rosae Crucis. There is, in fact, no connection whatsoever between the two organizations.

HISTORY

According to Rosicrucian legend, a high spiritual teacher with the symbolic name of Christian Rosenkreuz appeared in Europe in the fifteenth century, charged, he claimed, with explaining the mysteries of the cross. Born in 1378 in Germany, he took an interest in the occult at a young age and traveled to Syria, Egypt, and Morocco, where he sought out spiritual masters. Returning to Germany, he began the Rosicrucian Order with three monks from the cloister in which he had been raised. He died at the age of 106 and was buried in the Spiritus Sanctum, the monastery he and his followers had built.

Among modern Rosicrucians, there is a variety of opinions regarding the Rosenkreutz legend. Some believe he did actually exist, as the legend claims. Others believe his name is a pseudonym for some other historic person, such as Sir Francis Bacon (1561–1626). Still others believe the legends to be parables, symbolic tales that signify more profound truths. According to researcher J. Gordon Melton, research seems to indicate the idea of the Rosicrucian Order originated with a German Lutheran pastor named Johann Valentin Andrae (1586–1654). He envisioned a society for the reformation of social life, created the legend of Rosenkreutz, and published the documents describing the philosophy—and he acted alone. Naturally, some see the whole thing as a hoax, but most believe that Andrae formed the society combining his interests in mysticism, the occult, and the reformation of society, which the published documents promoted.

The response to the documents was rapid and dramatic, as Rosicrucian societies arose. Suddenly, the twin symbols of the cross and the rose—which seem to have been taken from Andrae's coat of arms—became popular across Europe. For example, in England, it was championed by Robert Fludd (1574–1637) and Michael Maier (1588–1622), and in Germany, it found exponents in Johann Jacob Zimmerman and his disciple, Johannes Kelpius (1673–1708), who brought the society to the United States in 1694.

Rosicrucianism almost disappeared in the eighteenth century, but it was a major component of the revival of the occult in the next century. Oddly enough, it emerged out of Masonry when, in 1866, Robert Wentworth Little (1840–1878) formed a society open only to Masons. Other branches were soon formed in Scotland and France, and the order was on the rise again.

The founder of the Rosicrucian Fellowship in the United States is Max Heindel (1865–1919). Born Carl Louis Von Grasshoff, in Denmark, he emigrated to America around the turn of the century. An engineer by profession, he also studied the occult and metaphysics, searching for spiritual knowledge. In 1907, on a trip to Germany, there appeared to him several times one of the "Elder Brothers of the Rosicrucian Order," as he described his visitor. Then he was sent to work with a master teacher, probably Rudolf Steiner, founder of the Anthroposophical Society.

Returning to the United States, he put in writing all that he had been taught and published it under the title of *The Rosicrucian Cosmo-Conception* (1909), which is today the main text of the Rosicrucian teachings. About the same time, the first Rosicrucian center was founded in Columbus, Ohio, but the organization moved to California the following year. Heindel, recuperating in a hospital from a cardiac condition, had a vision of the future center in Mt. Ecclesia in Oceanside, California, and indeed, it became so. It remains the organization's headquarters to this day.

Upon Heindel's death, he was succeeded by his wife, Augusta Foss Heindel, a well-known occultist in her own right, who carried on his work. The Rosicrucian Fellowship has grown into an international body, disseminating the Western Wisdom Teachings around the world and preparing the people for the New Age of Aquarius.

BELIEF SYSTEM

The Rosicrucian philosophy is Christian, as taught through the medium of occult or esoteric knowledge. The teachings provide accounts of the nature of the visible world and of the invisible worlds, the evolution of man, the nature of soul and of the spirit. The divine essence of the spirit, the past, present, and future evolution of man, and the applications of the laws of Nature—for example, the Law of Consequence and the Law of Rebirth—are the focus of the Western Wisdom Teaching. These beliefs are supported by reason and logic, as well as the personal experiences of the believer. The purpose of presenting the Rosicrucian philosophy is to:

- Explain the hidden sides of life, so that, by knowing what forces are at work within himself, man can make the best of his present faculties;

- Teach the purpose of evolution. This enables man to work in harmony with the plan of God and develop still unrecognized possibilities;

- Show why service to others is the most direct path to spiritual enlightenment.

The Rosicrucian Fellowship spreads the Western Wisdom Teachings mainly through correspondence courses of philosophy, biblical studies, astrology, and the occult, thus enabling people to understand and to accept the Christian religion through the medium of occult or esoteric knowledge. The Rosicrucian Fellowship is also involved in spiritual healing and spiritual astrology.

RITUALS AND HOLY DAYS

Daily services are performed, and a Sunday service is held at the Rosicrucian Fellowship headquarters in Oceanside, California. The services are similar to those of other Christian churches, but the sermons are much more esoteric and metaphysical.

FOR ADDITIONAL INFORMATION

Recommended Contact

The Rosicrucian Fellowship
P.O. Box 713
2222 Mission Avenue
Oceanside, CA 92054
Phone: (619) 757–6600
Website: www.cts.com/browse/rosfshp/index.html

Recommended Readings

Heindel, Max. *The Rosicrucian Mysteries*. Oceanside, CA: Rosicrucian Fellowship, 1929.

Heindel, Max. *The Rosicrucian Cosmo-Conception*. Oceanside, CA: Rosicrucian Fellowship, 1909.

BUILDERS OF THE ADYTUM

The Builders of the Adytum, or BOTA, is a Western mystery school whose teachings are based on the Holy Kabbalah and the Sacred Tarot.

HISTORY

BOTA was founded in 1922 by Dr. Paul Foster Case for the study of practical occultism. As a recognized world authority on the Tarot and Kabbalah, Dr. Case was given the task by the "Inner School" of reinterpreting the Ageless Wisdom into terms understandable to the modern Western mind. According to Case, the "Inner School" has no corporeal reality in this physical world, but exists in the realm of psychic awareness with which he was able to communicate.

Dr. Case had studied the Holy Kabbalah present in the Mystery Wisdom Teachings of ancient Israel. The great prophets of the Bible, including Jesus of Nazareth, were versed in the Kabbalah and recognized it as their source of spiritual training. The Kabbalah is based on a diagrammatical and symbolic glyph called the Tree of Life. It is a pictorial-symbolic representation of the One God, and man's relationship to that God and to creation. The Tarot is a pictorial textbook on Ageless Wisdom.

BELIEF SYSTEM

The primary purpose of BOTA is to teach and practice the doctrine of the Oneness of God, the brotherhood of man, and the kinship of all life. The beliefs are patterned after the Ageless Wisdom mystery schools of spiritual training, as particularly exemplified by the Kabbalah. The major objective of BOTA is to promote the welfare of humanity, which is embodied in their seven-point program: (1) universal peace, (2) universal political freedom, (3) universal religious freedom, (4) universal education, (5) universal health, (6) universal prosperity, (7) universal spiritual revelation.

Dedicated work with the tarot techniques, as embodied in the BOTA curriculum, transmutes personality. A transformed personality will bring the ability to change the environment, bringing it ever closer to the heart's desire. A fulfilled life becomes a positive radiating center, an effective channel through which the Higher Self can function; it also serves as a living example for others.

RITUALS AND PRACTICES

The reading of the Sacred Tarot serves as the ritual that invokes the spirit, provides the message, and cultivates the brotherhood of the member.

FOR ADDITIONAL INFORMATION

Recommended Contact

BOTA offers courses in the Kabbalah and the Sacred Tarot, and correspondence courses are also available. For information, contact:

Builders of the Adytum, Limited
5105 North Figueroa Street
Los Angeles, CA 90042
Phone: (213) 255–7141
Website: www.atanda.com/bota

Recommended Readings

Case, Paul Foster. *The Book of Tokens*. Los Angeles: Builders of Adytum, 1974.

Case, Paul Foster. *The Tarot: A Key to Wisdom of the Ages*. Los Angeles: Builders of Adytum, 1974.

SHAMANISM

The word *shaman* is derived from the Tungusic language of Siberia, and refers to the mystical practices associated with spiritual guides and healers of central Asia, where it probably originated. At that point, it embraced a belief that powerful spirits existing in animals or natural phenomena could be influenced by the shaman. This person, known as the witch doctor, tribal priest, or physician, used spells, symbolism, incantations, and other primitive rituals to commune with the spirit world and shape the fortunes of man.

However, today Shamanism is used more generally to refer to those native or indigenous people from all parts of the world who call upon spirits, forces of nature, and altered states to confer spiritual insight or communion with higher planes of consciousness, with spirit realms, or with God directly. In order to induce altered states of consciousness, shamanistic practitioners may chant, dance, pray, and use incantations. They may also ingest hallucinogenic plants, such as opium, coca (from which cocaine is made), peyote cactus, jimsonweed (datura), psilocybin mushrooms, marijuana, or even wild tobacco. It is common for shamans to have "out-of-body" experiences, see astral projections, and enter lucid dream states in order to gather the information they need.

Quite often, spirits are called upon for help and guidance. These spirits could come from other worlds, from heaven or the underworld, from deceased relatives still existing on the Earth, from spirits of animals or plants, and from spirits alive within other people.

In this section, we will examine four shamanistic traditions. First, we will discuss the Native American peoples and their beliefs about Mother Earth and the human's connection to her. Second, we will delve into the Hawaiian tradition, called Huna. Third, we will explore the strange world of voodoo, and finally, we will take up Rastafariansim, a Jamaican sect. Each tradition calls upon the role of the shaman in some way.

The shaman's role is to help, heal, and guide the community in which he or she lives. The shaman generally sees life on this planet as only one aspect of a greater existence that serves God in a typically mysterious and unfathomable way.

FOR ADDITIONAL INFORMATION

Travel abroad and make the effort to investigate those traditions which interest you. Visit tribes far removed from industrialized society and spend time with the elders to learn their ways. You really won't get it from a book. Also, see "Native American Traditions" on page 238, "Huna" on page 242, "Voodoo" on page 244, and "Rastafarianism" on page 247.

Recommended Readings

Included here are a series of books that may provide some insight from a wide variety of shamanistic traditions:

Berndt, R. M. *The Australian Aboriginal Religion.* Brill Academic, 1997.

Campbell, Joseph. *The Power of Myth.* New York: Anchor Books, 1991.

Castaneda, Carlos. *The Teachings of Don Juan: A Yaqui Way of Knowledge.* New York: Pocket Books, 1974.

Eliade, Mircea. *Shamanism: Archaic Techniques of Ecstasy.* Princeton, NJ: Princeton University Press, 1972.

Kharitid, Olga. *Entering the Circle: A Russian Psychiatrist's Journey Into Siberian Shamanism.* Gloria Publishers, 1995.

McKenna, Terence. *Food of the Gods: The Search for the Original Tree of Knowledge.* New York: Bantam Doubleday Dell, 1993.

Some, Malidoma Patrice. *Of Water and the Spirit: Ritual, Magic, and Initiation in the Life of an African Shaman.* New York: Penguin USA, 1995.

Tedlock, Dennis, trans. *Popol Vuh: The Mayan Book of the Dawn of Life.* New York: Touchstone Books, 1996.

NATIVE AMERICAN TRADITIONS

Native American traditions refer to the numerous and diverse spiritual cultures of the original Native Americans and their descendants.

HISTORY

About eleven thousand years ago, during the last glacial period, our North American ancestors came from Siberia by way of a land bridge across the Bering Strait. From there, they spread east and south, populating the Americas, even to what is now Cape Horn.

At the time of westward migration by Europeans, there were already over a million Native Americans in North America. European subjugation of the Native Americans decimated their numbers, integrated them into the European culture, and converted the majority to Christianity.

On the North American continent today, there are over 250 distinct tribal languages. Tribes range from small local communities to large federations covering whole regions. During the later part of the twentieth century, both Native Americans and others have developed a growing interest in Native American culture and spiritual beliefs.

BELIEF SYSTEMS

One general commonality among Native American theology is in the nature of spirit. Native Americans believe the Great Spirit created all existence, inhabits that existence, and directs its development. They place great emphasis on soliciting advice from and following the examples of deceased ancestors, whose spirits still live in this world. They seek the guiding influence of natural spirits through human intervention (a shaman, or medicine man), as well as through animals, plants, and inanimate objects (talismans).

Native Americans place a great emphasis on living in concert with nature, and live very close to the land and all of its inhabitants. They see the Earth (generally) as a living Being, and animals as their brothers and sisters. Generally speaking, they perceive God as a Great Spirit associated with the heavens, and the Earth as the Mother of creation. North American mythology is full of heroes who initiated the laws, culture, and traditions that the Native Americans follow. Humans are viewed as being only one part of the greater workings of nature; they serve as part of a Divine ecology and order on the planet. Most tribes believe that each human has a spirit that lives beyond the physical life, in another realm or dimension that is not completely separate from our physical existence.

Humans, both individually and collectively, abide here on Mother Earth to learn to live within the greater workings of the whole of creation.

RITUALS AND HOLY DAYS

Within Native American traditions, each person serves a different role in the scheme of things. You may be a medicine man, diviner, hunter, leader, or ritual dancer. In the latter role, you might sometimes take on the character of a spirit, or you might commune with the spirit of a deceased relative, animal, plant, or angelic being. Often, the medicine man (or woman) will enter into ecstatic states of consciousness in order to make contact with the spirit world, and may even visit with spirits in their heavenly abode. The medicine man, or Shaman, may also play the role of "psychopomp," escorting the deceased soul to the domain of the dead.

In the Native American context, religion is not a separate identifiable entity within a larger culture, but an integral part of daily living and societal interaction. Rituals and observances vary with the regional ecology; some tribes emphasize the planting, growing, and harvesting of crops, while others focus on hunting and gathering.

In agricultural tribes, prayer and alms are given to the planting and harvesting of crops, whereas in hunting and gathering tribes, the rituals involve paying tribute to the animals they hunt and the foliage they gather. Special rituals may include observances to the deities or spirits that have influence over the sun, rain, and crops.

In some tribes, hallucinogenic plants, such as peyote, mushrooms, or wild tobacco, are smoked or eaten to invoke divine visions or communion with the spirit world. Special rites may also be performed when a child reaches puberty, or adulthood. Sometimes the seasons are observed, and other special occasions, such as marriages, births, and deaths, are noted with appropriate ceremonies.

Rituals typically include dancing and chanting or singing, accompanied by bright costumes and the beating of drums and feet. Feasts and smoking may also be integral forms of ritual. On special occasions, a "medicine wheel" may be constructed in order to create the power to connect human beings to the infinite. At a medicine wheel gathering, special stones are placed in various configurations within a circle, and a "peace pipe" is passed around—after being offered to the spirits of the four directions—to foster solidarity among the participants, which may include members of other tribes.

One of the most demanding disciplines performed is the "vision quest." During such a ritual, the participant goes off into the wilderness by himself or herself for several days; typically without eating. During this time, the trekker severs all worldly attachments, and calls upon God to show a sign for direction and guidance—which often takes the form of a vision. Thus, the successful quest provides the insight, direction, or answer the seeker is after, and may serve as a rite of passage.

Another common Native American practice is purification in a "sweat lodge." This practice begins when "stone people"—spirits of the mineral kingdom located within stones—are scouted out at special times, and then heated up in a ceremonial fire. At the appropriate time, you are "smudged," or covered with smoke from a sacrificial fire. You then pay your respects to your relatives and guiding spirits, and enter the sweat lodge—usually a dome-like structure covered with skins or blankets. Once you and the others are seated, the heated "stone people" are brought in and placed in a pit in the middle of the lodge; the openings are closed to keep the heat in. While the intensity increases and you sweat from the heat of the stone people, you and the others take turns letting go of those feelings that have been troublesome. In the sweat lodge, you pray to the spirits and ask for guidance; you pray to purge yourself of negative feelings, and to prepare yourself for changes in your life. You emerge from the experience refreshed and exhibiting a new sense of direction, a new harmony with nature.

Native Americans generally believe that we are here to learn to live in peace with our Creator, with our universe, and with each other.

FOR ADDITIONAL INFORMATION

Look up a tribal group or representative in your area. The Bureau of Indian Affairs—listed under "Federal Government" in the blue pages of your telephone book—may be able to direct you. You may also look under the "Native American Church," mostly in southwestern states, for additional information.

Recommended Contacts

The following resources should prove helpful:

The Bear Tribe	The Deer Tribe
P.O. Box 9167	P.O. Box 1519
Spokane, WA 99209	Temple City, CA 91780
Phone: (509) 326–6561	Phone: (818) 285–9062
	Website: www.dtmms.org

Recommended Readings

Barrett, S. M., ed. *Geronimo, His Own Story*. New York: Plenum, 1996.

Black Elk, Wallace. *The Sacred Ways of a Lakota*. San Francisco: Harper, 1991.

Erdoes, M., and C. Ortiz. *American Indian Myths & Legends*. New York: Pantheon Books, 1985.

Harrod, Howard L. *Becoming and Remaining a People: Native American Religions on the Northern Plains*. Phoenix, AZ: University of Arizona Press, 1995.

Hirschfeldere, Arlene B., ed. *The Encyclopedia of Native American Religions*. New York: Facts on File, Inc., 1992.

Neihardt, John G. *Black Elk Speaks*. Lincoln, NE: University of Nebraska Press, 1988.

Sun Bear, Wabun, and Barry Weinstock. *The Path of Power*. New York: Prentice-Hall, 1992.

Recommended Websites

Native American and First Nation Resources
www.geocities.com/Paris/9840/na.htm

Native American Church
www.nativeauthors.com
ionet.net/hochunk/nacnal.html

Native American Sites
www.pitt.edu/lmitten/indians.html

HUNA

Huna is a Hawaiian spiritual tradition, part of a Polynesian heritage. The word *huna* means *that which is hidden*, or *not obvious*. A related word, *kahuna*, designates the Hawaiian shaman, or, in the Polynesian language, *the transmitter of the secrets*.

HISTORY

Huna is not a religion, but rather an esoteric philosophy and science that has been passed on through Hawaiian family lineages for some three to five thousand years, or more. The Huna teachings were an integral part of Hawaiian culture until the first Christian missionaries came to Hawaii in 1820. These missionaries rapidly began altering the culture and customs of the Hawaiian people and eventually outlawed the practice of Huna in Hawaii. Due to this alienation from their culture and condemnation by the Christians, the kahunas became reclusive. They did not reveal themselves to any *haoles*, or white people, and their teachings remained a mystery to the uninitiated. However, these days, Huna can be practiced more openly, and several kahunas have opened up to share their philosophy with others. The Huna practice is now gaining in popularity, particularly on the West Coast and in Hawaii.

BELIEF SYSTEM

Huna is not a philosophy that can be easily understood by reading about it. It is an interactive system between an individual and the environment. In Huna, everything is interrelated. In the Huna teachings, God is everything, and everything is of God. Moreover, all things have a higher spiritual nature called *aumakua* or *akuas*, and the personal god or god-self is not limited to mankind but is innate in all creation. The spiritual and material worlds are creations resulting from the interplay between male and female aspects of God. Kane is the principal male god, expressing the masculine (expansive) forces of nature, and Wahine is the primary female god, expressing the feminine (contractive) forces of existence. This dual nature of the god-self lies within all creation, and it is the interaction of these energies that creates our existence.

The teachings of the kahunas have historically been passed on by word of mouth. The only historical writing of Huna is found in the ancient creation chant called the "Kumulipo."

The practice of Huna involves looking within all that you perceive; there is a being within a being, and a universe within a universe, and the center of the universe lies within you. This awareness develops as you observe the natural rhythms working within you and around you, interconnected to you. Huna is the practice of attuning to the energies around you, and working in concert with those energies. One of the principal energies utilized by the kahunas is that of *Aloha*, or complete unconditional love. The practice of Huna involves expressing the Aloha Spirit in yourself, as well as bringing it out in others and in all things.

Kahunas have a reputation for being very psychic. They practice telepathy and mind reading, are clairvoyant, and have the ability to leave the physical body and return at will. Several kahunas are even said to be able to raise the dead. However, kahunas typically do not give public demonstrations of their abilities; rather, they concentrate on helping others learn about the nature of self, and assisting them to live in harmony with their surroundings. Some kahunas focus on certain areas, such as intuitive navigation or healing. In Hawaii, they are often consulted before you launch a ship for the first time, build a house or holy site, or make a major decision in your personal life.

The kahuna sees you and other humans as instruments of the spirit. You are here to serve this spirit and bring it into your daily life. This achieves greater happiness and peace within you and those around you.

FOR ADDITIONAL INFORMATION

Recommended Contacts

Aloha International
P.O. Box 665
Kilauea, HI 96754
Phone: (808) 828–0302
Website: www.huna.org

Hawaiian Church of Life
P.O. Box 4878
Hilo, HI 96720

Recommended Readings

Hoffman, Enid. *Huna: A Beginner's Guide*. Atglen, PA: Schiffer Publishing, 1997.

King, Serge. *Urban Shaman*. New York: Simon and Schuster, 1990.

King, Serge. *Mastering Your Hidden Self: A Guide to the Huna Way*. Theosophical Publishing House, 1985.

Recommended Websites

Kahunas
www.hooponopono.org
www.lava.net/kaha/hahu.htm

VOODOO

Voodoo is a polytheistic religion practiced chiefly in the West Indies. It is derived from various cult worship in West Africa and borrows from Roman Catholicism, as well. The word *voodoo* probably comes from the Creole French *voudou*, or from the West African *vodu*, meaning *introspection into the unknown*, and the religion is based upon experiences in the spirit realms.

HISTORY

As a result of the slave trade that flourished during the eighteenth and early nineteenth centuries, native tribal religions of the black Africans from, primarily, the western coast of Africa, were introduced to the New World and integrated into Christian culture. Of the some 15 million slaves who were seized from West Africa during that terrible period, approximately half were taken to South America, 42 percent were brought to the Caribbean Islands, and the others were sold in North America. As the slaves integrated into the Christian, and primarily Roman Catholic, cultures in the Caribbean and in Central and South America, tribal ritual and spiritual practices were commingled with Catholicism and modified to suit the new culture.

The most prominent of these religions is voodoo, or voudoun, which comes mainly from Haiti in the West Indies, but which has spread throughout the Caribbean and parts of the Americas. Similar religious practices are known as Macoumaba (Macumba) in Brazil, and Santeria (or Lucumi) in Cuba. Other Neo-African religions are smaller and tend to remain within their respective communities. Typically, these religions are practiced discreetly, due to religious prejudices and racism; however, during the early part of the twentieth century there was a proliferation of various "voodoo" sects, and today the religion is practiced a little more freely.

BELIEF SYSTEM

Voodoo and the other Neo-African religions are based on the premise that the material body houses an *esprit*—a soul or spirit—which is eternal. Moreover, the soul is able to achieve divinity, and can become the "archetypal representative" of some natural or moral principal.

There is a whole spectrum of loa, or gods, that represent different aspects of existence. These loa are known by different names in different tribes, but generally have the same attributes. Voodoo originated in the mystical city of Ife, a replica of which exists in Yoruba in southern Nigeria, from which the revelation or spirit descends through the form of double serpents Danbhalah Wedo and Aida Wedo. These spirits represent the male and female aspects of divinity, which are also represented by Legba (male/Sun) and Erzulie (female/lunar).

RITUALS AND HOLY DAYS

Voodoo ritual is practiced by the houn'gan and mam'bo, male and female priests, who can summon the loa, or *mysteres*, into a special pottery jar called a *govi*, or may be incarnated into the physical world by *mounting* or taking possession of another's body. The various loa perform different functions in ritual, such as providing protection, conferring various powers, curing illnesses, and punishing the guilty. Rituals are typically performed in the *peristyle*, or courtyard, or the *oum'phor*, or temple. In the center of the peristyle lies the *poteau-mitan*, a center post around which the ceremonies revolve. The top of the poteau-mitan represents the sky or heavens, and the bottom, the center of hell.

Rituals typically involve the use of music, incorporating the beating of rada, pethro, or conga drums, chanting and singing, and dancing. They might also involve prayers, feasts, sacrifices of cattle or other animals, and possession by loa, or *mysteres*, in French. Other spiritual services performed by the houn'gan or mam'bo include divination, healing, and exorcisms. Additional unique features of Neo-African religions would include ritual floor paintings, or *veves*, and a variety of objects, such as ceremonial dishes, pitchers, bottles, flags, and *asson*—calabash rattle, which is a symbol of office.

Generally, in voodoo, we are here both to serve spirit as well as to be served by spirit. Human existence is just one level of the manifestation of spirit, and as we evolve, we ascend to higher levels. Many sects of voodoo are heavily influenced by Christian ideology and ascribe to the notion of salvation through Jesus Christ, and ascension into heaven after death.

FOR ADDITIONAL INFORMATION

Recommended Contacts

African Theological Archministry
C/o Oyotunji African Yoruba
   Village
P.O. Box 51
Sheldon, SC 29941
Phone: (843) 522–9393

Church of Lukumi Babalu Aye
345 Palm Avenue
Hialeah, FL
Phone: (305) 887–1901
Website:
   www.home.earthlink.net/clba
E-mail: clba@earthlink.net

Church of the Seven African
   Powers
P.O. Box 453336
Miami, FL 33245

Monastery of the Seven Rays
P.O. Box 1554
Chicago, IL 60690–1554

Orisha Net
4748 University Way, NE
Seattle, WA 98105
Phone: (206) 729–1000
Website: www.seanet.com/
   efunmoy/wa/ochanet.html

Recommended Readings

Deren, Maya. *Divine Horsemen, the Living Gods of Haiti*. McPherson and Company, 1985.

Haskins, Jim. *Voodoo and Hoodoo: Their Tradition and Craft as Revealed by Actual Practitioners*. Scarborough House, 1990.

Karade, Baba Ira. *The Handbook of Yoruba Religious Concepts*. York Beach, ME: Samuel Weiser, 1994.

Murphy, Joseph M. *Santeria: African Spirits in America*. Boston: Beacon Press, 1993.

Rigaud, Milo. *Secrets of Voodoo*. San Francisco: City Lights Books, 1985.

Recommended Websites

African Ritual Sites
www.asheonline.com
www.members.tripod.com

RASTAFARIANISM

Rastafarians are part of a messianic movement originating in Jamaica. They worship the god Jah, and believe that Haile Selassie, the emperor of Ethiopia, is the Messiah of the black race. Ras Tafari, the great-grandson of King Saheka Selassie of Shoa, was crowned negus of Ethiopia and took on the name of Haile Selassie (Might of the Trinity). *Jah* is an abbreviation of *Jehovah*, who is the god of the black races from Egypt and Ethiopia, as well as other religions.

HISTORY

The Rastafarian movement has its origins with the slave trade and the repression of the black people in Jamaica by the white ruling class. Years of socioeconomic struggle and a lack of religious identity of the black majority fostered the rebellious Back-to-Africa Movement, which was started by a black Jamaican named Marcus Garvey in the early 1900s. This movement spurred sentiments of black supremacy, and called for the abolition of white dominance.

The ideology gained a spiritual connotation and fervor with the crowning of Haile Selassie as emperor of Ethiopia in 1930, as it was seen as a revelation of God and fulfillment of the biblical prophecy in Psalm 68: "Princes shall come out of Egypt; and Ethiopia shall soon stretch out her hands unto God."

The redemption of Africa by the Messiah of Africa, Haile Selassie (Ras Tafari), spurred several members of the Back-to-Africa Movement to consolidate the members under the name of Rastafarians. Four members in particular—Leonard Howell, Joseph Hibbert, Archibald Dunkley, and Robert Hinds—played major roles in driving the movement.

As heads of rebellious and militant movements, the leaders were at odds with the presiding authorities. By 1953, "Rastas" had begun wearing their hair in long curling locks, now known as "dreadlocks," as a form of group identity, and had formed a commune called "Pinnacle" in the hills twenty miles from Kingston. However, as the Rastafarians had been growing *ganga* (marijuana, an illegal substance in Jamaica) at Pinnacle for ritual purposes, the police raided the commune. In the process, they destroyed the buildings, burned the crops, and arrested many members of the movement. This was certainly a blow to its growth.

Eventually, the movement grew less militant, and the followers became a peaceful, loosely structured, multiracial body. Thus transformed, they find fellowship through the music and a cultural identity known as "reggae." This music, with its Rastafarian themes, first spread throughout the Caribbean nations, and now has spread throughout the rest of the world. Reggae music has become popular with millions of people of every race.

BELIEF SYSTEM

Rastafarians generally believe that Jamaica is Babylon, or Hell, and that Africa, and Ethiopia in particular, is the Promised Land. Moreover, Haile Selassie is the Messiah who will deliver the black race from the oppression of the white race in Jamaica and bring them to live in Ethiopia (or Africa). The Ethiopians, or black race, are the Israelites, who will one day rule over the world as Jah's chosen people. Jah, or Jehovah, is the one supreme God, who is considered black according to several biblical translations, namely, Jeremiah, 8:21, "For the hurt of the daughter of my people am I hurt; I am black; astonishment hath taken hold of me"; and Daniel, 7:9, describing God as one with "hair of his head like pure wool; his throne was like the fiery flame, and his wheels as burning fire" (fire being associated with the black race). Rastafarians generally consider the Bible holy, but believe other faiths have interpreted the scriptures incorrectly.

Most Rastafarians are vegetarians, and don't believe in killing for any reason, although their symbol is the lion. They are identified with wearing the colors red, black, and green.

The vision of the Rastafarians is to create a universal brotherhood, all living together in peace. Having accomplished that, they believe they will ascend to heaven upon death.

RITUALS AND HOLY DAYS

Rastafarian rituals involve prayers, the smoking of ganga, reciting poems, and most often playing or singing reggae music.

The controversial use of the ganga plant, which is smoked for religious experiences, is supported by the following biblical passages: Genesis 1:12, "And the earth brought forth grass, and herb yielding seed after his kind, and the tree yielding fruit, whose seed was in itself, after his kind: and God saw that it was good"; and Psalm 104:14, "He causeth the grass to grow for the cattle, and herb for the service of man."

FOR ADDITIONAL INFORMATION

The best way to learn more about the Rastafarian movement is to listen to their recorded music, or watch a Rasta group perform. Check the calendar section of your newspaper. Or go to Jamaica!

Recommended Readings

Barrett, Leonard. *The Rastafarians*. Boston, MA: Beacon Press, 1997.

Chevannes, Barry. *Rastafari: Roots and Ideology*. Syracuse, NY: Syracuse University Press, 1994.

Hausman, Gerald, ed. *The Kebra Negast: The Book of Rastafarian Wisdom and Faith from Ethiopia and Jamaica*. New York: St. Martin's Press, 1997.

Recommended Listening

Because so much of Rastafarian culture and practice is associated with reggae music, it seems appropriate to recommend the work of the following artists:

Bob Marley

Steel Pulse

Peter Tosh

Third World

PART FOUR

CONTEMPORARY SPIRITUAL TEACHINGS

Something unprecedented in world history is now occurring on this planet: Mankind is evolving its consciousness into a higher awareness of itself in relation to God. On a scale broader than before, people are beginning to take a good look at themselves, searching for meaning and purpose in their lives, and not relying entirely on a prescribed religion, blind faith, or a single sacred text. Individuals are beginning to recognize their own divine nature, and are looking within to find answers and to commune with God. In the search for deeper meaning within and closer communion with God, the traditional churches and spiritual paths have always been available to the seeker, but in recent years, there have been a number of contemporary teachings that have provided alternatives. Many new teachings have evolved to facilitate a greater understanding of truth, self, and God. It is those teachings we will investigate in this section of the book.

We will use the term contemporary to convey the mass change of consciousness occurring on the planet. The term means different things to different people, depending on which vehicle they have used or which organization they have adopted. For example, it may refer to the Aquarian Age, in which mankind is expected to commune with God and live in peace, or it may refer to a variety of attempts to unify science, religion, and philosophy and discover the fundamental essence in all religions.

No one organization is responsible for this movement or transition, but rather various individuals and groups have mobilized to address the needs of individual seekers. Some of these groups are drawing upon arcane teachings from Eastern or Western cultures, while others are adapting traditional theology to more modern modes, in an effort to completely understand their role in the plan of creation. However, the commonality among most contemporary teachings is that they are addressing the human being's innate need to discover, or experience, the Truth for himself or herself. Contemporary teachings are directing the responsibility for self-awareness back to the individual; the power of realization is being acknowledged within mankind. The various forms by which these vehicles express themselves are as wide and divergent as the societies that create them.

As you read about the various spiritual movements, think about what must have occurred to manifest such beliefs and create such a response within our society. Many of these teachings may seem far-fetched—and they may actually be far-fetched—but you must also acknowledge the enormous changes that have occurred in society because of them. Not only have the alternative teachings prompted internal questioning and personal investigation in search of the Truth, but many individuals are living fuller, happier lives due to their greater understanding of themselves. Moreover, many people who had either developed apathy or disillusionment in their spiritual lives are now enthusiastically exploring their spirituality again. More than anything else, the contemporary teachings have been a catalyst for change and renewal.

In this section, we will explore some of the largest and better-known among these contemporary teachings. We begin with theosophy, a belief that attempts to unify the triad of science, religion, and philosophy, to distill the fundamental essence in all religions and unite these findings with science in the mind of the individual. We will examine a number of teachings that all attempt to achieve similar goals but do so in different ways. These would include Religious Science, Unity, Scientology, Mentalphysics, Baha'i, and more. These are teachings both from the West and from the East. Some are more philosophical, others, more mystical, still others, more scientific, but each is based on individual investigation of the meaning of things, the purpose of life, and the role of the individual in that purpose.

We will also delve into the teachings of the Monroe Institute that try to explain unnatural phenomena outside ourselves, and we will look at Alcoholics Anonymous and the many twelve-step programs that try to help their members deal with torments inside themselves through a relationship with God. These groups seek a higher meaning, a higher source of inspiration and strength. In the search for Truth, we will examine the phenomenon of channeling and meet many of its practitioners.

FOR ADDITIONAL INFORMATION

Recommended Contacts

Valuable sources of contemporary information are the Whole Life Expos, which are held around the country. For more information contact:

The Whole Life Expo
c/o Universal Mind
147 Carondelet Street, Suite 1059
New Orleans, LA 70130
Phone: (504) 639–9302
Website: www.universalmind.com

The Whole Life Expo
Phone: (888) 444–3612
Website: www.wholelife.com

Recommended Periodicals

Body Mind Spirit Magazine
P.O. Box 3035
Southeastern, PA 19398-9978
Phone: (401) 351–4320
Website: www.consciousnet.com/
　bmsmag.htm

Common Ground
305 San Anselmo Avenue,
　Suite 313
San Anselmo, CA 94960
Phone: (415) 459–4900
Website: www.comngrnd.com

New Age Journal
P.O. Box 51162
Boulder, CO 80321-1162
Phone: (800) 782–7006
Website: www.newage.com

Personal Transformation
4032 South Lamar Blvd.,
　#500–137
Austin, TX 78704
Phone: (800) 775–6887

The Quest
The Theosophical Society in
　America
P.O. Box 3000
Denville, NJ 07834-3000
Phone: (800) 669–9425

Recommended Website

New Age–Metaphysical: Whole Again Resource Guide
www.wholeagain.com

THEOSOPHY

The word *theosophy* comes from the Greek *theos*, meaning *god*, and *sophia*, meaning *wisdom*. It is generally considered to be a strain of Western mystical philosophy.

HISTORY

Theosophical thought can be traced back to the Greek philosopher, mathemetician, and mystic Pythagoras, through the Renaissance philosopher Paracelsus, to the nineteenth century thinkers Helena Petrovna Blavatsky and Henry Steel Olcott, cofounders of the Theosophical Society in 1875.

Helena P. Blavatsky (1831–1891) was born in Ekaterinoslav, Russia, the daughter of a Russian colonel and a princess. In 1851, she went to London and met the legendary Master Morya (see "The Ascended Masters" on page 266), who began guiding her inner development and work for mankind. She made several trips through Asia and into Tibet to complete her training in occult powers. Henry Steel Olcott (1832–1907) was born in Orange, New Jersey. He was a lawyer, but through his interest in the occult, came under the influence of Madame Blavatsky. In 1875, Blavatsky, Olcott, and W. Q. Judge founded the Theosophical Society in New York, to "collect and diffuse a knowledge of the laws which govern the Universe." At various times, theosophical followers have included Jakob Boehme (see page 202) and Emanuel Swedenborg (see page 206).

In 1878, the founders moved the international headquarters of the Theosophical Society from New York to Adyar, India, where it continues to this day. Theosophy is now studied throughout the world, with centers in many countries, with thousands of members and numerous others who contemplate the doctrines independently.

Blavatsky wrote several books that form the basis for contemporary theosophy, including *Isis Unveiled* (1877) and *The Secret Doctrine* (1888).

BELIEF SYSTEM

Theosophy is the study of the science of God, or "Divine Wisdom." It seeks to "gather the oldest of the tenets together and to make of them one harmonious and unbroken whole." The teachings are not those of any one Eastern or Western religion, but rather the distilled essence of all the world's spiritual teachings. It may be described as "eclectic," in that it draws on many religions, including Brahmanic and Buddhistic teachings.

The "Secret Doctrine" of theosophy is stated as being the synthesis of science, religion, and philosophy. It proposes to explain the fundamental unity in all religions and unite these findings with science. Because of the adherents' belief in the absolute essence of God, they deduce the essential spiritual nature of creation. In that creation, man is finite, subject to temptation but capable of good—so long as he exercises his latent spirituality. This requires discipline, and theosophy draws much of this discipline from Eastern sources.

Believers hope to form the nucleus of the universal brotherhood of man, without distinction of race, creed, sex, caste, or color; to encourage the study of comparative religion, philosophy, and science; and to investigate unexplained laws of nature, as well as to discover the powers latent in man himself.

FOR ADDITIONAL INFORMATION

Recommended Contacts

The Theosophical Society
P.O. Box 270
Wheaton, IL 60189-0270
Phone: (708) 668-1571
Website: www.blavatsky.net
    www.theosociety.org
    www.theosophy.com
    www.theosophy.org
    www.theosophycompany.org
    www.ult.org

Theosophical University Press
P.O. Bin C
Pasadena, CA 91109
Phone: (818) 798-3378

Recommended Readings

Blavatsky, H. P. *Isis Unveiled*. Pasadena, CA: Theosophical University Press, 1994.

Blavatsky, H. P. *The Secret Doctrine*. Pasadena, CA: Theosophical University Press, 1989.

de Purucker, G. Fountain. *Fundamentals of Esoteric Philosophy*. Pasadena, CA: Theosophical University Press, 1979.

RELIGIOUS SCIENCE

Religious Science is a spiritual teaching that attempts to integrate the laws of science, the convictions of philosophy, and the revelations of religion. Once accomplished, this discipline can be applied to the needs and the aspirations of man.

HISTORY

This teaching was founded by Ernest Holmes (1887–1960), who synthesized his personal spiritual studies into the basic text for Religious Science, *The Science of Mind*, first published in 1926.

Holmes started lecturing on his insights in 1916 in Los Angeles. By 1927, he had formed the Institute of Religious Science and School of Philosophy, which became known as the Church of Religious Science in 1954. Later, in 1967, the organization adopted the United Church of Religious Science as its legal name. Religious Science is now represented internationally, and its *Science of Mind* magazine is read by hundreds of thousands.

BELIEF SYSTEM

The teachings of Religious Science emphasize belief in a living, loving God who manifests himself in and through all creation. Adherents believe in the incarnation of the Spirit in man's immortal soul; and profess that each man and woman must become conscious of that Kingdom within. They believe in the direct revelation of truth through the spiritual nature of man; and indeed, that any man may become a revealer of that truth. They accept the healing of the sick through the power of the Spirit, and profess man's control over his own destiny.

As Holmes wrote in an article called "What We Believe," published in the first issue of *Science of Mind*, in October of 1927, "We understand that the life of man is God . . . that the ultimate goal of life [is to achieve] a complete emancipation from all discord of any kind."

FOR ADDITIONAL INFORMATION

Recommended Contact

Look up the local member church in your telephone directory, or contact:

United Church of Religious Science
3251 West 6th Street
P.O. Box 75127
Los Angeles, California 90075
Phone: (213) 388–2181
Website: www.scienceofmind.com
        www.wmop.org
        www.scienceofmind.org

Recommended Readings

Holmes, Ernest. *The Science of Mind.* New York: Putnam, 1998.

Holmes, Ernest. *This Thing Called You.* New York: Putnam, 1998.

Recommended Periodical

Science of Mind Magazine
Science of Mind Communications
P.O. Box 18087
Anaheim, CA 92817-8087
Phone: (800) 247–6463

UNITY

Unity is a religious movement that is both a church and a teaching that crosses denominational lines.

HISTORY

Unity was founded in the 1880s by Charles and Myrtle Fillmore. Both had serious medical problems: Charles had a withered leg and Myrtle had tuberculosis. However, they both claimed to have been cured through the power of prayer. It was after this miracle that they began expressing their new ideas about the purpose of life and the power of prayer. When others saw how the Fillmores had been healed through prayer, they sought out the couple, requesting assistance with their own problems.

The Fillmores had no thought of starting a new religion. However, when others came to them asking questions and looking for help, the Fillmores shared what information they had, and this eventually led to the publication of a magazine. *Modern Thought* was first published in 1889, but was renamed *Unity* a few years later to better reflect the views of its founders. A new religion had begun.

Over the last century, Unity has become an international church, publishing several magazines—including *Unity* and *Daily Word*—which are the main vehicles for spreading its teachings to its estimated three million readers. Unity has over 915 member and satellite ministries and over 60 international ministries. The church has grown almost entirely because individuals who have been helped by its ideas have told others needing help, or, perhaps, donated a subscription to *Daily Word* in their name.

BELIEF SYSTEM

The precepts of Unity are described quite simply in their literature: "One, God is good. Two, God is available; in fact, God is in you. If God is good, God's will is good. It is impossible to believe that a good God— a God who is love and intelligence—could have made you in any other way except to be healthy, happy, prosperous, loved and loving, courageous, and strong. If you are not healthy and happy, it can only be because you have separated yourself in mind from God—the only place you *can* separate yourself from God and God's good. You have only to reunite in mind with God, and your life is certain to be full and fulfilling. You do this best by getting still and realizing your oneness with God."

Unity is the practical application in everyday life of the principles of Truth thought and exemplified by Jesus Christ, as interpreted by Unity School of Christianity. Unity puts great emphasis on the healing power of prayer, and in the individual study and application of principles of Unity.

As Christians, Unitarians accept that through receiving Christ, they are assured greater peace on Earth, and communion with God in heaven.

RITUALS AND PRACTICES

In addition to attendance in Unity churches and independent study, Unity offers a program called Silent Unity. In this program, students are encouraged to join an international Circle of Prayer that begins at 9:00 in the evening. Each session is based on the affirmations presented that day in the *Daily Word* magazine.

FOR ADDITIONAL INFORMATION
Recommended Contact

For more information on Unity look in your phone book under that heading, or contact:

Unity School of Christianity
1901 NW Blue Parkway
Unity Village, MO 64065-0001
Phone: (816) 524-3550

Recommended Readings

Bach, Marcus. *The Unity Way.* Unity Village, MO: Unity Publishers, 1994.

Butterworth, Eric. *Unity: A Quest for Truth.* Unity Village, MO: Unity Publishers, 1978.

Freeman, James Dillet. *The Story of Unity.* Unity Village, MO: Unity Publishers, 1978.

SCIENTOLOGY

The term *scientology* means *knowing how to know*. Scientology, also known as Dianetics, is an applied religious philosophy dealing with the study of scientific knowledge. Its adherents believe that, through the application of its technology, they can raise mankind to a higher level of consciousness and thereby effect desirable changes in the life of man.

HISTORY

Scientology was founded by the prolific writer and philosopher L[afayette] Ron[ald] Hubbard. Born in Tilden, Nebraska, on March 13, 1911, Hubbard attended Woodward Preparatory School and George Washington University. At the age of sixteen, he began to travel extensively, exploring the globe, observing his fellow man, and putting a great deal of his ideas in writing. From the culmination of these observations, he developed a philosophy and science he called Dianetics, which means *through thought of mind*. Hubbard published this new concept of the nature of life and the human mind in 1950 in his book *Dianetics: The Modern Science of Mental Health*, which quickly became a bestseller. In 1951, he released his findings on the spirit of man in his book *Science of Survival*, which contained the foundation of the religion of Scientology.

In 1954, the first Church of Scientology was founded by a zealous group of followers in Los Angeles, and in 1955, Hubbard became the executive director of the Founding Church in Washington. A few years later, he moved his base to East Grinstead, England, but resigned his position in 1966 to devote more of his time to writing and research. He later returned to his first love, science fiction, with the publication of *Battlefield Earth: A Saga of the Year 3000*, followed by the ten-volume *Mission Earth*.

Hubbard died in 1986. In all, he had published over 589 works, delivered over 4,000 lectures, and spread the science of Dianetics to every continent, using the people power of over 600 churches, missions, and other groups.

BELIEF SYSTEM

Scientology evolved from Dianetics. Its aim is for humanity to evolve, individually and collectively as a society, to a higher state of being. The aims of Scientology, according to L. Ron Hubbard, are to create a "civilization without insanity, without criminals, and without war, where the able can prosper and honest beings can have rights, and where Man is free to rise to greater heights." The faith is in man, and the teaching is concerned with how to show man how he can set himself free. The belief is that the route to freedom lies in knowledge, in knowing how to know.

The greater realization in Scientology is to know yourself as "that which is aware of being aware," to know your own identity, to know your own spirit. The purpose of life, then, is to realize your self, and by doing so find greater meaning to your existence.

RITUALS AND PRACTICES

Scientology is practiced in classes that allow the student to realize a greater self. The student would be considered a "preclear," a person whose vision of the world, or of reality, was distorted or out of focus. Thus, much of the work involves "clearing" the "preclear" of unwanted behavior patterns and discomforts. The goal is to become a "clear," an individual who, as a result of Dianetics therapy, has neither active nor potential psychosomatic illness or aberration. Such "clearing" allows the student to come to know his true self, or Thetan.

FOR ADDITIONAL INFORMATION
Recommended Contact

Scientology Information Center
4833 Fountain Avenue
Los Angeles, CA 90029
Phone: 1 (800) FOR-TRUTH
Website: www.scientology.org
           www.lronhubbard.org

Recommended Readings

Hubbard, L. Ron. *What Is Scientology?* Los Angeles, CA: Bridge Publications, 1998.

Hubbard, L. Ron. *Scientology, the Fundamentals of Thought.* Los Angeles, CA: Bridge Publications, 1997.

Hubbard, L. Ron. *Dianetics: The Modern Science of Mental Health.* Los Angeles, CA: Bridge Publications, 1995.

MENTALPHYSICS

The science of Mentalphysics is known in the East as Brahma Vidya. It professes to be a methodology for self-realization.

HISTORY

Brahma Vidya was brought from Tibet to the West by Edwin John Dingle in the early part of the twentieth century. Edwin John Dingle was born in England on April 6, 1881. His mother and father both died while he was young, and he was raised by his paternal grandmother in Cornwall. Edwin was a solitary boy who developed a marvelous imagination. For example, he used to take imaginary trips to Tibet and yearned to travel there. After completing school, Edwin was apprenticed in the printing trade and later became editor of the *Strait Times* of Singapore. In that capacity, Edwin met a sage who recognized his seriousness of purpose. This learned personage instructed him in certain methods and practices for spiritual development, and then encouraged him to make a pilgrimage to Tibet.

When Edwin arrived in western China, he was surprised to find his spiritual masters and brothers waiting for him. He soon began his arduous training in the mysteries of the East. Dingle spent twenty-one years in the Orient, where he built a large publishing company with offices in Shanghai and Hong Kong. He also developed a reputation as a geographic authority on China. During the Boxer Rebellion, he served as a war correspondent. Despite all the demands upon his time, he nevertheless kept up his studies of the mysteries of the East. Later, he was honored with the Chinese name of Ding Le Mei, and went on to teach disciples the mysteries of the ancient science of Brahma Vidya, or what he referred to in the West as the Science of Mentalphysics.

In 1927, Ding Le Mei founded the Institute of Mentalphysics in New York. It was this institute that pioneered the evolving Western interest in Eastern esoteric teachings. To date, the organization has inspired over 200,000 students from all over the world. After Edwin Dingle died in 1972, the guidance of the Institute was assumed by Chancellor Donald L. Waldrop at their headquarters in Yucca Valley, California.

BELIEF SYSTEM

Mentalphysics is based on the "Eternal Truth of Life." It serves to spread the Light of Divine Wisdom, working through Natural Law in the Holy Trinity of Body, Mind, and Spirit of Man. The underlying belief is that there is a spark of the divine in every human being, and through the practice of Mentalphysics that divinity can be realized more clearly. Through this practice, man will see "the universality and oneness in life, embodied in all substance, energy and thought." Moreover, "man is the Temple of the Living God, and the knowledge of God's Universal Law . . . enables him to demonstrate 'a perfect mind in a perfect body.'"

Mentalphysics is more of a practice or discipline than a creed. The truth cannot be fully understood by our intellect, but must be "felt" within the depth of the soul, and made "a *mainspring* of every thought and action from within us." Students absorb the universal truths as they are offered in the teachings. They then bring them into the laboratory of their own lives in order to prove the truth for themselves, to "feel" the truth in the core of their soul. Thus, the teachings are called the science of mentalphysics.

Humans are evolving and, through self-realization, they can find fulfillment in their purpose in existence. In this manner, they can contribute more to awakening humanity so that we can all live together in happiness and peace.

RITUALS AND PRACTICES

Central to the practice of Mentalphysics is the use of the breath, or pranayama, as it is referred to in the East. Within the air we breathe is the vital life force that provides the energy to sustain the body. By cultivating this energy, we increase our vitality and expand our capacity for higher awareness. Various breathing techniques are used to develop and direct the Prana—the "vital air"—for specific applications such as health, clarity of mind, and inspiration. Sometimes affirmations and visualizations are designed to create an optimal physical, mental, and spiritual state, and they are included as part of the meditation process. Also prescribed are a particular healthy diet and regular exercise—something similar to yoga—to enhance the body's capacity for utilizing its spiritual energy.

FOR ADDITIONAL INFORMATION

Recommended Contact

Institute of Mentalphysics
P.O. Box 1000
Joshua Tree, CA 92252
Phone: (760) 365–8371

Recommended Readings

Dingle, Edwin John. *Breaths that Renew Your Life*. Joshua Tree, CA: Institute of Mentalphysics, 1984.

Dingle, Edwin John. *My Life in Tibet*. Joshua Tree, CA: Institute of Mentalphysics, 1984.

THE ASCENDED MASTERS

The teachings of the Ascended Masters are the Universal Truths taught by the "Great White Brotherhood," which is comprised of all those who have become enlightened, or attained God-consciousness. They have dedicated their lives to helping humanity to awaken to the revealed truths. These Ascended Masters have psychically transmitted their teachings to Mark L. Prophet and Elizabeth Clare Prophet.

HISTORY

The Great White Brotherhood is a spiritual order of Western and Eastern Saints known as the "Ascended Masters." They work with earnest seekers and public servants of every race, religion, and walk of life to assist humanity in their forward evolution and to save the planet. Considered to be among the Ascended Masters are Jesus Christ, Gautama Buddha, Saint Michael the Archangel, Maitreya, Kuthumi, El Morya, Saint Germain, and the Mother Mary. In the middle of the twentieth century, Mark and Elizabeth Prophet were anointed as messengers for the Ascended Masters. It was their mission to deliver God's prophecy and to convey the truths necessary for a change in consciousness that would allow humanity to live together in peace.

Mark L. Prophet was born on December 24, 1918, in Chippewa Falls, Wisconsin. He was a very religious child; he was raised in the Pentecostal church and received all nine gifts of the Holy Spirit before finishing high school. Later, he studied the teachings of Paramahansa Yogananda in the Self-Realization Fellowship (see page 355), was associated with the Rosicrucian Order (see page 227), and was apparently inspired by Theosophy (see page 255). Prophet lectured on Christian and Eastern mysticism from 1945 to 1952, then began publishing a series of letters to his students called "Ashram Notes." These letters were comprised of materials that he claimed had been dictated by the Ascended Master El Morya. In 1958, Prophet founded The Summit Lighthouse to publish the teachings of the Ascended Masters and launch a worldwide movement.

In February of 1973, Mark L. Prophet died, and his ministry was carried on by his wife and partner, Elizabeth Clare Prophet, nee Wulf. Born in Red Bank, New Jersey, in 1939, Elizabeth had always been interested in finding Truth. She acknowledged she could even hear Jesus speaking to her in her heart as she pursued her quest. From the span of nine to eighteen years of age, she studied the works of Mary Baker Eddy and attended the Christian Science Church. In 1961, she attended a meeting of The Summit Lighthouse in Boston and met Mark Prophet. Soon, both of their lives would change.

While Elizabeth was studying for her bachelor's degree in political science at Boston University, the Ascended Master El Morya appeared to her in a vision. He told her to go to Washington, D.C., to study with Mark Prophet, who would train her to become a messenger. With Mark, she underwent intense spiritual training, and three years later, she received the anointing of another Ascended Master—Saint Germain—to be the messenger of the Great White Brotherhood. Mark and Elizabeth were married on March 16, 1963, and over the years, raised a son and three daughters.

Today, the Teachings of the Ascended Masters are disseminated throughout the world. Elizabeth has lectured in over thirty countries and written more than fifty books, selling over a million copies. The Ascended Masters operate more than 250 centers in 35 countries, and their cable television shows have a viewing audience estimated at 36 million.

BELIEF SYSTEM

According to the traditions of the Ascended Masters, cosmic councils had long ago determined that no further opportunity should be given to humanity, so great was their departure from cosmic law and their desecration of life. It was at this time that Sanat Kumara, one of the Seven Holy Kumaras who focused the light of the seven rays, offered his heart to serve the people of earth until the few, and eventually the many, would once again keep the flame of Life and come to know their True Self as God.

The traditions maintain that the solar lords granted Sanat Kumara this dispensation, and he proceeded with his spiritual sons and daughters to Earth and established the retreat of Shamballa in what is now the Gobi Desert. This sanctuary, once physical, was withdrawn to the etheric octave, or heaven-world, in subsequent dark ages. It is one of many retreats on the etheric plane from which the Ascended Masters minister to those on earth and work together to uplift the consciousness of the world.

The Masters teach that your soul has the potential to externalize its own divine nature, and that you have the ability to realize the Light of God, as the Inner Christ or the Inner Buddha, within. Moreover, you have the ability to walk the path of personal Christhood and to ascend, as Jesus did. The ascension is a spiritual awakening of your consciousness that takes place at the natural conclusion of your final lifetime on earth.

RITUALS AND PRACTICES

The practice of the Ascended Masters focuses on the science of the spoken Word through "dynamic decrees," which combine prayer, meditation, and visualization, with a special emphasis on affirmations using the name of God: "I am that I am." Emphasis is also placed on reading and contemplating the Teachings of the Ascended Masters. Students of the Ascended Masters use decrees to direct God's light for the solving of personal and planetary problems. Some students practice independent study, while others may subscribe to the weekly "Pearls of Wisdom" discourses, dictated by the Ascended Masters. There is also a Keepers of the Flame fraternity, a secular organization "dedicated to keeping the flame of Life in earth's evolutions and to planetary enlightenment." The movement is based at the 33,000-acre Royal Teton Ranch in Park County, Montana, which is home to a self-sufficient spiritual community. It is the international headquarters for Church Universal and Triumphant, The Summit Lighthouse, Summit University Press, and Summit University—which sponsors twelve-week retreats and summer courses.

FOR ADDITIONAL INFORMATION

Recommended Contact

The Summit Lighthouse
Department 793, Box 5000
Corwin Springs, MT 59030-5000
Phone: (800) 245–5445
Website: www.tsl.org

Recommended Readings

Prophet, Elizabeth Clare. *How to Work with Angels*. Corwin Springs, MT: Summit University Press, 1999.

Prophet, Elizabeth Clare. *Saint Germain's Prophecy for the New Millennium*. Corwin Springs, MT: Summit University Press, 1999.

Prophet, Mark L., and Elizabeth Clare Prophet. *The Lost Teachings of Jesus*. Corwin Springs, MT: Summit University Press, 1989.

INTERNATIONAL BIOGENIC SOCIETY

The International Biogenic Society is a nonsectarian, nonpolitical, scientific, educational "association of Individual Associate Members and Associate Teachers." They focus on the teaching of the various aspects of Biogenic Living—celebrating life, learning to use natural foods, and interacting properly with the environment—and emphasize many modern applications in our daily lives of the ancient Essene teachings.

HISTORY

The International Biogenic Society was founded in Paris in 1928 by the Nobel prize-winning author Romain Rolland and the philosopher Edmond Bordeaux Szekely. The International Biogenic Society evolved out of Dr. Szekely's research on ancient civilizations and religions, and in particular on the Essene brotherhood of first century A.D. Judaea. Early in his education, Dr. Szekely had earned the privilege of studying ancient manuscripts at the Archives of the Vatican, under the direction of Monsignor Mercati, the curator. His research began with the study of the venerable Saint Francis, which led him to the writings of Saint Benedict. The manuscripts that Benedict had preserved dated back to the fourth century A.D. These manuscripts were Saint Jerome's translations of first-century biblical codices, which included Hebrew writings of the Essene Brotherhood.

During the middle of the fourth century A.D., Jerome spent twenty years traveling in the Holy Land deciphering fragments of these ancient first-century A.D. manuscripts. During this time, he gathered letters from an ancient brotherhood of the desert known as the Essenes (see "Essenes" on page 178), and began translating these fragments from Hebrew into Latin.

Based on this work, Jerome gained a reputation as a scholar of first-century Hebrew manuscripts. Pope Damasus I (304–384), who founded the Papal Library and was also later canonized a saint, commissioned Jerome to revise the New Testament, using the newly translated first-century letters. These new translations included a number of "Apoc-ryphal Documents" that have been preserved at the Vatican. It was these same documents that had been rediscovered and translated by Dr. Szekely in the 1920s. These writings revealed the philosophy practiced by the ancient Essenes. Dr. Szekely called it "Biogenic Living."

In 1928 Dr. Szekely translated "The Essene Gospel of Peace" into the modern vernacular, and today over 10 million readers have absorbed its message. Moreover, the International Biogenic Society is now repre-sented around the world, instructing people in "The Essene Way of Bio-genic Living."

BELIEF SYSTEM

The philosophy of the International Biogenic Society can be summed up in one of Dr. Szekely's most famous statements: "We believe in the Fatherhood of God, the Motherhood of Nature, and the Brotherhood of Man," making clear the interdependent nature of all three. Adherents profess that our most precious possession is life. They believe we must preserve instead of waste our natural resources, the heritage of our chil-dren. Therefore, we must avoid the pollution of our air, water, and soil.

In the social realm, they believe that mutual understanding leads to mutual cooperation and peace; the only way mankind can survive. They understand that the improvement of life and of mankind must start with their own individual efforts.

They believe in living naturally. Thus, they eat only fresh, natural, wholesome foods, without chemical treatment or artificial processing. They enjoy a simple, natural, creative life, absorbing all the sources of energy, harmony, and knowledge in and around them.

RITUALS AND PRACTICES

The major spiritual practice of the International Biogenic Society involves "dynamic communion," which is a way of "tapping a source of knowledge which does not depend on superficial dogmatic convictions, but is eternal and timelessly valid from which our own human existence was formed, and with which we are forever connected."

Biogenic Living also involves self-analysis and reflection on life's pur-pose. It is not based on abstract theories. Rather, these ideas are arrived at through empirical life experiences. Biogenic Living is considered by its adherents to be the most natural, healthy, and happy way of living.

FOR ADDITIONAL INFORMATION

Recommended Contacts

IBS International   First Christians' Essene Church
Box 205 Matsqui, B.C.   2536 Collier Avenue
Canada VOX 1SO   San Diego, CA 92116
Phone: (530) 926–0260   Phone: (877) 808–8098
Website:
  www.awarenessinstitute.com

Recommended Readings

Szekely, Edmond Bordeaux. *The Essene Gospel of Peace of Jesus Christ.* London, UK: C. W. Daniel, 1994.

Szekely, Edmond Bordeaux. *The Teachings of the Essenes from Enoch to the Dead Sea Scrolls.* London, UK: C. W. Daniel, 1992.

Szekely, Edmond Bordeaux. *The Way of the Essenes: Christ's Hidden Life Remembered.* Rochester, VT: Inner Traditions, 1992.

THE BAHA'I FAITH

Baha'i is a faith founded by Baha'u'llah, and is based on the tenets of the unity of all religions and of mankind. Baha'i is the outgrowth of a movement within Islamic culture known as Babism. Note that it is an outgrowth of Islamic *culture*, not Islamic religion. In fact, it has no clergy but focuses, rather, on the individual devotee.

HISTORY

In 1844, a young man named Siyyid'Ali Muhammad from Shiraz, Iran, who was a direct descendent of the prophet Muhammad, proclaimed himself to be the Bab (the "gate" or "door"). Within the Shi'ite sect of Islam, it is believed that the Imam Mahdi, or "rightly guided imam," will come forth and bring in an era of justice and peace. By proclaiming himself the Bab, Siyyid'Ali Muhammad was declaring himself as the expected imam and forerunner to "He whom God shall make manifest" who, adherents believe, was Baha'u'llah.

The Bab was rapidly gathering disciples, but this threatened the established clergy in Iran. They quickly put him to death by firing squad in 1850, and many of his followers, or Babis, were massacred or exiled.

One such exiled follower was Mirza Husayn-'Ali, who was known as Baha'u'llah. He had been born in Teheran, Iran, in 1817, the son of a nobleman and minister. In 1863, after the death of the Bab and his own exile, he declared himself to be "He who God shall make Manifest" to a small group of followers. Shortly thereafter, he was banished to Istanbul and then to Adrianople, Turkey. There, he publicly proclaimed his mission.

While in exile, he wrote many letters to world rulers and developed the unifying concepts that characterize the Baha'i faith. In 1868, Baha'u'llah was exiled to Akka, Palestine, where he suffered harsh imprisonment for two years. This ordeal was followed by a house arrest that lasted until his death in 1892. Leadership passed to one of Baha'u'llah's sons, who was known as "Abdul-Baha," or "The Servant of Baha." Abdul-Baha was released from prison in 1908 and promptly set out on missionary journeys to Egypt, Europe, and America. After the death of Abdul-Baha in 1921, his grandson, Shoghi Effendi Rabbani, was appointed the Guardian, or next leader of the Baha'i religion. After Shoghi Effendi's death in 1957, the administrative duties were delegated to the Universal House of Justice in Haifa. Baha'i is currently represented throughout the world, with over 5 million believers, among them large followings in Iran, India, Europe, and the United States.

BELIEF SYSTEM

The main tenet of the Baha'i Faith is the unification of all religions and teachings and the promotion of the unification of humanity. Baha'is perceive God as an essence that manifests itself in numerous ways. Their theology recognizes the great prophets and saviors of all major religions, but emphasizes the most recent revelations given by Baha'i prophets such as the Bab, Baha, and Ullah, as their wisdom is designed for the scientific age. The teachings and laws of the Baha'i are set forth in such books as the *Kitab al-Aqdas,* or *The Most Holy Book,* and the *Bayan,* or *Statement of Explanation* by the Bab.

Baha'i teachings have as their goal the improvement of the conditions of human life.

RITUALS AND HOLY DAYS

The Baha'i Faith is a religion without a clergy. Each individual in the faith is encouraged to look into religious teachings with an unbiased mind and be responsible for his or her own individual beliefs and actions. Spiritual assemblies are elected to carry on various activities such as marriages and funerals. Baha'is often meet for small-group discussions called "firesides" and observe various Holy Days such as the birth and death of the Bab and Baha'u'llah. Fasting is observed, from March 2 through March 20, when believers abstain from all food and drink from sunrise to sunset. The Baha'i Faith also has the institution of obligatory prayer; believers are responsible to say one of three obligatory prayers each day.

FOR ADDITIONAL INFORMATION
Recommended Contact

Baha'i National Center
536 Sheridan Road
Wilmette, IL 60091
Phone: (847) 869–9039

Recommended Readings

Baha'u'llah. *The Kitab-I-Aqdas: The Most Holy Book.* Wilmette, IL: Baha'i Publishing Trust, 1993.

Baha'u'llah. *Gleanings from the Writings of Baha'u'llah.* Wilmette, IL: Baha'i Publishing Trust, 1983.

Waging Peace: Selections from the Baha'i Writings on Universal Peace. Novato, CA: Kalimat Press, 1985.

Recommended Websites

www.angliacampus.com
www.bahai.org
www.bounty.bcca.org
www.worldtrans.org

EMISSARIES OF DIVINE LIGHT

The Emissaries of Divine Light was founded in 1940 by Lloyd Arthur Meeker. They focus on trying to regenerate interior spirituality in the human race—with the guidance of God.

HISTORY

Lloyd Arthur Meeker was born in Iowa in 1907 and moved to Colorado at the age of two. He was the son of a poor farmer and minister, whose strict interpretation of religious dogma prompted Meeker to question the spiritual values he had been taught, and to contemplate the deeper meaning of life. In September 1932, Meeker had "an experience of enlightenment" that opened his eyes to the purpose of existence and man's relationship with God. Lloyd quickly began to find others who shared his spiritual values and who found great benefits from his insights on God and man. His following grew, and in 1940, he incorporated his program into a church under the name of Emissaries of Divine Light.

In 1939, Meeker was introduced to a cattle rancher from British Columbia named Martin Cecil. A member of the English aristocracy, Cecil was instrumental in developing and spreading the work of the Emissaries. In 1945, the Emissaries established its international headquarters at Sunrise Ranch near Loveland, Colorado. In 1948, another spiritual community was formed in British Columbia at Cecil's 100-Mile House Lodge. The work of the Emissaries inspired many, and other communities soon formed around the world.

In 1954, Lloyd Meeker died in a plane crash, and Martin Cecil assumed the leadership of the Emissaries. Under his administration, the Emissaries continued to prosper. In 1981, Cecil succeeded to the title of seventh Marquess of Exeter with the death of his brother, David, and took his seat in England's House of Lords in March of 1982. In 1987, the Emissaries held their "The Signs of the Times" public event, which was broadcast to seventy locations in twenty-three countries, reaching many thousands around the world. In 1988, Martin Cecil died, and now his son

Michael Cecil provides leadership for the Emissaries. Michael succeeded his father as the eighth Marquess of Exeter and has taken his seat in the House of Lords.

BELIEF SYSTEM

The purpose of the Emissaries is "to assist in carrying forward a work of Spiritual regeneration of the human race, under the inspiration of the Spirit of God." The Emissaries provide a forum to align the individual with the true character of the spirit. No specific teachings are adhered to, but rather individuals are assisted to release the spiritual nature within themselves. As Lloyd Meeker affirmed, "Incarnate within all people dwells an aspect of the spirit of God, eternal and perfect, having no need to evolve or to grow." He held that where there is a willingness to "align" with that spirit, the mind and emotions become "clear channels through which the essence of that incarnate spirit may find release," and all problems immediately begin to dissolve. This is the secret of inner peace and the foundation of the Emissaries' message.

RITUALS AND PRACTICES

The Emissaries have established spiritual communities that provide a setting where people have the opportunity to awaken the spirit within themselves. Classes and seminars are offered regularly. As Martin Cecil stated, "Such awakening is easier, in many ways, when one shares the process with others; as when a team climbs a mountain, there is the advantage of comradeship, mutual encouragement, and shared purpose." Each individual in the community is encouraged to exemplify the Truth, to become a walking example of the very nature of spirit.

However, many Emissaries do not live in these communities, which have developed as regional headquarters, but merely visit as time permits. Thus, twice monthly, transcripts of Michael Exeter's recent addresses are sent to those interested. In addition, a correspondence course, featuring introductory material, is available at no charge.

The Emissaries now have centers throughout North America and in South America, South and West Africa, Australia, and Europe, serving thousands of members and guests. Visitors are welcome to visit their communities or attend their Sunday services, which include reading, prayer, meditation, and discussion.

FOR ADDITIONAL INFORMATION

Recommended Contact

The Emissaries of Divine Light
5569 North County Road 29 .
Loveland, CO 80538
Phone: (970) 679–4229
Website: www.emissaries.org

Recommended Reading

Exeter, Martin. *Thus It Is*. Denver, CO: Foundation House, 1989.

ECKANKAR

Eckankar is the ancient path to God-Realization through the inner light and sound and the Living Eck Master, or Mahanta. It is geared to the spiritual needs and goals of the individual.

HISTORY

Eckankar has always existed. It predates history as we know it, and is practiced not only throughout the physical universe, but also throughout all higher levels of consciousness, or Heaven. Eck Masters have always been available on earth to assist seekers in reaching God-Realization. However, since very few people were ready for such a direct path to God, the teachings were not made available to the masses. As many evolved souls are now incarnating in preparation for the Aquarian Age in the near future, the Eck teachings are becoming more readily available.

It was Paul Twitchell who brought Eckankar to Western civilization in the early 1960s and made it accessible to the masses. Twitchell was an American, born in Kentucky, who had been chosen by the Eck Masters to reveal their sacred teachings. Eckankar is now practiced around the world by many thousands, and is growing rapidly as more people make contact with the inner light and sound.

The current Living Eck Master—chosen by Sugmad, or God—is Harold Klemp, who works with seekers in two ways: *outwardly*, through his writings, correspondence, and speaking engagements; and *inwardly* through his interpretation of dreams and promotion of soul travel, or out-of-body experiences.

BELIEF SYSTEM

Like many of the contemporary teachings, Eckankar guides you on the basis of direct personal experiences. It is more of a practice or a discipline than a formal religion with a dogmatic position on spiritual issues. Eckists believe that through the purification of the soul—through meditation, introspection, contemplation, and good works—believers can reach higher states of consciousness and become coworkers with Sugmad, or God.

RITUALS AND PRACTICES

As part of the Eckankar discipline ritual, you receive spiritual exercises as the vehicles for learning. There are also written discourses, which can be experienced in private or in classes. These spiritual exercises connect you (the Chela) with an inner light and sound, which are seen and heard from within. This light and sound connect you, via the Eck (holy spirit), to the Sugmad (the all that is, or God). To overcome the limits of physical awareness, the Mahanta (Living Eck Master) assists you to ascend, as soul, into the higher levels of consciousness (heaven) where greater truths can be realized through direct experiences.

FOR ADDITIONAL INFORMATION

Recommended Contact

Eckankar
P.O. Box 27300
Minneapolis, MN 55427
Phone: (612) 544–3001
Website: www.eckankar.org

Recommended Readings

Klemp, Harold. *The Dream Worlds*. Minneapolis, MN: Eckankar Press, 1997.

Klemp, Harold. *The Spiritual Exercises of Eckankar*. Minneapolis, MN: Eckankar Press, 1997.

Twitchell, Paul. *Eckankar, the Key to the Secret Worlds*. Minneapolis, MN: Eckankar Press, 1997.

THE MONROE INSTITUTE

The Monroe Institute is a school that provides research and education in the field of human consciousness.

HISTORY

The Monroe Institute was founded by Robert Monroe in 1971. Monroe is a former broadcasting executive who, in 1958, began to have spontaneous out-of-body experiences. On these occasions, he would find that his spirit left his body to wander the area; he could look down and see himself; he could move through walls or other obstacles. These occurrences went on for over thirty years. These experiences led him to investigate the nature and causes of such phenomena.

His research has resulted in the publication of two best-selling books, *Journeys Out of the Body* and *Far Journeys*. He has also lectured extensively throughout the country; has trained thousands how to access other states of awareness; and is considered one of the world's foremost scientists in the field of human consciousness. Moreover, the Monroe Institute has developed audio tapes with sound patterns that create electrical patterns in the brain. These assist in focusing the consciousness toward desired results, such as health, learning, and expanding consciousness. These "Hemi-Sync" tapes act by synchronizing the energy frequencies of the left and right hemispheres of the brain, which creates a stimulus that activates higher levels of awareness. It is estimated that over 200,000 people have experienced the Hemi-Sync tapes to date.

BELIEF SYSTEM

Monroe does not claim to have the Truth, and the Monroe Institute does not pretend to have all the answers to the nature of human consciousness. However, the Institute does provide a facility for individuals to have personal, direct experiences that will assist them in determining the Truth for themselves.

The underlying premise to be tested through his methods for having out-of-body experiences is that there is something more to our existence than our physical world. Monroe reasons that "our physical reality is only one band or frequency in a vast spectrum of realities in the 'universal energy system.'"

Monroe goes into considerable detail as to how he manages to enter into these alternate states, and explains to the best of his ability what these other realities are like. His methodology is scientific and his approach is objective, almost clinical. Most interestingly, he is able to document and repeat his experiences, and has been able to teach his techniques to many others with positive results.

RITUALS AND PRACTICES

There are higher forms of consciousness that you can achieve with Monroe, as well as the others who practice his techniques. These include the following:

- Seeing your physical body from outside yourself, which, Monroe estimates, is an experience over 20 percent of the population has had;

- Visiting entities that have either physically died, or are from other universes or energy systems;

- Going forward or backward in time, and even beyond time; and

- Transcending the limits of your physical consciousness.

Various techniques are employed to initiate out-of-body experiences, including the following:

- Empty all your thoughts and worries into an "Energy Conversion Box" in your imagination;

- Practice "Resonant Tuning," a form of chanting combined with rhythmic breathing;

- Recite the prescribed affirmation, which states that you are more than your physical body, that you desire to experience other energy systems, and that you desire assistance from beings "whose wisdom is equal to or greater than" your own.

This technique is best practiced just as you fall off to sleep. It is also recommended that you practice remembering your dreams and other experiences you may have. To assist in developing the ability to have control over expanded states of consciousness, the Monroe Institute recommends that you use the Hemi-Sync cassette tapes, which are played in a sequence to enhance your experience.

The Monroe Institute provides training to help you explore your own consciousness, but does not advocate any particular spiritual theology.

FOR ADDITIONAL INFORMATION

Recommended Contact

The Monroe Institute
Route 1, Box 175
Faber, VA 22938
Phone: (804) 361–1252
Website: www.za.spiritweb.org

Recommended Readings

Monroe, Robert A. *Far Journeys*. New York: Doubleday, 1971.

Monroe, Robert A. *Journeys Out of the Body*. New York: Doubleday, 1971.

ALCOHOLICS ANONYMOUS

Alcoholics Anonymous is a society of alcoholics that help each other to keep sober and to enjoy life more fully. Like the Monroe Institute, it does not advocate any particular spiritual theology. Rather, it accepts God as you perceive him.

HISTORY

This fellowship started when an alcoholic stockbroker from New York made the acquaintance of a physician from Akron, Ohio, in 1935.

Six months prior to their meeting, the stockbroker, Bill W., had had a spiritual experience that had relieved him of his obsession with drinking. Bill had learned of the "grave nature of alcoholism" from the late Dr. William D. Silkworth, a specialist in alcoholism, and became convinced of the "need for moral inventory, confession of personality defects, restitution to those harmed, helpfulness to others, and the necessity of belief in and dependence upon God."

Bill W. had been working with other alcoholics in New York, on the premise that only another alcoholic could help an alcoholic. Nevertheless, he had not been successful. However, during a business trip to Akron, Bill met Dr. Bob S., and their lives changed dramatically. Dr. Bob had also been struggling with alcoholism. He had tried a variety of strategies to overcome his dependency, but so far he had failed. This time, however, Bill's W.'s words and support were effective in mustering Bob's resolve, and Bob remained sober until his death in 1950.

With much inspiration and mutual support, Bill and Bob set off to the Akron City Hospital to offer assistance to other alcoholics in overcoming their disease. At first, they had many failures, but they also achieved several successes. After refining their approaches, they started the first self-help group in the fall of 1935. Shortly thereafter, a second group started in New York, and others picked up the basic idea in other cities.

In 1939, the first edition of *Alcoholics Anonymous* was published as a cooperative effort of the group, which began to refer to itself as "Alcoholics Anonymous," or "AA." Because of the publication of this book, the message quickly spread to many thousands. Over 300,000 copies were sold in the first printing, and the second edition, published in 1955, sold over 1,150,000 copies. By September, 1983, the combined total of the three editions distributed totalled over 4,000,000. By 1987, AA had grown to approximately 67,000 groups. Alcoholics Anonymous is now represented in almost every country in the world, with countless millions who actively participate in the fellowship of this society, and who have been able to remain sober and enjoy life more fully.

BELIEF SYSTEM

Alcoholics Anonymous has two basic underlying premises: first, that fellow alcoholics can assist each other through the process of becoming and remaining sober, and second, that there is a power greater than themselves whom they can call upon. (See the inset regarding the "Twelve Traditions" of AA on page 286.) That power is God—however you may perceive him.

The process of overcoming alcoholism through AA is one of recognizing and acting upon the reality of your life. Through the help of others in similar situations, and with a power greater than yourself, you become sober. You can live a happier life.

Achieving this goal is not easy. Alcoholism is a disease of the mind and the body, but it must be fought with mind, body, and spirit. Remember, the only requirement for AA membership is a desire to stop drinking. So when you are ready, the twelve-step process begins. For some details, you may refer to the inset on page 287. You begin with a moral inventory, confess your personality defects, make restitution to those whom you have harmed, show helpfulness to others, and accomplish all this with a belief in and dependence upon God.

You are never alone in the process; you have your fellow members, and you have God, however you perceive him.

Literally millions of people from all classes and all walks of life have come to AA and found fellowship, hope, and solutions to their problems. AA works with alcoholics, but for assistance for the friends and relatives of alcoholics you might look into Al-Anon and Alateen.

Alcoholics Anonymous and the Twelve Traditions

Alcohol Anonymous, or AA, functions in accordance with what is termed the "Twelve Traditions." A summary of these traditions might read as follows:

1. Our common welfare should come first; personal recovery depends upon AA unity;

2. For our group purpose there is but one ultimate authority: a loving God as He may express Himself in our group conscience. Our leaders are but trusted servants; they do not govern;

3. The only requirement for AA membership is a desire to stop drinking;

4. Each group should be autonomous except in matters affecting other groups or AA as a whole;

5. Each group has but one primary purpose, i. e., to carry its message to the alcoholic who still suffers;

6. An AA group ought never endorse, finance, or lend the AA name to any related facility or outside enterprise;

7. Every AA group ought to be fully self-supporting, declining outside contributions;

8. Alcoholics Anonymous should remain forever nonprofessional, but our service centers may employ special workers;

9. AA, as such, ought never to be organized; but we may create service boards or committees directly responsible to those they serve;

10. Alcoholics Anonymous has no opinion on outside issues; hence the AA name ought never to be drawn into public controversy;

11. Our public relations policy is based on attraction rather than promotion; we need always maintain personal anonymity at the level of press, radio, and films; and

12. Anonymity is the spiritual foundation of all our Traditions, ever reminding us to place principles before personalities.

Alcoholics Anonymous and the Twelve Steps

The stages through which you must pass are known in AA as the "Twelve Steps," and they are as follows:

1. We admitted that we were powerless over alcohol, that our lives had become unmanageable;

2. We came to believe that a Power greater than ourselves could restore us to sanity;

3. We made a decision to turn our will and our lives over to the care of God as we understood Him;

4. We made a searching and fearless moral inventory of ourselves;

5. We admitted to God, to ourselves, and to another human being the exact nature of our wrongs;

6. We were entirely ready to have God remove all these defects of character;

7. We humbly asked Him to remove our shortcomings;

8. We made a list of all persons we had harmed, and became willing to make amends to them all;

9. We made direct amends to such people wherever possible, except when to do so would injure them or others;

10. We continue to take personal inventory and when we are wrong, promptly admit it;

11. We sought through prayer and meditation to improve our conscious contact with God as we understood Him, praying only for knowledge of His will for us and the power to carry that out; and

12. Having had a spiritual awakening as the result of these steps, we tried to carry this message to alcoholics, and to practice these principles in all our affairs.

These twelve steps are difficult to accomplish. More than once, an alcoholic will "fall off the wagon" and begin to drink again. However, with the assistance of their fellow members and of their God, the problem drinker will begin again, face the problem, and succeed eventually.

FOR ADDITIONAL INFORMATION

Recommended Contacts

Look up "Alcoholics Anonymous" in the phone directory, or contact:

The General Service Office:
Alcoholics Anonymous
P.O. Box 459
Grand Central Station, NY 10163
Phone: (212) 870–3400
Website: www.alcoholics-anonymous.org

For the friends and relatives of alcoholics, there is also a support group called Al-Anon. To find an Al-Anon group, look in your phone book for the nearest group, or contact the organization itself at:

Al-Anon Family Groups, Inc.
P.O. Box 182
Madison Square Station, NY 10159
Phone: (888) 4AL-ANON
Website: www.Al-Anon.org

Similar groups have formed for those with other abuses, such as drugs, gambling, or overeating. You can get additional information through AA groups in your area.

Recommended Readings

Alcoholics Anonymous. Third Edition. New York: World Services, Inc., 1976.

The Twelve Steps of Alcoholics Anonymous. New York: World Services, Inc., 1996.

CHANNELING

Channeling is a spiritual vehicle whereby individuals in this world act as conduits, mediums, or channels for the expression of thought from another world, or another level of consciousness. The channel generally allows a physical body to be used by an element, or entity of "higher" consciousness, to communicate concepts to our physical world. The messages are generally presented to humanity to raise or increase its spiritual awareness. Channeling can generally be divided into two kinds. Subjective channeling occurs when the channel makes conscious contact with a higher level of consciousness, or even God, and recalls the experience. Many of the world's great spiritual texts, such as the Holy Bible, the Koran, and the Vedas, are "God's" word given to man—the channel, or messenger—to commit, ultimately, into writing. Subjective channeling is generally not what we consider channeling in the contemporary use of the term. On the other hand, objective channeling occurs when the channel makes contact with an entity in another world, which then uses the channel's physical faculties to communicate with people in this world. The channel may or may not even be conscious of what the entity is saying through him or her. During the channeling experience, the practitioner is generally in an altered state of consciousness such as sleep, trance, deep meditation, or out-of-body state. Most of what is currently referred to as channeling is objective channeling.

Accounts of channeling have been recorded throughout history from many cultures. The source of the information being imparted has been attributed to various entities, including: God, various deities, prophets, saints, saviors, and enlightened beings, as well as universal mind, collective consciousness, and unnamed thought-form personalities. Channels have also been known by many names, such as prophets, apostles, saviors, masters, holy ones, and evangelists. They have also been referred to as oracles, seers, psychics, savants, soothsayers, fortune tellers, shamans, healers, medicine men, witches, and witch doctors, and, in esoteric schools, as light markers, teachers, and initiates.

Most of the contemporary objective channels appear to be ordinary people with little or no previous spiritual inclination. Currently, there is a plethora of channels expressing a wide variety of spiritual teachings.

Many of these are only discovered by word of mouth, but some may have relatively small followings.

I have limited the following section to those channels who are widely known and have made their teaching readily available to the public. The following sections will briefly cover a few of the more well-known entities and teachings being channeled. We begin with one of the most famous channels of all time, Nostradamus, the sixteenth-century doctor known for his predictions into the fourth millennium. Then we take up Edgar Cayce, an American channel who could connect with the past as well as the future; he could also make medical diagnoses even though he was not a physician. Then we will look at the phenomenon of Jane Roberts, a channel who made repeated contacts with an entity named Seth, who dictated over 6,000 pages of notes across two decades. Next, we examine the channel Helen Schucman, who wrote down "A Course in Miracles," authored by none other than Jesus Christ. For an Eastern perspective, we will explore the case of J. Z. Knight, the foster daughter of Ramtha in another lifetime—and his channel in this one. Finally, we will delve into the channeling of Jach Pursel, a Florida businessman, who began his trances in 1974, communicating with "Lazaris," an entity that possessed consciousness yet had no form.

NOSTRADAMUS

For centuries Nostradamus (1503–1566) has been cited to have predicted the outcome of future events. He is one of the best known seers of modern history.

HISTORY

Nostradamus is a Latinization for Michel de Notre Dame. Born in 1503 in St. Remy, France, of Jewish parents who converted to Catholicism, Nostradamus was a doctor with the gift of visionary powers, and interests in astronomy and astrology. Married twice, he was blessed with six children. Nostradamus moved to Lyons where he distinguished himself for his fearlessness in treating plague victims. In 1540, he published an almanac of weather predictions based on his astrological research, and in 1555, at the age of 52, he published his first set of one hundred quatrains prophesying the future. This collection, known as *Centuries*, makes predictions of the future, from the birth of Louis XIV in 1215 to events in the year A.D. 3797. By 1557, he had completed ten sets of one hundred quatrains, which had come to him while in an altered state, or trance. He was appointed Counsellor and Royal Physician to King Charles IX and died in 1566.

BELIEF SYSTEM

Nostradamus believed he had a "sixth sense," and while focusing his mind and gazing into crystal, fire, or water, he experienced visions of events that were yet to occur. His followers claim that many of the events have indeed occurred, such as the sinking of the Spanish Armada, the Napoleonic Wars, Hitler's rise to power, World War II, and the development of the atomic bomb.

Other predictions, such as World War III and the rise of the Antichrist, are considered likely to happen soon. Consider the following prediction, found in CX Q72:

> *In the year 1999, and seven months from the sky*
> *will come the great King of Terror. He will bring*

> to life the great King of the Mongols.
> Before and after war reigns happily.

Most interpret this quatrain to predict the advent of the Anti-christ—an evil person or power that will corrupt the world but then be conquered by Christ in his second coming. The specific year—1999—is rare in Nostradamus's writing, only one of seventeen out of hundreds of predictions. Most of the others are ambiguous, at best, and because of the author's metaphysical style, difficult to "prove" with any certainty.

FOR ADDITIONAL INFORMATION

Recommended Readings

Paulus, Stefan. *Nostradamus, 1999: Who Will Survive?* St. Paul, MN: Llewellyn Publishing, 1996.

Roberts, Henry, trans. *The Complete Prophecies of Nostradamus.* Pittsburgh, PA: Three Rivers Press, 1999.

Recommended Websites

Nostradamus Home Page Website:
ftp.netcom.com/poub/nanomius/home.html

Nostradamus Questions Website:
http://saturn.las.ox.ac.uk/internet/news/faq/by_category.
    nostadamus.html

EDGAR CAYCE

Edgar Cayce is probably the most widely known American channel. In a hypnotic state, he was able to predict the future and even make medical diagnoses.

HISTORY

Edgar Cayce was born in Hopkinsville, Kentucky, in 1877, and made a living as a photographer. After he mysteriously lost his voice, a doctor suggested that he learn to hypnotize himself to deal with the symptom. While attempting the hypnosis, Cayce went into a trance state and was able to "tune in" to another awareness.

Apparently, Cayce never had another entity enter into his body or consciousness. Rather, he would be connected with another aspect of his own being. Even when he was communicating with the minds of those people, either living or dead, Cayce's flow of information came through his own voice and consciousness. Cayce was a mild-mannered Christian gentleman who shied away from acclaim and offered himself to be tested by many skeptics.

Cayce's unique gift among channels is that he was able to provide accurate clairvoyant medical diagnoses for people whom he never even met. Before his death in 1945, he had accurately diagnosed over 30,000 cases. These are made available to the public at the Association for Research and Enlightenment in Virginia Beach, Virginia.

BELIEF SYSTEM

Cayce was able to see things that had occurred in the past, and knew about the life and times of famous people, such as Jesus Christ. Like Nostradamus, he could also see into the future and foretell events yet to come. For example, he predicted a shift in the Earth's polarity, a millennium disaster, and a return of Christ at the end of the century.

FOR ADDITIONAL INFORMATION

Recommended Contact

Association for Research and Enlightenment
P.O. Box 595
Virginia Beach, VA 23451
Phone: (888) 273–0050
Website: www.edgarcayce.com

Recommended Readings

Cayce, Edgar. *Edgar Cayce, Modern Prophet*. Richmond, VA: Outlet Publications, 1998.
Cayce, Edgar Evans. *Edgar Cayce on Atlantis*. Hugh L. Cayce, ed. New York: Warner Books, 1996.

SETH CHANNELED BY JANE ROBERTS

Seth is an "energy personality essence," that is, he is no longer incarnated in the physical world. However, speaking through the channel of Jane Roberts, he has a message for this world.

HISTORY

Jane Roberts, now deceased, was an aspiring poet and novelist who was contacted by Seth in September of 1963. While composing poetry, Jane had an out-of-body experience, during which she was somehow introduced to concepts radically different from anything she had ever considered before. Later that year, while she was experimenting with a ouija board, the entity who had contacted her on the previous occasion identified himself as Seth. From that point on, Jane began going into trances regularly in order for Seth to communicate through her, while her husband Rob took down notes of what Seth had to say. While in the altered state, Jane was generally not conscious of what Seth was saying, but she was instrumental in editing the material after it had been transcribed. During the twenty years Jane had been channeling, over 6,000 pages of Seth's material was written down. Ironically, Seth, a noncorporeal entity, is now one of the best known and widely published "authors" of this century.

BELIEF SYSTEM

Seth's central theme is that we each create our own reality by the beliefs we hold and desires we have. Moreover, Seth maintains that man is a manifestation of a soul that is incarnated in this physical world—as well as in alternate "realities." He maintains that man needs to experience each respective reality to its fullest extent in order to fulfill the totality of his being. Man is constantly learning that he must awaken to discover—or rediscover—his true nature as a God-like being. Seth instructs the seeker in practices designed to realize this inner being. Seth also discusses other topics, including the nature of time and space, the concepts of energy and matter, the reality of God, the philosophy of reincarnation, the improvement of health, and commentary on the historical Christ.

FOR ADDITIONAL INFORMATION

Recommended Reading

Roberts, Jane. *Seth Speaks: The Eternal Validity of the Soul*. Novato, CA: New World Library, 1994.

A COURSE IN MIRACLES

A *Course in Miracles* is the result of a channeling encounter experienced by Helen Schucman. The document that was dictated is designed to teach us to make the choices that will heal our inherent inner conflicts and bring us inner peace.

HISTORY

A *Course in Miracles* was authored, through inner dictation, by Jesus Christ himself. The course was channeled through Helen Schucman, who previously worked in the Psychiatry Department at Columbia University College of Physicians and Surgeons. As a consequence of Helen's determination to find "a better way," she began to hear an inner voice. This channeled voice kept repeating, "This is a course in miracles." With the encouragement of her associate Bill Thetford, she started taking down the notes from the other world. This began in the 1970s and continued over a seven-year period. Her data developed into what is now known as A *Course in Miracles*.

The text comprises 1,200 pages in three volumes, consisting of a text setting forth the theoretical system; a workbook for students, containing 365 daily lessons; and a manual for teachers, based on the premise that "to teach is to demonstrate."

The course employs a self-study method, so the learners—hundreds of thousands have taken the course to date—can move at their own pace. Also available are national and international classes, seminars, workshops, study groups, and spiritual counseling.

BELIEF SYSTEM

The premise of the course is summed up in the introduction, which states: "This is a course in miracles. It is a required course. Only the time you take for it is voluntary. Free will does not mean that you can establish the curriculum. It means only that you can elect what you want to take at a given time. The course does not aim at teaching the meaning of love, for that is beyond what can be taught. It does aim, however, at removing the blocks to the awareness of love's presence, which is your natural inheritance.

"The opposite of love is fear, but what is all-encompassing can have no opposite. This course can therefore be summed up very simply in this way: 'Nothing real can be threatened. Nothing unreal exists.' Herein lies the peace of God." The course emphasizes developing inner awareness, letting go of fear and guilt, and identifying with the peace and love that is heaven.

RITUALS AND PRACTICES

There are 365 lessons with exercises, one set for each day of the year. As you read each day's message and meditate upon its meaning in your life, the process gradually changes your point of view and your perception, enabling you to overcome negative feelings of fear and guilt, and develop positive feelings of altruism and love.

FOR ADDITIONAL INFORMATION
Recommended Contacts

Foundation for "A Course in
   Miracles"
RD2, Box 71
Roscoe, NY 12776
Phone: (607) 498–4116

Miracle Distribution Center
1141 E. Ash Avenue
Fullerton, CA 92631
Phone: (714) 738–8380
Website: www.miraclecentere.org

Foundation for Life Action
902 S. Burnside Avenue
Los Angeles, CA 90036
Phone: (213) 933–5591

Recommended Reading

Helen Schucman. *A Course in Miracles*. New York: Viking, 1996.
The texts may be ordered directly from:

The Foundation of Inner Peace
P.O. Box 1104
Glen Ellen, CA 95442
Phone: (415) 388–2060
Website: www.acim.org

RAMTHA CHANNELED BY J. Z. KNIGHT

J. Z. Knight is a woman who had been Ramtha's foster daughter in a previous lifetime, and now channels his messages. She describes him as a "Sovereign Entity" who lived on earth over 35,000 years ago. Subsequently, he ascended to a higher level of consciousness so as to teach mankind how to rediscover the "God who lives within you."

HISTORY

Knight was first contacted by Ramtha in 1977, during a fit of laughter prompted by putting a cardboard pyramid on her head while enjoying a light moment with her husband. Since then, Knight has become one of the best known channels, especially after having been mentioned in Shirley MacLaine's book *Dancing in the Light*.

Knight grew up in the South. A child of a poor family, she nevertheless found the resources to attend business school. It was during this period that she began having psychic experiences. She later married a dentist and, while they were living in Tacoma, Washington, Ramtha came to her. He wished to speak through her. She agreed and since that time, she has devoted her life to channeling his teachings.

The Knight/Ramtha channeling sessions are lively and often humorous. They can be seen live at seminars or on videocassettes as well as heard on audiotapes.

BELIEF SYSTEM

Ramtha's message is that we human beings are divine and immortal entities who have forgotten our true nature as, over the years, we have become more and more entrenched in the materialistic world. God is the essence that loves us so much as to provide complete freedom for us to experience beingness without limitation.

Moreover, God lies within you, and there is no other redemption than for you to realize your Godhood. Ramtha explains in great detail the science of knowing, and the actual process of achieving a state of complete God-awareness, something akin to Adam and Eve living in Eden.

RITUALS AND PRACTICES

Spiritual exercises are explained and practical guidelines are provided in the literature and on the tapes. Topics include: death and ascension, creation and evolution, reincarnation, and the purpose of existence, among others. The spiritual practices include deep introspection, intense contemplation, and positive affirmations.

FOR ADDITIONAL INFORMATION
Recommended Contact

Ramtha Dialogues
P.O. Box 1210
Yefin, WA 98597
Phone: (206) 458–5201
Website: www.ramtha.com

Recommended Readings

Knight, J. Z. Introduction. *A Beginner's Guide to Creating Reality: An Introduction to Ramtha and His Teachings.* Yelm, WA: JZK, Inc.: 1997.

Knight, J. Z. *Ramtha, Channeled by J. Z. Knight.* Yelm, WA: JZK, Inc.: 1997.

LAZARIS CHANNELED BY JACH PURSEL

Lazaris is a consciousness without form, an energy that has never chosen to take human form. This nonphysical entity is often referred to as "the one who waits for us at the edge of our reality."

HISTORY

Jach Pursel thought of himself as a rather ordinary person, an insurance supervisor in Florida. In October of 1974, at the suggestion of his wife, Penny, he tried meditating, and something extraordinary occurred. During a deep trance, an entity Jach later named "Lazaris" started speaking with Penny—through Jach. This phenomenon continued, and soon Penny and Jach were taping the channeling sessions and making the information available to the public.

When Jach was channeling, he was unaware of what Lazaris was saying, and his eyes remained shut. Lazaris spoke with an accent that might be described as Chaucerian Middle-English. His sessions were quite lively, humorous, and informative.

Lazaris has developed quite a large selection of audio and videocassettes, which are available to the public, and his patronage is growing rapidly, as thousands call, write, or use the Internet to contact his organization.

BELIEF SYSTEM

Lazaris' premise is that we humans are essentially evolving, spiritual, immortal beings within and at one with a universe that he refers to as the "God-Goddess, All That Is." He claims that, in order to realize our true nature as immortal souls, we must work to overcome our negative programming, our debilitating self-image, and our limited worldview.

Some of the topics covered in the Lazaris material include the following: the new age, loving yourself, forgiveness, dealing with the ego, creating reality, the higher self, the nature of existence, and the journey home. Lazaris offers to guide you on your journey home to a higher consciousness.

RITUALS AND PRACTICES

At Lazaris seminars, lectures, and workshops held around the country, contemplative exercises or meditations are offered to the attendees. Guided meditations and visualization exercises of the Lazaris materials are provided on the audiocassette tapes.

FOR ADDITIONAL INFORMATION

Recommended Contact

Concept Synergy
302 So. Country Road, Suite 109
Palm Beach, FL 33480
Phone: (407) 588–9599

Recommended Reading

Lazaris. *Working With Your Shadow*. Orlando, FL: NPN Publishing, 1995.

OTHER CHANNELS

In the last decade, a plethora of new channels have come forth. There are literally hundreds, if not thousands, of new channels in the contemporary metaphysical marketplace. For more information on channeling, check advertising in New Age periodicals and metaphysical bookstores.

Recommended Readings

Carroll, Lee. *Kryon: The End Times*. Del Mar, CA: Kryon Writings, 1993.

Hoodwin, Shepherd. *The Journey of Your Soul: A Channel Explores Channeling and the Michael Teachings*. Laguna Beach, CA: Summerjoy Press, 1999.

Marciniak, Barbara. *Bringers of the Dawn: Teachings from the Pleidians*. Santa Fe, NM: Bear & Company, 1992.

The Urantia Book. Chicago, IL: Urantia Foundation, 1955.

Recommended Websites

www.llamalinks.com
www.master.spiritweb.org

PART FIVE

EASTERN MASTERS AND MOVEMENTS

In this section, I describe the more well-known and accessible teachings of enlightened, or self-realized, Eastern spiritual masters of the twentieth century, and the organizations that developed from their teachings. There have been innumerable spiritually evolved beings working to raise the consciousness of mankind, but not all of them attract a large following or have their teachings disseminated to the masses. In fact, many spiritual masters will work only with a select few who have demonstrated their sincerity and perseverance, and do not make themselves accessible to the curious or unprepared. Still other masters work on meditation or dreams. The various Eastern masters and movements described here are those that make themselves readily available to the public.

There is an ancient saying that "when the student is ready, the teacher will appear." From my personal experience, and from listening to the accounts of students from many different masters, this adage appears to hold true. There are so many different teachers and instructional methods that one or more is sure to accommodate the different personalities and proficiencies of those who seek them out.

Common Eastern Names and Titles

Very often, people react negatively to strange experiences, unusual terminology, and odd names that seem bizarre to them. Consequently, they reject that which they do not immediately understand. However, if you did that, you would be missing out on some truly profound and important truths, ideas that could provide inspiration and direction in your life. In order to assist you in making the names and titles less peculiar—or more familiar—I have provided you with a brief listing of the more common names and titles you will see in the pages that follow:

- *Baba* refers to a *holy man,* or *father,* and is used as a term of endearment. *Swami* literally means *one who possesses,* or *lord,* referring to someone in a high position, but it is used more loosely to describe any spiritually dedicated man. Many renunciates, monks, and spiritual aspirants are referred to as *Baba* or *Swami,* and it does not necessarily refer to a spiritual master, but acknowledges the spirituality of the individual.

- The title *Ji* is a sign of respect added to other names to show additional reverence, such as in *Babaji* or *Swamiji.* One who is referred to by such a name is held in high esteem as a spiritual teacher.

- A *guru* is a *teacher,* generally a spiritual teacher; and in the strictest sense, one who is awakened, or realized, and therefore capable of teaching others the Truth.

- A term of endearment is *dev,* so one who loves or appreciates the teacher may refer to that person as *Gurudev,* or *beloved teacher.*

- A *yogi* is one who practices or teaches yoga, the science of the self, and when used as a title refers to one who has attained the goal of yoga, which is self-realization, or God realization.

- A *rishi* is a *seer,* one who sees through illusion, or maya, and a *raj* is a *king.* *Maha* means *great,* thus a *maharishi* is a *great seer,* and a *maharaj* is a *great king.* A *yogiraj* is the *highest yogi,* and a *yogini* is a *female yogi.*

- *Ma* and *Mata* refer to the *holy mother*. A female spiritual aspirant may be referred to as *Ma*, or *Mataji*. The term *Sri, Shri*, or *Shree* is also used as a sign of respect, similar to the English *Sir*.

- *Bhagawan*, or *Bhagavan*, refers to a God-man, or a venerable saint, as does the word *Sant*. An *avadhuta* is a saint who has transcended body-consciousness, and whose behavior is not bound by social conventions.

- A *sadhu* is a dedicated spiritual aspirant, usually an *ascetic*.

- A *brahmacharya* is generally a spiritual aspirant who has taken a vow of celibacy, and a *sannyasan* is one who has completely renounced all worldly obligations to pursue self-realization. Nowadays, these terms may refer to any spiritual aspirant, although this is not technically correct, according to tradition.

- *Ram, Hari, Vishnu, Krishna*, and *Shiva* are all names of *God*, and are frequently used in spiritual names and titles.

- *Das* or *Dass* refers to a *devotee* of God, thus *Ram Dass* or *Krishna Das* refers to a devotee of Ram or Krishna.

- *Mukti* is *liberation; sat* is *beingness* or *truth; chit*, or *chid*, is *absolute consciousness;* and *ananda* means *bliss*. Thus, when these words are combined, *Muktananda* refers to *one who has attained bliss through liberation,* and *Satchidananda* is *one who has realized beingness-consciousness-bliss*. Both terms refer to one who has attained self-realization.

- *Master* generally refers to one who has mastered the discipline of yoga, or is the head of a spiritual lineage.

Some of the confusion people experience comes because some of the Eastern titles and names are compounded. Examples might be combining baba and ji into babaji. The term ananda means perfect bliss, and this is attached to the first two Eastern masters you will read about, Sivananda and Satchidananda. They seem like strange names indeed, but when you realize that they are compound words, they may seem less so.

When you look at all the different kinds of people in this world, it is not surprising that so many different kinds of spiritual paths and movements evolved. In fact, it would be surprising if they had not evolved as they did. After all, we are all here to learn different lessons in life, and each master has his own special talents and abilities to assist us on the path of self-awareness.

Each teacher is unique, with his or her own message, personality, and method of communicating. In a grade-school curriculum, studying many different subjects can round out your education; but at some point in the higher grades, you must concentrate in one area to really comprehend the subject. So it is in working with one of the masters. When you have found the one who matches your innate tendencies, you can concentrate, master one discipline, and rise to a new level of spirituality.

Studying with a spiritual master transcends intellectual speculation and conventional understanding. It stretches your awareness beyond the limited grasp of your mind and physical senses. These student-teacher relationships go to the very depths of the soul. Most of what occurs within you lies beyond normal experience. The master can discern a side of you that you don't even acknowledge yourself, and can help you to perceive it for yourself. Ultimately, the master's role is to help you discover and evolve something within you that is the very essence of who and what you are.

Each individual must travel the path to the Truth for himself, but the trail is fraught with pitfalls. Thus, it is imperative that you seek the guidance of one who knows the way. Think of a spiritual master as a pathfinder on your own road to Truth and self-discovery.

The descriptions I've written are from a limited perspective—my own. Each of you receives something different from each teaching, and from each master. Your understanding should be based on your own personal experience with the master and his or her teachings.

As you become familiar with the various masters I discuss in the pages to follow, you will find numerous names and titles given to the various teachers. These names can get confusing to a Western reader unfamiliar with the Eastern vernacular, so I have provided brief explanations of the more common terms. (See "Common Eastern Names and Titles" on page 307.)

The general purpose of all spiritual masters is to help the student, or chela, realize the Self, or God. As more and more individuals attain realization, the whole world begins to awaken to its highest potential.

All spiritual masters work to uplift humanity so that we may all live together in happiness and peace. In the section that follows, you will encounter almost forty such masters and the groups or organizations that follow their teachings. For example, you will meet charismatic teachers like Sivananda, Swami Rama, Sivabalayogi, Paramahansa Yogananda, Ram Dass, and Krishnamurti. You will come upon many who espouse one kind of yoga or another, including Integral Yoga (Swami Satchidananda), Raja Yoga (Brahma Kumaris), Kripalu Yoga (Amrit Desai), Hatha Yoga (B. K. S. Iyangar), Kundalini Yoga (Gopi Krishna), Sahaja Yoga (Shri Mataji), Kriya Yoga (Harihanananda Giri), Surat Sabdah Yoga (the Radhaswami Movement), Ashtanga Yoga (Baba Hari Dass), and Bhakti Yoga (Mata Amritanandamayi). In addition, you will encounter many different philosophies and views of the world and your place in it, including "The Way of the Heart" (Da Avabhasa), meditation upon the Self (Siddha Yoga), life as "divine play" (Osho Rajneesh), the path of personal experience (Saiva Siddhanta), "The Pathless Way" (Krishnamurti), Dhyan meditation (Shivabalayogi), and Transcendental Meditation (Maharishi Mahesh Yogi). There is a master named Yogi Bhajan who founded the Healthy, Happy, Holy Organization, and there is one who, before his death, predicted his reincarnation eight years in the future—and fulfilled the prophecy (Sai Baba).

There are so many groups, so many strange names, so many ideas, so many paths to God. There are so many ways to perceive the reality around you, so many ways to achieve serenity within you. Let us begin again to search the paths and help you find your way.

FOR ADDITIONAL INFORMATION
Recommended Periodicals

Hinduism Today
107 Kaholalele Road
Kapaa, HI 96746
Phone: (808) 822–3152

Inner Directions Journal
P.O. Box 231486
Encinitas, CA 92023
Phone: (619) 471–5116

What Is Enlightenment?
P.O. Box 2360
Lenox, MA 01240
Phone: (413) 637–6000

Recommended Website

Electronic Ashram: http://HinduismToday.kauai.hi.us/ashram/

SIVANANDA

Swami Sivananda was born as Kuppuswami Iyer in nineteenth-century India. He grew to become a world-wide influence on yogic practice and philosophy.

HISTORY

Kuppuswami Iyer was born of a pious family in Pattamadai, South India, in 1887. At a young age, he was inspired to serve humanity. As a medical student, Kuppuswami published a popular medical journal called *Ambrosia* from 1909 to 1913. He threw himself into the project, serving as editor, manager, dispatcher, and journalist. However, in response to an appeal for medical care for thousands of Indian workers on the rubber plantations, Dr. Kuppuswami left for Malaysia in 1913.

By 1923, his ceaseless compassionate service had generated such a dispassion for material life that Dr. Kuppuswami renounced the world to follow *parivrajaka*, a traditional practice of wandering as an ascetic. In 1924, his wanderings brought him to the Himalayan village of Rishikesh, an enclave for yogis striving for God-realization. It was here on the banks of the Ganges that he was initiated into the Sringeri line of Sri Sankaracharya. The ritual was performed by his guru, Swami Viswananda Saraswati.

Kuppuswami soon plunged himself into sadhana, the practice of yoga. His austerities included intense meditation along with asanas, pranayama, study, and service. He used his medical skills to serve sick and needy ascetics in the area. Inspired by these practices, the local populace began to call him Sivananda.

In 1938, Swami Sivananda began his monthly review, *The Divine Life*. He soon built the Sivananda Ashram in Rishikesh, which provided a myriad of services: a printing press, a hospital, a post office, and a yoga training center. By the time Sivananda died in 1963, he had authored over three hundred books on yogic theory and practice.

His many disciples continue to travel the world over, serving as personal representatives of his teachings. Some of the better-known in the West are Swami Chidananda, Swami Satchidananda, Swami Venkatesananda, and Swami Vishnu Devananda. The yoga teacher Lilias Folan, who has appeared on the PBS-TV show, *Lilias, Yoga & You,* was also trained by Swami Sivananda.

One of Sivananda's main disciples, Swami Vishnu Devananda, carried on his work around the world. Vishnu-Devananda became the founder and president of the International Sivananda Yoga Vedanta Centers. In 1957, the Swami was sent to the West by Sivananda with the words, "People are waiting."

After traveling coast to coast by car, with a brief residence in New York City, Swami Vishnu-Devananda founded the first Sivananda Ashram Yoga Camp in Val Morin, Quebec, Canada. This 350-acre facility offers retreats and courses in Hatha Yoga, meditation, and Vedantic philosophy. By 1977, other camps had opened in India, New York, California, and the Bahamas. Swami Vishnu-Devananda's instruction has reached millions through his Yoga Centers, which are now found on five continents, and to date, over 5,300 teachers have been trained.

BELIEF SYSTEM

Swami Vishnu Devananda presented yoga as a popular discipline in the West with a series of five principles, namely:

1. Proper exercise. This involves yoga postures for overall health and well-being;

2. Proper breathing to recharge the body and control the mental state by regulating the flow of prana, or life-force energy;

3. Proper relaxation, releasing tension from the body and carrying that awareness to all daily activities. This will conserve energy and shed fears and worries;

4. Proper diet. This means a natural vegetarian diet, which will keep the body both light and supple, and the mind calm; and

5. Positive thinking. According to Vedantic philosophy, meditation (Dhyana Yoga) will put one in control, purify the intellect, and bring one peace with one's Self by transcending the mind itself.

Through the proper exercise of the discipline, the followers of Sivananda strive to achieve control, peace, and health in body, mind, emotion, and spirit. Ultimately, they hope to transcend life itself.

FOR ADDITIONAL INFORMATION

Recommended Contact

Sivananda Ashram Yoga Camp
673 8th Avenue
Val Morin, Quebec,
Canada JOT 2RO
Phone: (819) 322–3226
Website: www.sivananda.org

Recommended Readings

Sivananda. *Yoga, Mind and Body*. New York: DK Publishing, 1996.

The Sivananda Yoga Center. *The Sivananda Companion to Yoga*. New York: Simon and Schuster, 1983.

SRI SWAMI SATCHIDANANDA

Like Sivananda, Satchidananda was an Indian, but born of a different generation. His major emphasis was the achievement of inner peace and serenity through Integral Yoga.

HISTORY

Sri Swami Satchidananda was born as C. K. Ramaswamy Grounder in Chettipalayam, South India, on December 22, 1914. He came from a family of landowners who were devout and often took in sadhus and holy men who would instruct the young Ramu, as he was called. After graduating from agricultural college, Ramu took a position with his uncle's firm, which imported motorcycles. At the age of twenty-three, he married, but five years later, his wife died suddenly, and he turned all his attention to spiritual development.

In 1945, at age thirty-one, Ramu went to Palani to study with several siddhas, including Sri Sadhu Swamigal, Sri Swami Badagara Sivananda, and Sri Swami Ranga-Nath. The next year, he entered the Ramakrishna Mission at Tirupurraiturai. Here, he received his brahmacharya diksha (monastic vows), and was given the name Sambasiva Chaitanya.

During the next two years, Ramu went to Kalahasti to study with Sri Swami Rajeshwarananda, then to Tiruvannamalai to study with Sri Ramana Maharishi. He also visited Pondicherry to experience the "darshan" philosophical system of Sri Aurobindo. In May of 1949, Swamiji went to Rishikesh to meet his Gurudev, H. H. Sri Swami Sivanandaji Maharaj. Two months later he was initiated into the Holy Order of Sannyas and was named Swami Satchidananda.

Two years later, Sivanandaji requested that Satchidananda undertake an "all-India tour," lecturing and teaching yoga. In the following years, Satchidananda began organizing branches of the Divine Life Society in many parts of India and what is now known as Sri Lanka.

Swamiji made his first world tour in 1966, traveling to Europe and the United States, and founded the first Integral Yoga Institute (IYI) in

New York City. From here, Swamiji's list of contacts reads like a Who's Who, with regular world tours and meetings with other spiritual authorities, such as Pope John Paul II and the Dalai Lama. Satchidananda became visible to many Westerners by opening the Woodstock Music and Peace Festival in 1969 to a gathering of over 400,000 people.

Today there are over forty Integral Yoga Institutes all over the world, offering classes in nutrition, yoga postures, and meditation. Satchidananda Ashram-Yogaville, in Buckingham, Virginia, encompasses about a thousand acres and is the international headquarters for Integral Yoga International.

BELIEF SYSTEM

Sri Swami Satchidananda believes there is but one god, that he is omnipresent, without gender, and infinite. Yet this being *is* knowable: "Only when the mind expands to a greater capacity can we understand infinite things. That is why . . . the Infinite One reduces Himself to a lower level. God appears in different names and forms to suit the taste, temperament and capacity of every individual." Swamiji teaches from an interdisciplinary perspective, recognizing that "although the paths are many, the Truth is One."

Swamiji has stated the objective of this path as follows: "The Goal of Integral Yoga, and the birthright of every individual, is to realize the spiritual unity behind all the diversities in the entire creation and to live harmoniously as members of one universal family. This goal is achieved by maintaining our natural condition of a body of optimum health and strength, senses under total control, a mind well-disciplined, clear and calm, an intellect as sharp as a razor, a will as strong and pliable as steel, a heart full of unconditional love and compassion, an ego as pure as crystal, and a life filled with Supreme Peace and Joy."

Swamiji teaches that it is our true nature to be peaceful and happy. However, since some are not usually in touch with these emotions, he offers various methods for clearing away the toxins and other disturbances that made us diseased, so we can regain our ease and realize our true Self. These methods include Hatha Yoga (see "Yoga" on page 17), Karma Yoga (selfless service), Raja Yoga (concentration and meditation, based on ethical perfection), Japa Yoga (repetition of a sound vibration), Bhakti Yoga (love and devotion to God), and Jnana Yoga (self-inquiry).

FOR ADDITIONAL INFORMATION

Recommended Contact

Integral Yoga International Headquarters
Satchidananda Ashram-Yogaville
Buckingham, VA 23921
Phone: (804) 969–3121
Website: www.integralyogaofnewyork.org

Recommended Readings

Satchidananda. *Integral Yoga Hatha*. Buckingham, VA: Integral Yoga, 1998.

Satchidananda. *The Golden Present: Daily Readings*. Buckingham, VA: Integral Yoga, 1994.

BRAHMA KUMARIS

Brahma Baba was the founder of Brahma Kumaris, the world-famous university located in India. It is known for its curriculum devoted to spirituality, meditation, and Raja Yoga. Its influence is now international, with study centers dotting the world landscape.

HISTORY

Brahma Kumaris World Spiritual University was founded in Karachi—now a part of Pakistan, then India—in 1936. Its founder, Brahma Baba, was a wealthy businessman who had experienced a spiritual awakening and Self Realization. For the next fourteen years, he led a self-sustaining spiritual community that devoted its time to yoga and meditation. Then, in 1951, he moved his headquarters to Mount Abu, in Rajasthan, India, and prepared the site for the growing university's international headquarters. When Baba died in 1969, the responsibility for the university's activities were assumed by two female teachers, Dadi Prakashmani and Didi Man Mohini. Currently, Brahma Kumaris is represented in eighty countries, with 3,500 centers and 450,000 students around the world.

BELIEF SYSTEM

The programs that Dada Lekhraj initiated at Brahma Kumaris center on the practice of Raja Yoga. The meditation focuses upon the internal workings of the mind; no mantras or special postures are needed. Students gradually gain experience at calming the mind, creating positive thoughts and forming a connection with God.

The underlying belief is that when the mind becomes intelligible, inner clarity develops. Toward this end, Brahma Kumaris offers classical yoga training, including yoga postures, breathing exercises, deep meditation, introspective practices, and philosophical discourse.

FOR ADDITIONAL INFORMATION

Recommended Contact

Brahma Kumaris World Spiritual University
46 South Middle Neck Road
Great Neck, NY 11021
Website: www.bkwsu.com

Recommended Readings

Brahma Kumaris. *Pathways to Higher Consciousness*. New York: BK Publications, 1996.

Brahma Kumaris. *The Art of Life*. New York: BK Publications, 1995.

KRIPALU YOGA

It was Yogi Amrit Desai, known as Gurudev (Beloved Teacher) to his many followers, who developed the Kripalu Yoga form of meditation that is called "meditation in motion."

HISTORY

The teachings of Kripalu Yoga have their origins in the Pasupata Siva sect from India. Gurudev studied under the reclusive yoga master Swami Kripalvananda—lovingly referred to as Swami Kripalu, or Bapuji—who maintained his extraordinary meditation practice for twelve hours a day over thirty-three years. Under the guidance of Bapuji—or beloved grandfather—Gurudev's kundalini energy was awakened, and he experienced heightened states of ecstasy and awareness. In 1969, after years of practice under Bapuji, Gurudev earned the title of Yogi and was authorized to teach yoga.

In America in 1961, Gurudev had started out working from four o'clock to midnight in a paper-bag factory in Philadelphia, Pennsylvania. In addition to earning a paycheck and supporting a family, Gurudev would teach yoga to Western aspirants. By 1966, he had started the Yoga Society of Pennsylvania, and also taught daily yoga classes throughout the day and into the night.

Today, Gurudev has the largest yoga ashram in the United States, the Kripalu Center for Yoga and Health, located on 350 acres in Massachusetts. The ashram houses approximately 300 staff members and nearly as many guests. It serves over 15,000 guests annually, and oversees 75 affiliate groups around the country and in Canada. Kripalu Yoga is one of the most popular and authentic forms of yoga in the United States—practiced most widely on the East Coast—and continues to grow under Gurudev's leadership.

BELIEF SYSTEM

Kripalu Yoga is based upon the utilization of prana, the life-force energy of the universe. According to Gurudev, it is explained in Samkhya Yoga philosophy not only as the Cosmic Spirit, God, but also as the individual spirit, "the spark of divine within us." He describes how prana works in the Kripalu Yoga practice: "At the usual level, prana merely sustains life, whereas at the evolutionary level, awakened prana accelerates healing, rejuvenation, and purification of body, mind, and emotions. The power of this secret science of awakening prana lies not just in accessing it, but in also knowing how to raise it for the unfolding of the higher consciousness."

Kripalu Yoga is practiced through a unique combination of disciplines: physical exercises (asanas), meditation, devotion (bhakti), and selfless service (Karma Yoga). The intention of the discipline is to establish conscious communication with the body wisdom, prana, and allow it to carry out automatically all the evolutionary purification processes of the body and mind at an accelerated rate. The technique involves moving through progressive stages of relaxation, absorption in sensation and movement, conscious attunement to experience, and free expression of released energy. This process is what Gurudev calls "meditation in motion."

RITUALS AND PRACTICES

The Kripalu Center is open year-round to support the transformational process of its guests and residents. Programs and workshops are offered on yoga, spiritual attunement, health and fitness, personal growth, and physical discipline. Retreats at the ashram provide participants a chance for healing and integration of the body, mind, and spirit. Teacher training and intensive seminars are also available.

FOR ADDITIONAL INFORMATION
Recommended Contact

Kripalu Center
P.O. Box 793
Lenox, MA 01240
Phone: (800) 741–7353
Website: www.kripalu.org

Recommended Readings

Desai, Amrit. *Working Miracles of Love*. Lenox, MA: Kripalu Shop, 1994.

Desai, Amrit. *Kripalu Yoga: Meditation-in-Motion*. Lenox, MA: Kripalu Shop, 1985.

Kripalvanandaji, Swami. *Premyatra: Pilgrimage of Love, Books I, II and III*. Lenox, MA: Kripalu Shop, 1996.

SWAMI RAMA OF THE HIMALAYAS

Swami Rama is the founder and spiritual head of the Himalayan International Institute of Yoga Science and Philosophy.

HISTORY

Swamiji was born into a learned, wealthy Brahmin family in 1925, in the state of Uttar Pradesh, India. Orphaned at an early age, Rama was raised in the Himalayas and instructed in a variety of subjects by his Bengali teacher and surrogate father, Sri Madhavananda Bharati. Swami spent many years traveling throughout India and the Himalayas meeting with some of the world's great masters such as Neem Karoli Baba, Ramana Maharishi, Sri Aurobindo, Rabindranath Tagore, and Harikhan Baba. At the age of twenty-four, Swami Rama was initiated into the Order of Shankarachariya, and served as spiritual leader in Karvirpitham, South India, from 1949 to 1952. Rama then renounced his position and went back to the Himalayas to spend eleven months of solitary meditation in a cave. Swami was then directed by his spiritual master to head west, where he studied psychology and philosophy at Hamburg University in Germany, at the University of Utrecht in Holland, and at Oxford University in England.

In 1969, Swami Rama came to the United States at the instruction of his guru, who stated, "You have a mission to complete and a message to deliver." At the Menninger Foundation in Topeka, Kansas, Swami Rama astonished scientists with his abilities of yogic control over involuntary autonomic nervous system functions, such as his heartbeat, pulse rate, and skin temperature. In 1971, Swami Rama founded the Himalayan International Institute of Yoga Science and Philosophy in Glenview, Illinois.

In 1978, he moved the entire operation to its present location in Honesdale, Pennsylvania. This 422-acre campus tucked away in the Poconos is populated by devotees with M.D.'s and Ph.D.'s who are working to advance the science of yoga. The institute holds annual conferences and teacher training courses in Hatha Yoga. The facility accom-modates 190 residents and guests, and oversees 21 branch centers around the world.

BELIEF SYSTEM

Swami's teachings are based upon the yogic sciences of personal experi-ence. He follows the Smarta Sampradaya, a popular nonsectarian tradi-tion of Hinduism. Rama asserts that "all the religions of the world have come out of one Truth," and that "if we follow religion without practic-ing the Truth, it is like the blind leading the blind. Those who belong to God love all. Love is the universal religion."

Swami teaches that Truth is wisdom that is gained through deep meditation. His belief is that one must know Truth through his own per-sonal experience.

RITUALS AND PRACTICES

Today, Swami Rama's work is being applied to methods of fighting high blood pressure, heart attack, headaches, and other ills. His "holistic health" programs are gaining credibility among conventional Western medical practitioners, and the Institute now offers M.A.- and Ph.D.-level programs. His training seminars for health professionals include courses in biofeed-back, diet and nutrition, Hatha Yoga, and meditation. In addition, semi-nars, training programs, and retreats are available to the general public.

FOR ADDITIONAL INFORMATION
Recommended Contact

The Himalayan Institute of Yoga Science and Philosophy
RR 1, Box 400
Honesdale, PA 18431
Phone: (800) 822-4547
Website: www.himalayaninstitute.org

Recommended Readings

Rama, Swami. *Living with the Himalayan Masters*. Honesdale, PA: Himalayan Institute Press, 1999.

Rama, Swami. *The Art of Joyful Living*. Honesdale, PA: Himalayan Insti-tute Press, 1989.

B. K. S. IYENGAR

B. K. S. Iyengar is one of the best-known and respected yoga teachers in the Western world, with over fifty years of experience.

HISTORY

B. K. Sunderaraja was born in Karnataka, India, in 1918. At the age of sixteen he went to Mysore to study with the yoga-adept Sri Krishnamacharya for several years during the 1930s. After completing his yoga training with his guru, Sunderaraja was given the name Iyengar and began teaching yoga classes in Pune, India. He became popular in the West when one of his students brought him from his home in Pune to live and teach in Europe in 1954.

Iyengar traveled to the United States for the first time in 1956. During the early 1960s, he trained many Western students throughout Europe and America, and in 1966, published his first book, *Light on Yoga*, which has become a classic yoga text.

With San Francisco as a base, Iyengar founded the Iyengar Yoga Institute, which is currently one of the nation's largest and most visible yoga institutions. There are over 150 Iyengar centers around the world, with 100 centers in the United States, and over 500 Iyengar-trained teachers in the country. Over 500 students a week take courses at the San Francisco studio alone. Some of the West's most respected yoga teachers have been trained by Iyengar, and his books on yoga are considered by many to be the best.

BELIEF SYSTEM

Iyengar integrates both Hatha Yoga and Raja Yoga in his training courses, and draws upon the classics of Hindu teachings, such as the *Yoga Sutras* and the *Bhagavad Gita* to explain his philosophies. He believes that everything is permeated by the *Paramatma*, or God, of which the *jivatma*, or your individual human spirit, is but a part. The system of yoga teaches you the means to unite the *jivatma* with the *Paramatma* and so secure *moksha*, or liberation. This communion is accomplished through the discipline of the body, mind, and emotions, that is, through Hatha and Raja Yoga.

RITUALS AND PRACTICES

Iyengar's yoga system is popular in the West because it is very practical in its approach and applications, and is oriented to you who live "normal" householder lives. Emphasis is placed on maintaining your health and well-being. The practice primarily involves yoga asanas—physical exercises—and pranayama—breathing exercises. These disciplines develop your physical, emotional, and mental strength and open up an awareness of yourself at many levels. You develop a relationship with and understanding of God by evolving a greater awareness of the self.

FOR ADDITIONAL INFORMATION
Recommended Contact

Iyengar Yoga Institute
2404 27th Avenue
San Francisco, CA 94116
Phone: (415) 753–0909
    or (800) 889–0909
Website: www.comnet.org/iynavs
        www.yogagroup.org

Recommended Readings

Iyengar, B. K. S. *The Concise Light on Yoga*. New York: Schocken Books, 1995.

Iyengar, B. K. S. *The Tree of Yoga*. Boston, MA: Shambhala, 1989.

MAHARISHI MAHESH YOGI

It was Maharishi Mahesh Yogi who introduced the practice of Transcendental Meditation [TM] to the world. Its purpose is to help you to realize pure consciousness.

HISTORY

Maharishi was trained as a physicist in college, but was not satisfied with the depth of knowledge he gained. Soon after graduation, he met the Shankaracharya of Jyotir Math, Shri Guru Dev Maha Yogiraj—a highly revered yogi—and decided to study with him. Maharishi spent the next thirteen years serving as Maha's personal assistant.

In 1953, Mahesh retired to the caves of the "Valley of the Saints" in Uttar Kashi, high in the Himalayas. After two years, he decided to make a pilgrimage to Rameshvaram, and then to the southern tip of India. It was here that Maharishi was first inspired to give the Vedic wisdom to the people. Although Maharishi did not actually speak his feelings, the people of Trivandrum spontaneously fulfilled his calling by asking him to give a series of lectures. Soon the Maharishi was traveling all over Kerala, lecturing and instructing the people in Transcendental Meditation.

After the Maharishi's six-month stay in Kerala, followers of Guru Dev and Maharishi formed the Spiritual Development Movement. In 1955, they organized the Spiritual Development Conference, attended by religious leaders of many disciplines. At the Seminar of Spiritual Luminaries in Madras in 1957, saints from all over India and over 10,000 other seekers of Truth heard the Maharishi's message.

On New Year's Day of 1958, Maharishi inaugurated the worldwide Spiritual Regeneration Movement "to bring the direct experience of pure consciousness to everyone in the world through the simple, natural, effortless technique of Transcendental Meditation." Since this time Maharishi has made numerous world tours, founded several universities, and established TM centers in over 120 countries around the world. To date, over 4 million people have been initiated into TM, which makes it by far the largest meditation movement in the world today.

BELIEF SYSTEM

Transcendental Meditation is based on the timeless Vedic truth that there is a higher nature in man that is eternal and absolute, and that it is man's purpose and birthright to realize this "state of being," or pure consciousness, within himself. Moreover, it is held that, through this realization, all suffering is alleviated. The process of attaining this realization and applying it to daily living is what the Maharishi calls "the Science of Being and the Art of Living." Through the process of TM, you are able to experience directly that eternal Being, at the deepest level of your own consciousness, a field of pure creative intelligence—the source of all thought and creation.

Transcendental Meditation is not practiced as a religion, but rather as an effortless, natural practice for unfolding the full potential of human consciousness.

RITUALS AND PRACTICES

The actual practice of Transcendental Meditation consists of simply sitting for fifteen to twenty minutes twice daily in a comfortable position with eyes closed, and repeating a personal mantra. A mantra is a sound, one chosen especially for the meditator, which is repeated in a prescribed manner. A common mantra, for example, is the sound, "Om."

During this simple meditation, the meditator's bodily functions and mental activity slow down, and the practitioner is able to experience deeper and deeper states of relaxation, serenity, and awareness.

Over five hundred scientific research studies conducted at two hundred independent universities around the world have shown that TM benefits an individual by increasing mental clarity, heightening psychic awareness, and significantly improving physical, emotional, and mental health.

FOR ADDITIONAL INFORMATION
Recommended Contact

You might look up the nearest Transcendental Meditation Center listed in the telephone book, or contact the following:

Maharishi Continental Capital for the
    Age of Enlightenment in North America
1600 North Fourth Street
Fairfield, IA 52556

Phone: (202) 723–9111
    or (800) 532–7686
Website: www.tm.org

Recommended Readings

Denniston, Denise. *The TM Book*. Fairfield, IA: Fairfield Press, 1986.

Mahesh, Maharishi. *Science of Being and the Art of Living*. New York: Meridian Books, 1994.

YOGIRAJ VETHATHIRI MAHARISHI

Yogiraj Vethathiri Maharishi, or Swamiji, is a kundalini master from a line of Tamil Siddhas in South India. He founded the World Community Service Centre, which seeks world peace through the individual practice of Simplified Kundalini Yoga.

HISTORY

Vethathiri was born in 1911 in Guduvancheri, a small village near Madras in South India. He came from a family of weavers, and by the age of seven, he had taken up that trade to augment the family finances. From an early age, Vethathiri sought after truth. He served an apprenticeship for many years under his master Vaidya Boopathi, Dr. Krishna Rao, who instructed him in the spiritual science of kundalini and the healing method of the ayurvedic—the ancient Indian medical science.

After many years of meditation practice, Swamiji evolved his consciousness to the realization of the self, and was called upon to share his insights and awareness with others. He quickly gained a large following. Today, the Vethathiri movement has hundreds of thousands of students, with centers throughout India and around the world.

In 1958 Swamiji founded the World Community Service Centre, which strives for world peace. The belief is that when individuals practice Simplified Kundalini Yoga, they will achieve interior peace as individuals. When a sufficient number of individuals have achieved this state, we will achieve world peace.

Since 1972, Yogiraj Vethathiri Maharishi has traveled around the world teaching Simplified Kundalini Yoga to many thousands. He is one of the few enlightened masters who works individually with spiritual aspirants. He often lectures at universities, explaining the theory of Unified Force, and has addressed the United Nations to announce his plan for world peace.

BELIEF SYSTEM

Swamiji explains the workings of the Universe, God, and the nature of man through a very scientific method involving the mechanics of "magnetism." The Divine Consciousness is the Absolute Space, or "Plenum," which is the latent potential within and beyond the Universe. From the static state, a fractionalized portion of consciousness creates fundamental energy particles with whirling motion. From this whirling motion of life-force energy particles, a spreading wave is generated, creating a field of magnetism with attractive and repulsive forces. Mass is created out of the joint functioning of these energy particles. Whenever the magnetism in the Universe gets intensified, it evolves into physical transformations as six characters: pressure, sound, light, smell, taste, and mind. Thus the world of our senses is created. To evolve the mind and awareness beyond limited perception, one must observe the life-force energy (kundalini) and merge the individual consciousness with the total consciousness.

RITUALS AND PRACTICES

Swamiji has developed an advanced practice of yoga so that it may be practical for householders and Westerners. He calls this practice Simplified Kundalini Yoga, or SKY, and has made it available for anyone regardless of age, religion, or culture. Through the initiation into Kundalini Yoga, your life-force energy, or Kundalini Shakti, is awakened and brought up, initially, to the *ajna chakra*, or "third eye" point, and then to the *sahasrara chakra*, or "crown center." After awakening these powerful centers of higher consciousness, you discover how to ground the energy through the practice of Shanti Yoga, and learn to integrate your higher awareness into daily living. This is one of the most powerful paths of awakening consciousness available.

Swamiji also teaches the ancient discipline of Kaya Kalpa. This practice rejuvenates the body's life-force energy in order to withstand the aging process and optimize good health and well-being.

FOR ADDITIONAL INFORMATION
Recommended Contact

Self Awareness Institute
219 Broadway, #714
Laguna Beach, CA 92691

Phone: (888) 881–4541
www.selfawareness.com

World Community Service Centre of California
926 La Rambla
Burbank, CA 91501
Phone: (818) 848–1509
Website: www.karnatakainfo.com

Recommended Readings

Vethathiri, Yogiraj. *World Peace*. Madras, India: WCSC Press, 1993.

Vethathiri, Yogiraj. *Karma Yoga*. Madras, India: WCSC Press, 1992.

Vethathiri, Yogiraj. *Yoga for Modern Age*. Madras, India: WCSC Press, 1991.

GOPI KRISHNA

Gopi Krishna was a kundalini yoga master who lived from 1903 to 1984. It was to further his teachings regarding spiritual awareness that the Kundalini Research Foundation was established.

HISTORY

Gopi Krishna was born in Srinagar, Kashmir, India, in 1903. During his teenage years, he undertook the discipline of deep meditation that he was to maintain for the rest of his life. As a young man, he married, raised a family, and established a career working for the Public Works Department. At the age of thirty-four, after seventeen years of meditation, he experienced an awakening of his Kundalini Shakti, or life-force energy. This phenomenon activated the centers of higher awareness from within him, creating heightened spiritual awareness. He spent many years exploring the nature of this kundalini and wrote fourteen books on the subject.

In 1970, an American friend and colleague, Gene Kietter, organized the Kundalini Research Foundation. His purpose was to disseminate the teachings and writings of Gopi Krishna, who died in 1984. The foundation is not organized by membership, but has affiliated groups in America, India, Switzerland, and Canada. To spread the message, it also sells thousands of books internationally every year.

BELIEF SYSTEM

The basic belief espoused by the Kundalini Research Foundation is that your life-force energy or innate intelligence is located at the base of your spine, in the root chakra. This Divine energy will start awakening naturally as you evolve your consciousness, but you can accelerate the process by learning how to tune into and work with this energy. Often depicted as a coiled snake, the kundalini, when awakened, will start to move up your spine and into the top of your head where it activates your centers of higher awareness, the Crown Chakra or thousand-petaled lotus. As the kundalini awakens, you naturally become aware of your true nature, the nature of God, and the purpose of your existence. It is an accelerated path to God-Realization, and can create many extraordinary experiences and realizations. To awaken your kundalini, you may practice various breathing exercises, improve concentration, and use a variety of meditation techniques.

FOR ADDITIONAL INFORMATION

Recommended Contact

Kundalini Research Foundation
P.O. Box 2248
Darien, CT 06820
Website: www.stn.net/icr/gopikris.html

Recommended Readings

Krishna, Gopi. *Kundalini: The Evolutionary Energy of Man*. Boston, MA: Shambhala, 1997.

Krishna, Gopi. *Living With Kundalini*. Boston, MA: Shambhala, 1993.

SRI RAMAKRISHNA

The great Indian saint Sri Ramakrishna experienced enlightenment at an early age and led such an exemplary life that he became an inspiration and model for others. The leader of his disciples, Swami Vivekananda formalized the worship of Ramakrishna by founding a society in his name. The Ramakrishna Order is connected to the ancient Vedantic tradition in its discipline and teachings.

HISTORY

Ramakrishna was born Gadadhar Chatterjee in the Bengali village of Kamarpukur, northeast India, in 1836. As a young man, he went to Calcutta and became a priest at the Kali temple at Dakshineswar. While serving as a priest, Ramakrishna began *sadhana,* or intensive training, in various Hindu spiritual traditions. He was unique among saints in that he had experienced "enlightenment" in both Shivaism (God as Shiva) and Vaishnavism (God as Vishnu), as well as in both dualist and nondualist modes of Vedanta.

Ramakrishna served as an archetypal figure who inspired a renaissance of Hindu spirituality at the end of the nineteenth century. His wife, Sarada, who was known as "the Holy Mother," also became recognized as a fully realized saint. A group of disciples formed around him, which became known as the Ramakrishna Mission, the leader of which, Swami Vivekenanda, became instrumental in bringing Hindu, and specifically Vedantic, teachings to Western civilization.

Ramakrishna's spiritual heir was Vivekenanda. The latter's original name was Narendranath Datta, and he was born in Calcutta in 1863. He was brought up in a Western-educated, middle-class family, and later studied at Calcutta University. In 1881, Datta met the great saint Sri Ramakrishna, and shortly thereafter, set aside his plans for a legal career and became a sannyasin, that is, a renunciate of material life.

Following Ramakrishna's mahasamadhi, that is, his death and final union with God, in 1886, Vivekenanda embarked on a pilgrimage across India, speaking on Vedanta and inspiring thousands toward a more spiritual life. In 1893, he traveled to Chicago to represent Hindus at the World's Parliament of Religions, which opened the West to Vedanta and initiated a worldwide interest in Eastern philosophy. He later helped found the Ramakrishna Order in India and the first Vedanta centers in America and England. Today, there are Vedanta centers throughout the United States and Europe, and the Ramakrishna Order is one of the largest spiritual organizations in India.

BELIEF SYSTEM

The Ramakrishna Order teaches Vedanta, which is a philosophy taught by the Vedas, the most ancient scriptures of India. Its basic teaching is that our real nature is divine. God, the underlying reality, exists within every being. The purpose of the religion is then to search for God within ourselves, a search for self-knowledge. The Vedantic view of God is that "it is not possible to define God as being only this or that. God is conceived according to our state of mind. God has form when called Christ, Buddha, or the Divine Mother, and again is without form when thought of as a Divine Force or Consciousness."

Some of the main tenets of Vedanta are:

- Brahman, or Existence-Consciousness-Bliss Absolute, is the ultimate reality. It is the unchanging Truth that is beyond name and form, and is devoid of qualities, without beginning or end;

- The universe is perceived through space, time, and causation, which begins when you receive your body and start thinking. But like water in a mirage, the limited perception of the tangible universe disappears when one enters the state of samadhi.

- The real nature of the human being is the Atman, which is eternal, infinite, and identical with Brahman. The goal of your human life is to free yourself from the limited illusion that you are separate from the Divine, and to become free in the Realization of God.

- The divinity that lies within you can be manifested through the practice of yoga, which signifies the union between your individualized soul and the universal soul.

Vedanta is practiced in various ways, depending on your personal characteristics. It stresses personal effort and direct experience as a means for knowing Truth. The four yogas that are prescribed for realization might be described as follows: Bhakti Yoga is the cultivation of a devotional relationship with God through prayer, ritual, and worship. In this practice, the human emotions are given a Godward turn. Their energy is used in the search for God within. Jnana Yoga is the approach to God through discrimination and reason. The goal is freedom. All of our miseries in life are caused by seeing differences, and so the jnana yogi tries to break through this delusion by seeing God everywhere. Karma Yoga is the path to God through selfless service to others. By working in this spirit, the God within each person is worshipped. Raja Yoga is sometimes called the yoga of meditation. It is the soul of all yogas. The emphasis here is on controlling the mind through concentration and meditation." (See "Yoga" on page 17.)

FOR ADDITIONAL INFORMATION
Recommended Contact

The Vedanta Society of Southern California
1946 Vedanta Place
Hollywood, CA 90068
Phone: (323) 465–7114
Website: www.vedanta.org

Recommended Readings

Nikhilananda, Swami. *The Gospel of Sri Ramakrishna*. St. Louis, MO: The Ramakrishna Vedanta Center, 1942.

Nikhilananda, Swami. *Vivekenanda: The Yogas and Other Works*. St. Louis, MO: The Ramakrishna Vedanta Center, 1942.

Vivekenanda, Swami. *Vedanta, Voice of Freedom*. Swami Chetanananda, ed. St. Louis, MO: The Ramakrishna Vedanta Center, 1991.

KRISHNAMURTI

Jiddu Krishnamurti was a great spiritual philosopher of this century, who taught "the pathless way" to find Truth and experience Beingness.

HISTORY

Krishnamurti was born in 1895 in Andhra Pradesh, south India, to a Brahmin family. At the age of twelve, he was "discovered" by C. W. Leadbeater, Annie Besant, and other Theosophists, who believed him to be the Messiah. Henceforth, he was reared and educated by them in Adyar, outside Madras, to prepare him to become a vehicle for the Lord Maitreya, or World Teacher. A religion called the Order of the Star was organized around him to deliver his message. However, in 1929, Krishnamurti resigned as head of the Order after a series of psychic and physical experiences, and renounced all religions and philosophies regarding enlightenment.

After disassociating himself from the Theosophical Society, he began teaching through discussions and lectures held throughout India, Western Europe, and North America. He is believed to have achieved enlightenment in 1948, at the age of fifty-three, but he had already gathered a large following, even though he clearly stated that he wanted no "followers." Until his death in 1986 at the age of ninety-one, Krishnamurti circled the globe giving lectures and discourses. His work is now known internationally, and several schools have been founded in India, Europe, and North America.

BELIEF SYSTEM

Krishnaji's taught that Truth is a "pathless land," that is, you cannot approach it by any path whatsoever, by any religion, or by any sect. "Truth, being limitless, unconditioned, unapproachable by any path whatsoever, cannot be organized; nor should any organization be formed to lead or to coerce people along any particular path." The object of Krishnamurti's teaching was to set man free by experiencing truth unencumbered by dogma or mental concepts.

Krishnamurti also taught the importance of being aware. To do this, you must give up your preconceived ideas, theories, and beliefs, and investigate the source of your knowledge. The objective is to get out of the state of *having* experiences, and to remain in the *state of experiencing;* to veer away from the collection of thoughts and ideas, and to simply "be." As Krishnamurti explains, "Truth is the understanding of what *is,* from moment to moment, without the burden or the residue of the past moment." Obviously, this is a difficult concept to grasp; it would be much clearer if you would simply *be* in the moment, if you would simply *experience* the moment.

FOR ADDITIONAL INFORMATION

Recommended Contact

Krishnamurti Foundation
P.O. Box 1560
Ojai, CA 93023
Phone: (805) 646–2726

Recommended Readings

Krishnamurti, Jiddu. *The Future Is Now: Last Talks in India.*

Krishnamurti, Jiddu. *Commentaries on Living (Vols. I–III).*

Krishnamurti, Jiddu. *The Awakening of Intelligence.*

Krishnamurti, Jiddu. *Freedom from the Known.*

Krishnamurti, Jiddu. *Think on These Things.*

SHRI SHRI SHRI SHIVABALAYOGI MAHARAJ

Shivabalayogi is regarded as a living saint in India. He has had visions and special blessings, but he lives only to guide and heal others.

HISTORY

Shivabalayogi was born with the given name of Sathyaraju on January 24, 1935, in the small village of Adivarapupeta in Andhra Pradesh, southeast India. When he was quite young his father died, and he was forced to work as a weaver to help support his family. On August 7, 1949, at the age of fourteen, an amazing thing happened to Sathyaraju.

On his way home after playing with his friends, he passed under a tree, and a piece of fruit fell into his hands. He squeezed the fruit and began to tremble all over. As he gazed into his hands, he saw a jyoti, or bright light, shining from the fruit, followed by the omkar duani (sound of Om) coming from his palm. Following this, a Shivalinga—a symbolic emblem of Lord Shiva—appeared in place of the fruit, and a sadhu (holy man) approached him and touched him between the eyebrows. With this, Sathyaraju lost outer consciousness and went into deep samadhi (the superconscious state).

Sathyaraju's experience prompted him to begin a period of deep and intense meditation known as tapas. The next twelve years were spent completing the Yoga's Tapas. These exercises consisted of meditating for twenty-three hours per day for eight years, and then for twelve hours per day for the next four years. Finally, on August 7, 1961, at the age of twenty-six, Shivabalayogi (as he became known) emerged from his samadhi with extraordinary spiritual powers received through Self-Realization. In front of a crowd of over 300,000, Shivabalayogi appeared with a strange luster, exuding peace and grace, although his body had been almost deformed by the rigors he had experienced over the past dozen years.

Shivabalayogi has guided and healed people from all over the world, and to date, he has initiated over 2 million into Dhyan meditation. He is now regarded as one of India's greatest living saints, and thousands of holy men and women come from all over the world to receive his darshan (blessings).

BELIEF SYSTEM

Shivabalayogi's message is, "World Peace through Inner Peace." Although Shivabalayogi is of the Hindu tradition, he teaches no doctrine. In his own words: "Know Truth through meditation (dhyan). Then you will yourself know who you are, your religion, your caste, and your nature. Do not believe what others say and become a slave to religious prejudices." Through Shivabalayogi's meditation techniques and spiritual guidance, willing aspirants will be led into ultimate union with God. All answers come through the individual's direct personal experience in meditation.

Shivabalayogi is also renowned for his ability to heal, with numerous accounts of the lame walking, the blind seeing, and other ailments being miraculously healed.

Shivabalayogi has several ashrams in India, and he makes regular world tours.

RITUALS AND PRACTICES

After having been initiated by Sri Swamiji, the devotee practices regular Dhyan meditation. During the initiation, aspirants are given Vibhuthi (Holy Ash), which has been consecrated by Sri Swamiji. The followers are then asked to concentrate on that spot, and the Swamiji will guide them from there. The initiation is solely for the deepening of meditation. Initiates may follow the spiritual path of their choice.

Sessions with Swamiji consist of the singing of bajans (devotional songs), followed by meditation in Swamiji's presence, and Prasad, that is, partaking in food that has been blessed. Afterward, those who have personal questions or need healing may approach Swamiji for his assistance.

Shivabalayogi does not typically give discourses or lectures, but rather encourages aspirants to learn the truth for themselves through inward-turned consciousness. There are no dogmas to follow, for all things can be known from within during deep meditation.

FOR ADDITIONAL INFORMATION

Recommended Contacts

National Organizer Ninu
    Durgesh Kumari
816 S. Vermont Street
Smithfield, NC 27577
Phone: (919) 934–3534
Website: www.shiva.org

Shri Shivabalayogi Maharaj Trust
6770 N.W. Jackson School Road
Hillsboro, OR 97124
Phone: (503) 693–1582

The Self Awareness Institute
219 Broadway, Suite 714
Laguna Beach, CA 92651
Phone: (888) 881–4541
Website: www.selfawareness.com

Recommended Readings

Palotas, Thomas L. *Darshan*. Seattle, WA: Sri Sri Sri Shivabalayogi Trust, 1992.

Palotas, Thomas L. *Tapas Shakti*. Seattle, WA: Sri Sri Sri Shivabalayogi Trust, 1992.

SHRI MATAJI

Devi, as she was known in her earlier years, is a twentieth-century female guru. She knew she had achieved enlightenment and wanted to pass on her gift to others.

HISTORY

Shri Mataji Nirmala Devi was born in 1923 into a Christian family in India. As a child, she and her parents lived in the ashram of Mahatma Gandhi, and were very involved in India's independence movement. Devi's start as a guru began when she became disappointed with some of the other gurus who were coming to the West from India, and sought to achieve enlightenment on her own initiative. On the evening of May 5, 1970, she sat all evening under a bilva tree, whereupon her kundalini shakti (Divine Life Force energy) arose to the top of her head and opened her Crown Chakra, which provided a Divine spiritual awakening. Devi is believed to be connected with this Divine energy, and transmits it to her students in order to help them awaken their higher consciousness. Her students bestowed Devi the honorific "Mataji" out of devotion and respect.

Later, she married a prominent Indian civil servant, Sir C. P. Srivastua, and spent her days teaching and promoting her beliefs. Centers bearing her name and teaching her ideas have opened in the United States, Canada, and Eastern Europe.

BELIEF SYSTEM

In order to awaken the kundalini, Devi transmits energy through a personal presence or, if necessary, through a photograph of herself. Through the students' receptivity, the shakti energy is activated within them and rises to the tops of their heads, activating their kundalini.

With an awakened consciousness, all answers are known and the purpose of life is fulfilled. The underlying belief is that we are here to evolve our consciousness to full Self-Realization. This is accomplished through meditation, receptivity, and serene concentration.

FOR ADDITIONAL INFORMATION

Recommended Contact

Sahaja Yoga Center
13659 Victory Blvd., Suite 684
Van Nuys, CA 91401
Phone: (805) 371–7717
Website: www.shrimataji.org

Recommended Reading

Meta Modern Era. *Sri Mataji*. Calcutta, India: Vishwa Nirmala Dharma, 1997.

SRI RAMANA MAHARSHI

Bhagavan Sri Ramana Maharshi was the enlightened Master of Nonduality. His message spread to the West because of his "cave of the heart" idea promoted in his extensive writings.

HISTORY

Ramana Maharshi was born in the small village of Tirucculi near Madurai, in southeast India, on December 30, 1879. He was born with the name Venkataraman, the second oldest son of Sundaram Ayyar, a local pleader, or unofficial lawyer. In his family, there was a history of one member from each generation becoming a person dedicated to spiritual pursuits. At the early age of seventeen, Venkataraman experienced a sudden profound introspection, which established him in the Realization of the Self, the Absolute. He left his home, leaving only a brief note and taking three rupees for train fare to Tiruvannamalai in the State of Madras.

At the Arunachala Temple in Tiruvannamalai, Venkataraman gave up all his possessions and remained silently absorbed in the nondual state, wherein the meditator is absorbed in Absolute Union with Being, a union that cannot be explained, cannot be voiced. The young "Brahmana Swami," as he was called, would sit for many hours on a bare floor, in a dark pit, or under a tree, unaffected by external distractions.

He soon gained quite a reputation, and within a year received his first disciple, who would take care of him. The silent sage soon attracted quite a following, and by the early 1900s began teaching aspirants from all over the world. By 1935, his devotees rose to considerable numbers, and later an ashram was built at Arunachala Hill. By the time of Sri Ramana Maharshi's translation into Mahanirvana in 1950, his teachings on Nonduality were known throughout the world.

BELIEF SYSTEM

The Bhagavan taught that you are not separate from truth, from God. Rather, there is unity between you and God, not duality. He believed that duality implies ignorance, but the Knowledge of the Self is beyond relative knowledge and ignorance; the Self is all alone.

Ramana Maharshi's teachings focused on obtaining enlightenment: "To know the truth of one's Self as the True Reality and [to] merge and become one with it is the only True Realization." The emphasis of his teachings is not on reading or on intellectual operations, but rather on a constant process of introspection and union with the Absolute in "the cave of the heart." Inquiring within as to, "Who am I?" or following the "I-thought" back to its source, and the discovery of limitless Love or God through self-surrender (nondual devotion) are also integral parts of the teaching.

FOR ADDITIONAL INFORMATION

Recommended Contacts

Arunachala Ashram
66-12 Clyde Street
Forest Hills, NY 11374
Phone: (718) 575–3215
Website: www.ramana-
    maharshi.org

Ramana Publications
P.O. Box 1326
Sarasota, FL 34230
Phone: (813) 951–0431

Recommended Readings

Godman, David, ed. *Be As You Are*. New York: Arkana, 1985.

Osborne, Arthur. *The Collected Works of Ramana Maharshi*. York Beach, ME: Samuel Weiser, 1997.

H. L. POONJA

The message of Poonjaji was deceptively simple—you are already what you seek—and it was this simplicity in approach that drew his disciples to follow his path.

HISTORY

Harivansh Lal Poonja, affectionately known by his students as Poonjaji, was born in 1910 in Gujranwala, India (now a part of Pakistan). He lived a fairly normal life as a devoted Hindu, marrying and serving in the army, until his spiritual yearnings caught up with him, and he set off to find his guru. In 1944, he met Ramana Maharshi (see "Sri Ramana Maharshi" on page 343) and stayed with him for many years. Having rediscovered his absolute oneness, he settled in Lucknow, India, and began receiving students from around the world for Satsang. During the nineties he developed a large Western following, and recently died in 1997. He is succeeded by several teachers who had awakened with him, the best known of which are Andrew Cohen and Gangaji.

BELIEF SYSTEM

Poonjaji's message is very simple: You are already what you are looking for. Human beings are pure consciousness and hence are absolutely free. There is no teaching, no path, nothing to do but acknowledge what already is. The purpose of life is to realize the Self, and the Truth is that the Self itself is already realized, and it is only the mind that creates the illusion of having to realize anything.

FOR ADDITIONAL INFORMATION
Recommended Contacts

Gangaji
Satsang Foundation and Press
4855 Riverbend Road
Boulder, CO 80301
Website: www.gangaji.org

Moksha Foundation
39 Edison Avenue
Corte Madera, CA 94925
SEC 20/144A Indirangar
Lucknow, V. P.
India, 226016
Phone: 0091-522-346-342
E-mail: Poonja@lwl.vsnl.net.in

Vidya Sagar
P.O. Box 1654
San Anselmo, CA 94979
Phone: (415) 289-7976
Website: www.poonja.com

Recommended Readings

Cohen, Andrew. *Autobiography of an Awakening*. Corte Madera, CA: Moksha Press, 1992.

Gangaji. *You Are That*. Boulder, CO: Gangaji Foundation, 1996.

Poonja, H. W. L. *Wake Up and Roar*. Kula, HI: Pacific Center Press, 1993.

SRI CHINMOY

Sri Chinmoy teaches that you have within your soul an "Infinite Consciousness" and a "Self-illuminating Light" that will allow you to connect with the Supreme through the "Path of the Heart" and find serenity in this world.

HISTORY

Sri Chinmoy was born in Bengal, northeast India, in 1931. At the age of twelve, he entered an ashram and remained there in intense spiritual practice for the next twenty years. While in the ashram, he would write poetry, essays, and devotional songs, perform selfless service, and meditate up to fourteen hours a day. While still in his early teens, he had many profound inner experiences and attained self-realization.

In 1964, the Supreme commanded Chinmoy to come to New York to serve sincere seekers in their aspirations to achieve enlightenment. It was here that he founded the Sri Chinmoy Center, which still attracts thousands of students from around the world. Currently, there are over eighty centers around the world, mostly in North America, Europe, and the Far East.

Sri Chinmoy is very active in lecturing in universities and has written over 650 books, composed some 5,000 devotional songs, and painted over 140,000 mystical paintings. In addition, he conducts peace meditations twice each week for ambassadors and staff at the United Nations headquarters in New York, and he frequently does the same for government officials at the United States Congress in Washington, D.C. He also meditates with his students regularly at his center in Jamaica, New York, and accepts students at all levels.

BELIEF SYSTEM

Sri Chinmoy teaches that "God is the Infinite Consciousness [and] the Self-illuminating Light," that there is no human being who does not have within him these two elements. Moreover, he states that "Consciousness is a spark that lets us enter into the Light. It is our consciousness that connects us with God. It is the link between God and man, between Heaven and earth."

The human body is considered the temple, and the heart, the shrine where the soul resides. The soul works in and with the body in order to manifest and evolve consciousness. As Sri Chinmoy explains: "For the realization of the highest Truth, the body needs the soul; for the manifestation of the highest and deepest Truth, the soul needs the body."

RITUALS AND PRACTICES

The practice involved in this spiritual discipline is called the "Path of the Heart," in which love is the most direct way for the seeker to approach the Supreme. In this life, "man fulfills himself in the Supreme by realizing that He is his own highest self. The Supreme reveals Himself through man, who serves as His instrument for world transformation and perfection." The path does not end with realization, however, as it is necessary to manifest this reality in the world around us. Meditation and selfless service are emphasized in this practice.

FOR ADDITIONAL INFORMATION
Recommended Contacts

The God-Adoring Song
P.O. Box 280934
San Francisco, CA 94128
Phone: (415) 584–1027

Sri Chinmoy Center
86-24 Parsons Blvd.
Jamaica, NY 11432
Phone: (718) 523–3471
Website: www.webcom.com/
_shanti/chinmoy.html

Recommended Readings

Chinmoy, Sri. *Meditation, Man-Perfection God-Satisfaction*. New York: Aum Publications, 1986.

Chinmoy, Sri. *Beyond Within*. New York: Aum Publications, 1985.

Chinmoy, Sri. *Samadhi and Siddhi*. New York: Aum Publications, 1985.

SRI AUROBINDO

Sri Aurobindo was a man of enormous potential for worldly success, but gave it up to follow the path of a student of yoga and philosophy. Revered in his day as a poet, philosopher, and mystic, he founded an ashram in southern India that is an international influence to this day.

HISTORY

Aurobindo Ghose was born in Calcutta, India, in 1872. He was the son of wealthy Bengali parents who sent him to a private grammar school in England, and then to Kings College, Cambridge, where he was awarded a number of scholarships for academic achievement. At the age of twenty, he returned to India to begin a career of teaching at Baroda College, where he became politically active in India's nationalist movement against the British colonial regime. In January 1908, Aurobindo met Vishnu Bhaskar Lele, a Mahashtrian yogi, in Baroda, from whom he learned to silence his mind and experience the spaceless and timeless Brahman.

In May 1908, Sri Aurobindo was imprisoned for one year on charges of sedition, whereupon he began an intensive study of the *Bhagavad Gita* and underwent a spiritual transformation. Henceforth, he would devote his life to yoga and Hindu philosophy.

After his release from prison, Sri Aurobindo went to the French colony of Pondicherry, in South India, where he devoted himself completely to the study and practice of yoga. In 1910, he founded an ashram, known as Auroville, as an experiment in communal living. His writings on "integral yoga" and philosophy became increasingly popular, and followers from all over the world flocked to his ashram.

On November 24, 1926, Sri Aurobindo experienced "The Day of Siddhi," where the oversoul consciousness (Krishna) descended into the physical and touched him. Subsequently, he retired to concentrate on his sadhana (spiritual practice). At this point, Mira Alfassa, a French woman and his most devoted follower, who was known as "The Mother," assumed the running of the ashram and the spiritual studies. In 1950, Sri Aurobindo died, and The Mother acted as the temporal head of the ashram and the international spiritual community until her death in 1973.

Today, Sri Aurobindo's teachings are considered classic to spiritual seekers, and study centers are active throughout the United States and abroad. Moreover, Auroville is one of the most popular stops for spiritual seekers traveling in India. It is also the site of numerous reforestation and other regional projects.

BELIEF SYSTEM

Sri Aurobindo's spiritual premise is that life is a field for the evolution of spirit involved in mind, life, and matter: "Man has been evolving, now self-consciously, from the lowest to the highest levels of existence; his latest evolutionary stage will integrate the physical, vital, and mental in a synthesis made possible by the Supermind." Sri Aurobindo conceived seven elements in the evolutionary stages—with the Supermind as the bridge between the lower and higher hemispheres of existence. Moving from the lowest to the highest, they are:

1. Matter (physical, inorganic);

2. Life (vital, organic);

3. Mind (intellect and intuition);

4. Supermind (perfect unity in diversity): the bridge element;

5. Bliss (Ananda);

6. Consciousness-Force (Chit); and

7. Existence (Sat).

Just as the lower levels of consciousness—matter, life, and mind— need to be transformed by the higher three, the latter are not fulfilled until they have been completely spiritualized in the realms of physical, vital, and mental existence. This can only be accomplished in the mind of the meditator, through discipline, austerities, and yogic exercises, a process that Sri Auribindo called "Integral Yoga."

Sri Aurobindo does not offer any strict or prescribed set of spiritual disciplines. His "Integral Yoga" is a synthesis of the forms of yoga discussed in the *Bhagavad Gita*, namely, Jnana (knowledge), Karma (action), and Bhakti (devotion or love). However, he adds a fourth one,

The Yoga of Self-Perfection, developed to focus on physical transformation.

However, his emphasis does not lie only in striving for your individual liberation. He states that your spiritual aspiration should be to transform the "spiritual, mental, vital and physical orders of existence." Emphasis is placed on directing your attention on your own divine nature, and devoting yourself to selfless service in order to bring about that transformation.

FOR ADDITIONAL INFORMATION
Recommended Contacts

Matagiri
HC 1 Box 98
Mt. Tremper, NY 12457-9711
Phone: (914) 679–8322

Sri Aurobindo Associates
2550 9th Street, Suite 206
Berkeley, CA 94710
Phone: (415) 848–1841
Website:
www.sriaurobindoinstitute.org
www.miraura.org

Recommended Readings

Aurobindo, Sri. *The Integral Yoga*. New York: Lotus Press, 1998.

Aurobindo, Sri. *The Life Divine*. New York: Lotus Press, 1985.

KRIYA YOGA

Lahiri Mahasay was the leading exponent of Kriya Yoga, the science of Self-Realization. The term *kriya* literally means *action,* and kriya occurs "when one acts to combine the action of the mind with breath, with the view to dissolving the mind at its Source." (See "Yoga" on page 17.)

HISTORY

Kriya Yoga is a science that has been passed on through different ages by the ageless and ethereal Master of Master Yogis, Mahamuni Babaji. In recent history it was Babaji who drew the father of Kriya Yoga, Yogiraj Sri Shyama Charan Lahiri Mahasay, up to the Himalayas to reveal again the authentic Kriya Yoga.

Lahiri Mahasay was born in the village of Ghurni on the bank of the Jalangi river in Krishna Nagar, India, on September 30, 1828. Raised in the Brahmin caste, Lahiri Mahasay was educated in the Vedic tradition, and received the sacred thread, becoming "Dwija," or "twice born," in 1836. Lahiri Mahasay was married in 1846, and fathered two sons who later became Kriya masters. In 1851, Lahiri Baba joined the Bengali Military Engineering Service as a clerk. He traveled extensively and was eventually transferred to Ranikhet in the Himalayas. It was here at age thirty-three that Lahiri Mahasay at last followed his compulsion to climb into the mountains in search of his guru, and it was at the top of Dunagiri Hill that he met the great Mahamuni Babaji and subsequently was initiated into Kriya Yoga.

After several weeks of training every day with Babaji, Lahiri Mahasay was instructed to give initiation to several disciples who had been waiting for him. Then, in 1865, Lahiri Mahasay's attainment of Realization was affirmed publicly by the famous saint Trailanga Swami, and many seekers started coming to see him. Mahasay gathered fourteen disciples to work with him, and, although he did not start any formal organization, the lineage branched out into several directions.

Many of his disciples developed a following of their own, and most of them remained within India with a small following of dedicated Kriyabans. Kriya Yoga is now one of the most widely known and respected yogic paths in the world. Nevertheless, there are very few people authorized to initiate in true Kriya, and they do not accept many students. One of the most respected authentic teachers available in the West is Swami Hariharananda Giri.

BELIEF SYSTEM

The underlying Truth in Kriya Yoga is this: "The Self is Absolute and One; there is nothing outside of It." All activities and manifestations are then a Divine Play of Consciousness. This Consciousness is much like a screen on which all of the world's happenings, activities, etc., are seen occurring, but is not separate from the Self. The multiplicity of states that are perceived by the mind are simply transitional phases on the way to Pure Consciousness.

The Awareness of this reality is grasped through vibrations. Vibrations are radiations of the Inner Light, which find dimension in various degrees and rhythms of dispersal. Those vibrations, which are perceived through our physical senses, are merely a reflection of a range of vibrations we know as our physical world. The seer and the seen are in the same state, or level of vibration, as the object and its reflection. The mind is the object, and the world its reflection. However, those who are able to become established in higher levels of vibration transcend the lower states of form and become one in Pure Consciousness. The object of Kriya Yoga is to attain this level of awareness, to Realize the Self, or make conscious union with the One Absolute.

RITUALS AND PRACTICES

In order to establish oneself in the Absolute, you must learn to look within yourself and attune to frequencies of vibration that lie beyond your physical perception. Meditation and introspection are the tools for focusing your attention within and attaining peace and harmony in your life. Kriya Yoga involves a meditation that "acts to combine the action of the mind with breath, with a view to dissolving the mind at the Source." Attaining the state of Pranayam—the tranquil or still state of Breath—and thereby "eternal Tranquillity" (Sthirattva), is the aim of Kriya science. Kriya Yoga is considered to be a more highly developed form of Raja Yoga, a synthesis of Karma, Bhakti, and Jnana Yogas.

FOR ADDITIONAL INFORMATION

Recommended Contact

Kriya Yoga Ashram
4904 Cloister Drive
Rockville, MD 20852

Recommended Reading

Giri, Hariharananda. *Kriya Yoga.* Rockville, MD: Kriya Yoga Ashram,
1986.

PARAMAHANSA YOGANANDA

In 1920, Paramahansa Yogananda founded the Self-Realization Fellowship for the worldwide dissemination of Kriya Yoga. This branch of yoga is the universal science of Self Realization, and strives for the development of physical, mental, and spiritual harmony.

HISTORY

Paramahansa Yogananda was born on January 5, 1893, in Gorakhpur in northeastern India, near the Himalayas. His name at birth was Mukunda Lal Ghosh. In 1915, after completing his college studies, Mukunda was admitted to the ancient monastic Swami Order by his master, Swami Sri Yukteswar, and given by him the monastic name Yogananda.

Yogananda came to America in 1920. He was the first great spiritual master of India to live in the West for an extended period—over thirty years. In 1917, Paramahansa Yogananda founded the Yogoda Satsanga Society of India, and in 1920 established a branch in America, where it is known as the Self-Realization Fellowship, headquartered in Los Angeles, California. Yogananda's classic book, *Autobiography of a* Yogi, has introduced many thousands of Westerners to the methods of Self-Realization and the science of Kriya Yoga. In 1936, Swami Sri Yukteswar bestowed upon him the revered spiritual title of Paramahansa.

Today the Self-Realization Fellowship disseminates the teachings of Kriya Yoga through temples, centers, and meditation groups throughout the world. They also publish a curriculum for home study.

Yogananda entered mahasamadhi—a yogi's final conscious exit from the body—in Los Angeles on March 7, 1952. Since then, Sri Daya Mata is carrying on the work as president and spiritual leader of the Self-Realization Fellowship.

BELIEF SYSTEM

The aims of the Self-Realization Fellowship are to disseminate throughout the world the knowledge of scientific techniques for attaining direct personal experience of God. The Fellowship teaches that the purpose of life is the evolution, through self-effort, of man's limited mortal consciousness into God-consciousness. Through daily, scientific, devotional meditation on God, man can be liberated from physical disease, mental disharmonies, and spiritual ignorance, and demonstrate superiority over body, mind, and soul.

RITUALS AND PRACTICES

The Self-Realization Fellowship relies primarily on Kriya Yoga, "an advanced Raja Yoga technique that reinforces and revitalizes subtle currents of life energy in the body, enabling the normal activities of heart and lungs to slow down naturally. As a result, the consciousness is drawn to higher levels of perception, gradually bringing about an inner awakening more blissful and more deeply satisfying than any of the experiences that the mind or the senses of the ordinary human emotions can give."

The initial techniques of the Self-Realization teachings are: (1) Energization, which enables you to draw energy consciously into your body from the Cosmic Source; (2) Concentration, which assists you to develop your latent powers of concentration; and (3) Meditation, which helps you to use your powers of concentration to discover and develop the divine qualities of your own true Self. By assisting you in these disciplines, the Self-Realization Fellowship hopes to serve you as your larger self.

FOR ADDITIONAL INFORMATION
Recommended Contact

Self-Realization Fellowship
3880 San Rafael Avenue
Los Angeles, CA 90065
Phone: (213) 225–2471
Website: www.yogananda_srf.org

Recommended Readings

Daya, Sri Mata. *Finding the Joy Within You*. Los Angeles: Self-Realization Fellowship, 1998.

Yogananda, Paramahansa. *Autobiography of a Yogi*. Los Angeles: Self-Realization Fellowship, 1998.

Yogananda, Paramahansa. *The Divine Romance*. Los Angeles: Self-Realization Fellowship, 1998.

Yogananda, Paramahansa. *Man's Eternal Quest*. Los Angeles: Self-Realization Fellowship, 1998.

Yukteswar, Swami Sri. *The Holy Science*. Los Angeles: Self-Realization Fellowship, 1998.

KRIYANANDA

It was Kriyananda, born James Donald Walters, who founded the Ananda Church, an offshoot of the Self-Realization Fellowship of Paramahansa Yogananda. It also employs Kriya Yoga as its main discipline to evolve toward God-consciousness. (See "Paramahansa Yogananda" on page 355.)

HISTORY

James Donald Walters was born of American parents in the Rumanian expatriate colony of Teleajen, on May 19, 1926. Because his father worked for Esso Oil in Europe, he lived most of his childhood abroad, attending boarding schools in Switzerland and England. With the advent of World War II, his family moved back to the United States and he completed high school in Connecticut and New York. He then spent the next three and a half years at Haverford College and at Brown University, where his interests in the spiritual became the primary focus in his life.

After leaving college, Walters began working as a playwright at the Dock Street Theater in Charleston. It was during this time that he developed an interest in Eastern philosophy. His curiosity had been piqued by reading first the Hindu classic *Bhagavad Gita*, and then *Autobiography of a Yogi*, by Paramahansa Yogananda.

In 1948, after reading Yogananda's work, Walters was compelled to come to California and meet with the master himself. Due to his "good karma" (spiritual merits), Walters was soon accepted as a "Brother" and began to live and study at the Self-Realization Fellowship (SRF) ashram at Mt. Washington in Los Angeles.

Walters was privileged to work closely with Yogananda, to whom he devoted his life, and was rapidly given more responsibilities and privileges in the organization. While working with the master at their retreat at Twenty-nine Palms, in the California desert, Walters was asked to edit Paramahansa's *Commentary on the Bhagavad Gita* and write articles for the group's newsletter. He was also asked by Yogananda to lecture on his behalf, and to give Kriya initiations.

On March 7, 1952, Paramahansa Yogananda entered mahasamadhi, a yogi's final conscious exit from the body. Walters spent the next few years reorganizing the SRF offices in the United States and centers around the world. In 1955, Walters was initiated into the Giri Swami Order and was given the spiritual name Kriyananda. From 1955 to 1958, Kriyananda was the main minister of the Hollywood Church. He was elected to the board of the Self-Realization Fellowship in 1960.

In 1962, Kriyananda was removed from the board of SRF due to personal differences with other board members. He began writing and lecturing on his own in San Francisco. It was during this period that he wrote his first book, *Crises in Modern Thought*. In 1967, with the help of friends, he purchased some land in the Sierra Nevada foothills, where by 1968, he began construction of the Ananda Cooperative Village. This spiritual society has set the example of a successful self-sustaining spiritual community. Annually, thousands come to learn how to live harmoniously and to practice yoga.

BELIEF SYSTEM

Kriyananda was trained by the realized master Paramahansa Yogananda in the practice of Kriya Yoga, a more highly developed form of Raja Yoga. The objective of the practice is to realize the Self, which "is absolute and one; there is nothing outside of it." Moreover, "our egos are nothing but vortices of conscious energy that, within the vast ocean of consciousness, take on the appearance of a separate reality of their own." Through the practice of Kriya, these "separate vortices of consciousness are dissolved in infinite consciousness." The purpose of life is the evolution of man's consciousness from mortal- to God-consciousness.

The Ananda Church fosters spiritual living and makes it easier for the seeker to go into "deep communion with God." Classes in yoga and meditation are offered and vegetarian dining is provided.

RITUALS AND PRACTICES

Kriya Yoga is the principal practice at Ananda. The word *kriya* literally means *action*, and it occurs when "one acts to combine the action of the mind with breath, with the view to dissolve the mind at its source." So kriya meditation, a form of pranayam, involves the breath.

Ananda's guest facility, "The Expanding Light," is open every day of the year, and a "Spiritual Renewal Week" is held during the last week of August each year.

FOR ADDITIONAL INFORMATION

Recommended Contact

Ananda's Expanding Light
14618 Tyler Road
Nevada City, CA 95959
Phone: (800) 346–5350
Website: www.ananda.org

Recommended Reading

Kriyananda. *The Path.* Nevada City, CA: Crystal Clarity Press, 1977.

SIDDHA YOGA

Siddha Yoga is a spiritual path based on the highest principles of life. The heart of Siddha Yoga lies in meditation upon the Self.

HISTORY

Gurumayi Chidvilasananda is the living Siddha master of Siddha Yoga, and the successor of a great unbroken lineage of spiritual masters. She was born into Siddha Yoga and grew up at the feet of her master, Swami Muktananda. At a very young age, she dedicated herself entirely to her guru and his teachings, and at the age of twenty-six, she took the vows of monkhood. Before Swami Muktananda died in 1982, he empowered Gurumayi with the vast spiritual legacy that his own Guru, Bhagawan Nityananda, had left to him.

Swami Muktananda was born in Mangalore, south India, in 1908. He came from a wealthy family, but became a renunciate as a teenager, whereupon he was given the name Muktananda. For the next twenty-five years, he wandered throughout India on foot, learning from many of the great sages and saints of his day. In 1947, at age thirty-nine, Baba met Bhagawan Nityananda, one of the greatest saints of India in recent times and master of the Siddha lineage. Baba studied under Nityananda for nine years and achieved self-realization under his guidance.

Swami Muktananda introduced Siddha Yoga to the West, and initiated hundreds of thousands into the Siddha path. Since then, Gurumayi has continued to evolve the teachings and makes regular world tours, initiating many thousands into Siddha Yoga. Today, Siddha Yoga enjoys one of the largest followings of yoga practiced in the West.

BELIEF SYSTEM

Through the pursuit of Siddha Yoga the inner conscious energy called kundalini shakti is awakened. Kundalini shakti is a great spiritual power that lies dormant within the body. Anyone who wishes to experience kundalini must do so with his own conscious body. He then tastes divine bliss and ecstasy. This is the secret of Siddha Yoga. The awakening of kundalini in the great initiation called Shaktipat occurs through the grace of the guru during a program of meditation called the Siddha Yoga Meditation Intensive. After initiation, a seeker is encouraged to practice Siddha meditation.

Siddha meditation is a very simple and easy process that consists of repeating a mantra given to you by the guru. With the practice of the mantra, the power of the kundalini unfolds within you, which induces the state of meditation within the aspirant. In time, you progress more and more deeply into your own being, until your mind is purified, your emotions become clear, and you experience a profound inner peace.

In the final stage of meditation, the knowledge, "I am complete and I am perfect," arises spontaneously within. There are some who believe that if they say the words, they will experience the kundalini shakti, but it is not so. There is no other way except through the path of meditation and self-discipline.

Siddha Yoga teaches you to identify and love the light, the truth, and the peace within each human being. It endeavors to help you achieve knowledge, search for the inner consciousness, bring about oneness on earth, and realize your own Self.

FOR ADDITIONAL INFORMATION

Recommended Contacts

Centers Office SYDA
  Foundation
P.O. Box 600
South Fallsburg, NY 12779
Phone: (914) 434–2000
Website: www.siddhayoga.org

Guru Siddha Peeth
PO Ganeshpuri (PIN 401206)
District Thana, Maharashtra,
  India

Recommended Readings

Chidvilasananda, Gurumayi. *Kindle My Heart*. South Fallsburg, NY: SYDA Foundation, 1992.

Muktananda, Swami. *Play of Consciousness*. South Fallsburg, NY: SYDA Foundation, 1987.

Muktananda, Swami. *Where Are You Going?* South Fallsburg, NY: SYDA Foundation, 1987.

Swami Rudrananda

Culturally, Swami Rudrananda was from the West, but he found his fulfillment in the philosophies and teachings of the East. Because of his influence, we today have the Nityananda Institute and numerous disciples to carry on his message.

HISTORY

Albert Rudolph—who was later known as Rudi and then as Swami Rudrananda—was born in New York City in 1928. At an early age, Rudi showed signs of psychic development, and was exposed to Buddhist, Hindu, and Western mysticism. He studied under several spiritual teachers, the most notable of them being Sri Shankaracharya of Puri and Bhagawan Nityananda of Ganeshpuri. After many trips to India, studying and practicing spiritual exercises with his teachers, he was recognized as a Swami—one of the first Westerners to be recognized as such. He became known internationally as Swami Rudrananda. Perhaps, because he was culturally of the West, he was able to teach the secrets of the East in a way that was more easily accessible to Westerners. Rudi became a well-known spiritual leader, with thousands of followers in the United States and Europe.

Tragically, Rudrananda died in a plane crash in 1973. Nevertheless, his teachings are still being carried out in the ashrams he established through his students. One of his most notable disciples is Swami Chetanananda at the Nityananda Institute.

BELIEF SYSTEM

Rudrananda's teachings involve coming to an understanding that "everything is a part of perfection and must be taken in a state of surrender; it must be digested and transcended." Thus, all experiences become spiritual exercises. Difficult experiences in our lives force us to change the patterns in our lives that keep us from complete realization. Rudi emphasizes the role of the teacher, or guru, to serve as a role model and catalyst for spiritual development.

RITUALS AND PRACTICES

Rudi's spiritual disciplines included both sitting meditations and yoga. He emphasized awareness of the energies affecting you all the time during any activity.

Moreover, he claimed that all barriers must be broken down and all energies must be utilized for spiritual unfoldment. In this way, all experience becomes our teacher.

FOR ADDITIONAL INFORMATION

Recommended Contact

Nityananda Institute
P.O. Box 1973
Cambridge, MA 02238
Phone: (617) 497–6263

Recommended Readings

Chetanananda, Swami. *The Breath of God*. New York: Rudra Press, 1988.

Hatengdi, M. U. *Divine Presence*. New York: Rudra Press, 1998.

Hatengdi, M. U., and Swami Chetanananda. *Nitya Sutras*. New York: Rudra Press, 1990.

Rudi. *Spiritual Cannibalism*. New York: Rudra Press, 1990.

DA AVABHASA

Da Avabhasa, which means *"the Bright,"* is a God-Realized master whose teachings are called "the Way of the Heart."

HISTORY

Da Avabhasa was born "already Awake" on Long Island, New York, in 1939. His name at birth was Franklin Jones. He entered Columbia College at seventeen and studied Western philosophy. He did graduate work in English at Stanford University, and later, he studied for the priesthood at three Christian seminaries.

But from the beginning of his college years, Jones immersed himself in a spiritual quest. His primary breakthroughs in understanding occurred before he met his human spiritual teachers, Albert Rudolph (See "Swami Rudrananda" on page 363), and Rudi's own teachers, Swami Muktananda and Swami Nityananda of India. He received the spiritual transmissions of each of these great yogis and was blessed by them to enter into an esoteric devotional relationship with the Divine Goddess, or Shakti. After an extraordinarily rapid spiritual evolution, which included three sacred pilgrimages to India, Jones passed into the most radical or absolute Realization of the Divine Self in a temple of the Vedanta Society in Los Angeles, California, on September 10, 1970. He soon came to be called Da Avabhasa.

Since then, he has been involved in a remarkable demonstration of the nature and work of a Divine Incarnation. He has provided a thoroughly new sacred literature of revealed wisdom for modern men and women, established and empowered three meditation and retreat sanctuaries—two in America, one in Fiji—and has many thousands of appreciative readers. Over a thousand dedicated devotees all over the world follow his Way of the Heart. His disciples and many others regard Da Avabhasa as the Divine World-Teacher of our epoch.

BELIEF SYSTEM

Da Avabhasa's "Teaching Message" revolves around two principal revelations. The first is that every *ego* is an addict, chronically locked in the adventure of self-created separation, suffering, and fruitlessly seeking for relief, union, or consolidation. The second principle is that Da Avabhasa is himself the Source of Divine Grace that makes our freedom from egotism possible.

The practice of Da Avabhasa's "Way of the Heart" thus proceeds along two lines. The first involves an increasingly deep understanding of how you create the sense of egoistic separation, and why all of your searches are futile. The second endures this joyous and, in many ways, miraculous ordeal, because the core of it is increasingly deep communion with Da Avabhasa as the agent of very tangible grace in your life. Thus, the "Way of the Heart" is to be found through the grace of Da Avabhasa himself.

Speaking ecstatically in oneness with the Divine, Da Avabhasa writes in his simplest and most popular scripture, *The Love-Ananda Gita,* "Separation is the first gesture made by anyone who has a problem, who is seeking, or who is trying to account for anything whatsoever. Perfect understanding is the capability to directly . . . transcend dilemma, all problems, and all seeking. Perfect understanding is the capability inherent in Love-Bliss itself. I have . . . thoroughly elaborated the great process wherein and whereby Love-Bliss-Unity is . . . perfectly realized. Contemplation of my bodily (human) form, my spiritual (and always blessing) presence, and my very (and inherently perfect) state is the principle wherein and whereby the great process of the Way of the Heart is accomplished."

FOR ADDITIONAL INFORMATION

Recommended Contact

Free Daist Communion
P.O. Box 3680
Clearlake, CA 95422
Phone: (707) 928–4936
Website: www.adidam.org

Recommended Readings

Bonder, Saniel. *The Divine Emergence of the World-Teacher.* Middletown, CA: Dawn Horse Press, 1998.

Da Avabhasa. *Feeling Without Limitation.* Middletown, CA: Dawn Horse Press, 1998.

Da Avabhasa. *The Love-Ananda Gita.* Middletown, CA: Dawn Horse Press, 1998.

GURDJIEFF

Gurdjieff was a Russian Georgian whose ideas had enormous influence on twentieth-century philosophy and practice, especially in his espousal of the concept of the "Fourth Way."

HISTORY

Georges Ivanovitch Gurdjieff was born in Russian Georgia on January 13, 1877. He was a mysterious man who valued his privacy and managed to cover his tracks well during his years of searching for Truth. However, there are suggestions that he traveled a great deal throughout the Middle East and even ventured into Tibet. During this quest, he studied with several spiritual masters of various backgrounds and disciplines, and developed a unique style and process of learning, now referred to as the "Fourth Way."

He returned to Russia before the war in 1914, and met his most noted disciple, P. D. Ouspensky, in 1915. It was this devotee who wrote the first book on Gurdjieff's philosophy, and who contributed to making Gurdjieff's teachings known the world over. Gurdjieff later fled from Russia with a number of his disciples and settled in France in 1922.

While in France, he created the "Institute for the Harmonious Development of Man," at Prieure of Avon. At the institute, he developed "sacred dances," which he began teaching in Europe and in the United States around 1924. After these tours, he returned to France to write his three major works in the "All and Everything" series.

Gurdjieff is responsible for changing the direction of Western thought. After he died in 1949, his teachings were carried on by Ouspensky and other disciples of the Fourth Way path. His methods are still practiced at Gurdjieff/Ouspensky Centers around the world. There are over forty such centers throughout the United States alone.

BELIEF SYSTEM

Gurdjieff held that "every man is a three-brained being." These mental centers are identified as follows: The *physical* center, which is functional, instinctual, and sexual in nature; the *emotional* center, which focuses on one's feelings and emotions; and the *intellectual* center, which is the source of the mind. Gurdjieff's premise is that it is our fate to be unbalanced and out of touch with these centers. This imbalance keeps us living under a "false personality." Moreover, he believed that most of us are operating primarily under the control of *one* of these centers. He taught that each individual among the whole of mankind could be classified as being one of the three types, depending on which center was most predominant in one's character:

1. The *first* kind of individual is controlled by his instincts and desires, and basically copies others' behavior patterns as a means of survival.

2. The *second* type of person is a slave to his or her emotions, and is caught up in achieving immediate emotional gratification.

3. The *third* kind of being is preoccupied with mental concepts and ideas, and is limited by theories and idle speculation.

In order to make the transformation into the more highly evolved *fourth* kind of being, the mechanical patterns associated with each respective type of person must be broken. This process is referred to as the "Fourth Way."

The Fourth Way is an interactive process, rather than a philosophy or faith. The process not only involves the *evolution* of man's consciousness, but also the *involution* of consciousness within man. In a letter to P. D. Ouspensky in 1916, Gurdjieff wrote: "In speaking of evolution it is necessary to understand from the outset that no mechanical evolution is possible. The evolution of man is the evolution of consciousness and 'consciousness' cannot evolve unconsciously. The evolution of man is the evolution of his will and 'will' cannot evolve involuntarily. The evolution of man is the evolution of his power of doing, and 'doing' cannot be the result of things which 'happen.'"

The Fourth Way is a way of living, and to understand the process is to participate in the process; Fourth Way Centers and their trainers provide the tools to undergo the transformation. The key to the process is to become conscious of your own consciousness and its need to evolve, to become conscious of an awareness within yourself. The next step is to discipline the mind to be conscious of being conscious, to become aware of your own consciousness and mindful of not being unconscious. This is the beginning of the evolution of your consciousness.

FOR ADDITIONAL INFORMATION
Recommended Contacts

The Fellowship of Friends
P.O. Box 500
Renaissance, CA 95962
Phone: (916) 692–2244

Gurdjieff Foundation
85 St. Elmo Way
San Francisco, CA 94127
Website: www.gurdjieff.org

Recommended Readings

Gurdjieff, G. I. *Beelzebub's Tales to His Grandson*. New York: Penguin USA, 1999.

Gurdjieff, G. I. *Meetings With Remarkable Men*. New York: Dutton, 1991.

Ouspensky, P. D. *In Search of the Miraculous*. New York: Harcourt Brace, 1974.

THE RADHASOAMI MOVEMENT

Shiv Dayal Singh, a retired money lender and mystic, introduced the Radhasoami Movement to India. Today, the movement boasts over a million adherents.

HISTORY

Shiv Dayal was responsible for introducing the spiritual discipline of Surat Shabdah Yoga to the world. Shiv Dayal was a retired businessman, with a family from Puntaos. As is typical of retired men in this culture, he dedicated the rest of his life to the pursuit of God. During meditation, he experienced mystical awareness of the inner worlds and proceeded to show others various methods to gain this higher awareness. His reputation began to spread, and the movement was born.

The Radhasoami Movement was started in 1861 in Agra, north India. The movement is split into two major divisions, one in Agra and the other in Beas. The *Agra* Radhaswamis, which comprises the parent branch, known as Swami Bagh, has been without a Guru since 1949. The Dayal Bagh sect was established in 1907 and later formed the Dayal Bagh colony in 1915.

The *Beas* branch is referred to as Sant Mat, or Faith of Holy Men, and the movement is known as Satsang Beas. The Sant Mat sect was founded in Beas, Punjab, by Baba Jaimal Singh, a Sikh soldier who died in 1903. Sawan Singh then became the Living Master of the Sat Mat group in Beas.

The Satsang Beas movement was *further* split into two factions. One is the Satsang Beas Living Guru, better known as Radhasoami Satsang Beas, which was started in 1951 by Maharaj Jagat Singh Ji. He was succeeded by Maharaj Charon Singh, who died in 1990, and proclaimed Maharaj Gurinder Singh the spiritual head and living guru.

The other faction was the Ruhani Satsang Delhi, which was founded in New Delhi by Sant Kirpal Singh. Upon his death in 1974, three devotees emerged as Spiritual Masters and founded new orders, although

Ruhani Satsang presently has no incarnate masters. Sant Thakar Singh founded the Kirpal Light Satsang; Sant Darshan Singh—Kirpal Singh's son—founded the Sawan-Kirpal Ruhani Mission, and then passed it on to his son Rajinder Singh; and Sant Ajaib Singh founded the Sant Bani Ashram, which also has a following in the United States.

By his own estimate, Sant Ajaib Singh had initiated between eight and ten thousand devotees. Today there are estimated to be over 1.2 million devotees, divided into several major sects represented around the world.

RITUALS AND PRACTICES

The similarities between the sects lie principally in the practice of Surat Shabdah Yoga, which involves connecting with the Audible Life Stream, or the inner light and sound. Radhasoamis also practice vegetarianism, abstain from drugs and alcohol, uphold prescribed high moral values, work for a living—no renunciation of the world—and hold allegiance to the Sant Guru, or Spiritual Master. The initiations are secret and the spiritual experiences one has during the spiritual exercises are not to be shared with others. The sects utilize various forms of chanting the names of God, referred to as sumiran, or simran, and listening to the sound current, which is referred to as bhajan.

Generally, the Agra Radhaswamis consider Shiv Dayal Singh as an avatar of the Supreme Being Radhasoami and founder of a new world order. On the other hand, the Sant Mat sect see him as a revivalist master in the line of saints such as Kabir and Nanak. The Delhi faction see Shiv Dayal as a great successor to the tenth Guru of the Sikhs, Gobind Singh. (See "Sikhism" on page 26.) The spiritual practices and beliefs among the various Radhasoami factions are similar. The primary differences concern who are the true Sat Gurus, or Living Masters.

FOR ADDITIONAL INFORMATION
Recommended Contacts

Kirpal Light Satsang
Merwin Lake Road
Kinderhook, NY 12106
Phone: (518) 758–7521

Radha Soami Satsang Beas
10901 Mill Springs Dr.
Nevada City, CA 95959

Radhasoami Satsang Association   Sawam Kirpal Ruhani Mission
PB Nam Prasad Bhatia   8605 Village Way, No. C
5166 Down West Ride   Alexandria, VA 22309-1605
Columbia, MD 21044

Recommended Readings

Maharaj, Soami Ji. *Sar Bachan*. Beas, India: Radha Soami Satsang Beas, 1987.

Singh, Huzur Maharaj Sawan. *Spiritual Gems*. Beas, India: Radha Soami Satsang Beas, 1980.

Singh, Kirpal. *Spirituality—What It Is*. Delhi, India: Ruhani Satsang, 1965.

Singh, Maharaj Charan. *Divine Light*. Beas, India: Radha Soami Satsang Beas, 1983.

Singh, Maharaj Sardar Bahadur Jagat. *The Science of the Soul*. Beas, India: Radha Soami Satsang Beas, 1987.

Singh, Sant Thakar. *Five Interviews*. Kinderhook, NY: Kirpal Light Satsang, 1984.

YOGI BHAJAN

Yogi Bhajan is the founder of the Healthy, Happy, Holy Organization (3HO), a group that espouses Kundalini Yoga, encourages a vegetarian diet, and takes its name as its philosophy.

HISTORY

Yogi Bhajan was born in Punjab, north India, in an area that is now a part of Pakistan. He was raised as a devout Sikh, and introduced early to yoga and meditation. At an early age he mastered Kundalini Yoga, and advanced to study White Tantric Yoga. After receiving a degree in economics, he began working for the government, married and raised three children, all the while maintaining his yogic discipline. At age thirty-nine he left India for the United States, where he began teaching Kundalini and White Tantric Yoga.

He is founder of the Healthy, Happy, Holy Organization (3HO), which offers courses in Kundalini Yoga and related areas. The 3HO has expanded rapidly, with ashrams throughout the United States, Canada, Mexico, Europe, Israel, and Japan.

BELIEF SYSTEM

Yogi Bhajan teaches that one should look inward to find God, and that in order to find the divine within, one must purify oneself through conscious living and regular meditation. The universe is described as being in "a constant state of vibration manifested to us as light, sound, and energy," and "the Word" mentioned in the Bible is actually the "totality of vibration that underlies and sustains all creation."

Moreover, although our external senses only perceive a fraction of this eternal vibration, one can "tune into" this universal essence of creation through meditation, using a mantra. This mantra is that given by Guru Nanak. He is the first of the ten Sikh Gurus, namely, *Sa Ta Na Ma*, which comes from *Sat Nam*, which means *truth manifested*. Using the mantra in deep meditation, you can connect with the eternal vibration, find the divine within, and rise to new levels of spirituality.

RITUALS AND PRACTICES

The Kundalini practice as taught by Yogi Bhajan involves physical postures (asanas), breath control exercises (pranayams), and various meditations, including the chanting of mantras. He teaches methods in conscious living and encourages a vegetarian diet.

FOR ADDITIONAL INFORMATION

Recommended Contacts

Healthy, Happy, Holy
    Organization
House of Guru Ram Das
1620 Preuss Road
Los Angeles, CA 90035
Phone: (213) 275–7769

Yogi Bhajan
Rte. 3, Box 1320
Espanola, NM 87532
Phone: (505) 753–0423
Website: www.yogibhajan.com

Recommended Readings

Bhajan, Yogi. *Kundalini Yoga: The Flow of Eternal Power*. New York: Perigee, 1998.

Bhajan, Yogi. *The Mind: Its Projections and Multiple Facets*. Los Angeles: Kundalini Resource Institute, 1998.

OSHO RAJNEESH

Osho Rajneesh, also known as Bhagwan Shree Rajneesh, is one of the world's best known and most controversial spiritual masters of this century. As a philosopher, teacher, writer, and meditator, he has had a profound influence on spiritual thinking and practice.

HISTORY

Born Rajneesh Chandra Mohan in central India in 1931, Osho Rajneesh was raised by his grandparents until the age of seven. He lived a simple childhood, and by the age of fourteen, he experienced his first satori, and for the next seven years he experimented with various forms of meditation. In 1952, he experienced his second satori. Thus, at the age of twenty-one, he entered into the natural state of enlightenment. He then went on to college, where he was an excellent student and was awarded the All-India University Debating Trophy.

After completing his studies, he went on to become a professor of philosophy at Jabalpur and traveled all over India lecturing. In 1966 he resigned his professorship and devoted all his energies to his spiritual work, holding his first meditation camp in Rajasthan. First settling in Bombay, he gave controversial lectures to audiences of over fifty thousand people.

In 1974 he established the Shree Rajneesh Ashram in Poona, India. This ashram has become the largest "humanistic therapy" center in the world and attracts people from all around the world. Over the past two decades, about 540 books on the teachings of Rajneesh have been published. Thousands of audio and video cassettes are available featuring his daily discourses. Meditation centers—Osho Centers—have been established all over the world, and his followers number over half a million. Since he died in 1990, an appointed council has overseen the ongoing practical affairs of the ashram and its wide variety of activities.

BELIEF SYSTEM

Osho Rajneesh does not teach a belief system or philosophy. Rather, his message is to give total commitment to life itself and celebrate each and every moment. Although raised in a Hindu culture, Rajneesh draws upon the eternal truths from all the world's great teachings. His views often run contrary to traditional interpretations, and his approach to teaching is controversial. For example, as a means of awakening your consciousness and stimulating your awareness, he might explore some deeply personal areas with you.

The structure of his teaching is dynamic, designed to let you see reality, not as some theoretical abstract concept, but as a continuous exchange with life—in other words, as a living reality. Life is considered a "divine play," and God is something you experience. His credo is "love, life, and laughter."

RITUALS AND PRACTICES

Rajneesh employs many spiritual practices for his sannyasins. Typically this word, sannyasin, refers to a renunciate, but here it refers to one who has entered into a deep acceptance of life. Loving and laughing are important elements of the spiritual practice, but cathartic meditation is also encouraged. Typically, high-energy movements, such as deep breathing, shaking, compulsive dancing, and whirling, are followed by a quiet period of silent witnessing. Other meditation techniques include laughing and crying, chakra sounds and chakra breathing, and the cathartic meditation followed by complete stillness. Group meditations and workshops are held at hundreds of meditation centers around the world, as well as at the ashram in Poona.

FOR ADDITIONAL INFORMATION
Recommended Contacts

Chidvilas
P.O. Box 17550
Boulder, CO 80308
Phone: (800) 777–7743
Website: www.osho.org

Osho International
570 Lexington Avenue
New York, NY 10022
Phone: (212) 588–9888
Website: www.osho.com

Recommended Readings

With over five hundred books in print, it would be a good idea to review the booklist from Chidvilas. Some of the classics for beginners would be:

Rajneesh, Osho. *The Everyday Meditator*. New York: Charles E. Tuttle,

1993.

Rajneesh, Osho. *Meditation: The Art of Ecstasy*. Poona, India: Rebel Publishing, 1991.

Rajneesh, Osho. *Sex Glimpses of a Golden Childhood*. Poona, India: Rebel Publishing, 1991.

Rajneesh, Osho. *The Book of Secrets*. Poona, India: Rebel Publishing, 1990.

Rajneesh, Osho. *Sex*. Poona, India: Rebel Publishing, 1990.

Recommended Website

Friends of Osho
www.sannyas.net/osho

BABA HARI DASS

Baba Hari Dass is a silent monk who has been teaching Ashtanga Yoga to the West since 1971.

HISTORY

The man who would become Babaji was born in 1923 in the Almora District of north India. At the age of eight, he went to a brahmacharya school for spiritual instruction, and later went off to perform his sadhana (spiritual practice) on his own. During this time, he had several experiences with various Indian saints, although he has not discussed his personal instruction or association with other spiritual teachers. Since 1952, Babaji has been a mauna, or silent saddhu, and only communicates with others either through inner communication or by a chalkboard that he carries with him.

Several American aspirants traveling in India discovered Baba Hari Dass, and persuaded him to come to the United States to teach. In 1971, Babaji arrived in America and began teaching the classical "eight-limbed" path of Patanjali known as Ashtanga Yoga. In 1974 a group of his students founded the Hanuman Fellowship to foster the teachings inspired by Babaji. In 1978, the Mount Madonna Center for the Creative Arts and Sciences was established as a spiritual community and a seminar and retreat facility. Its purpose was to "nurture the creative arts and health sciences within the context of spiritual growth." This center comprises 355 acres in the redwoods overlooking Monterey Bay in California. There are generally more than one hundred residents at the facility, which includes a children's boarding school, a bookshop and a library, as well as the retreat and seminar facility itself. There are also centers in Canada—at British Columbia and Ontario—and in Mexico—at Mexico City.

BELIEF SYSTEM

Babaji teaches the classical form of Yoga from Patanjali's Yoga Sutras, known as Ashtanga Yoga. Babaji describes God as: "the creator of the world. We don't see his form. We don't know how he came into existence. His creation is He—But God is beyond name and form. Our desires have created the form and we worship our desire. It's a good method, but after reaching a higher stage, the name and form disappear." Babaji states that our sole purpose in life is to find God, and to find God you must "open your heart in front of God and He will listen to your prayer. A yogi searches for God in the world and says, 'This is not God . . . this is not God . . . this is not God,' and he rejects everything. As soon as he finds God, he says, 'This is God . . . this is God . . . this is God.' He begins to see God in everything, and accepts everything."

RITUALS AND PRACTICES

Babaji's practice of Ashtanga Yoga consists of eight parts:

1. Yama, the restraints of nonviolence, truthfulness, nonstealing, continence, and nonpossessiveness;

2. Niyama, the observances of purity, contentment, austerity, scriptural study, and surrender to God;

3. Asana, the physical exercises (postures) of well-being;

4. Pranayamathe, control of the breath;

5. Pratyahara, withdrawing the mind from sense perception;

6. Dharana, concentration;

7. Dhyana, meditation; and

8. Samadhi, superconsciousness.

Through a series of exercises designed to take you through a progression of the eight stages, you would evolve your awareness to total consciousness, or self-realization.

Ashram life also consists of a vegetarian diet, kirtan (devotional singing), and Karma Yoga, or selfless service, all designed to complement the eight stages. Three-week teacher-training courses and retreats are available to the public.

FOR ADDITIONAL INFORMATION

Recommended Contact

Mount Madonna Center
445 Summit Road
Watsonville, CA 95076
Phone: (408) 847–0406
Website: www.mountmadonna.org

Recommended Readings

Dass, Baba Hari. *Fire Without Fuel*. Santa Cruz, CA: Sri Rama Publishing, 1988.

Dass, Baba Hari. *Ashanta Yoga Primer*. Santa Cruz, CA: Sri Rama Publishing, 1987.

Dass, Baba Hari. *Silence Speaks*. Santa Cruz, CA: Sri Rama Publishing, 1986.

Ram Dass

The term *ram dass* means "servant of God." The man named Ram Dass, an American formerly known as Dr. Richard Alpert, was a student of the Eastern discipline Karma Yoga, which he introduced to the West.

HISTORY

Ram Dass was born as Richard Alpert in 1933. He was the son of a prominent attorney and founder of Brandeis University. He was a natural student, earning his Master's degree in psychology from Wesleyan and his Ph.D. from Stanford. In his career in the 1960s, Dr. Alpert was a psychology professor at various universities such as Harvard, Stanford, and the University of California. It was during this time of the counterculture in America that Alpert met Timothy Leary, a Harvard University colleague, and began experimenting with psilocybin mushrooms and, later, with other psychedelic drugs such as LSD. According to Alpert, these experiences expanded his awareness of himself, and of life in general, and served as an impetus for focusing his attention on finding the answers to the purpose and meaning of life.

In 1967, Dr. Alpert went to India in search of Truth. There, he met an American who had taken the Eastern name of Bhagwan Dass and who had studied various Eastern spiritual disciplines such as yoga and Buddhism. The two struck up a friendship, and Dass began teaching Alpert various yogic techniques. Eventually, he took Dr. Alpert to his guru, Neem Karoli Baba, whom the Western devotees called Maharajji.

Dr. Alpert stayed with Maharajji for several months, and during this time, he studied Karma Yoga, and later took the spiritual name Ram Dass. His daily routines consisted of observing a vegetarian diet, assuming yoga postures, performing breathing exercises, and practicing meditation.

One day Maharajji came up and touched Ram Dass on the forehead in such a way as to open up his spiritual awareness. Shortly thereafter, Maharajji instructed Ram Dass to go back to the West to share what he had learned, and he has since become one of the best-known lecturers and writers in the field of spiritual development.

BELIEF SYSTEM

The gist of his teachings is summed up in the saying, "Be Here Now," which is also the title of his very successful book, outlining his experiences and philosophies. Ram Dass suggests that you should look within for the answers to life's great questions. You should go beyond your analytical understanding of things and develop an awareness based on your personal experience.

To illustrate his points, Ram Dass draws upon many Western and Eastern teachings. The emphasis is on learning by doing and being, rather than by intellectual speculation. The teachings are designed so that you become your own teacher and follow your own unique spiritual path—even though other spiritual teachers may be invaluable in your efforts toward self-realization. Emphasis is placed on learning by doing selflessly for others.

FOR ADDITIONAL INFORMATION

Recommended Contacts

Hanuman Foundation
524 San Anselmo Avenue,
   Suite #201
San Anselmo, CA 94960
Phone: (415) 457–8570

Ram Dass Tape Library
]524 San Anselmo Avenue, #203
San Anselmo, CA 94960
Phone: (415) 499–8587
Website: www.ramdasstapes.org

Recommended Readings

Dass, Ram. *Miracle of Love, Stories about Neem Karoli Baba*. New York: Dutton, 1979.

Dass, Ram. *Be Here Now*. New York: Crown Publishers, 1971.

Dass, Ram, and Paul Gorman. *How Can I* Help? New York: Knopf, 1985.

Dass, Ram, and Stephen Levine. *Grist for the Mill*. Berkeley, CA: Celestial Arts, 1988.

SATYA SAI BABA

Sai Baba is an avatar, "a descent of deity to earth in incarnate form." He is said to have performed miracles such as curing illnesses and foretelling the future.

HISTORY

Satya Sai Baba had been incarnated in a previous life and lived as an itinerant fakir, settling in the Bombay State in India, around 1872. He was known to have performed astounding miracles and gave spiritual instruction to those who gathered around him in Shirdi, where he was known as Shirdi Sai Baba. Before leaving his earthly body in 1918, he told one of his devotees that he would be reincarnated and return as a male infant in eight years' time.

In 1926, eight years after the death of Sai Baba of Shirdi, a boy was born in the remote village of Puttaparti. The baby was named Satyanarayana, or "Satya." At an early age, the child demonstrated supernormal powers, such as materializations, making objects appear out of emptiness. Later, he was able to quote long passages in Sanskrit, an ancient language that he allegedly had never learned.

Puzzled by such phenomena, his father asked Satya who he really was. Satya answered "I am Sai Baba," but no one in the village knew what that meant. However, as word spread about the advent of "Sai Baba," devotees who knew of the original Sai Baba began to gather around the young teacher. In 1957, Satya Sai Baba first began giving discourses in public, and thousands of people flocked to hear him.

Today, hundreds of thousands still come to see him during religious festivals in India. He is known internationally, and he has a following of millions. Several Indian colleges have been founded by Satya Sai Baba, and over 1,200 centers in 137 countries have been established around the world.

BELIEF SYSTEM

Satya Sai Baba is perhaps best known for the many miracles he performs, such as materializing objects out of emptiness, "vibhuti," in which holy ash miraculously appears on the hands, curing people of various "incurable" diseases, foreseeing the future, and causing events to occur. All these miracles are Baba's way of illustrating the power of Divine Love for us. The demonstrations are not meant to inspire us to perform miracles, but rather to illustrate that the Divine is within us, and to inspire us to seek the God within.

Baba espouses the path of love and devotion. He teaches that inward contentment, peace, and bliss are found by liberation from the bondage of the trivial and the temporary through daily contemplation on the Highest Self. Constant dwelling on the name (any name) of the Lord, cultivating love, and giving up hatred, envy, anger, cynicism, and falsehood constitute Baba's prescription for spiritual development.

FOR ADDITIONAL INFORMATION
Recommended Contact

Satya Sai Book Center of America
305 West First Street
P.O. Box 278
Tustin, CA 92680
Phone: (714) 669–0522
Website: www.sathyashi.org

Recommended Readings

Murphy, Howard. *Sai Baba Avatar: A New Journey Into Power and Glory*. San Diego, CA: Birth Day Publishing, 1977.

Steer, Brian, ed. *The Satya Sai Compendium*. York Beach, ME: Samuel Weiser, 1997.

Recommended Website

Sai Baba Links
www.premamusic.com/sai

MEHER BABA

Meher Baba, whose name means *compassionate father*, is believed to be the incarnation of God among men. He welcomed all castes, all faiths, all social strata to his teaching. Notably, as part of his internal austerities, he maintained silence for over forty years.

HISTORY

Merwan Sheriar Irani was born in Poona, India, on February 25, 1894. His parents were of the Zoroastrian religion, but they sent him to a Catholic high school in Poona, and later to Deccan College, where he excelled in academics and sports.

On his way home from college, Merwan would regularly stop to visit a woman saint known as Hazrat Babajan, who was his first spiritual master. It was Babajan who awakened Merwan to his realization of the Self through a kiss on the forehead, and who made him aware of his high spiritual destiny. Over the next seven years, Merwan visited with several perfect masters. The last of these was Upasni Maharaj, who gave Merwan the experience of gnosis, or Divine Knowledge. Having thus attained spiritual perfection in 1921, Merwan began drawing together a group of disciples. They soon gave him the name Meher Baba, which means "Compassionate Father."

After years of intensive training under Meher Baba, his disciples established a colony near Ahmednagar called "Meherbad." This complex boasted a free school for spiritual training, a free medical clinic for the needy, and shelters for the poor. Baba turned no one away but welcomed people of every caste and creed. He criss-crossed the country, feeding and clothing the poor and demonstrating such selfless acts as cleaning the latrines of the untouchables and bathing lepers. Baba also spent time seeking out "advanced souls" to assist them in the completion of their spiritual evolution.

On July 10, 1925, Meher Baba began to observe silence, which lasted for the next forty-four years of his life. To communicate with his students he used an alphabet board, and later just hand gestures. His following quickly grew, and sometimes as many as 100,000 people would come to be with him on a single day. Beginning in 1931, Baba began the first of six trips to the West, visiting such regions as Europe, North America, and Australia.

On January 31, 1969, Baba died, but in keeping with his request, no formal organization was created to perpetuate his teachings. Nevertheless, students continue to gather informally in centers around the world to discuss his teachings and express—through music, poetry, dance, or drama—their reflections on his life.

BELIEF SYSTEM

Meher Baba was the avatar of this age; an avatar being the periodic incarnation of God in human form. He had come "not to teach but to awaken" mankind to the revelation of all religions of "that One Reality which is God." Baba taught that "the goal of all life is to realize the absolute oneness of God, from whom the universe emanated . . . to know itself as conscious divinity." To gain this realization, you must walk an inward spiritual path, eliminating all false impressions of your individuality and coming to the knowledge of *your real self as God*. Baba saw his work as awakening the world, through love, to a new consciousness of the oneness of all life.

Baba's teachings emphasized practicing love and compassion, the elimination of the selfish ego, and the potential of realizing God within yourself. Meher Baba has no dogma, and does not place any importance on religious ceremonies or rites. He directs his students to an understanding of the Seven Realities, as follows:

1. The only *real existence* is that of the One and Only God;

2. The only *real love* is the love for this God;

3. The only *real sacrifice* is that in which, in pursuance of this Love, all things, body, mind, position, welfare, and even life itself are sacrificed.

4. The only *real renunciation* is that which abandons all selfish thoughts and desires;

5. The only *real knowledge* is that God is the inner dweller in good people and bad, in saint and sinner;

6. The only *real control* is the discipline of the senses, avoiding the indulgence in low desires;

7. The only *real surrender* is that in which the poise is undisturbed by any adverse circumstance, and the individual, amidst every kind of hardship, is resigned with perfect calm to the will of God.

This discipline requires you to help all equally as circumstances demand, without expectation of reward. When you are compelled to take part in a dispute, you must act without the slightest trace of enmity or hatred. You must try to make others happy with brotherly or sisterly feeling for each one. Baba's teaching requires that you harm no one in thought, word, or deed, not even those who harm you.

FOR ADDITIONAL INFORMATION

Recommended Contact

Meher Spiritual Center
10200 Highway 17 North
Myrtle Beach, SC 29572
Phone: (843) 272–5777
Website: www.avatarmeherbaba.org

Recommended Readings

Meher, Baba. *The Everything and the Nothing*. Myrtle Beach, SC: Sheriar Foundation, 1996.

Meher, Baba. *God Speaks*. New York: Sufism Reoriented, 1977.

MATA AMRITANANDAMAYI

Mata Amritanandamayi is considered something of a living saint in India, ever since she achieved "realization" at a very young age, achieving unity with the Divine Mother.

HISTORY

Mata Amritanandamayi was born with the name Ammachi on September 27, 1953, on a small island in Kerala, south India. She manifested an unusual dark-blue complexion reminiscent of the Hindu gods Lord Krishna and Divine Mother Kali. From an early age, she demonstrated an inborn devotion to the Lord by constantly thinking about the Lord and repeating his name. By the age of seven, Ammachi was composing and singing devotional songs, which were soon known by the whole village. A few years later, she began a rigorous and austere penance, living only on tulasi leaves and water, being absorbed in meditation on the Divine Mother throughout the day and night.

During her penance, the Divine Mother appeared to her and became a "mass of effulgence, merged in her." From this day on, Ammachi declares, "Nothing could be seen as different from my own formless Self, wherein the entire universe exists as a tiny bubble."

From this point on, Ammachi has been recognized as being one with the Divine Mother. Having attained this "Divine Realization," she has been known as Mata Amritanandamayi. She has been receiving thousands of seekers from all over the world, men and women who come to learn or be healed, to experience her compassion, blessings, and grace. Mata Amritanandamayi is now recognized as one of India's greatest living saints, and makes regular tours to Western countries.

BELIEF SYSTEM

Ammachi's teachings are basically bhakti, or devotional, and come from the heart. The learning is not just a mental process, but an experience that is felt in the heart. Although the context from which her teachings are imparted is that of an Indian culture, her message is universal: Love God with all your heart, and love your fellow man. God can be worshipped as a male form such as Krishna or Christ, or as a Devi (Divine Mother), but the essence of the Divine dwells within you. Establishing contact with, and merging into, this Divine Realization is the focus of her teachings. The key is in opening up your heart to God.

RITUALS AND PRACTICES

The practices involve primarily devotional singing and the chanting of holy mantras (empowered names of God). Devotees practice various meditation techniques, and carry out devotional service. Although the Divine Mother does impart oral teachings, answers questions, and gives spiritual advice, the power of her teachings comes from the heart and is felt while in her presence. Sessions are provided in which Ammachi will see every individual who comes to see her, and she will give a hug to the aspirants and impart her love directly to them.

FOR ADDITIONAL INFORMATION
Recommended Contact

Mata Amritanandamayi Centers
P.O. Box 613
San Ramon, CA 94583-0613
Phone: (510) 537–9417
Website: www.ammachi.org

Recommended Readings

Amritanandamayi, Mata. *For My Children*. San Ramon, CA: M.A. Center, 1992.

Amritanandamayi, Mata. *On the Road to Freedom*. San Ramon, CA: M.A. Center, 1992.

Amritanandamayi, Mata. *Awaken, Children! I–III*. San Ramon, CA: M.A. Center, 1991.

MOTHER MEERA

The young woman who would one day be called Mother Meera showed extraordinary spiritual awareness at a very young age. After years of intense meditation, she taught Cosmic Shakti, preparing the way for the Divine to enter each heart, and for the awakening of consciousness of each human being.

HISTORY

Mother Meera was born Kamala Reedy in a small village in Andhra Pradesh, India, in 1960. Her parents were not particularly religious people, she had no guru, and the young girl was given no particular spiritual training, but at the age of six, she entered into her first samadhi, or deep meditative state of transcendence. By the age of fourteen, her uncle noticed her unusual spiritual activities, such as going into deep meditation, and took her to the ashram of Sri Aurobindo and his colleague, the Mother, where she—Meera—continued to have extraordinary spiritual experiences.

She left after a short stay and started conducting her own darshan, where she would meet with devotees and impart a divine presence. In 1979, she left India with her uncle for Europe and Canada, where the Mother Meera Society was initially formed. In 1985 she settled in Frankfurt, Germany, where a large group of followers from around the world come to enjoy her company and grace.

BELIEF SYSTEM

Mother Meera teaches no specific philosophy or practice. She describes her work as that of the Cosmic Shakti bringing down the light of the Paramatma (Divine Soul) to prepare the way for humanity's spiritual awakening. Followers are reminded to remember the Divine in everything they do. They offer everything to the Divine. They revere her for the transformations they undergo and the miraculous healings that take place in her presence.

The basic underlying belief is that human beings are undergoing an awakening of consciousness, and that this is their destiny.

FOR ADDITIONAL INFORMATION
Recommended Contacts

Mother Meera
26 Spruce Lane
Ithaca, NY 14850
Website: www.mothermeera.com

Mother Meera Society
Oberdorf 4A
65599 Dornburg-Thalhelm
Germany
Phone: 011–49–6436–2361

Recommended Reading

Harvey, Andrew. *Hidden Journey*. New York: Penguin USA, 1992.

HARE KRISHNA MOVEMENT

The Hare Krishna movement is dedicated to spreading the science of Krishna (KRSNA, or God) consciousness throughout the world for the good of all suffering humanity. To focus the mind and achieve greater discipline, devotees employ a ritual mantra. The term *mantra* means *that which delivers the mind*.

HISTORY

The founder of Hare Krishna movement was His Divine Grace A. C. Bhaktivedanta Swami Prabhupada. Swami was born in 1896 in Calcutta, India, and was initiated by his spiritual master, Srila Bhaktisiddhanta Sarasvati Gasvami in 1933. For years, he led an outwardly normal life, marrying and following a career, but in 1950, at the age of fifty-four, Prabhupada retired from married life, and in 1959 accepted the renounced order of life (Sannyasa). During this period, he devoted his life wholly to the worship of Lord Krishna.

Srila Prabhupada came to the United States in 1965 to fulfill the mission of his spiritual master—to spread the teachings of Krishna to the Western world. In July 1966, he established the International Society for Krishna Consciousness, and before his death on November 14, 1977, he had established the movement through over one hundred ashrams, schools, temples, institutes, and farm communities all over the world.

Swami Prabhupada has written more than sixty volumes of authoritative translations and commentaries of the philosophical and religious classics of India. His writings have been translated into twenty-eight languages, and the Bhaktivedanta Book Trust, which publishes his works, has become the world's largest publisher of books in the field of Indian religion and philosophy. He is perhaps best known for his translations of the eighteen-thousand-verse *Srimad Bhagavatam* as well as the *Bhagavad Gita, As It Is*.

The Hare Krishna movement today is well established in centers around the world, and its message is carried through "devotees," or "sannyasans," as well as through the writings of Prabhupada.

BELIEF SYSTEM

In the Hare Krishna faith, Lord Krishna (KRSNA) is recognized as the Supreme Personality of Godhead, and, as the highest form of God, is found within all life and substance. Lord Krishna is the absolute truth and the highest object of devotion. Sri Krishna is seen as the creator of the universe, and the destroyer. Periodically, the Lord incarnates into human form in order to teach humanity how to live correctly. Some of the best-known incarnations are known as Hari, Rama, Buddha, and in the Kali Yoga, of the current modern age of darkness, Lord Caitanya. The Gods Brahma and Vishnu are believed to have been created by Lord Krishna.

RITUALS AND PRACTICES

In the Hare Krishna movement, devotees use a form of Bhakti Yoga devotional discipline in which you place all your attention on Krishna and think, act, and speak in his name. This phenomenon is achieved by chanting the holy names of God either silently during meditation or out loud in a congregation. The classical mantra is as follows:

> "Hare Krsna, Hare Krsna,
> Krsna Krsna, Hare Hare
> "Hare Rama, Hare Rama,
> Rama Rama, Hare Hare."

By chanting the mantra in this ritual form, you purify your mind, develop greater mental control, attain a heightened sense of awareness, and awaken to the pure love of God. The aim is to reach your highest state of consciousness, or understanding of truth, which is Krsna Consciousness or God consciousness. When you achieve this higher awareness, you are delivered from the perpetual cycle of reincarnation; subsequently, you will reside in eternal ecstasy with Lord Krishna.

The Hare Krishna movement also promotes a vegetarian diet, and advocates refrain from the killing of animals. Respect for all life forms is promoted through its numerous vegetarian restaurants and books on the subject.

FOR ADDITIONAL INFORMATION

Recommended Contact

International Society for Krishna Consciousness (ISKON)
3764 Watseka Avenue
Los Angeles, CA 90034
Phone: (213) 836–2676
Website: www.iskon.org

Recommended Readings

Prabhupada, A. C. Bhaktivedanta. *The Bhagavad-Gita As It Is*. Los Angeles, CA: Bhaktivedanta Book Trust, 1972.

Prabhupada, A. C. Bhaktivedanta. *The Science of Self Realization*. Los Angeles, CA: Bhaktivedanta Book Trust, 1972.

Prabhupada, A. C. Bhaktivedanta. *The Srimad Bhagavatam, First Canto*. Los Angeles, CA: Bhaktivedanta Book Trust, 1970.

GURUDEVA SIVAYA SUBRAMUNIYASWAMI

Gurudeva Sivaya Subramuniyaswami is the foremost exponent and teacher of Saiva Siddhanta in the West. He is a self-realized Western spiritual master of an age-old Saivite tradition. Through his churches, newspapers, and personal magnetism, he promotes that Hindu sect to the West.

HISTORY

Gurudeva was born on January 5, 1927, in Oakland, California, and grew up near Lake Tahoe. He began studying yoga and meditation as a youth, and spent many hours in meditation daily. In 1947, at the age of twenty, he traveled to Sri Lanka, renounced all worldly possessions, and trekked to remote caves to practice yogic disciplines until he attained the enlightenment of Self-Realization.

Two months later, he met Siva Yogaswami at his ashram in Columbuthurai. Yogaswami initiated him into the Saivite Hindu religion (Siddhar line) and gave him his spiritual name Subramuniya.

It was also Siva Yogaswami who gave him new direction in his life. From this point on, his life mission would focus on his role as a spiritual teacher to the West.

After returning to America, Gurudeva spent seven years in continued spiritual practice in Denver, Colorado, where he had a series of kundalini experiences. This discipline enabled him to bring about many siddhis—occult experiences—such as clairvoyance and clairaudience.

In 1957, at the age of thirty, Gurudeva established a branch of the Saiva Siddhanta Church in California, and began teaching Westerners the ancient yoga practices of Saiva Diddhanta. He also opened the Palani Swami Temple in San Francisco that year, and founded the Himalayan Academy to promote a greater understanding of ancient Hindu culture and spirituality.

In 1970, Gurudeva established the Kauai Aadheenam ashram and temple on the Hawaiian island of Kauai, where he lives and guides the advanced disciples of his yoga order. In 1975, he founded a ten-acre spiritual sanctuary on Kauai called the San Marga Sanctuary, and in 1979 Gurudeva founded the international newspaper *Hinduism Today*, which is now published in five countries and reaches an international readership in the hundreds of thousands. Gurudeva lectures around the world, initiating thousands into Saivite Hinduism.

BELIEF SYSTEM

Saiva Siddhanta is the path of personal experience of Siva consciousness and self realization. Gurudeva believes that the Self "is the very core of you," that you can only know this through personal experience. If you can visualize your Self surrounded on all sides by nothingness, that would be a beginning of self-realization. But the nothingness would still be something; in fact, it would be "the fullness of everything: the power, the sustaining power, of the existence of what appears to be everything."

Saiva Siddhanta is a path that places stress on the all-embracing nature of human spirituality, that is, it seeks to reveal that every dimension of life is sacred. It teaches seekers to see God everywhere, and in everyone, inside and outside ourselves. It is a tolerant path, accepting wholeheartedly the many ways of seeking God, and denying emphatically that any path is the one or only path. A traditional manual of this ideal is found in Gurudeva's book, *Living with Siva*.

RITUALS AND PRACTICES

Some of the practices found in Saiva Siddhanta grow out of the ancient Vedic wisdom of the Hindu culture. Some of these practices include:

- Bhakti Yoga, or devotion to the God Siva, through acts of worship and the observance of certain acts of moral conduct;

- Karma Yoga, or serving God selflessly through your thoughts, words, and actions;

- Raja Yoga, which involve yogic exercises and meditation; and

- Jnana Yoga, which is the path of intense mysticism and wisdom. This comes from the direct knowledge of the divine as personal experience transcending all other knowledge.

A catechism for Saiva Siddhanta called *Dancing with Siva* is available through the Himalayan Academy.

FOR ADDITIONAL INFORMATION

Recommended Contact

Himalayan Academy
1819 Second Street
Concord, CA 94519
Phone: (415) 827–0127
Website: www.hinduismtoday.kauai.hi.us
      www.shaivam.org

Recommended Readings

Subramuniyaswami, Sivaya. *Lemurian Scrolls: Angelic Prophecies Revealing Human Origins*. Concord, CA: Himalayan Academy, 1998.

Subramuniyaswami, Sivaya. *Living with Siva*. Concord, CA: Himalayan Academy, 1997.

Subramuniyaswami, Sivaya. *Hindu Catechism*. Concord, CA: Himalayan Academy, 1978.

Subramuniyaswami, Sivaya. *Raja Yoga*. Concord, CA: Himalayan Academy, 1977.

THE INTERNATIONAL SUFI MOVEMENT

Pir-O-Murshid Inayat Khan founded the Sufi Order as "an interfaith approach to spiritual growth." He wanted to "spread the message of unity and promote the awakening of humanity to the divinity in all."

HISTORY

Hazrat Inayat Khan was born in Baroda, India, on July 5, 1882. He was born into a family of musicians and became a master musician himself. Later in his career, he was initiated by his Sufi teacher, Abu Hashim Madani, and trained in the four main schools of Sufism in India. After completing his training in 1910, he was instructed to spread the Sufi message to the West. For seventeen years, he traveled and taught throughout Europe and the United states, inspiring those he met with the message of spiritual liberty and world unity. His work became the foundation of the Sufi Order of the West based on the twin ideals of service to God and to mankind.

Before his death in 1927, Inayat Khan initiated his eldest son, Vilayat Inayat Khan—who was only ten years old at the time—as his spiritual successor. In the next decade, Vilayat Inayat Khan was educated in psychology, philosophy, and music, in both the East and West. He holds an undergraduate degree from the University of Paris, and did postgraduate work at Oxford University in England. He has also undergone extensive training in meditation and contemplation. Pir Vilayat has since successfully taken the Sufi message worldwide, and integrated the principles of the teachings into practical applications, such as counseling and therapy. Pir Vilayat is a recognized speaker, and holds seminars, camps, and retreats throughout the United States and abroad.

The Sufi Order of the West changed its title to the "International Sufi Order Founded in 1910," the name it now bears. Currently, the organization has a network that spans the United States and Europe, and has members from around the world.

BELIEF SYSTEM

A brochure on the Sufi Order describes it as "a community of seekers who are drawn to the . . . ideals of service to God and to humanity. Its purpose is to work toward unity, bringing humanity closer together in the deeper understanding of life. It seeks to bring the world that natural religion which has always been the religion of humanity: to respect one another's belief, scripture, and teacher. Humanity must awaken to its inherent divinity."

Sufism is not so much a religion or doctrine, but rather a system of practices that immerse you in life, bringing your highest ideals into everyday practice. They often refer to themselves as the "Religion of the Heart," because they seek to discover God in the heart of mankind. The Sufi Order describes its approach as "a school for personal transformation and a preparation for service to humanity." Its esoteric teachings deepen a philosophical understanding of life.

Personal guidance helps you deal with problems in both your interior and exterior lives. Retreats help strengthen the effect of the teachings in your being. The Sufi Order operates as an umbrella organization for a number of different activities that it sponsors. These would include the Sufi Order as an esoteric school; as a healing order; as a Universal Workshop, uniting the themes underlying all the world's religions; as a Ziraat, an application of Sufi principles to planetary consciousness; and as Brother/Sister Work, which is dedicated to serving humanity.

FOR ADDITIONAL INFORMATION

Recommended Contacts

The Abode of the Message
RFD 1, Box 1030D
New Lebanon, NY 12125
Phone: (518) 794–8090

Sufi Order North American
P.O. Box 85569
Seattle, WA 98145
Phone: (206) 525–6992
Website: www.sufiorder.org

Recommended Readings

Khan, Hazrat Inayat. *The Inner Life*. Boston, MA: Shambhala, 1997.

Khan, Pir Vilayat Inayat. *The Call of the Dervish*. New Lebanon, NY: Omega, 1999.

THE FALUN DAFA MOVEMENT

Falun Dafa is an advanced system of cultivation and practice of Falun, or energy of the universe, introduced by Master Li Hongzhi. It is also known as Falun Gong.

HISTORY

Falun Dafa has its roots in the ancient Taoist practice of Qigong and Buddhist philosophy. Its founder, Mr. Li Hongzhi, was born into an ordinary intellectual family in GongZhuLing, JiLin Province, China, on May 13, 1951. At the age of four, Li received personal instructions from the Buddhist Master Quan Jue. At the age of eight, he suddenly came to the realization of "Zhen Shan Ren," that is, "Truthfulness-Compassion-Forbearance." With this realization came great supernatural powers, and the strong desire to help others. At the age of twelve, Mr. Li was further taught by a second Master of Taoist Gongfu, who taught him energy cultivation techniques.

Beginning in 1984, Mr. Li devoted his whole body and mind to the development of Falun Buddha Law, which evolved into the current practice of Falun Dafa. In 1992, he came into public prominence teaching Falun Dafa, and became a part of the Qigong Science Research Institute of China, which gave further support to the practices that he had evolved. Today the Falun Dafa movement techniques are practiced in over 30 countries with over 100 million practitioners.

BELIEF SYSTEM

The foundation of the Falun Dafa practice lies in your cultivation of a fundamental knowledge of how the universe works, and in cultivating the Falun (Law Wheel) energy located in your *dan-tian* (lower abdomen). Through prescribed Falun Dafa exercises, an intelligent spinning body of high-energy substance is cultivated. This facilitates the absorption of energy from the universe and relieves your body of its negative elements.

This Falun center within your body has the same characteristics as the universe but is a miniature of the universe. The Taoist Yin-Yang and Buddha's Dharma-wheel both have their reflections in the Falun.

The Falun Dafa movement and practice gives top priority to the cultivation of Xin Xing (mind nature) and its assimilation to Zhen-Shan-Ren (Truthfulness-Compassion-Forbearance), which is considered the supreme nature of the universe. Falun Dafa distinguishes itself from other Qigong practices in that it focuses its purpose in the enlightenment of the individual. (See "Qigong" on page 56.) It is neither a religion nor a cult, but rather a practice for developing your higher nature.

RITUALS AND PRACTICES

The precepts emphasize the development of your Falun through various movement and breathing exercises, as well as the development of greater awareness. The goal is to become enlightened to the truth of human life and to cultivate your spiritual awareness to higher levels. The focus is on your self-examination and self-improvement, rather than on the development of an organization or a group.

FOR ADDITIONAL INFORMATION

Recommended Contact

Universe Publishing Company
P.O. Box 2026
New York, NY 10013
Phone: (212) 343–3056

Recommended Readings

Master Li. *China Falun Gong*. New York: Universe Publishing Co., 1999.

Master Li. *Zhuan Falun*. New York: Universe Publishing Co., 1999.

Recommended Websites

The Internet has a complete listing of Falun Dafa centers:
www.falundafa.ca
www.falundafa.org

CONCLUSION

It is my sincere hope that you never come to a conclusion about God, but rather that you continue to expand your awareness, knowledge, and love for God. When you stop searching, when you accept the status quo, when you begin to believe there is only one way to see your world, your life, your Creator, or yourself, then you stop growing—and you must never stop growing.

THE HAND EXTENDED

I believe the more you look for God, the more you will find. There are no great secrets, only great opportunities for those who take the time to look. Examine yourself, explore your life, search the world around you, ponder the experiences you have had; they all reflect the Truth back to you. The whole Universe is the Divine presence, and your life is part of it, not separate from it.

Use what you have learned—and are learning—from the spiritual paths that attract you, but do not stop there. Your reality must be dynamic and alive.

Your experiences with your Creator are personal. God isn't a concept. God is a reality, a profound presence in your life. Realize this presence, and you will realize who you are and why you were born. Get in touch with God's presence as deeply as you can, as soon as you can. Accept that it is because of this presence that you are holding this book and reading it. It is what makes you conscious of what you are reading, and enables you to reflect upon what you read.

Be conscious of your consciousness. Realize who you are. Enjoy the presence of God. It is this presence that causes events, large and small, in all of creation, from the beating of your heart to the spinning of the planets in the heavens. Observe and celebrate this connection with your Creator.

Question what you have read and what you have been told—even by me. Think for yourself. Believe you are being guided. Trust your intuition. Follow your heart. Explore the possibilities presenting themselves in your life, and look for the signs that are guiding you on your path. Whenever you have a question, when there is something for you to learn or pass on to another, an opportunity will present itself. By becoming increasingly more conscious of what is going on around you and within you, you will begin to see this invisible hand of God directing and guiding you. Take that hand and walk with it.

In so doing, you find yourself, you find God, you find the purpose of your existence, and you find how to accomplish that purpose. It is in finding and achieving your life's purpose that you find fulfillment and meaning in your existence.

Do you recall the famous image painted by Michelangelo on the ceiling of the Sistine Chapel in the Vatican? In it, God is seen as reaching out to man. You can realize God's presence in your life as easily as understanding that God's hand *has already been extended*. Now it is your turn. Reach out and take that hand.

Every breath you take is given to you by a power greater than your own. Recognize this higher power within you and work with it. Celebrate your existence by realizing God's living presence in your life.

DEVELOPING SPIRITUALITY

I am often asked what one can do to develop spirituality. The best answer is to follow your own heart. However, here are several common practices that may be useful to you. Let me suggest a few:

Find Quiet Time

Take some time each day to have some quiet time alone with yourself and God. Whether alone in nature or in a place where you feel close to God, walk or sit in silence and allow your mind to calm down. You need not use formal prayer, just observe the quiet places between your thoughts. Meditate on the stillness. Allow the thoughts to flow out of your being naturally, and enjoy the quiet within your own mind. You don't "try" to quiet your mind; just allow your mind to relax by putting your attention on the emptiness. Within that emptiness is a deep peace, a bliss, a clarity that develops over time. Open your heart and let your spirit guide you naturally and effortlessly into that infinite abyss of pure bliss.

"Retreat" from the World

When you can, or when you feel the need, take off and find some time to be alone with yourself. Whether an afternoon, a weekend, a month, or longer, take a retreat to find yourself. You may wish to take a pilgrimage to a holy place or just get out into nature. Distance yourself from your daily activities long enough to regain your perspective. If you don't "make the time," business and other activities will consume your life. But if you do make the commitment to your spiritual side and make your "retreat" from the cares of the world, you will get back in touch with your Self and regain your sense of perspective.

Use Contemplation and Prayer

Take some time to reflect upon your Self and your purpose in life. Who are you? Why were you born? Why are the different events taking place in your life? Who, or what, is God? Try and connect with your Creator, with God. Look within yourself and bare your own soul to yourself. Speak to your own spirit and let your spirit speak to you. Get in touch with what you are thinking and feeling.

Pray. I consider prayer to be conversation with God, however you conceive Him. It doesn't have to be a formula or come from a book. Just conversation with that Presence, using your own language and your own ideas, is all you need. Ask for guidance and direction. Give your soul the time to be heard and acknowledged.

Keep a Journal

Keep a journal handy, and write out whatever you feel compelled to write. Your soul will speak through your mind and hands as you give it free rein. Describe who you think you are, and why you were born. Explain what it is that is testing you, or bothering you. What are your life's lessons teaching you? What have you learned, and what do you still have to learn? What might you have to experience in order to discover what you need to learn? How might you be tested? What is your purpose in life? What opportunities are there for you to make a difference in the world? What could you change about yourself to improve your life? What steps do you need to take in order to implement those changes?

Learn Love and Compassion

What could you do to increase your capacity to receive and give more love in your life? To begin with, forgive others. Make peace with those who angered or hurt you, and/or others that you love. Forgive yourself. Provide more space for love to grow in your life. Let go of the guilt and shame, the feelings of inadequacy or unworthiness. Focus your attention on the ideal within your nature, and demonstrate it to others—exercise it.

Observe the negative thinking and judgments that your mind makes regarding others—and break the habit. Don't think, speak, or act negatively or violently. Tell the Truth. Appreciate all that you have, and open yourself up to receiving the grace of the Divine. Realize that it takes practice, and that it is fun. Celebrate life!

Fall in love with God. Realize that at the heart of life is God, and God dwells within your own heart. Your heart beats because of its presence. Creation itself is alive within you; creatively express yourself. Let your love grow by letting it flow. Cultivate awareness of love by focusing your attention on it. Stop, take a deep breath, and feel God's presence in your life regularly. Share that love with everyone you see, everywhere you go, all the time, every day, without exception. Enjoy it.

Live Your Service to Others

The very quality of life is measured by what you leave for this world. The more that you allow your spirit to guide you, the more it will. The more you are guided, the more opportunities are provided to be of service to those who need you. This flow of helping each other is what makes the whole world go around. When we block this flow by being self-centered, or thoughtless, we get depressed and dissatisfied with our life. It is in making others happy that we find greater happiness and peace.

Have you noticed that all the great teachers, prophets, and saints have worked selflessly to help others? We all have this capacity, and we all have this need. The more that we honor this part of ourselves the happier we are with ourselves and with our own lives.

Consider what you can do to be of service to others, then act accordingly. Every day. You will find you will be happier and more fulfilled because you have done so.

CREATING THE CRITICAL MASS

We would all like to live in a better world, a happier, healthier, cleaner, and more peaceful world. However, the world is not going to change until we as individuals do. We must all make the effort, and through our efforts, inspire others to make similar efforts. It's a matter of attitude, and commitment. We *can* create the world that we want to live in through the collective efforts of a critical mass making a unified effort to do so. The world awakens one consciousness at a time. You have only to follow your own soul.

FOR FURTHER READING

The following recommended reading list represents a broad cross section of some of the most popular and important works to shape the minds of individuals, facilitate an awakening of consciousness, and herald a contemporary age of spiritual exploration. In addition, you may consult the many other important works that have been mentioned in the other sections of this book.

Most of the recommended authors have had several books published, and these should be available in any major bookstore, through the Internet, or at your local library. Moreover, many of these writers also give lectures, hold workshops, or conduct retreats. To get more information on their activities, consult the recommended books themselves for appropriate addresses, or contact the authors through their publishers.

Although they are arranged alphabetically, the following recommended readings range from the older classics to the more contemporary, and they include both fiction and nonfiction.

Bach, Richard. *Illusions*. New York: Dell Publishing, 1998.

Bailey, Alice A. *Discipleship in the New Age*. New York: Lucis Publishing, 1968.

Bradshaw, John. *Creating Love*. New York: Bantam Books, 1994.

Cameron, Julia. *The Artist's Way*. Los Angeles, CA: J. P. Tarcher, 1992.

Campbell, Joseph. *The Power of Myth*. Anchor Books, 1991.

Canfield, Jack, and Mark Victor Hansen. *Chicken Soup for the Soul*. Deerfield Beach, FL: Health Communications, 1993.

Capra, Fritjof. *The Tao of Physics*. Boston, MA: Shambhala, 1991.

Chopra, Deepak. *The Seven Spiritual Laws of Success*. San Rafael, CA: Amber-Allen Publishers, 1995.

Clason, George S. *The Richest Man in Babylon*. New York: New American Library, 1997.

Cohen, Andrew. *Enlightenment Is a Secret*. Lenox, MA: Moksha Press, 1995.

Dossey, Larry. *Healing Words: The Power of Prayer and the Practice of Medicine*. San Francisco, CA: Harper, 1995.

Dyer, Wayne. *You'll See It When You Believe It*. New York: Avon Books, 1990.

Einstein, Albert. *Albert Einstein on Humanism*. Secaucus, NJ: Citadel Press, 1993.

Emerson, Ralph Waldo. *Essays*. New York: Vintage Books, 1990.

Ferguson, Marilyn. *The Aquarian Conspiracy*. Boston, MA: J. P. Tarcher, 1987.

Gibran, Kahlil. *The Prophet*. New York: Random House, 1996.

Gwain, Shakti. *Creative Visualization*. New York: Bantam, 1983.

Hay, Louise L. *You Can Heal Your Life*. Carlsbad, CA: Hay House, 1999.

Hesse, Hermann. *The Journey to the East*. New York: Noonday Press, 1989.

Houston, Jean. *A Passion for the Possible*. New York: HarperCollins, 1997.

Huxley, Aldous. *The Perennial Philosophy*. New York: HarperCollins, 1990.

Jampolsky, Gerald G. *Love Is Letting Go of Fear*. Berkeley, CA: Celestial Arts, 1988.

Jung, Carl Gustav. *Modern Man in Search of a Soul*. New York: Harcourt Brace, 1955.

MacLaine, Shirley. *Out on a Limb*. New York: Bantam, 1986.

Magil, Frank N., ed. *Masterpieces of World Philosophy*. New York: Harper-Collins, 1991.

Maltz, Maxwell. *Psycho-Cybernetics*. New York: Pocket Books, 1987.

Maugham, W. Somerset. *The Razor's Edge*. New York: Penguin USA, 1992.

Millman, D. *The Way of the Peaceful Warrior*. San Francisco, CA: H. J. Kramer, 1985.

Moore, Thomas. *Care of the Soul*.

Myss, Caroline. *Anatomy of Spirit*. New York: Random House, 1997.

Nietzsche, Friedrich. *Thus Spoke Zarathustra*. New York: Penguin, 1978.

Peck, M. Scott. *The Road Less Traveled*. Cutchogue, NY: Buccaneer Books, 1995.

Pirsig, Robert M. *Zen and the Art of Motorcycle Maintenance*. Quilcene, WA: Quill, 1999.

Quinn, Daniel. *Ishmael*. New York, Bantam Books, 1995.

Rand, Ayn. *Atlas Shrugged*. New York: Signet, 1996.

Redfield, James. *The Celestine Prophecy*. New York: Warner Books, 1997.

Robbins, Anthony. *Unlimited Power*. New York: Fireside, 1997.

Sadleir, Steven. *The Awakening: An Evolutionary Leap in Human Consciousness*. Laguna Beach, CA: Self Awareness Institute, 1992.

Steiner, Rudolf. *Knowledge of the Higher Worlds*. Hudson, NY: Anthroposphic Press, 1993.

Thoreau, Henry David. *Walden*. Princeton, NJ: Princeton University Press, 1989.

Walsch, Neale Donald. *Conversations with God*. Charlottesville, VA: Hampton Roads Publishers, 1998.

Wilber, Ken. *No Boundary*. Boston, MA: Shambhala, 1991.

Williamson, Marianne. *Return to Love*. New York: HarperCollins, 1997.

INDEX

About the Author

Steven Sadleir balances his life between two worlds, the material and the spiritual. Born and raised in Newport Beach, California, he received his B.S. from Menlo College and M.A. in Financial Economics from the University of Wales, United Kingdom, as a Rotary Scholar. He currently works as an investment banker in Southern California, assisting companies to grow and prosper, and in raising capital for ventures that will make positive contributions to society.

In addition to studying firsthand virtually all the spiritual paths described in this book, Sadleir is also a Yogi, with training in numerous forms of the yoga discipline. For example, he undertook a ten-year apprenticeship with the Kundalini Master Vethathiri Maharishi, and at another time, experienced forty consecutive days and nights of continuous meditation (yoga tapas) with Shivabalayogi Maharaj.

In 1985, wanting to share his knowledge and experience with others, Sadleir founded the Self Awareness Institute in California. To date, the institute has taught meditation to thousands all over the world.

Sadleir is also the author of several books and tapes on yoga and meditation. He is a frequent speaker at retreats, lectures, and conferences. He also teaches classes in yoga and meditation at local institutions in California, and is preparing an Internet course.

For further information, contact:

Steven S. Sadleir
The Self Awareness Institute
219 Broadway, Suite 417
Laguna Beach, CA 92651
Website: www.selfawareness.com

With written inquiries, please enclose a self-addressed, stamped envelope.